The Best
AMERICAN
ESSAYS
2014

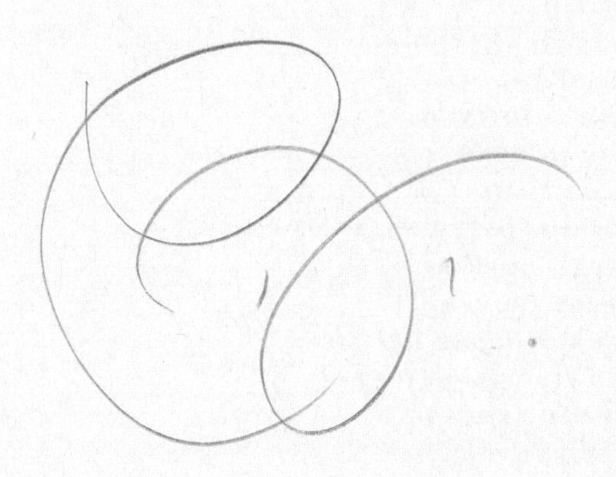

GUEST EDITORS OF
THE BEST AMERICAN ESSAYS

1986 ELIZABETH HARDWICK
1987 GAY TALESE
1988 ANNIE DILLARD
1989 GEOFFREY WOLFF
1990 JUSTIN KAPLAN
1991 JOYCE CAROL OATES
1992 SUSAN SONTAG
1993 JOSEPH EPSTEIN
1994 TRACY KIDDER
1995 JAMAICA KINCAID
1996 GEOFFREY C. WARD
1997 IAN FRAZIER
1998 CYNTHIA OZICK
1999 EDWARD HOAGLAND
2000 ALAN LIGHTMAN
2001 KATHLEEN NORRIS
2002 STEPHEN JAY GOULD
2003 ANNE FADIMAN
2004 LOUIS MENAND
2005 SUSAN ORLEAN
2006 LAUREN SLATER
2007 DAVID FOSTER WALLACE
2008 ADAM GOPNIK
2009 MARY OLIVER
2010 CHRISTOPHER HITCHENS
2011 EDWIDGE DANTICAT
2012 DAVID BROOKS
2013 CHERYL STRAYED
2014 JOHN JEREMIAH SULLIVAN

The Best AMERICAN ESSAYS® 2014

Edited and with an Introduction
by JOHN JEREMIAH SULLIVAN

Robert Atwan, Series Editor

A Mariner Original
HOUGHTON MIFFLIN HARCOURT
BOSTON • NEW YORK 2014

www.hmhco.com

ISSN 0888-3742
ISBN 978-0-544-30990-6

Printed in the United States of America
DOC 10 9 8 7 6 5 4 3 2 1

right © 2013 by Mary Gordon. Reprinted by permission of the author and *Salmagundi.*

"Letter from Greenwich Village" by Vivian Gornick. First published in *The Paris Review,* #204, Spring 2013. Copyright © 2013 by *The Paris Review.* Reprinted by permission of *The Paris Review* and Vivian Gornick.

"Slickheads" by Lawrence Jackson. First published in *n+1,* Winter 2013. Copyright © 2013 by Lawrence Jackson. Reprinted by permission of the author.

"The Devil's Bait" by Leslie Jamison. First published in *Harper's Magazine,* September 2013. Copyright © 2013 by Leslie Jamison. Reprinted by permission of Leslie Jamison.

"Thanksgiving in Mongolia" by Ariel Levy. First published in *The New Yorker,* November 18, 2013. Copyright © 2013 by Ariel Levy. Reprinted by permission of the author.

"Dear Friend, From My Life I Write to You in Your Life" by Yiyun Li. First published in *A Public Space,* #19, Fall 2013. Copyright © 2013 by Yiyun Li. Reprinted by permission of The Wylie Agency, LLC.

"Sliver of Sky" by Barry Lopez. First published in *Harper's Magazine,* January 2013. Copyright © 2013 by Barry Lopez. Reprinted by permission of Sterling Lord Literistic.

"Someone Else" by Chris Offutt. First published in *River Teeth,* Fall 2013. Copyright © 2013 by Chris Offutt. Reprinted by permission of Chris Offutt.

"Joy" by Zadie Smith. First published in *The New York Review of Books,* January 10, 2013. Copyright © 2013 by Zadie Smith. Reprinted by permission of Zadie Smith.

"Little X" by Elizabeth Tallent. First published in *The Threepenny Review,* Spring 2013. Copyright © 2013 by Elizabeth Tallent. Reprinted by permission of the author.

"The Old Man at Burning Man" by Wells Tower. First published in *GQ,* February 2013. Copyright © 2013 by Wells Tower. Reprinted by permission of Wells Tower.

"How to Make a Slave" by Jerald Walker. First published in *Southern Humanities Review,* Fall 2013. Copyright © 2013 by Jerald Walker. Reprinted by permission of Jerald Walker.

"On Being Introduced" by Paul West. First published in *The Yale Review,* January 2013. Copyright © 2013 by Paul West. Reprinted by permission of the author.

"Becoming Them" by James Wood. First published in *The New Yorker,* January 21, 2013. Copyright © 2013 by James Wood. Reprinted by permission of James Wood. Excerpt from "How Shall I Mourn Them?" by Lydia Davis from *The Collected Stories of Lydia Davis.* Copyright © 2009 by Lydia Davis. Reprinted by permission of Farrar, Straus and Giroux, LLC.

"Legend: Willem de Kooning" by Baron Wormser. First published in *Grist,* #6, 2013. Copyright © 2013 by Baron Wormser. Reprinted by permission of Baron Wormser

Contents

Foreword

In recent years we've heard a lot about the issue of truth in nonfiction, the impetus for this topic deriving mainly from a stream of disingenuous memoirs. By truth—and I'll avoid the customary nervous quote marks—we generally mean how honestly and accurately the writing represents the actions and events the writer depicts. Is the writer telling us exactly what happened? Is he embellishing, fabricating, making things up, in an attempt to tell a compelling story (ah, that potentially deceitful narrative arc!) or to characterize himself as attractively virtuous or appealingly naughty? Sounding frank, honest, and sincere is, of course, a rhetorical strategy in itself, known from ancient literature as parrhesia. It's often employed by liars.

I've addressed the topic of truth in nonfiction in several talks and essays (including the foreword to the 2008 edition of *The Best American Essays*), maintaining essentially that unless the incidents or factual references are in some ways verifiable, we usually—short of confession or recantation—have no way of knowing whether a nonfiction writer is telling the truth, especially when details remain unconfirmed, utterly private, or trivial. No one has ever verified the now famous deaths of George Orwell's elephant or Virginia Woolf's moth, though the passing of E. B. White's poor pig can actually be documented.

But truth in nonfiction involves more than accuracy, sincerity, documentation, or verifiability. Not all essays take the form of personal narratives that recount a string of events in a candid tone of voice; many offer personal opinions on various topics, whether general (growing old) or topical (health care). Most such nonnarrative essays pose a different set of criteria for assessing truth. In the territory of argument and exposition, we look at claims, evidence, consistency, and logical coherence. If all we can hope for in nonfiction narrative is verifiability, in opinion essays we demand validity. We want to see at the minimum that conclusions follow from premises. But testing the premises is another matter. Three essays, all demonstrating dramatically different opinions, can all be grounded in valid arguments.

So, as useful as they are in establishing degrees of truth and truthfulness, verifiability and validity do not always take us very far. And, of course, they have little to do with the literary value of essays and creative nonfiction in general. I remember in college courses we made a rough distinction between the essay as a literary genre (whether belletristic or experimental) and the essay as *functional* prose that explained, proposed, persuaded, or argued. In my writing class we were asked to write both. I distinctly recall one assignment requiring a stylistic imitation of Addison and Steele's *Spectator* papers, and another asking us to express an opinion about whether teachers should unionize. One instructor along the way called the later type "purposeful prose." To appreciate the literary essay required the application of aesthetic criteria similar to those used for works of the imagination; to appreciate the purposeful essay it helped to know the rules of rhetoric.

A useful rough distinction, but it's not that simple. Too many essays emerge out of a blend of rhetoric and poetics, and the line between aesthetics and purpose can be blurry at best. When purposefully engaged in a topic, a talented essayist will still offer fresh observations and even surprising conclusions, and do so while attending closely to style and voice. The problem with most topical essays—especially those caught up in current controversies—is that from a literary standpoint they are usually predictable: the conclusions predictable, the prose predictable, the perspective predictable. By a stretch, we may still call these "essays," but they don't behave like essays that want to engage in the struggle of ideas, attack stale thought, or suggest new insights.

I've come to think that one reason for the oppressive predictability of polemical essays can be found in today's polarized social and political climate. To paraphrase Emerson: "If I know your party, I anticipate your argument." Not merely about politics but about everything. Clearly this acrimonious state of affairs is not conducive to writing essays that display independent thought and complex perspectives. Most of us open magazines, newspapers, and websites knowing precisely what to expect. Many readers apparently enjoy being members of the choir. In our rancorously partisan environment, conclusions don't follow from premises and evidence but precede them. Some classical fallacies I once learned and respected—ad hominem, hasty generalization, either-or reasoning, slippery slope, guilt by association—appear to be no longer flimsy fallacies but fundamental strategies of argument. It's worrisome to think that we may be approaching a writing situation that worried Robert Frost: that thinking would become equivalent to voting.

Such an opinionated, partisan atmosphere makes essaying a risky and endangered method of communication. The essay genre, as Montaigne invented and nurtured it, thrives on the attempt to see the multiple sides of issues and conflicts, to suspend judgments and conclusions, to entertain opposing opinions. That's why he modestly called the work he was doing "essays," that is, attempts, trials, thought experiments (but see John Jeremiah Sullivan's introduction for a brilliant in-depth examination of Montaigne's tricky term). For Montaigne, truth was essential, but it lived only in its quest. He perfectly describes his project in a late essay, "Of the Art of Discussion": "I enter into discussion and argument with great freedom and ease, inasmuch as opinion finds in me a bad soil to penetrate and take deep roots in. No propositions astonish me, no belief offends me, whatever contrast it offers with my own. There is no fancy so frivolous and so extravagant that it does not seem to me quite suitable to the production of the human mind." He goes on in the same essay (I'm relying on the Donald Frame translation) to condemn the self-satisfied "stupidity" of those who cling stubbornly and happily to their beliefs and opinions: "Nothing vexes me so much in stupidity as the fact that it is better pleased with itself than any reason can reasonably be. It is unfortunate that wisdom forbids you to be satisfied with yourself and trust yourself, and always sends you away discontented and diffident, whereas opinionativeness and heedlessness fill their hosts with rejoicing and assurance."

For Montaigne, wisdom was not the product of accumulated knowledge—a convenient set of all the conclusions we've reached in life. *Au contraire:* wisdom instead meant developing the habit of continually and rigorously testing that accumulated knowledge. Some writers and readers today, I'm sure, still endorse Montaigne's radically open-minded disposition, but how many would agree with John Stuart Mill's even more radical way of assessing public opinion? In "Of the Liberty of Thought and Discussion," an essay once well known and respected in academia, Mill famously wrote: "If all mankind minus one were of one opinion, and only one person were of the contrary opinion, mankind would be no more justified in silencing that one person, than he, if he had the power, would be justified in silencing mankind." Yet we see in the news nearly every day someone censured for "offensive," "objectionable," "inappropriate," "unacceptable," or "insensitive" remarks. Lately, each spring as I work on this annual foreword, I come across reports of commencement-day speakers who have had their campus invitations rescinded, usually because one group or another is "offended" by a speaker's comments, beliefs, opinions, or affiliations.

And as I write now, I see in the *New York Times* an item on a new college trend, "trigger warnings." These, the *Times* explains, are "explicit alerts [to students] that the material they are about to read or see in a classroom might upset them." I imagine these "triggers" would be boldly noted in a syllabus, like warnings on a pack of cigarettes. For *Moby-Dick* I see the following: *Caution: this classic American novel depicts no women characters, graphically portrays the inhumane treatment of ocean wildlife, and features an obsessive amputee intent only upon pursuing and slaughtering a majestic sperm whale.* Or Henry David Thoreau's *Walden: Caution: This noted work of nonfiction, though it shows respect for the environment, nevertheless may promote a life of self-reliance and antisocial behavior.* Or Montaigne's *Essais: Caution: These essays may cause you to think about things you shouldn't, which in turn may result in a disturbing sense of mental disorientation and ideological tolerance.* Potentially upsetting incidents or information, of course, can be encountered not just in literature but in all kinds of reading. In "Someone Else" (p. 140), Chris Offutt recalls feeling "uneasy" after reading an article in a psychology class about victims of sexual abuse, he having been one of them.

One hopes that "trigger warnings"—however well-intentioned or psychologically prophylactic they might be—don't indicate an American society becoming increasingly censorial and overly protective. I recall, growing up in the Catholic Church, how many educated people used to sneer at the index of forbidden books that "endangered faith and morals." In my parochial high school the sisters told me that I could not read *The Brothers Karamazov* for a book report (I chose a safer book but sinned and read *Brothers* anyway, and my mind exploded). Will "trigger warnings" simply be a way of establishing a new secular index, a cautionary list of books and other works dangerous not for religious reasons but because they may offend or upset certain groups or individuals or that contain material which can be viewed as insensitive or inappropriate? Would *Grapes of Wrath* be upsetting to someone with bad memories of rural poverty? Will the near future necessitate warning labels in front of all published material? Will future editions of *The Best American Essays,* for example, include a trigger warning in front of each selection so readers can avoid material that might upset them? And will trigger warnings in themselves eventually cause upsetting reactions, just the words and images sufficing to evoke unpleasant memories or anxious responses? Says our impressionable liberal arts student, "Why did you even mention cruelly harpooning sperm whales? Now I can't sleep at night."

Until the censors control the day, I hope our intrepid readers will enjoy the essays collected here, despite their many unsettling subjects and themes. So, caution: you might feel your skin crawl as you read Leslie Jamison's vivid depiction of a demonic disease; or completely shaken up by what happens in Ariel Levy's hotel room during a Thanksgiving trip to Mongolia; or discomfited by John H. Culver's visit to a Rome emergency room; or distressed by the vicious and systematic sexual abuse Barry Lopez suffered as a child; or wholly on edge with Jerald Walker's tense dialectics of racism; or grossed out by the antics of Wells Towers's unembarrassed old father at a drug-enhanced Nevada festival; or shocked by Kristen Dombek's sexual candor; or disoriented by Lawrence Jackson's dangerous trips through a *Clockwork Orange*–like Baltimore. Also in store are recurring nightmares, obsessive behavior, the fears and anxieties of aging, suicide, and—as they say in those infomercials—a whole lot more.

The Best American Essays features a selection of the year's outstanding essays, essays of literary achievement that show an awareness of craft and forcefulness of thought. Hundreds of essays are gathered annually from a wide assortment of national and regional publications. These essays are then screened, and approximately one hundred are turned over to a distinguished guest editor, who may add a few personal discoveries and who makes the final selections. The list of notable essays appearing in the back of the book is drawn from a final comprehensive list that includes not only all of the essays submitted to the guest editor but also many that were not submitted.

To qualify for the volume, the essay must be a work of respectable literary quality, intended as a fully developed, independent essay on a subject of general interest (not specialized scholarship), originally written in English (or translated by the author) for publication in an American periodical during the calendar year. Today's essay is a highly flexible and shifting form, however, so these criteria are not carved in stone.

Magazine editors who want to be sure their contributors will be considered each year should submit issues or subscriptions to The Best American Essays, Houghton Mifflin Harcourt, 222 Berkeley Street, Boston, MA 02116. Writers and editors are welcome to submit published essays from any American periodical for consideration; unpublished work does not qualify for the series and cannot be reviewed or evaluated. Please note: all submissions must be directly from the publication and not in manuscript or printout format. Editors of online magazines and literary bloggers should not assume that appropriate work will be seen; they are invited to submit printed copies of the essays to the address above. Because of the increasing number of submissions from online sources, material that does not include a full citation (name of publication, date, author contact information, etc.) will no longer be considered.

I would like to dedicate this book to a very close friend who died as I was at work on this foreword, Bruce Forer. Bruce and I edited several books together, and he helped me conceptualize this series back in 1985. This will be the first foreword he didn't get a chance to read. As always, I appreciate all the assistance I regularly receive from my editors, Deanne Urmy and Nicole Angeloro. I was fortunate that Liz Duvall once again handled copyediting. I'd like, too, to thank my son Gregory Atwan for calling my attention to a few of the outstanding essays that appear here. It was a great pleasure to work with John Jeremiah Sullivan, whose 2011 essay collection *Pulphead* has helped revitalize the genre and sent the essay spinning in new directions. The prose energy that can be found in *Pulphead*—the way Sullivan brilliantly maintains the momentum of a story while casually slipping surprising information into traditional forms—can also be seen in this impressively diverse collection of essays, one that is simultaneously intense, intellectual, and inventive.

R. A.

Introduction: The Ill-Defined Plot

For Scott Bates, 1923–2013

A BIT OF ETYMOLOGICAL TRIVIA noted in certain dictionaries is that the word *essayist* showed up in English before it existed in French. We said it first, for some reason, by not just years but a couple of centuries. France could invent the modern essay, but the notion that someone might seize on the production of these fugitive-seeming pieces as a defining mode was too far-fetched to bear naming. Rabelais had written *Pantagruel,* after all, and people hadn't gone around calling themselves Pantagruelists (in fact they had, starting with Rabelais himself, but the word meant someone filled with nonjudgmental joie de vivre). Had a Bordelais born with the name Michel Eyquem titled his books *Essais* in the 1580s? Fine—Montaigne was Montaigne, a mountain in more than name. One didn't presume to perpetuate the role. France will cherish his example, but the influence it exerts there is partly one of intimidation. In France the essay constricts after Montaigne. It turns into something less intimate, more opaque, becoming Descartes's meditations and Pascal's thoughts. It's said that even a century and a half after Montaigne's death, when the marquis d'Argenson subtitled a book with that word, *Essays,* he was shouted down for impertinence. Not a context in which many people would find themselves tempted to self-identify as "essayists." When the French do finally start using the word, in the early nineteenth century, it's solely in reference to English writers who've taken up the banner, and more specifically to those who write for magazines and newspapers. "The authors of periodical essays," wrote a French critic in 1834, "or as they're commonly known, *essayists,* represent in English letters a class every bit as distinct as the *Novellieri* in Italy." A curiosity, then: the essay is French, but essayists are English. What can it mean?

Consider the appearance of the word in English—which is to say the appearance of the word—in the wintertime of late 1609 or early 1610, and most likely January 1610. A comedy is under way before the court of King James I of England, at the Palace of Whitehall in London, or maybe at St. James's Palace, where the prince resides, we're not sure. The theaters have been closed for plague, but there must be diversion for the Christmas season. Ben Jonson has written a new piece, *Epicœne, or The Silent Woman,* for his favored company, the Children of the Whitefriars, boy actors with "unbroken voices," several of whom have been "pressed"—essentially kidnapped (sometimes literally off the street, while walking home from school)—into service for the theater. For most of them it's an honor to number among the Children of the King's Revels. They enjoy special privileges.

January of 1610: James is forty-three. The biblical translation he has sponsored is all but done. John Donne holds a copy of his first published book, *Pseudo-Martyr,* and gives it to James, hoping in part to flatter him into forgiving past wildnesses. "Of my boldness in this address," he writes, "I most humbly beseech your Majesty to admit this excuse, that, having observed how much your Majesty has vouchsafed to descend to a conversation with your subjects by way of your books, I also conceived an ambition of ascending to your presence by the same way." Galileo squints at Jupiter through a telescope he's made and finds moons (he can see them so faintly they look like "little stars") that evidently obey no gravity but Jupiter's own, proving that not all celestial bodies circle the earth, a triumph for proponents of the still-controversial Copernican theory of heliocentrism, but one suggesting an important modification to it as well, for Copernicus had placed the sun at the center of the world, whereas Galileo was sensing that there might be no center, not one so easily discerned. James receives a dispatch about it from his Venetian ambassador. "I send herewith unto His Majesty the strangest piece of news," it reads, "that he has ever yet received from any part of the world," for a "mathematical professor at Padua" had "overthrown all former astronomy." What is opening is the multiplicity of worlds. Sir Walter Raleigh sits in the Tower writing his *Historie of the World,* begging to be sent back to America, saying he'd rather die there "then to perrish" in a cell. We're at the court of the Virginia Company, which days before has published a pamphlet, a *True and Sincere Declaraccion,* extolling the virtues of the new colony, that "fruitfull land," and struggling to quiet horrific accounts that are starting to circulate. Across the Atlantic in Jamestown it's what they're calling "this starveing Tyme." Of roughly five hundred settlers, four hundred and forty die during this winter. Survivors are eating corpses or disappearing into the forest.

James draws our notice here not for being king—not as shorthand for the period, that is—but because he plays a significant if unmentioned part in the evolution of this slippery term and thing, the essay. All his life he has loved learning. We may imagine him as a stuffed robe-and-crown who gives a thumbs-up to the *Authorized Version* and fades into muffled bedchambers, but James was a serious man of letters. He fashioned himself so and was one, in truth. Not good enough, perhaps, to be remembered apart from who he was, but given who he was, better than he needed to be. He held scholarship in high esteem, while himself indulging certain sketchy ideas, among them the power of demons and witches. In his youth, in Edinburgh and at Stirling Castle, he'd been at the center of a loose-knit and blazingly homoerotic band of erudite court poets, dedicated to formal verse and the refinement of the Middle Scots dialect, his native tongue. Most of what King James wrote had to be translated into plain English before being published, but one text—because it took for its subject partly the use of Middle Scots for poetic purposes—got published in the original language. It consisted mainly of poems but contained also, in the most remarked-upon part of the book, a nonfiction "Treatise" of twenty pages, laying out "some reulis and cautelis"—precepts and pitfalls—"to be obseruit and eschewit in Scottis Poesie." The title of James's book? *Essayes of a Prentise.*

This book was first published in 1584, a full thirteen years before the appearance of Francis Bacon's famous 1597 *Essayes,* traditionally held to mark the introduction of the essay as a formal concept into English writing. Granted, Bacon doesn't quite hold up as the first English essayist even when we do omit James: some person—we're not positive who, but almost certainly an Anglican divine named Joseph Hall—had published a collection of essays a year before Bacon, titled *Remedies Against Discontentment,** and it's

* The authorship of the *Remedies* has been wondered about since it was written, and its obscurity depends heavily on our failure to crack its "Anonym[o]us" mask. But a linguist at Princeton, the New Jersey–born Williamson Updike Vreeland, discovered that the book was Joseph Hall's more than a century ago, and published the information in his *Study of Literary Connections Between Geneva and England Up to the Publication of* la Nouvelle Héloïse (1901). Vreeland didn't care about Bishop Hall, not much—he was interested in the book's translator, the zealous Swiss Calvinist Theodore Jaquemot, who rendered at least a dozen of Hall's books into French—but Vreeland had gone to the library in Geneva and seen the only known French copy of the *Remedies,* titled by Jaquemot *Remèdes contre les mécontentements,* and it read right there on the title page, "Traduit nouvellement de l'anglais de révérend Seigneur Joseph Hall . . . 1664." Sixteen sixty-four: Bishop Hall was seven or eight years dead by then—Jaquemot didn't need to worry about protecting his friend's identity. Plus, once you introduce Vreeland's evidence, other things line up: Hall, it turns out, favored the phrase "Remedies Against" in the chapter heads of his later books, the ones he claimed; and he knew fairly well the man to whom the book is personally dedicated, Sir Edward Coke, the attorney general under Elizabeth I. The *Remedies* is all but certainly Joseph Hall's. But Vreeland, not really caring about Hall and maybe not even knowing that the *Remedies* had long been considered a frustratingly mysterious book, didn't broadcast the discovery, and it's safe to say scant few scholars of English came across his study, so this tiny datum has hunkered there since 1901, waiting for the magic of just the right database and search-term combination to conjure it forth. Well, you might say, who cares? Fair enough. Probably hardly anyone anymore. But sometimes a little fact like that will ignite a constellation of things, the way you can make a strand of Christmas-tree lights come on by replacing one burned bulb. Specifically, this is how it becomes intriguing: Bishop Joseph Hall, though largely forgotten, is major. I won't wear you out quoting four-hundred-year-old accolades. Suffice it to say that his impact and influence in and on his own time were enormous. They called him "the English Seneca." He argued with Shakespeare in taverns and quarreled with Milton in print. He resolved spiritual controversies. He pioneered multiple prose forms in English, among them the satire, the dystopia, the Theophrastian character sketch, and the Neostoical meditation. In the 1650s, when he was old and fallen from power and sick—suffering from, among other ills, "strangury" (painful, constricted urination)—he was attended and his life prolonged by a younger, admiring friend, the writer-physician Sir Thomas Browne, who went on to quote from Hall in his own work. Thomas Browne closed Hall's eyes. Alexander Pope read Bishop Hall. Laurence Sterne knew Bishop Hall's sermons and used them. But most significant of all: *Francis Bacon* knew Hall, and is highly likely to have read his *Remedies.* A year later, Bacon publishes his own *Essayes.* Granted, Hall hadn't used that word in his book. He'd used *Discourses.* But the formal and stylistic overlap between the two productions is huge. Which means we need to consider the likelihood that Joseph Hall is, if not the father, at minimum a coparent of the English essay. There is more to be learned about him.

likely that one or two of the "later" writers—William Cornwallis or Robert Johnson or Richard Greenham—had already begun writing their pieces when Bacon's book came out. Even so, Bacon is the greatest in that little cluster of late-sixteenth-century English essayists and would seem to possess the clearest claim to the word in English. Yet King James's book had preceded them all by more than a decade. Indeed, when James published his *Essayes of a Prentise,* Montaigne was still publishing his own *Essais* (the Frenchman was in between volumes I and II).

The most available conclusion for leaping to is that James is using the word in a general sense. An "essay," we're frequently told, means an attempt, a *stab.* Perhaps King James had been saying, self-deprecatingly, "I'm a mere *prentise* [an apprentice] here, and these are my *essays,* my beginner's efforts." It makes sense.

A problem is, *essay* wasn't supposed to be used *that* way either in the 1580s. If we were to impute that meaning to James's use of the word, it would mark the first occurrence of that particular sense in English (or Middle Scots), which is not proof that we shouldn't do it. That may be precisely what's going on. But whatever James means by *essay,* he means something new by it, new in English. That we know.

Could James have meant something closer to what Montaigne did? On the face of it, the idea seems far-fetched. Montaigne's book had been published just a few years before James finished his. An English translation would not appear for another twenty years. Doubtless there existed English men and women who'd already heard about the book, perhaps even seen it, but what are the odds that one of them was the eighteen-year-old king of Scotland?

Rather good, believe it or not. James's tutor in the 1570s, the years during which Montaigne was composing his first volume of pieces, happens to have been a man named George Buchanan, a Scottish classicist and Renaissance giant who'd spent part of his life in France, where his poetry was much admired ("Easily the greatest poet of our age," said his French publishers, an opinion echoed by Montaigne, among others). Buchanan was placed in charge of young James's education and made on his pupil a lifelong impression of both respect and fear, deep enough that decades later, when James saw a man approaching him at court who looked like Buchanan, he started to tremble (Buchanan had drunkenly beaten the hell out of the boy James on at least one occasion).

Why does this matter? Because James was not the only pupil of Buchanan's who never forgot him. There had been another, in France, in the 1530s and early '40s. For several years George Buchanan had taught at the Collège de Guyenne, in Bordeaux, and one of his students there, a young boarder who also came to him outside of class for private instruction, was a local boy named Michel Eyquem. The boy, whose precocity in Latin astonished his professors, was also a talented actor and performed in a few of Buchanan's plays. Buchanan even considered him something of a favorite student and, running into Montaigne at the French court many years later, honored him by saying that their time together had inspired certain of Buchanan's subsequent theories of humanistic pedagogy. Montaigne returned the compliment by praising his former teacher more than once in the *Essais*. They were well aware of each other, these two men, and remained so. And precisely as the younger was starting to publish in France, the elder became the tutor in Scotland to King James. Who, four years after Montaigne's *Essais* were published, published his own *Essayes*.

What was it, then? Could this appearance of two books titled *Essays*—the first two ever titled that way in any language, and within a mere few years of each other, and written by two men who shared a childhood teacher—really be a coincidence? Or was it the case, as seems vastly more plausible, that the two were connected somehow—that King James knew of Montaigne, or at least knew of his book (but probably both), and was appropriating the word from him? And if that's true, why is James's book rarely, if ever, cited in histories of the essay form, from England or France?

Partly it's that the work consists mostly of poems, so it wouldn't have jumped into anyone's mind to link it with Montaigne, apart from the title. On the other hand, the book does include, as mentioned, a piece that today (or in 1600) would be described as an essay, the "Reulis and Cautelis" treatise. And that piece—unsurprisingly, given the bare adequacy of the king's poetry—became by far the best-known part of his book. In fact, at some point later in the sixteenth century, the work appears to have been republished (or rebound) not as the *Essayes of a Prentise* but instead as *Reulis and Cautelis,* such that its true title could have remained unknown even to one who spotted the work in bibliographies or catalogues.

I wish to argue—or should say, this being an essay, float the suggestion—that something other than either coincidence or appropriation is going on in James's use of the word as a title. Namely, misinterpretation. Or maybe it's more correct to say simply interpretation. James had an acknowledged gift for languages, after all, and the greatest teachers in the world. No one is accusing him of not knowing what *essai* meant in French. The problem is, it meant lots of things—in French, and already in English by then too—but the king in his title seems to have battened on and emphasized one sense above all others, winding up with a usage of the word that differed slightly from what Montaigne had intended. The choice can be seen to have exercised an invisible but crucial effect on the evolving English conception of the essay.

French scholars have been debating what precisely Montaigne meant by *essai* for going on half a millennium, and I don't pretend to be qualified to intervene in that discussion. I've read a lot about it, but as an interested and biased practitioner, not a linguist. Rest assured that when the French see us walk up to the front of our classrooms and intone the familiar explanation, "An essay . . . from the French *essai* . . . meaning 'attempt'" (as I have watched professors do, as I have done in turn before students), ruthless Gallic laughter is occurring on some level.

You can read about the Latin roots of the word, *exagere, exagium,* words that come from the context of Roman coinage, which have to do with measuring and weighing. A sense of "drive out" or "swarm" supposedly knocks around in there somewhere (a swarm of thoughts, like bees, fast and done?). There was the phrase "coup d'essay," meaning, according to a contemporary bilingual dictionary, the "maister-peece of a young workeman." And yes, there was also, simultaneously, King James's sense, of "a beginning, entrance, onset, attempt . . . a flourish, or preamble, whereby a tast[e] of a thing is given." That was undoubtedly present, in both Montaigne's France and his title—but it was not the primary shading, not what Montaigne had foremost in mind (in his ear) when he took that word, *essais,* as a description of his work.

We know what the primary meaning was not only because it comes first in period dictionaries (though it does), nor because it pops up most frequently in period usages (though it does), but also because it's the sense Montaigne himself, when using the word outside of his title—that is, elsewhere in his books—tends to employ, not in every single case but in the vast majority of them. It's the sense of "a proofe, tryall, experiment." To test something—for purity, or value (going back to coinage; the *essayeur* was "an Officer in the Mint, who touches everie kind of new coyne before it be delivered out"). There was the *essay de bled,* the "trial of grain," in which the wheat was carefully weighed, a custom Montaigne may have had in mind when he wrote: "Je remets à la mort l'essay du fruict de mes estudes" ("I put off until my death the essay of the fruits of my studies"). The Rabelais scholar E. V. Telle, in a 1968 essay titled with delightful transparency "A Propos du Mot 'Essai' Chez Montaigne," pointed out that the usage most ready to mind for many of Montaigne's readers would have come from a university context, in which before a candidate's examination for some degree, placards would be posted reading ESSAI DE JEAN MARIN or whoever it was. The students were tested, probed, *essayed,* to find out if they really knew their shit. Montaigne was toying with that meaning too—he would essay himself and his own "jugement" (as he repeatedly writes), become his own essayer. Wasn't this his great guiding question, *Que sçay-je?* ("What do I know?") Which he seems to have meant both literally and in our idiomatic sense (*You really think I'm gonna die?* "Seems like it, but what do I know?").

The task is not to say that Montaigne meant *this* and not *that* by *Essais,* but to understand that the above-sketched polysemia of the word was precisely what he was up to with it, and indeed the reason he chose it, for if a book would be a true mirror, it must always reflect back in the direction from which it's approached. He will leave not one but many doors open to his readers. You may enter him through his likable talkativeness, his confessional, conspiratorial intimacy (he remains one of the few writers in history to have possessed the balls to admit he had a small penis), through his learning, through the possibly un-reattained depth of his psychological penetration, through the consolation he offers in times of sorrow—come whichever way you want, the door is there in the writing, and it's there in the title.

Nevertheless, at the center of it all, when you've peeled back every visible layer, there dwells this binary, this yin/yang, this Heisenbergian flickering between two primary meanings, between a stricter definition of the essay (the proof, the trial, the examination) and a looser one (the sally, the amateur work performed with panache, the whatever-it-is). The duality was noticed and articulated by one of Montaigne's earliest and most important readers, François Grudé, or, as he was better known, the sieur de La Croix du Maine. In his influential *Bibliothéques,* a kind of literary-biographical digest, he included Montaigne and praised him. This was in 1584, when the latter was still alive and writing (also the year in which King James's book came out). Grudé had read only Montaigne's first volume, but on that evidence alone put him into a company with Plutarch. Grudé gets credit for being one of the first people to realize that Montaigne was Montaigne. In 1584, among the lettered, the majority report on the writer was: lightweight, garrulous, and—interestingly for us—a woman's writer.* But Grudé got it, got that there was something very serious happening in the *Essais,* that here was a man inspecting his mind *as a means of inspecting the human mind.* Helpfully for us, Grudé gets into the meaning of the word, of the title, just a few years after Montaigne had introduced it (the first thing they noticed about it was the ambiguity!). He writes:

> In the first place, this title or inscription is quite modest, for if one takes the word "Essay" in the spirit of "coup d'Essay," or apprenticeship, it sounds very humble and self-deprecating, and suggests naught of either excellence or arrogance; yet if the word be taken to mean instead "proofs" or "experiments," that is to say, a discourse modeling itself on those, the title remains well chosen.

What's marvelous to observe is how this original dichotomy, which existed fully formed in Montaigne's mind, between the looser and stricter conceptions of the essay—the flourish and the finished, the try and the trial—transposed itself onto the one that

* An at-the-time disproportionate-seeming number of Montaigne's earliest readers were female, and he was made fun of for it. He dedicated several of his pieces to women and boasted that he would come to know more about that sex than any man before, because his book would become a tiny Trojan horse that would carry him even into their bedrooms, even into their *toilettes.* Among his most passionate early defenders, and his first posthumous editor, was the great Marie le Jars de Gournay, whom he called his *fille d'alliance* (something between a goddaughter and a female apprentice). Good on this topic is Grace Norton's *Montaigne: His Personal Relations to Some of His Contemporaries, and His Literary Relations to Some Later Writers,* which mentions the "peculiar interest Montaigne has inspired through all generations in women."

existed between France and England. If the French will largely repent of the essay's more casual and intimate qualities (and even its name), in the wake of Montaigne, England runs into their arms.* Something in Montaigne's voice, the particular texture of its introspection, opened a vein that had been aching to pop. Ben Jonson describes a literary pretender of the day, writing: "All his behaviours are printed, and his face is another volume of essays." And notice, it's clear from the start that the definition of *essay* the English are working with is the looser one, the one having to do with apprenticeship. That original tuning note King James had struck. Or perhaps one should say that the emphasis is on that signification, with the other one, the more serious one, now switching places and assuming the role of subfrequency. It isn't a unified national definition or anything like that; there are many definitions, as earlier in France, but they all strike that apologetic tone. In fact, in the first English attempt to pin down this odd new creature, the essay—William Cornwallis's "Of Essays and Books," from *Discourses upon Seneca,* published in 1601 (the year in which Robert Johnson defines his own *Essais* as "imperfect offers")—Cornwallis, with a comedy both intentional and un-, begins by arguing that Montaigne had actually been *misusing* the term. Whereas the English were using it correctly, you see. "I hold," he writes, "none of these ancient short manner of writings, nor Montaigne's, nor such of this latter time to be rightly termed *essays,* for though they be short, yet they are strong, and able to endure the sharpest trial: but mine are essays, who am but newly bound prentice."†

* Read Pierre Villey's *Montaigne en Angleterre* for both a tour de force treatment of this subject and an amusing instance of the French attitude to it, which is (or was for a long time) that we English are a little bit weird about Montaigne. Every country treasures him, but England has *loved* him. In the nineteenth century we tried to claim him, Villey points out, by seizing on a claim he makes, at one point in the *Essais,* that his father's family was descended from one situated in England and that he could recall seeing, as a boy, English relics in Eyquem family homes. Genealogies were drawn, more wishfully than carefully, tracing *Eyquem* back to *Ockham.* That would explain the English fixation on Montaigne, our drive to emulate him. *He was really ours.*

† Notice the self-canceling doubleness of even his syntax there. Those other pieces can't be "essays" (looser meaning) because they're strong, and able to endure the sharpest "trial" (stricter meaning). Cornwallis seems to be winking at us there, letting us know that he knows that the whole problem of the word is a linguistic ouroboros. Takeaway being, 1601 and you already have the ironic essay about essays.

From this initial mushroom ring of essayists that crops up on the island around 1600, the infestation spreads. Then comes the Grub Street explosion, and the essay is an eighteenth-century pop form. There are millions of pages of gazettes and daily journals and moral weeklies to fill. The word becomes a blazon for the early Enlightenment. It's the age of what Thackeray will christen "the periodical essayists of the eighteenth century." England becomes a nation of essayists every bit as much as it was ever one of shopkeepers, and the essay becomes . . . whatever we say it is. In the words of Hugh Walker—whose *English Essay and Essayists* remains the most lucid single-volume work on the genre a century after its publication—the genre becomes the "common" of English literature, "for just as, in the days before enclosures, stray cattle found their way to the unfenced common, so the strays of literature have tended towards the ill-defined plot of the essay."

But always—this is what I'm trying to say—with that original note hanging in the air, as both counterblast and guiding horn. Not King James's note, mind you. Montaigne's. The singularity. The word with its fullest, richest, Tiresian ambiguity, and the example of the writer himself, his bravery and rigor, his cheek. The modern essay develops not in any one country but within a transnational vibrational field that spans the English channel. It assumes many two-sided forms: trial/try, high/low, literature/journalism, formal/familiar, French/English, Eyquem/Ockham. The vital thing is that the vibration itself be there. Without it you have no "essays," you have only the *Essais*. To edit this anthology, I looked first for pieces in which the field was strong.

James was sitting there. It was January of 1610. Donne and Bacon and Joseph Hall and the rest of the gang were in the audience too—they may have been, so let's say they were. And the boys were performing Jonson's *Epicœne*. It's a lad who is playing, for the first time, the role of Sir John Daw, a knight. John Daw = Jack Daw = jackdaw, a bird that, like a magpie, likes to pick up and collect shiny things, such as classical quotations. Jack Daw may be a satirical representation of Bacon himself—more than one scholar has wondered. In the story, he has just been forced (it doesn't take much forcing) to recite some of his work. The work is ludicrous. But his listeners, meaning by flattery to draw him into further clownishness, tell him that it possesses "something in't like rare wit and sense." Indeed, they say—sounding already like us, when we go on about the essay's origins—"'tis Seneca . . . 'tis Plutarch."

Jack Daw, in the silliness of his vanity, takes the comparison as an insult. "I wonder," he says, that "those fellows have such credit with gentlemen!"

"They are very grave authors," his little crowd assures him.

"Grave asses!" he says. "Meere essayists, a few loose sentences and that's all."

Essayists: that's when it enters the world, with that line. The first thing we notice: that the word is used derisively and dismissively. And yet the character using it is one toward whom we're meant to feel derisive and dismissive. A pretentious ass. Who may be jibingly based on the inventor of the essay, Francis Bacon. On top of everything, the moment transpires before the eyes of the very monarch who had imported the word in the first place, initiating this long dialogue, and who is himself irretrievably but undoubtedly implicated somehow in the nesting doll of Jonson's wit.

How could we possibly trust any creature that comes into the world wearing such a caul of ambiguity? That's "essayists." Four hundred and four years later, they continue—as it was my privilege to find in editing this anthology—to flourish.

John Jeremiah Sullivan

The Best
AMERICAN
ESSAYS
2014

TIMOTHY AUBRY

A Matter of Life and Death

FROM *The Point*

> Now you become my boredom and my failure,
> Another way of suffering, a risk . . .
>
> —Philip Larkin

OFTEN AT NIGHT I dream that I've found some dangerous object lying on the floor and swallowed it. I sit up, coughing violently, trying to force it back out. I turn to my wife and tell her that I've ingested something potentially fatal, and what should I do? If she wakes up grouchy, she snaps, "Be quiet! I'm trying to sleep!" Startled, I recover myself, realize it's just the same nightmare I always have, and feel acutely embarrassed, hoping my wife won't remember the interruption the next morning. Other times she rubs my arm and says gently, "It's okay. You're fine. You didn't swallow anything. Go back to sleep, babe." The next morning she asks me, "How do you even know I'm there? I mean, aren't you dreaming? Why do you have to get me involved?"

Being left alone in my room in the dark used to be the scariest part of my life. I've been having night terrors as long as I can remember. At a pretty young age, I figured out that monsters hiding under the bed or even regular human intruders did not pose the greatest threat to my existence, and having seen a few too many episodes of Michael Landon's *Highway to Heaven,* about an angel who tends to the needs of dying children, I directed my fears at a more likely possibility: disease, and more specifically, Cancer.

One time, when I was around eight, I had a violent flu, and the whole time my older sister kept giving me significant looks, like she wanted to tell me something. Though I was pretty out of it, I couldn't help but notice, and I became convinced that this was it. Dr. Elisofon had already delivered the news to my family: I had Cancer, I was dying, my sister knew but she didn't want to tell me, and I was just going to have to accept it.

Eventually I discovered why she'd been giving me all those concerned stares. A couple nights before, my father, apparently, had gotten in very late. Still awake, my mother had said, "I don't expect you to come home for me anymore. But when your son is running a 103-degree fever, you might think about leaving the bar before 2 A.M." To which he had responded, "If you knew where I actually was tonight, then you'd be *really* mad." And thus it turned out that the big secret responsible for my sister's displays of anxiety was not Cancer but Divorce. My mom had decided to wait until I was feeling better to tell me. I wasn't dying, but my parents were splitting up. Life and death, marriage and divorce—ever since then, they've been all mixed up in my head, each one at times standing in for one of the others.

The problem with marriage, we all know, is the endlessness of it. Plenty of things we do will have long-term repercussions, but in what other situation do you promise to do something for the rest of your life? Not when you choose a college. Not when you take a job. Not when you buy a house. During childhood, you pick up many habits that are probably going to be lifelong, like walking, talking, reading, and sleeping, but once you've got those down, you start to feel like you're at greater liberty to decide what things you want to do and what things you want to stop doing. Especially when you're a young adult, the apparently infinite multiplicity of possible choices—possible jobs, possible friends, possible cities, possible girlfriends or boyfriends—can sometimes fool you into thinking you have an infinite amount of time to try out everything. But once you're married, you've significantly cut down the options, and it suddenly makes your life feel shorter—like now there's a direct line between you and your own death. You've just gotten on a train and you won't get off until the very end of the track. In your final moments, if you stick to your promise, you'll still be doing the same thing you're doing now, dealing with the same person, possibly having the same arguments. And that commonality between now and then makes that far-off time, when you're old and sick and about to die, a little more imaginable. Which is scary.

Apparently even my father didn't quite escape this predicament. Although they were no longer married, my mother was still there with him in the hospital on the day he died of lung cancer at age sixty. And she even managed to subject him to one of their old familiar rituals, though he wasn't exactly in a condition to notice. Apparently after the nurse declared him dead and shepherded me, my sister, and my two aunts out into another room, while we were all hugging and crying, my mother stayed in the room with my father's body in order to give him a final piece of her mind. "How *could* you?" she asked him. "How could you take such bad care of yourself and abandon your two kids like this?" My parents had been divorced for over fifteen years, and my father was dead, but my mother wanted to get in one last good fight.

I was stunned when my mother told me afterward what she had just done. You had to have some pretty strong feelings, after all, to stand there yelling at a corpse. Did my mother still love my father? Perhaps, but I also think his death had taken something important from her—something distinct from love that marriage offers to us all. Watching her two kids collapse into sobs, she'd looked at their faces and thought about how they'd have to spend the rest of their lives fatherless, with one less person really looking out for them. Though they were both technically adults, one pregnant with her first child, they'd seemed to her especially vulnerable and helpless, and she wanted someone to blame. The causes of their distress were too big to comprehend and pretty much beyond anyone's control: disease, aging, and death. So my dad, who could at least have tried to quit smoking, represented a much more tangible and more satisfying target for her grievances.

Marriage gives you someone to blame—for just about everything. Before you get married, when you feel depressed, you think to yourself, Is this it? And by "it" you mean life. Is this all life has to offer? Just one day followed by another? The same dreary routine? Etc. But after you get married, you think to yourself, Is *this* it? And by "it" you mean marriage. If your life feels monotonous, devoid of possibilities, static, two-dimensional, whatever, you don't blame your life; you blame your marriage. As a thing that's supposed to fill up your days until you die, your marriage becomes like an emblem of your life, like a kind of plastic insulation that's pressed all the way up against the very borders of your existence. It's much easier to blame the stuff lining the walls than the room itself. And there is, you sometimes remind yourself, just a little space between the lining and the outer boundaries, and thus it allows you to trick yourself into thinking if you could just get into that space between where your marriage ends and your life continues, or if you could somehow tear down the plastic, escape the confines of your marriage, life would suddenly be vibrant and rich and unexpected and mysterious again. So maybe the greatest gift marriage gives us is the chance to fantasize, to imagine that there's more to life than there actually is, and it accomplishes this by assuming responsibility for all the misery and dullness that we would otherwise equate with life itself.

But it's not actually marriage that does this: it's your spouse. One saintly individual steps forward and volunteers to be the fall guy, to absorb the entirety of your existential bitterness for decades to come, so that you can think life isn't quite as bad as you once feared, since everything that's wrong with it is actually your spouse's fault. Even if you don't ever act on your feelings, from this point forward you can believe that you don't have to die in order to escape from the dreary reality in which you sometimes feel trapped; you can just get divorced. Your marriage partner, in other words, allows you to hold on to your hope. It's a profound gesture of total, thankless altruism, if you think about it, but you don't think about it, because, by virtue of the particular service they're providing, you're too busy feeling resentful to feel the appropriate gratitude.

Much to her chagrin, and at the cost of her own hopes of sleeping soundly through the night, my wife's presence intrudes all the way into my private nightmares. Even when I should be getting away from everything that's troubling or annoying me, into some otherworldly place where I can forget who I am and what I believe my life has become, my wife is still somehow there. And not just an imagined version, but the actual physical person, right at the threshold of my bad dream, ready to pull me back into the room, either kindly or cruelly, so I can think, as I regain my sense of reality and watch her as she tries to get back to sleep, Thanks to you, I'm no longer afraid. I thought I had eaten something deadly, but I was wrong. What a relief to realize that you're still here, I'm not dead, and we're going to be together like this for as long as I can imagine.

WENDY BRENNER

Strange Beads

FROM *Oxford American*

> Virtually anything can become an amulet, depending on beliefs and resources.
>
> —*Harper's Encyclopedia of Mystical & Paranormal Experience*

THE PAIN IN MY MIDSECTION felt like a dull routine by the time I came across the *Vintage brass Made in India red and white mother of pearl bracelet,* a pretty little scallop-edged bangle that caught my eye as I was idly scrolling around on eBay. There was something charismatic about it, winking out from its dark tiny cell of a thumbnail photo. It seemed to appeal to me personally, like a particular kitten or puppy at the pound who makes eye contact. It gave me déjà vu, reminded me of some dim, distant place I couldn't quite identify. It recalled, suddenly and vividly, the doomed Pier 1 Imports store that opened a block away from my childhood home in the mid-1970s, not yet a brightly lit corporate clone but a dark warehouse full of a thousand genuinely foreign trinkets and uncategorizable tchotchkes, with aquariums of live tropical fish and hermit crabs lining the back wall. My sister and I stopped in daily to peruse, buy, or shoplift small mysterious items—worry dolls, Belgian gumdrops, incense cones—before the store's roof collapsed under the weight of wet snow in the Chicago blizzard of 1979. I was twelve that year, haunted by those fish and crabs freezing to death in the ruins. When spring came, the building was torn down and a nice new public library constructed in its place. No one said what happened to the hermit crabs.

The bracelet on eBay looked like something from the ruined store. But I never bought jewelry from eBay; I hardly even wore jewelry. Or hardly wore it anymore, I should say, since I never went out anymore, since I'd undergone five surgeries in five years' time, each leaving behind its own new circuitry of pain: damaged nerves, a colon held together by titanium clips, scar tissue where muscles used to be, tendinitis from premature attempts to exercise my way back to wholeness. All of these remained long after the cancer that started it all was eradicated. The invisible knife in my gut was not psychosomatic; my nerves had simply been cut too often, the doctors explained, and had regenerated new branches that went nowhere, a Möbius loop of pointless synaptic signals. Thus "recovered," months after my last operation, I could no longer remember what it felt like not to spend most of each day in wary negotiation with pain. I missed birthdays, weddings, and funerals. Many days it hurt to wear clothes; jewelry seemed beside the point. On the worst days, my body itself seemed beside the point.

Just before the last of the surgeries, I'd learned that my ex-fiancé had recently died—in late-stage alcoholism, he had "bled out" through his esophagus, alone in a residential hotel room in Phoenix, Arizona, far away from me and my narrow life as a professor in North Carolina. I was, by choice, not speaking to him at the time. I couldn't save him; I was *putting on my own oxygen mask first.* Jim had pulled me out of the dark again and again over the years, even after our engagement ended. Once, when I was stranded in a bed-and-breakfast in a strange town after a disastrous cross-country move—AWOL moving van, shyster landlord—Jim told me on the phone, *At least you're in a beautiful room.* It was a line I thought of often now, after his death, as I lay around waiting for my body to quit hurting. No day passed during those long months in which I did not think of following him. I lived alone; no one else was around to argue the point. A sentence floated to the top of my consciousness: *Ever since Jim died, I've had one foot out the door.*

There was no further description on eBay of the *Vintage brass Made in India red and white mother of pearl bracelet* besides its unwieldy title, its starting price of 99 cents, and a boilerplate backstory that appeared on all the listings posted by that seller, someone with the user name Bergbay310:

> This is one of many individual pieces or lots of vintage/costume jewelry I am listing every week over the coming months from a huge old collection. There are thousands of necklaces/sets and more bracelets earrings brooches charms than I can count that I am just getting to and all are in near perfect condition and more is coming . . . The collector frequented estate sales in Pasadena California for years and these items have sat safely in boxes . . . There is so much!!

I was struck by that breathless exclamation—*There is so much!!*—as if Bergbay310, whoever he was, had stumbled upon the treasure chest of the collective unconscious itself, the portal to those magical extra rooms that appear in our dreams, full of impossible abundance. Those rooms had been closed to me for a while. Shortly after I was diagnosed with cancer, I'd even had the opposite dream, in which I couldn't reach the real rooms of my real house. Only recently had I begun again to have the magical-extra-rooms dream, always the same house, familiar yet no place I'd ever seen in real life, with vast airy wings and corridors I would discover and realize I had neglected, sunken drawing rooms with vaulted sky-blue ceilings, ornate gilt furniture and grand pianos, oversized arched doorways leading to still more rooms—stretching out lavishly, improbably, a little scarily, in all directions. *There is so much!!*

Salespeople are supposed to operate on the principle of scarcity—*Only a few left in stock!*—but Bergbay310 seemed to be employing an opposite strategy on eBay, or no strategy at all, freely offering the key to Ali Baba's cave. Someone else had already bid 99 cents on the *Vintage brass Made in India red and white mother of pearl bracelet,* but I bid $1.04 and won. I sent my electronic payment to Bergbay310's PayPal account, which was registered under the name of a man I'll call Archie, with a Los Angeles PO box address. When the bracelet arrived a few days later, it did not disappoint; its colors were brighter than they appeared in the photo and had more depth—nothing obvious or easily definable, but you looked for a few moments longer than you might at some newer piece of jewelry. The brass had patina, which gave the piece a kind of authority. It felt good in my hand, a nice cold heavy little thing.

I logged back onto eBay, clicked on Bergbay310's page—and the portal swung open.

How can I communicate the vastness, the cognitive dissonance, the essential weirdness and sheer impossibility of Bergbay310's collection? As promised, he had *hundreds upon hundreds* of items for sale, but they were not lumped together in a big junky pile, the way most people sell off a grandmother's stash of costume jewelry. Rather, the goods were offered for our consideration in pages and pages of single-item listings, even though none of the items appeared to be remotely high-end (if there even is such a thing as "high-end" junk jewelry). Furthermore, none of the objects seemed to *go together.* There were brooches, necklaces, earrings, bracelets, sweater clips, scatter pins, cigarette cutters, tie tacks, scarf clasps, lapel pins, perfume bottles, pillboxes, hair combs, belt buckles, lighter holders, hundreds of pairs of cufflinks, and dozens of items so obscure that their purpose could not be determined. No two items were the same, nothing looked new or mass-produced, and there was no common thread or organizing principle I could detect. Every conceivable style, design, aesthetic, and time period was represented, and every region of the U.S. and world, from ancient Greek to Gilded Age glitz to midcentury regional Americana kitsch. A *Vintage/ Antique Brooch Pin GOLDTONE THREE GRACES CAMEO WITH HOOK* was listed alongside a *Vintage/ Antique Brooch Pin GOLDTONE AIRPLANE PROPELLER NEAT!*, a *Vintage/ Antique Pendant Charm egyptian style cat head SUPER COOL,* and a *Vintage/ Antique Brooch Pin Gold tone Totem Pole VANCOUVER GREAT!* Every item, large or small, antique or recent, had a starting price of 99 cents, from *Vintage/ Antique Set Earrings Necklace silvertone pink gems rhinestones FABULOUS* to *Vintage Brooch wooden head missing an ear still neat.*

The items ranged from stately and elegant to exotic and bohemian to bizarre and indecipherable. Each item had just one accompanying photo, underexposed against a black background, poor quality even by eBay standards. Some photos were so dark you couldn't see the item at all. The listing titles, such as *Vintage/ Antique clip of some sort orange plastic roses bakelite..???* suggested that Bergbay was not a jewelry expert or even a connoisseur. *Vintage/ Antique Pendant Charm 4 in long ostrich silvertone & lasso..???* appeared to be an obscure kitchen utensil, something in the whisk family, or maybe an ancient Roman sex toy. *Vintage/ Antique Pendant Charm of octopus style dangle silver bells?* looked like a pile of chains and beads in the process of metamorphosing into a small octopus. Sometimes the title and photo were clear but the object itself was inexplicable, like the *Vintage Antique Pendant Charm Miniature Real Tested Silver MOOSE TRAIN* (a moose hitched to a steam engine train), or the *Vintage/ Antique Real Tested Silver bracelet 7in marked sterling fish traffice,* which was a charm bracelet with only two charms, a fish and a traffic light. Some items did not seem to fall under the category heading "Vintage Jewelry" at all, such as *Small lot old Vintage one inch greenish rocks NEAT,* or *Large lot old Shark teeth each measures approx 1 inch long mixed grey brown NEAT.* (Like all of Bergbay's items, these teeth were automatically categorized by eBay as "pre-owned.") Many listing titles ended with smiley faces, as if Bergbay were simply shrugging his shoulders, with a wink, and giving up.

Most people who inherit or otherwise acquire large collections of stuff they don't want and on which they are not experts—stamps, postcards, costume jewelry—simply get an appraisal and sell the lots in their entirety. On eBay one can find huge lots of almost everything for sale, but it's rare to find a seller with more than, say, a dozen single-item costume jewelry listings, because why bother? Fifty is the maximum number of free listings eBay allows each seller per month—above that, the seller pays a listing fee—so why didn't Bergbay just put the whole huge lot up for sale at once and be done with it? Was the collection more personal than he was letting on? Did he care if his stuff sold at all? Maybe the display itself was the point, like the famous, possibly apocryphal Theatre of Memory, constructed by the sixteenth-century Italian scholar and/or charlatan Giulio Camillo in an attempt to gather together and display every facet of the entire universe, seen and unseen, via allegorical representation, in a wooden cabinet.

Some of Bergbay's item titles were so off-puttingly cryptic that they appeared to be anagrams, or code—*Vintage/ Antique Pendant Charm old goldtone with man woman scene needs, Vintage/ Antique Pendant Charm Miniature carved glass reverse paint hands pray*—and it occurred to me that English might be Bergbay's second language. Maybe Bergbay himself was the fabled anonymous collector of his description, a world traveler and importer of international antiques. But what kind of obsessed collector expresses such sincere-sounding bafflement before so many of his own items, doesn't recognize a simple jade horn charm *(Vintage/ Antique Pendant Charm green polished jade "tooth" or "fang"!),* consistently misspells *amber* as *ember,* yet is obscurely educated enough to describe a pendant as a *Tetragram astral zodiac planet?* Maybe, I thought, Bergbay was actually two people, an importer and his assistant. Maybe the assistant was his wife, or maybe there was a wife *and* an assistant. One of them, Bergbay, wife, or assistant, obviously did not speak English very well, and one of them kept calling everything *NEAT!*

Finally, though, I couldn't believe that Bergbay himself—or Bergie, as I had begun to think of him—was the original collector. Because of the proximity of Hollywood and the theatrical nature of so many of the items—*Vintage/ Antique Brooch Pin INCH MAGICIAN HAT AND WAND GEMSTONES NEAT, Vintage/ Antique Pendant Charm Miniature baby grand piano top opens NEAT*—I imagined some crazed celebrity behind it all. Someone famously eccentric, like Phil Spector, or secretly eccentric, like Nancy Reagan. Someone desperate to remain anonymous. At one point I had the thrilling revelation that the entire collection could very conceivably have belonged to Sid and Marty Krofft, creators of *H. R. Pufnstuf* and *Lidsville,* those druggy, trippy '70s children's TV shows. Support for this hypothesis grew with each new round of listings—brooches shaped like mushrooms, like pipes, *Vintage Brooch pin strange twisted silvertone spoon rock quartz crystal sugar, Vintage/ Antique Pendant Charm Miniature goldtone mother of pearl cuckoo clock.* But Bergie's collection was so large and wide-ranging that ultimately I couldn't believe it came from a single source, one person (or even one pair of whacked-out brothers) with a single set of aesthetic tastes.

Not that I cared. By now I was so infatuated that I bid on every item that even slightly appealed to me. Not long after I bought the red-and-white bracelet, I managed to win a *Vintage 3in diameter old clasp bracelet handmade in Greece brass & multi color* and a *Vintage/ Antique Pendant Charm 1.2x1 inch flower lucite block So Dakota NEAT!,* which was a clear cube with a tiny dried brown flower preserved inside, engraved "So. Dakota." I had never even visited South Dakota, but I no longer had any doubt that these items were meant for me.

Unfortunately, Bergbay310 had quickly developed a devoted following. Soon so many bidders were fighting over his items that it became difficult to win anything for less than $10. His photos had improved—he now used a white background and possibly even a flashbulb—and while everything still started at 99 cents, a glass bead costume necklace might now end up selling for $30; anything with rhinestones went for at least $20. A plastic Scottie dog brooch sold for $44, and a garden-variety locket—not precious metal, no stones, nothing special—went for $84.68. Most astonishing was the tiny silver "Flown Snoopy" lapel pin, a service award NASA has presented since 1968 to thousands of its employees. (The Snoopy pins are all flown on space missions first; there are Snoopys flying around up there right now.) *Does not have back or any paperwork,* Bergie noted in a rare addendum to his boilerplate description. *Collector said he acquired in San Diego and has had for while in Pasadena.* It sold for $355.

I resorted to trying to get the oddest, ugliest, or most inexplicable items, things nobody else would be likely to want, but even then I was almost always outbid at the last moment. After engaging in and losing a short bidding war over a *Vintage/ Antique NECKLACE strange beads shells acorns DIFFERENT :),* I realized I needed to step up my game and start sniping, the eBay term for lurking silently, bidding only in an auction's final seconds. In this manner I successfully snagged the *Vintage/ Antique Brooch Pin 2X.5INCH GOLDTONE CLOWN VERY DIFFERENT!,* a creepy smiling wicker-like creation with a cone-shaped hat and glittery blue rhinestone eyes, and a *Vintage/ Antique Brooch Pin UNIQUE orange splatter pain wooden? NEAT!,* which looked like a larval creature designed by Jackson Pollock. I had never once worn a brooch, nor could I recall ever saying the word *brooch* in my life. I came to understand that I was collecting the collection: *Anonymous collector, c'est moi.*

As a reality check, I started e-mailing select links from Bergie's eBay page to an old friend in Chicago, a consummate thrifter and expert on all things vintage. She wrote back: *That is seriously the most wacked out jewelry I've ever seen.* The next week she wrote: *So, I try to steel myself for whatever it is I'm about to see because it's definitely going to be bizarre, and yet, I'm still never prepared for what I actually see.* Then she wrote: *Bergie's subtitle for every piece should be: THE most bat-shit crazy jewelry man has created.* Finally she wrote: *I think he's some kind of jewelry wizard and he's conjuring it up somehow.*

It wasn't like this thought hadn't occurred to me. There were a large number of magical- and mystical-themed items in Bergie's collection *(Vintage antique miniature charm pendant neat hieroglyph key,*

Vintage charm pendant or miniature king titan sea god, Vintage Brooch Pin VERY INTERESTING serpents eagles upside down cross crest COOL), and while I still nurtured my Krofft Brothers theory, I now strongly suspected Bergie's entire story about the collection's provenance was a fabrication. This was eBay, after all, where there is no limit on how many dead grandmothers you can have, or how much jewelry each might have left you. I noticed that as the number of Bergie's listings multiplied by the week—he now had as many as 1,700 items for sale simultaneously—he kept updating his boilerplate. The mythical collector who had frequented Pasadena estate sales was still in there, but Bergie now claimed to have *over 3000 more signed brooches FEW THOUSAND MORE signed necklaces/sets and more bracelets earrings boxes full of undiscovered stuff than I can count . . . I have hundreds of pounds coming a week . . .*

Where in the known universe could anyone collect, steal, buy, or otherwise procure *hundreds of pounds* of antique costume jewelry per *week*? There were not enough little old ladies in the world, not even in Pasadena, to account for it. I thought of that scene in the movie *Poltergeist* in which a stream of dusty watches, bracelets, and brooches suddenly pours out of the living room ceiling, dropped by the dead from their world into ours. (The *living* room, get it?) There was a name for that stuff, according to my *Harper's Encyclopedia of Mystical & Paranormal Experience:* apports, defined as "object[s] certain mediums and adepts claim to materialize from thin air or transport through solid matter . . . including food, precious jewelry, religious objects." While most apports were small objects, the *Encyclopedia* said, some could be "large and quite unusual, such as flowers, books, serving dishes, and live animals, fish, and birds." I had in fact recently encountered a large peacock jogging on the sidewalk alongside my car past blocks of low-rent apartment complexes, on my latest trip to the post office to pick up a package from Bergie.

It was obvious from the comments on Bergie's Feedback Profile that I was not alone in my bewitchment:

Seller offered best price, quick and secure delivery magical item.

My totem animal is the elephant. I love these guys.

Unique dragon, great service. Thank you!

Thank you I lost a brooch just like this & finally found it again.

Not sure what it is, but love it!

The beads do look like a rainbow.

Even the negative reviews sounded like they came from other magicians matter-of-factly shopping on eBay for tools of the trade: *Ring shattered within 20 mins of putting on my finger,* wrote one customer.

So sorry—will send you another one!! Bergie replied.

Old but not "neat," beads missing (a lot) on one earring, wrote a customer with the user ID "ma2gical."

Hi! That is the design :) replied Bergie.

The person who outbid me on *Vintage/ Antique NECKLACE strange beads shells acorns DIFFERENT :)* wrote: *this was weirder than expected and not useful*—in his or her spells, presumably—which I found perversely satisfying. I was the rightful owner of that necklace and we both knew it.

By the time I finally worked up the nerve to contact Bergie, he had come to seem like a celebrity; when I saw his name on the reply in my inbox, I got that frisson you feel when you see a friend in person whom you normally only ever talk with on Facebook. In my e-mail I'd said I was a fan and frequent buyer of his items and that I wanted to write a story about the collection. The response, which came within a few hours, was not from Archie but from his wife—a cheerful young woman I will call Veronica. Her e-mail—and all her subsequent messages—were, like her thousands of listing titles, punctuated by smiley faces and multiple exclamation points. *I too am still totally shocked by the size of this guys collection and I have tried hard to get as much info as I can from him too but don't have a ton of "facts" ha ha,* she wrote. *I started selling this stuff off on ebay part time last summer and thought I would be done by now but it seems his collection is endless.* Her background was in real estate, she told me, and her husband had nothing to do with the operation; she only used his name on the account. His only involvement was to help her haul the heavy boxes she picked up every week from the mysterious collector. Yes, there really was a collector. He was a Hispanic man in his sixties (she referred to him as "elderly"), a retired jeweler who had lived in Mexico for twenty-five years and possibly also in Argentina at some point; she wasn't positive. He didn't speak much English, but Veronica happened to speak Spanish, so they communicated in both languages.

It all started at an estate sale in Altadena, where she and her husband went to look for art—and also, she said, she just liked looking at "neat old homes." Some of the collector's family members were at the sale, and they suggested that Veronica meet their relative and check out his wares, which he was looking to sell off. She herself rarely wore jewelry, she told me, besides her platinum wedding band, but after viewing some of the man's collection, she happily negotiated to purchase the entire lot, paid in advance by the pound—and thus began her relationship, her conscription, with the collector. He knew she intended to sell the lot piece by piece on eBay, and that was fine with him. She didn't know anything about costume jewelry, but she bought a few books so she could start researching it. Every week, then, he began delivering the goods—hundreds of pounds packed neatly in huge, moving-size cartons. They conducted these transactions at a public park, Veronica said, because he did not want his neighbors to see him moving so many boxes out of his house. (She also believed he kept a storage unit—there was simply too much to fit in any house.)

Seriously, a park? Argentina? Drugs had to be involved somehow, but I couldn't quite work it out. Smuggling cocaine inside a . . . *Vintage/ Antique Brooch Pin teeny miniature goldtone mouse green gems one gone*? A fence operation made no sense either, unless there was a black market for 99-cent costume jewelry. Anyway, I could not believe someone as open and seemingly wholesome as Veronica would involve herself in such a sketchy business, let alone tell a complete stranger the details. And then there was the problem of posting the thousands of pieces of evidence online, in plain public view. Plus Veronica sounded as bewildered by her story as I was. She felt like Scrooge McDuck, she said, shoveling through the mountains of jewelry in her house, trying to keep up with the supply, get it sorted, photographed, labeled, listed, sold, packed, and shipped. Archie was growing annoyed because he kept stepping on pins and rhinestones. Her father was worried about her. Veronica had enlisted her sisters to help, but there was still no end in sight. *He just dropped 1800 pairs of cufflinks (matching sets with tie tacks) off Sunday,* she wrote me in an e-mail. *UNBELIEVABLE—I almost had a heart attack—no more room in my house ha ha It just keeps coming . . .*

No matter how fast she worked, how much she sold, she did not appear to be making a dent. Like the sorcerer's apprentice, she might even have been making things worse. *Did I tell you he gave me 900 collectible old photo negatives of trains ships and trolleys?* she wrote to me. *And that he has over 200,000 collectible civil war time documents? We were supposed to have gotten to those by this summer but jewelry isn't ending and he hasn't said when it will! I ask him and he just exhales and laughs and says "OOHH LONG TIME MORE"* . . . .

Of all the jewelry I purchased from Bergie—I still think of Veronica that way—the *Vintage brass Made in India red and white mother of pearl bracelet* remains my favorite, though I've never once worn it. It sits atop a stack of Powell and Pressburger DVDs on my coffee table, an objet d'art keeping me company while I watch the 1947 movie *Black Narcissus* for the fiftieth time. The bracelet matches the movie's hyper-saturated reds and creamy, nuanced whites, colors the film's designers obsessed over and won Oscars for. "Vermeer was the sort of painter I had in mind on *Black Narcissus,*" the cinematographer Jack Cardiff said; he modeled shots in the film after Vermeer and Van Gogh paintings, which he liked to copy by hand in his free time as a hobby. "It's great art, and then it will be kitsch, and then it will be art again," said the contemporary director Alan Parker about the film, in 2009.

Based on Rumer Godden's 1939 novel, *Black Narcissus* is "a story about the disorientation of European nuns in India," according to Wikipedia, which is like calling *Alice in Wonderland* a book about a girl who takes a nap and has some dreams. The escalating hallucinogenic beauty of the remote, half-ruined Himalayan palace to which the British nuns are sent drives each of them slowly mad in her own way. One secretly mail-orders a bright red dress and lipstick from the city, another is haunted by relentless memories of an emerald necklace and earrings she gave up years ago, and the no-nonsense sister in charge of the garden finds herself surreptitiously planting beds of exotic flowers instead of the vegetables they all need to survive. *There is no escape from beauty,* the film seems to say. "There's something in the atmosphere that makes everything seem exaggerated!" exclaims one character.

I watched *Black Narcissus* for the first time in 2011 and quickly discovered that it worked better than any drug or therapy to break my mind and body out of their ever-constricting room of pain. All of Powell and Pressburger's films worked on me this way, alchemically, like great art, larger than the sum of its parts. I especially loved *The Red Shoes,* based on the Hans Christian Andersen fairy tale about a girl who gets her wish for magic shoes, then can't take them off and dances herself to death. "Time rushes by, love rushes by, life rushes by," says her Svengali, Boris Lermontov, in the film, "but the red shoes dance on."

I could so relate. In 2001, I was thirty-five years old with two published books and a tenured teaching job. I had never spent a single night in the hospital in my life. Then, overnight, it seemed, the warranty ran out. To quote Joy Williams's short story "The Route":

> A worn battery cable shorted out on the frame, setting fire to the engine at the same time an electrode from the spark plug fell into the combustion chamber, disintegrating the piston. The tires went flat the transmission fluid exploded the gas tank collapsed an armature snapped shooting the generator pulley through the hood the brake shoes melted the windshield cracked and the glove compartment flew open spilling my panties into the street.

In *The Red Shoes* I found a literal, practical kind of sustenance, watching perfect bodies move perfectly, knowing how much pain each had endured, tortured over a period of years in the interest of producing a bit of beautiful ephemera. "It was 1947," wrote the *Red Shoes* director Michael Powell in his autobiography. "A great war was over and a great danger to the whole world had been eliminated. The message of the film was Art. Nothing mattered but Art." There wasn't much else left to care about at my place either.

When Jim, my ex-fiancé, and I met, I was still in high school, and he owned and ran a successful comedy club and experimental theater—a sort of circus I hoped to run away to—but his true love had always been art. He attended design school before I knew him, and one of his last jobs before his death was at a Lucite studio, where he designed housewares and jewelry. By that point I was so busy working toward my imagined future that I had little time for his increasingly bitter phone calls, which seemed to come from my past. Now my body was failing and Jim was dead, the doors to both past and future closed and locked, and I was missing most of the present.

A few years before his death, Jim sent me a Lucite jewelry box he'd made for me—a simple, clear rectangular box with storage drawers, clean lines, nothing elaborate. Because I didn't wear much jewelry and already owned many other items he had given me over the years, and because I didn't know he was dying, I unthinkingly donated the box to a thrift store. It wasn't until I realized I was collecting Bergie's collection that I remembered the jewelry box and wished for it back, too late. Like everything else about Jim, the gift seemed prescient and miraculous—as if he had known someday I would need it.

"Cherish anything that wakes you up, if even for an instant," Joy Williams once wrote to me, a line which brought to mind a poem by Rumi: *The door is round and open. / Don't go back to sleep.* I still place bids on Bergbay310's offerings from time to time, surprised with each new round of listings at which items I win, which I lose. Like horoscopes, they are always uncannily, perfectly relevant. The latest shipment from Pasadena included a *Vintage/ Antique Pendant Charm Miniature mother of pearl clown.* For some reason I was the only one who wanted it—nobody else even placed a bid. Inside the package Bergie had added a tiny folded Post-it note that read: *To: The Home for Orphaned Clowns. Attn: Wendi.*

Like pain, like art, the collection is infinite. It has woken me up; I won't go back to sleep.

JOHN H. CULVER

The Final Day in Rome

FROM *The Gettysburg Review*

THE WAITING ROOM in the ER at Rome's Policlinico was a vast rectangle with four banks of chairs set facing each other in a much smaller rectangle. One group of chairs was missing a front stabilizer, which meant that any time someone sat down or stood up, the rest of the chairs moved in unison. Those not seated milled about in quiet conversation or stood near the faded tan walls that were covered with a variety of posters providing health tips and warnings. Two big-screen television sets hung from opposing walls. Reruns of *Starsky & Hutch* and *Quincy* dubbed in Italian aired across the gulf of the wide room. The ceiling was a good fifty feet above us. You could play field hockey in this place if you removed the chairs. The tile floor was grooved from foot traffic.

Ten hours earlier we had been on a tour bus seeing the sights. We had listened to the recorded dialogue in Spanish, French, English, and German announcing the various historic buildings we passed. The bus slowed at these but didn't stop. Rome was easing into its hot summer period, and I imagined how stifling the city would be if the temperatures were fifteen degrees warmer and there was no breeze to stir the air. Now I was standing in the emergency room wondering if she would live or die.

I alternated between scribbling notes on my small pad of paper and pacing the enormous room. I felt the need to record things, since my mind was not holding on to facts or the sequence of events that had brought me to a hospital in Rome at the end of what had been a glorious day. Occasionally I would glance at the TV screen to see a suspicious Jack Klugman in the autopsy room about to cut into a corpse. Before his scalpel touched flesh, he would say something that seemed to be of major importance, even dubbed in Italian. I never saw this show back home, but the Italian language made the scenes appear interesting. *Starsky & Hutch* was a chase-and-crash cop show, an insult in any language.

Across from me, a petite woman with the complexion and bone structure of someone from the Balkans sat quietly with her Italian partner. There was no indication of what they were doing in the medical facility. Neither of them had visible wounds or bandages, nor was there any blood on their clothes. They never approached the desk where several attendants recorded business. The woman, who was so small and delicate it seemed I could hold her in my hand, would periodically get up and go to both the men's and women's bathrooms and emerge with thick skeins of toilet paper wrapped around her hands. She would then patiently unwrap and rewrap the paper. The man never said a word, but every thirty minutes or so he would walk outside for a smoke. Everyone seemed to light up—nurses, patients, family—which left the outside patio carpeted with cigarette butts.

The ER was in Rome's largest hospital, which was also a teaching hospital. Ambulances, dented and scraped from numerous encounters with other vehicles, wailed into the bays at regular intervals, their service increasing as afternoon wore into evening in response to rush-hour incidents. The hospital was built in the postwar years, and different wings had been appended at various times over the decades. White-clad staff came and went, the waiting room a central passage point to the other medical areas. The tiny woman unraveled her toilet paper. An ancient man with a cleaning cart mopped around the chairs and the surrounding areas by the walls with regularity, tingeing the air with a whiff of disinfectant. After he did the bathrooms, the woman retrieved the replenished supply of toilet paper. We veterans of the ER were amused by newcomers who entered the respective bathrooms and emerged with quizzical looks on their faces; it had taken me two hours to realize that only the bathroom reserved for the handicapped contained toilet paper, something they would deduce for themselves if they remained in the ER long enough. Every now and then the loudspeaker would broadcast a message or request in rapid-fire Italian that would have been incomprehensible in any language; every hospital in the world has the same garbled public address system.

There was an orderly chaos to everything. No one was frantic.

Doctors and nurses hurried by; some stopped briefly at the time clock to punch in or out; others opened doors and quickly disappeared behind them. Periodically the main ER portal opened, and someone would call out the name of a waiting family and ask them to come inside or beckon someone waiting for treatment.

We had stopped at a small market after the tour ended to pick up a few things for the long flight home the next day. After a few minutes I realized she hadn't moved. She stood by a fruit bin. One hand was placed on the left back side of her head. "Pain," she said. I asked if it was like one of her migraines. "No, that's over here," and she tapped the back right side of her head. "This is different." After a few moments the pain lessened, and we slowly walked the several blocks back to the hotel. She felt better after resting and then went to the bathroom to pack her toiletries. She came out, grabbed the left side of her head again, and muttered, "Oh God." The pupils in both eyes vanished behind her eyelids, and she slowly folded into my arms. In the ambulance I showed one of the attendants her insurance card, but she just looked at me sternly and said, "No, free, free."

I finally heard the call of "Robertson," not my name but hers. A man in a white coat saw me respond and quickly came to guide me to a small office behind the desk, as if I couldn't navigate by myself. Three youngish women were there, two in white physician garb and the other in a nurse's uniform. One had tears in her eyes. Between the three struggling to find the right words in English, I heard "brain aneurysm," "wasn't expected to make it through the night," and "do you want to say goodbye?"

Contemporary American pop tunes were playing in the ER. The staff went about their business, giving injections, inserting tubes, and cleaning the gray-brown seepage from the brain of the man in the bed next to hers. Many sets of eyes were on me as I looked at her. She was comatose, her chest rising and falling with shallow breaths, a ventilator in her throat. I said goodbye for her daughters, two grandchildren, and myself. A beautiful woman, inside and out. I left through the ambulance doors, nodding to those taking a smoke break, and walked back to the hotel in utter disbelief at what had taken place over the four hours since she had collapsed in our hotel room.

I returned at six the following morning. There was an odd but different collection of souls in the waiting room from the previous evening. Now the televisions were showing Italian news. I alternated between pacing and sitting for three hours before "Robertson" was called out again. She had died moments earlier. I repeated the goodbyes and collected myself as best I could, sitting at a small desk that had the computer with the charts of the several people in the ER visible on the screen. Nurses and physicians patted my shoulders. Their touches and anguished looks were heartfelt. My final act in the hospital was to sign the form for organ and cornea transplants. Another gathering of medical staff stood outside smoking when I left. We traded single arm waves in the air.

The U.S. embassy was several miles from the hospital, a walk that went quickly. Italian soldiers were stationed in front of the embassy, sinister automatic weapons slung over their shoulders as if a terrorist movie scene were about to be filmed. I stated my business to one, went through the security check, and walked up the stairs to the second story, where a few of us gathered to report lost passports and other problems. I filled out the Report of Death in a Foreign Country form. The Italian man who assisted me anticipated my questions, probably from handling such reports too many times. I surrendered her passport and printed the contact information for her daughters. He asked if I wanted to use the embassy phone to call anyone back home, or if I needed additional funds to fly home. I didn't. He gave me a sheet with the names of several funeral homes in Rome that had experience—and staff fluent in English—in handling the deaths of Americans.

I arranged for her to be cremated and the ashes returned to me by air at an international airport, since the urn had to clear customs. I gave her clothes to a maid at the hotel who knew no more English than I did Italian, but her sorrowful look said she was aware of her *morte*.

My seatmate on the plane and I chatted a bit. She was several years older than I and was returning to the West Coast, where her third husband would meet her. She had outlived two previous husbands, and this one wouldn't travel with her, she reported with a laugh. She recommended the Nixon-Frost movie. We both put on our earpieces, and the movie began. We were flying west with the sun. I dreaded the return to earth.

KRISTIN DOMBEK

Letter from Williamsburg

FROM *The Paris Review*

THERE ARE MANY KINDS of prayer. There is a kind of prayer that's like breathing. There is a kind of prayer that's like talking to your best friend all day long. There is a kind of prayer in the face of beauty that lifts your hands up because it would be harder to keep them down. There is a kind of prayer for meaning that is answered by the one who wrote the book of the whole world and your life, so that the prayer is like waking up and finding yourself a character in the most elaborate of novels, as you've always suspected: authored, written into a world of meaning, a world meaningful because it was created by someone. There is a kind of prayer that is only a listening, the soft voice of God saying your name, saying "Come to me, come to me." There is the prayer of failure, and the answering voice that forgives you. There is the death prayer, your whole body crying "why" and the voice again, telling you that you will see your loved one again in heaven.

And there is one more kind of prayer. In this one, you are tired of wrestling with God—with the problems of evil and suffering and the way that anyone who doesn't believe in him is going to hell. You're trying not to masturbate, or think about girls, or about having sex with multiple people at the same time, but you're masturbating and thinking about girls and about having sex with multiple people at the same time anyway. So you give up. You nearly stop believing. You don't even have the words to ask God to come back, or be real; you slip down into the region below speech. And then he comes. He fills the bedroom with a presence that is unmistakably outside of you, the peace that passes understanding, a love that in its boundlessness feels different in kind from human love.

When God came into my teenage or college bedroom in that way, unasked and unmistakable, the next morning I would wake up changed. I'd go out into the world and give away everything I could. Wouldn't drive past a broken-down car without stopping to help, was kind and grateful even with my parents, couldn't stop singing, built houses for poor people, gave secret gifts to my friends, things like that. Sometimes it lasted for weeks; once, when I was in my early twenties, it lasted for nearly a year. It is called being on fire for God. It's like you've glimpsed the world's best secret: that love need not be scarce.

It has been fifteen years since I stopped believing, and I have been able to explain to myself almost everything about the faith I grew up in, but I have not been able to explain those experiences of a God so real he entered bedrooms of his own accord, lit them up with joy, and made people generous. For a long time it puzzled me why, if I made God up, I couldn't make up this feeling myself.

Like most women in Williamsburg, Brooklyn, I have spent thousands of hours and dollars on yoga classes attempting to manufacture unconditional love and moral bliss by detaching from my ego and my desires and also, not coincidentally, working on the quality of my ass. Because in the back of my mind, what I have been wondering (is this what the other women are wondering while we sit in lotus position on purple foam cubes, meditating in our jewel-toned leggings and tattoos?) is this: Isn't there some human who can make me feel this way instead?

After I stopped believing in God, I would sometimes wake in a panic at being alone without supernatural support. So I memorized Richard Wilbur's poem "Love Calls Us to the Things of This World" to say to myself in the morning. When I woke with someone in my bed, I would recite it to him or her:

> The eyes open to a cry of pulleys,
> And spirited from sleep, the astounded soul
> Hangs for a moment bodiless and simple
> As false dawn.
> Outside the open window
> The morning air is all awash with angels.

Wilbur is talking about laundry dancing on a clothesline outside the window in the morning, white sheets and smocks that one mistakes for angels. It is because one wants to see the laundry as spiritual that "the soul shrinks//From all that it is about to remember,/From the punctual rape of every blessed day,/And cries,/'Oh, let there be nothing on earth but laundry.'" Most people I recited the poem to found it a little melodramatic, but it calmed me down.

A few years ago I was living in a loft with a man and two cats and it started to happen again. In the morning, in the split second between sleep and waking, I would almost accidentally start to pray. I'd feel sunlight through the slits in the blinds, register that the alarm on my iPhone was going off, start hitting the bed and the windowsill and digging under myself to find it and tap its little snooze button. There were cats on either side of my head, and my human husband, to the right, was snoring hairily on his back, his hands curling and uncurling on his chest like the paws of a tickled kitten. But despite how many of us there were in the bed, I felt alone and too small to survive, too permeable, too disorganized, and trapped in something I didn't have the words to describe. And something in me stretched up in a physical way toward the place where God used to be. I'd wake up and remember: there is no God. But I wanted to give up anyway, as if in doing so I could be rescued.

There was a red armchair in the corner of the living room, and some days it was as far from the bed as I could get. The first few times I sat in the red chair it was just a comfortable place to think and cry. Then I would find myself in it for whole afternoons. I began to eye the chair, to tell myself not to sit in it. Then I'd tell myself I was just going to sit in it for a little bit. Then hours later the chair would still have me. The cats would sit a few feet from the chair and watch me warily—concerned, but mainly, I believed, judging me. One day when I left for work, I got only to the subway platform and turned back, and the second day, only to the street corner. I told the man about it, and the third day he walked me out and went down in the elevator with me and out the front door, but as soon as he was out of sight I snuck back upstairs to sit in the chair. I remember that for months I could not drive a car, but I cannot remember why I could not drive a car.

I do remember the shape of the sentences that were running

through my head while I was in the red chair, though not the words that were in them. They all went something like this: Is it this or that. Is it my job or my marriage. Is it my marriage or my mind. Is it him or is it me. It was him or me, him this or him that, and then always, But what if it's me this, me that. The sentences were all made of impossible twos. Knowing that the dilemmas did not make sense only made it worse; there was not even the smallest movement of my mind I could trust.

It took several years to get out of the red chair, and to do it I had to leave the loft, the man, and the cats too. I moved into another loft and took very little furniture with me. Soon I met a man at the bar across the street. He was gentle with me but angry at the world's rules. He made what little money he needed by less-than-legal means, and owned only five short-sleeved T-shirts, four long-sleeved T-shirts, two pairs of jeans, and a pair of Converse with holes in the soles. We saw other people and talked all about it, which made for a rare kind of understanding between us. The first woman he and I slept with together was tall and thin with long, expensive black hair. When we laid her down on the floor of my new loft and undressed her, we found, tattooed across her abdomen, just above her neatly waxed pussy, the word *Freedom.*

I'd found Freedom on a South Williamsburg street corner at two in the morning, unlocking her bicycle from a lamppost. She was in a filmy white blouse over shorts and thigh-high stockings, and when I said hello, she started kissing me. I said would you like to meet my boyfriend; do you have a problem with facial hair. He was not really my boyfriend at the time, but that's how it was clearer to talk in certain circumstances. She locked up her bicycle and walked inside the bar to meet him, and she didn't mind the beard. I said do you want to go home with us and she said yes. We walked up the six flights of factory stairs to my loft. We undressed one another and all ended up on the floor rather than on any comfortable piece of furniture. She and I were making out and he was kind of stroking his beard and watching us. And then he moved in and started eating her pussy, at which point she started saying these two sentences: "I want to steal you. I'm gonna steal you and take you home. I want to steal you. I'm gonna steal you and take you home." I was stroking her hair and kissing her neck and when she started saying that I said, "No, you're not gonna steal him, no you're not, just relax and let him make you come." And I held her so he could.

Actually, he didn't make Freedom come; I did. I reached inside her and did what I've only ever done before in secret, that is, away from the world of men, and he watched me. He'd never seen this, the way women can fuck each other; it is quite something to have a man who loves you watch you do it.

The next morning he and I ate egg-and-biscuit sandwiches, drank coffee, and went over the details of the previous night and morning. Then we talked about our childhoods, our dead parents, and other people we were seeing at the time. He was obsessed with a Mississippi girl who had trouble coming, and I offered some strategies. I told him about something sad that had happened to a man I was seeing. We moved on to discussing which of our friends were fighting, or having problems with love or sex, or depressed.

This man had also spent time in a chair, in a dark room, staring at a wall. We tried to remember how it happens, the giving up: how the mind turns on itself and pinions the body to furniture and then convinces you that it is the furniture that has pinioned your mind. The furniture, or the girlfriend, or the husband, with their supernatural ability to cause your feelings. But it is so hard to remember the demonic logic of the place. For our friends we should remember, when they think they're stuck with sadness forever and we're trying to shine some small light on the way out. But mainly it is a blank, like women with babies say labor was.

At one point we stepped outside for cigarettes and were quiet for a moment. It was spring and a new sun was shifting light across the brick buildings on every corner of the intersection. The air felt kind and the neighborhood good, down under the Williamsburg Bridge, just across the river from Manhattan. But it was more than just a nice day: there was a peace immanent and tangible as a body, some kind of giant embrace in the air, and it was most definitely not coming from my mind. I didn't tell him about it or ask him if he felt it. Because I knew this presence, or I'd known it before. It was the one I'd been wondering about, and we'd made it ourselves, but it didn't belong to us, any more than we belonged to each other. Between us, on days like this one, there began to be a very strong sense, quite often, that anything might happen next, a feeling like the opposite of anxiety, the opposite of a panic attack, whatever you would call that.

The second woman who came home with us had only four sentences, but she said them over and over again. The first one was to me: "You're so beautiful. You're so beautiful." Eventually she started kissing me. After a while she broke away from me and said, "You guys are strange. You guys are strange." She was from another country, and the limited sentences were in part because of this, but it was also as if she were, in the very process of seducing us, passing back and forth between two worlds. When she was in one, she would forget about the other. I said, "Do you want to be here, what do you want?" And she looked at me, quiet, and then, with the ferocity of a small puppy, leaned in to kiss me again for a while, and began to undress me. Then she stopped and leaned back and said, "You guys are strange," and I said, "But you decided to be here." This went on for a while. Later, in the middle of things, she started asking me, "Do you really like me or are you just doing this for him?" And I'd say, "I really like you." She'd suck his cock or I'd eat her pussy and then she'd turn to me and say, "Do you really like me or are you just doing this for him?" And I'd be like, "I really like you." And then, hours later, she started saying to me, "You're a boy. You're a boy. You're a boy." And I'd say, "No I'm not, sweetie." And he would say, "No she's not," and point out various parts of my body. "You've been all up in there." And she'd be quiet for a moment, and then say it again: "You're a boy." And I'd say, "No I'm not. I'm a girl."

I understand the trouble she was having very well. The first threesome I was in, before all this, I kept saying to the guy, over and over, "Your girlfriend is gay." I really did. The first time you feel yourself actually attracted to two people at the same time, in the same place, something very deep is shaken. You want to name the new thing, but you need new syntax to do it. Then you find yourself saying sentences like "Just relax and let him make you come," or "Don't be nervous, I can tell she really likes you, and I'll help you pick out a wine she'll love." The opposite of the red-chair and dark-room sentences. Sentences that in the speaking give you a feeling that is different in kind from ordinary human love, at least ordinary romantic love. If you try to find the word for this thing that is the opposite of jealousy, you end up at cheesy polyamory websites, where it is called *compersion:* when you feel happiness for another's happiness, even and especially when it doesn't involve you. Then your friends think you're delusional or stuck in the seventies, and you're basically relegated to having "your song" be George Michael's song "Freedom," which is why when we undressed the first woman who came home with us and found that word tattooed above her pussy, we looked at each other in wonder and a kind of fear.

A few months later, he moved in. The first time I laundered our clothes together I began to gather his underwear, and I didn't recognize it—it must have always come off in his pants, or we were usually drunk—and I thought, Who is this man. When I brought the clothes back from the laundrymat, as he calls it, hot and smelling of "meadow breeze," I put them on my bed and began to fold them, two black T-shirts, two navy T-shirts, one red T-shirt, two long-sleeved T-shirts, and two pairs of jeans, and I started sobbing and couldn't stop, as if doing a man's laundry were the most dangerous thing in the world.

The third woman we brought home had taken some care to lay the groundwork with each of us. With me she would talk about open relationships she'd been in, send me links to articles about unusual arrangements she'd heard of, talk to me about how much she understood. Him, she sexted. When we were together on my couch, there was a moment when she was sucking his cock with real enthusiasm and he was entirely absorbed, away from me, but I was stroking her hair and watching her and it would be the thing she talked about afterward, how much she felt I cared about her during that blowjob. There was a moment when I grabbed his hand and put his fingers inside of me and for a while it was just the two of us, together. There was another moment when he turned away and moved on top of her to fuck her and it was only them, but I was there. There is always a time when they turn away from you, together, and you panic, but if you can watch, just on the other side of the panic is a new kind of knowledge. We had come to think that this might be some part of why God forbade eating of the fruit of the tree of the knowledge of good and evil: eat it and you can no longer believe that your happiness comes from him or me, God or me, him this or her that, or me this or me that. People who are good at monogamy must know these things already.

We have structured our most common sacred relations in twos, but we cannot explain the feeling of God without resorting to threes, or at least the religion I grew up in couldn't. God the Father made and ordered the world, watched and evaluated us from afar, and punished. He was, in fact, a trap; he loved you more than anyone ever could, but only if you only loved him and no one else. There was no place to hide from him, except in Jesus, who drew close, in the flesh, to talk about real love, fuck with the Father's rules, suffer to save us, and retreat to heaven, allowing us to figure out for ourselves what we wanted to do. And then the Holy Spirit, who did not judge and didn't seem to care about these sacrificial games, who just pitched a tent in the air around you and filled it with this wild joy. The one who watched, the one who did, the one who felt. The one with power, the one who suffered, the bliss.

A few months after I first did his laundry, he left in much the same way he'd come, without really asking. He left his clothes in a dirty pile on my bedroom floor. He'd found a girl he wanted to be with, without me, or I'd begun to feel like giving up, or it's hard to do what we were doing and live under one roof. It was his thirty-third year and he wandered through Brooklyn, sleeping and eating where he could, full of new love, and homeless.

People often ask me what it's like to believe in God so completely and then stop. It is like leaving someone you love, or falling in love: when living in one world becomes more difficult than the difficulty of leaving without knowing if the new world will be better, you leave.

I thought about it for years before I did it, but it happened all in a moment. I was sitting in my bed, in my basement room in my college house, and I thought, I have no idea if there's anything else that is true but this can't be true. I closed my eyes and kind of threw myself off a cliff into an empty space. When I opened my eyes, I saw my bookshelf and my rug and my cat and I saw that I had been right. There was a world outside the world I'd known. I have never been so relieved in all my life. And the first thing I wanted to do, but I did not do it, was pray.

DAVE EGGERS

The Man at the River

FROM *Granta*

THERE IS AN AMERICAN sitting by a narrow caramel-colored river in South Sudan. His Sudanese friend, ten years his junior, has brought him to the area, and they have been touring around on bicycles, riding on dirt trails. This day, his Sudanese friend wanted to show the American man a town on the other side of the river, and so they rode a few miles to the riverbank, to this spot, where the river was shallow and slow-moving, and the Sudanese friend waded across.

But the American man decided he couldn't wade across the river. He had cut his shin a few days before, and the cut was unbandaged and deep enough that he is concerned that something in the river, some parasite or exotic microbe, will get into his body via this wound, and because they are hours away from any Western medical care, he might get sick and die here. So he's chosen not to wade across the river. He's chosen to sit on the rocks of the riverbed and wait.

The heat is extreme, and he and his Sudanese friend have been biking for hours, on and off, so the American is happy to have some time alone. But soon the American is not alone. There is a tall man wading across the river toward him, a friend of his Sudanese friend. The American fears what news this second friend could be bringing, why his friend hasn't come himself.

"Hello!" the second friend says.

The American says hello.

"Our mutual friend has sent me. He would like you to visit the village over the river. He has sent me to bring you across."

The American tells him that he's okay, that he's fine, that he would like to stay where he is. He is embarrassed to admit that he doesn't want to wade through the water, which is knee-deep, with his small wound, so he says he's tired and would like to stay.

The second friend stands above him, flummoxed. "Please will you come across the river with me?" he asks. "I was given this task."

The American explains that he's very tired and that he and their mutual friend agreed that he would stay here, on the riverbank, and that this is okay, that the second friend needn't worry.

The second friend's face is twisted, pained. "Well, you see, in our culture," he says, and the American winces, for these words usually precede an unpleasant request, "we must help our guests. It's my duty to help you get to the other side."

The American again insists that he doesn't want to or need to go across the river. As a last resort, the American shows him his wound and tries to explain the possibility that it might become infected.

"But this river is clean," the second friend says.

"I'm sure it is," the American says, hating himself for seeming fragile, "but I read about the many infections we can get here, given the different microbes . . ." The second friend is looking doubtful. "Just like if you came to the U.S.," the American continues. "You would be subject to diseases that were unfamiliar to you. You could get far sicker, far quicker, than we could in our own land . . ."

The second friend shakes off all this talk. "But in our culture," he says again, and the American wants to yell, *This has nothing to do with your culture. You know this and I know this.* "In our culture it is not permitted to allow a guest to sit here like this."

The second friend continues to look pained, and the American begins to realize that the friend will be in trouble—with their mutual friend, and the mutual friend's family, and with everyone else in the town—if the second friend does not accomplish this one task of getting the American across the river. Now the second friend is looking into the distance, his hands on his hips. He squints at a fisherman who is sitting in a small dugout canoe in the bend of the river, and an idea occurs to him. He goes running to the fisherman.

And soon he is back with the fisherman in tow. "This man will take you across."

To the American, the notion of this fisherman interrupting

what he's doing to ferry him across a shallow river is worse, in so many ways, than the thought of contracting some waterborne infection. He tries to refuse again, but he knows now that he's losing. He's lost.

"I don't want this," he says.

"Please. This man will take you. You will not get wet."

The American is smiling grimly, apologetically, at the fisherman, who is not happy to have been asked to do this. *No one wants this,* the American wants to say to the second friend, *no one but you.* But now, because the fisherman is waiting and the second friend has gone to such trouble, it seems that the path of least resistance is to get into the canoe and go across the river. So the American gets in, and notices that in the canoe are six inches of water, so he doesn't sit but only squats among a few nets and no fish.

The fisherman has nowhere to sit, so he stands in the water and begins to pull the canoe across the river in long, labored strides. The second friend is walking next to the fisherman and the two of them argue loudly in Dinka about what's happening. The fisherman is clearly annoyed that this American needs to be ferried across the river like some kind of despot, and the second friend is likely saying, *I know, I know, Lord knows I know.* And the two of them are forming, or confirming, an idea of this American and all Westerners: that they will not walk across a shallow river, that they insist on commandeering canoes from busy fishermen and being pulled across while they squat inside. That they are afraid to get wet.

But the American did not want to go across the river at all. He did not ask for this. He did not ask for any of this. All he wants is to be a man sitting by a riverbed. He doesn't want to be a guest, or a white man, or a stranger or a strange man, or someone who needs to cross the river to see anything at all.

EMILY FOX GORDON

At Sixty-Five

FROM *The American Scholar*

OVER THE PAST FEW YEARS, I've really begun to feel age. I feel it in my left eye, which sometimes leaks spontaneously—I swipe at it with the back of my wrist and people take me to be weeping. I feel it in my new habit of swinging both legs out of the car at the same time, apparently in unconscious response to a directive from the part of my brain that monitors muscle strength and balance. Having risen to my feet, I feel it in an embarrassing arthritic hobble that takes me ten seconds to walk off, hoping all the while that other parking-lot crossers aren't noticing, though several of them seem to be suffering from the same condition, or worse.

I hasten to add that though my muscles may be weakening and my joints stiffening, I'm not infirm. I'm as vigorous as I ever was, and reasonably healthy. Mentally I'm quite intact, though my memory, always bad, grows worse. People tell me I seem younger than my years.

But as I say, I'm feeling age. I feel it in my invisibility to strangers. I haven't been nubile for many years, and never got many glances when I was. I didn't mind that, or told myself I didn't. I saw my ordinary looks as protective coloration, a duck blind behind which I could comfortably observe and take my shots. But I'm not at all sure I like this new kind of anonymity, which is an absolute dismissal. Even in contextualized situations like readings and receptions, eyes slide past me; internal shutters fail to click.

When I was thirty, I felt sure that a paradoxical reward awaited me at sixty, if I made it that far. Having never had any beauty to lose, I reasoned, I'd be exempted from mourning its loss. But as

I've grown older, this proposition has turned inside out. I see now that I did have at least some beauty—not much, but some—and exactly because I had so little, I could hardly afford to lose it. Now, at this inconvenient moment, I realize that I do care about my looks. I find myself spending more energy compensating for my inadequacies than I used to. I search for becoming clothes. I color my hair. I experiment, in a gingerly way, with makeup. I suspect these efforts don't do a lot for me, though they do make some difference, if only in letting people know I'm trying.

But it's not easy to judge success or failure, when these days the reference class itself is collapsing. So many women my age have fallen victim to disqualifying conditions; it's hardly a consolation to congratulate myself on having escaped the ones I've so far escaped. After sixty, nearly every blessing is hinged to a curse that has fallen on someone else. Counting those blessings takes the form of saying to myself, At least I don't have varicose veins; at least I don't have a bald spot; at least I don't have a dowager's hump. Surely there's a diminishing utility in these kinds of comparisons, which extend seamlessly from minor gloating to deadly schadenfreude. (At least I haven't lost my mind. At least I'm not alone.)

There's a saving element of aesthetic disinterestedness in my new concern for superficialities. I find I can amuse myself for hours looking at clothes in stores. In the process, I learn about line and mass and balance, note that V-neck sweaters are flattering and that elbow-length sleeves are not. (Would that I'd learned these lessons earlier, when they were more applicable!) I take pleasure in rifling through racks, in running my fingers over fabrics, in holding garments at arm's length and appreciating the poignant way they seem to be offering themselves: *Choose me!* Saleswomen understand what I'm just now coming to acknowledge, which is the primitive imperative to decorate oneself, even if one is a crone—*especially* if one is a crone. "Ready to check out," they ask as I stand before a mirror, draping myself with scarves, "or still playing?"

I do most of this playing and self-decorating alone, but also sometimes in the company of other women. It's an odd surprise to me that these days I experience myself as more feminine than I ever did in my childbearing years, or at least more identified with other women. Now that all, or most, bets are off, I see that the deep alienation I felt from my gender for most of my life was largely defensive. Under the aspect of decline, I understand other women better. As our sags and wrinkles make us kin, I feel a tenderness for them, particularly for their—for our—slight shoulders and delicate wrists, those skeletal markers of femininity that no drag queen can approximate. I'm persuaded that we're alike, that we were alike all along. I feel a new sympathy for other women, and for myself.

Tiresias-like, I understand men better too, and make allowance for the lust that enslaves them all their lives. I think of the boys I knew when I was a teenager, of what was really going on in their minds. How could I have missed it?

Another small surprise: the intense pleasure I take in pure, strong, flamboyant color. A yellow hibiscus blossom, seen at a distance, will stop me in my tracks. Many years ago my husband and I spent a few nights in a New England guesthouse. One morning I came to breakfast in a bright red top, an unusual choice for me. Our hostess, a bent, muttering old thing, emerged from behind her dark desk under the stairs and trotted up to me, all animation now, her eyes alight. "RED!" she bellowed. "I LOVE RED!" I was baffled and amused. What was this about, this senile glee? Now I begin to understand.

Thirty years ago I assumed I would take the eccentric route as I aged, become one of those bluff, outspoken, truth-telling old women people claim to admire, even as they avoid them. That would have been in keeping with my strong contrarian impulse. But instead of growing bolder and more heedless, I seem to be growing more circumspect, more nervously observant of the proprieties, more conscious of other people's feelings.

At my age, motives are generally multiple. I can think of three explanations for this development in my behavior. Ranged along a continuum that moves from most to least cynical, they are as follows:

1. Age is unnecessary, as Lear observed. More and more I feel that I'm here on sufferance. If I don't want to be left out on an ice floe, I'd better try to be pleasant.
2. Being interesting is getting harder, but I can always be good.
3. Age is slowly melting away the outer layers of my personality, revealing the sweetness within.

*

I feel my aging in my moods, which have always been volatile, but are steadier now than they were when I was still menstruating and out of my mind for half the month. Even so, I can't say I often feel serene. A lot of the time what I feel is a buzzy muzziness, as though I need to give my head a good shake (perhaps it's tinnitus). And though my moods have stabilized, the background coloration of my subjectivity has darkened. This is a difficult distinction to make, because the concepts of mood and color seem inseparable, but a darkening of mood is not the same as a lowering of mood. It's an indelible staining, the result of a long immersion in the vat of years. Depression can occur concomitantly, of course. In fact, the darkening makes the lowering more likely.

I can't deny that often I am depressed, but I also find myself in the grip of an inalienable stoicism. Even when my moods are acutely painful, I no longer try to force my way out of them through explosion or confrontation or drinking. The price in shame would be too high: after sixty, one no longer gets the discounted rate. I simply wait for my moods to go away. What replaces them is nothing like euphoria. It's often the default state of muzziness I describe above, but sometimes—if the mood has been very bad, and I'm lucky—the muzziness lifts like a California fog and I enjoy an interval of steady, neutral clarity.

Not only am I better at containing my emotions, I'm also much more in control of my appetites, partly because many of them have shrunk. I'm improved in many other ways as well; I'm more conscientious, more prudent, better organized, more reliable. It amazes me that in my youth I was so morally careless and cheerfully self-destructive. I remember late nights in my early twenties, joyously rocketing along piney back roads in some drunk's car toward a party house rented by an older male reprobate. What was I after? I can't recall, though I do remember what I got. Now I feel poisoned if I drink two glasses of wine. Not that feeling poisoned stops me, though it does slow me down.

I'm proud of my newfound moderation and self-control, but I also must report that I've begun to notice in myself a certain age-related tendency to peevishness. Like the fussy old lady in C. S. Lewis's *The Screwtape Letters,* who only wants a properly made cup of tea and a piece of really crisp toast, I get seriously annoyed when the soup I've ordered comes to the table lukewarm. In earlier days I'd have bolted it obliviously, along with a sandwich, but a tiny disappointment like this really bothers me now: the only lunch I'll get today, ruined! Even so, I won't send it back to be reheated. That's not like me. That's the behavior of my alter ego, the grouse-stick-brandishing old bat I haven't become.

I also notice an age-related touchiness, an increased sensitivity to slights and insults to my dignity. I've always been easily hurt and quick to anger, but when I was young there was a robustness to my reactions. What I feel now instead of a straightforward rage is a quivering, querulous outrage that I have no choice but to conceal behind a tight smile. It's as if I suddenly expect chivalric treatment: How can people wound me when I'm old and I can no longer chalk their slights up to experience? How can they hurt me when I can no longer learn anything from it?

I've become much more sensible about my health, but also more relaxed about the prospect of getting sick. For many years I interpreted every flutter in my stomach as the sure sign of something terminal. Occasionally my panics took me to the emergency room, where irritated interns looked me over and sent me home, but mostly I avoided doctors because I feared that they'd catch me out. Diagnosis meant judgment, and sickness meant death. I lived much of my adult life in a state of medical dread. I look back on my earlier self with exasperation: so much of life wasted in vague neurotic terror, when now it turns out that all along I was quite well. Only a person who knew nothing of illness could have romanticized it the way I did, allowed it to carry so much existential freight.

Now I shrug off symptoms that thirty years ago would have had me calling an ambulance; but I also monitor my health. I take long conditioning walks, I floss faithfully, I keep regular hours, I seek balance. I actually find it comforting to stand in line at the pharmacy, to produce my Aetna card at the doctor's office. I suffer from none of the obscure and terrifying ailments I feared when I was younger, though I do require medication for elevated blood pressure and high cholesterol. I find it almost reassuring to have developed these garden-variety, though serious, conditions. I've joined the great citizen army of the elderly, and finally I'm like everyone else. In a few weeks I'll be eligible for Medicare!

My fear of death is considerably diminished, or perhaps it's only more diffuse, more mixed together with the other elements of my subjectivity. At any rate, I no longer sit bolt upright in bed, gasping at the thought of personal extinction. I suppose that aging is getting me used to the idea—limbering me up for it, so to speak. What fills me with dread these days is not the prospect of my own death but the thought of losing my husband.

I check in with a psychiatrist at irregular intervals, a cheerful man in his mid-seventies. I admire his graceful and realistic acceptance of his own aging, and would take him as a model if I could feel any certainty that the path of my aging will follow his—there are so many possible branchings. The last time I was in his office, I asked him, *What are the compensations of age?* "Well," he said, tentatively, "how about wisdom?" I was disappointed. That was it, wisdom? "Wisdom?" I said. "I'm wise enough already." He smiled faintly at this wise-guy riposte, lapsed into silence for a moment, and then quietly mentioned that old friends of his had been dying at an increasing rate lately. "Just one," he said, "after another."

Oh, how foolish I was in an essay I wrote a decade ago, to carry on as though I were ancient and resigned to it. Such presumption, and I was barely menopausal! The prematurity of this claim left me in an awkward position, like a sheepish party guest who has made a great show of saying goodnight to everyone and then finds she must return to retrieve her car keys.

Young people are forever professing shock when I mention my age. "You can't be," they say, and I assure them, with a certain grim relish, that I am. They continue to protest, but begin to take my word for it. I walk away from these encounters feeling like a fraud, partly because I've so obviously been fishing for compliments, but more importantly because I've left the impression that I'm an authority about age, that I know where I am in my life. I'm reminded of the shame I felt when I was twelve and I told my eight-year-old cousin some nonsense about sex in a falsely wised-up way.

This is a good time in my life. To say otherwise would be rank ingratitude. I've finally worked free of the agitation and misery of youth, which in my case extended well into middle age. I've learned better how to live, to do my part in maintaining my marriage, to master impulse and cultivate self-respect. If only, I find myself thinking, I can manage to keep it up for a while, I can shape the end of my life in a way that justifies and redeems what came before. But I'm suspicious of that ambition: it puts me in mind of some heresy I read about once—I forget its name.

I can't know, of course, how long I'll be able to keep it up. I can't know where I stand in relation to the end. What I do know is that a lot can happen during the time I have. It's a happening time: the late years are an avalanche of contingency. All the ways of going, all the ways that lead up to going—the ischemic episodes, embolisms, syncopes, infarctions, -omas! I could have a bad fall, drift into dementia, develop diabetes or pulmonary obstruction or heart disease or all three at once, discover I have cancer. I could lose my sight, my hearing, my colon, my husband. A sinister home health aide could steal my electronics and credit cards and disappear, leaving me without food for days. The state could take away my driver's license.

Any of these things, or any combination of them, could happen, and soon. Or not: I could continue moving along the gently tilted plateau I've been negotiating for years now, though the angle has been growing a little steeper. I could continue to write, to take walks and cook and travel and drink (moderately) and have lunch with friends and talk to my husband. Whatever happens, I continue to have a future. What will that future consist of? As always, I don't know, though the range of possibility has narrowed considerably. I don't know, and the reason I'm tempted to carry on as if I did is that I'm trying to bargain, in some primitive way, with my unknown fate. But there's no bargaining, no knowing the worst, no protecting myself from the shocks of age.

"Lord," says the psalmist, "make me to know mine end, and the measure of my days, what it is; that I may know how frail I am." The Lord, if I read the psalm correctly, gives no response. In the psalm's last line, the psalmist-petitioner drops his demand for knowledge in favor of a plea for an extension: "O spare me, that I may recover strength, before I go hence and be no more."

MARY GORDON

On Enmity

FROM *Salmagundi*

1—Trying for a Definition

The word *enemy* comes to my mind, and suddenly I hear it everywhere. It is a strong word, not only strong but powerful. To use it can have consequences, and those consequences can be and have been grave.

I am trying to understand the meaning of *enemy,* to consider what it might mean. I am trying, before anything else, to reach a definition.

What can be said of the word *enemy*? Can we at least begin by saying these things:
The enemy is one who does me harm.
My enemy is one who desires my harm.
I know my enemy because she is the one who desires to harm me.
Is everyone who has done me harm my enemy?

But then, there must be other questions.
Who defines the enemy, who is it that names him?
Is it the one harmed by him? Is the one harmed always right in his naming?
Is it possible to misname someone an enemy, because one feels harmed, feels that the harming is deliberate, personal, though in fact the one called the enemy had no desire to harm any particu-

lar person? Had only an unfocused, unformed impulse to harm? Perhaps felt a duty to do some sort of harm?

The enemy of my enemy is my friend.
The friend of my enemy is my enemy.

2—*On Hearing of the Death of an Enemy*

She wished me harm. She wanted to harm me. I never knew why. Others said that she was jealous, or that perhaps she loved me, and that her love was blocked, balked. She said that I had stolen her life. That I wanted too much of her, wanted us to be best friends, assumed that we were equals and we were not: she was a professor, I a graduate student, and by insisting that she link herself with me I was destroying her possibilities for professional advancement. It was the early seventies. We both had dogs. I phoned her one night to ask her to take care of my dog because I wanted to spend the night with someone I had just met. She agreed; it didn't occur to me that this would be a problem.

A few days later, I left for a three-week holiday. When I returned my mailbox was full: twenty-five letters, in which she told me how I had destroyed her life. In the three weeks that I was gone, she told everyone everything I had said about them. Repeated all the gossip we'd bred and stored in a year of being what I had thought was best friends. Many people felt betrayed by the things she told them and no longer wanted to see me. Others took her side because they felt that she was mentally fragile and I was strong, that she was a professor and deserved, therefore, their allegiance, and anyway I would be leaving soon. She told me that, as Haldeman or Ehrlichman said to John Dean (this was the time of Watergate), if I said anything to anyone she would "blast me out of the water."

Thirty-five years later, at lunch with mutual friends, I discover that she died, young, of breast cancer.

I think of all the hours I spent in torment connected to her.

At the table, a phrase comes to me:
Wasted sorrow.

3—A Story About a Baby

I heard this story many years ago, but it is a story no one can forget. I didn't know either the man or the woman, but I know people who knew them, knew them very well. They were poets. He was older. He had been her teacher, and established, successful, whereas she was only starting out. They had a child. The child was two years old. I don't know if they were married, but whatever their legal situation, she had understood, or perhaps it is better to say misunderstood, that he would be her partner, living beside her, involved with the rearing of the child. As it turns out, this was not his understanding. She was happy that they were both being offered jobs in the same city. A minor city in one of the less desirable (certainly for a poet) places in America. Then he was offered a better job in a more desirable city. There was no job there for her. She found herself abandoned, although he did not think of it as abandonment, though he left her in an undesirable city with a two-year-old child. She took a knife and stabbed her baby, whom everyone says was a beautiful boy, and then herself. His last sight on earth was of his mother coming at him with a knife. Was his last thought, My mother is my enemy?

4—Jerusalem

I am in Kennedy airport, waiting for a flight to Tel Aviv. A blond American couple complain about the extent of the security. An Orthodox boy, in yarmulke and tallit, says, "We have a lot of enemies." The American man says, "You've made a lot of enemies." Across the aisle from me, the American couple, and the Orthodox boy are a man and wife. The man, his hair in long side curls, seems to be dressed in a costume from the nineteenth century: black suit, black overcoat trailing the floor, black fedora. His wife is dressed in floor-length black as well; her hair is covered by a black wool scarf. During the exchange between the boy and the

American couple, they seemed to be praying. Silently, they rise and move several rows away. I can no longer see them.

5—My Husband Tells Me a Story About the War

My husband tells me this story, which took place in an army hospital in Paris at the end of the Second World War. There was a hideous colonel in charge of the hospital. The French workers who had worked, in turn, for the French, the Germans, and the Americans said he was worse than any of the Nazis they'd worked for. Inspecting the hospital with my husband, a young corporal, in tow, the colonel sees a broom leaning against the wall of a corridor. Enraged, he asks who left it there. My husband knows it is a little French cleaner whose husband or lover has just been killed in the war. He knows she is very poor. And so he says, "I left it there." The colonel knows that he is lying and storms off, furious. Then he comes back half an hour later to say he has fired the cleaning woman. Weeping, she says goodbye to all her friends, and knowing what my husband did for her, she whispers, "I will never forget what you did."

It immediately occurs to me that the colonel fired her to punish my husband, to make a point about the folly of his assumptions. My husband is shocked. He never thought of it this way. He wanted to revel in the good feeling of having someone who would never forget him.

Why did I have to tell him what I thought?

Does this mean that I am his enemy, or the enemy of his happiness?

Clearly the colonel was the enemy of the little cleaner. But why? Did he consider her his enemy, one enemy in his larger fight against disorder?

Who did she think of as her enemy?

Did she consider herself a person of so little consequence that she thought no one would believe her if she said someone had taken her seriously enough to define himself as her enemy?

6—Simone Weil and Georges Bernanos

Simone Weil and Georges Bernanos both, or each, traveled to Spain to cover the Spanish Civil War, Bernanos for the right-wing press, Weil for the left. Each wrote: This war is hopeless, it is impossible to tell good from evil, there is such evil, such cruelty, such barbarity on both sides. Simone Weil wrote to Bernanos, "I thought you were my enemy, but you are my brother."

7—Do Animals Have Enemies?

From watching my dogs, I know that the sight of certain dogs creates in my dogs the impulse to aggression, even though the other dog has done nothing provocative to warrant it. Is it the memory of past conflict that triggers the urge to aggression? Aggression toward themselves? Their ancestors? Do dogs have in their minds the category "enemy," into which they place an individual who fits the category, even if the individual is entirely innocent? If this is true of animals, what does it say about us? About the possibility for innocence, or reformation?

8—My Childhood Enemy

My childhood enemy was not another child. My enemy was an adult, who wished me harm. She wished me harm because I was a child and she was unable to have children. Because she was a polio victim and my mother was as well. She could bear being childless if she could understand that it was a result of her handicap. But my mother's fecundity made that explanation impossible. Therefore she hated me. She wished to do me harm. The harm: she wished me always to be unhappy. She wished that I would never admire myself. She was determined to kill any love I might feel toward myself. She humiliated me regularly, publically and privately. She accused me of vanity and selfishness. I still fear that she was right.

*

When I try to understand regarding a child as your enemy, or considering yourself the enemy of a child, I cannot. But because I walked beneath the magic carapace of my father's extravagant love, that woman's enmity could not pierce me. But this was not her desire; her desire was that life should be a misery to me. Perhaps in that way she could convince herself that it was better never to have borne a child.

9—Rachel Carson

At a lecture on the environment, a scientist says to the audience, "I am now going to project the face of the person responsible for more deaths in Africa than any political tyrant." He projects the face of Rachel Carson. He says that as a result of her campaign against DDT, millions of Africans have died of malaria.

Does that mean that Rachel Carson, friend of our fragile planet, is the enemy of millions of the dead?

10—Political Enemies

I grew up believing that Communists were my enemy. Many people would like me to believe that Muslims are my enemy. It is doubtless true that a certain group of Communists desired, in fact worked for, the destruction of America. The same is doubtless true of some Muslims. And I am American, and most of those dear to me, all of those connected by blood, are Americans living in America. Therefore, if those Communists who desired and worked for the destruction of America had achieved their wish, if the Muslims who desire and work for the destruction of America get their wish, I and those I love and have loved would have been in the past, and will be in the future, harmed. The work of my enemies. Though now I question what happens to the mind when it invites and houses the word *enemy*.

What harm is done by that commonplace word? What distinctions will not, cannot be drawn where *enemy* holds sway? Is the concept "enemy" the enemy of clear thought, therefore of justice? What is gained by its invocation? Perhaps as important, what is lost?

11—*Critical Enemies*

I believe that postmodern theorists who say that beauty is a socially constructed category and a threat, who say that there is no such thing as an author and that fiction is an outdated artifact, are my enemy.

I think the same of a student who believes that all literature must be read in the service of Catholic doctrine. This one wants to read Emily Dickinson as a crypto-Catholic. I tell her that her reading practice must be more open, that she must leave aside her preconceptions when she approaches the text. She is a pretty girl, with full rosy lips, but when she hears my words, her lips thin; her mouth hardens. She will resist me with all her will. I see in the thinness of her lips, the hardness of her mouth a desire to do me harm. I try to tell myself that this is ridiculous; she is very young, quite unsophisticated; she probably isn't interested enough in me and what I value to want to take any advice from me. Yet I perceive that she wants—should want—to take something from the world, a practice of open reading, and so she stands in my mind for a category of people who want to destroy what I value.

If I am honest, I have to say that I want to destroy what she values: a practice of reading that insists that the work of art fit into and confirm her own little idea.

Am I her enemy? Or the enemy of something that could be called a habit of mind? But whose mind? And who is harmed?

Increasingly, the beautiful things I value seem to me fragile. Susceptible to harm. Harm at the hands of an enemy.

12—*Shock and Awe*

We were told that our military might would inspire in our enemies shock and awe. Shock, yes: this is not difficult to understand. But awe? Doesn't awe imply admiration? What does it mean to admire your enemy? Isn't it to understand that your enemy is, in some way you can't help feeling, desirable? That you understand that submission to him might be, after all, the best, the truest course?

13—"The Spring Is My Enemy"

A friend of mine has a son who experiences severe asthmatic crises, requiring hospitalization every spring. Not knowing this, I meet my friend on a beautiful spring day and say, "Isn't it splendid, isn't it wonderful." She says, "Outside my office window there is a beautiful flowering cherry. It signals the arrival of spring. I look at it, and hate it; because of what it brings to my son, the spring is my enemy."

14—My Enemy, My Adversary

In an essay by a psychoanalyst, the following proposition is presented: civilization turns enemies to adversaries. What is the difference? An adversary can change. And is that the only essential difference? For the moment I can think of no other.

15—Encounters with the Enemy in Sacred Texts

"You prepare a table for me in the presence of my enemies": Psalm 23

"The last enemy to be destroyed is death": First Epistle to the Corinthians

VIVIAN GORNICK

Letter from Greenwich Village

FROM *The Paris Review*

FOR NEARLY TWENTY YEARS NOW Leonard and I have met once a week for a walk, dinner, and a movie, either in his neighborhood or mine. Except for the two hours in the movie, we hardly ever do anything else but talk. One of us is always saying, *Let's get tickets for a play, a concert, a reading,* but neither of us ever seems able to arrange an evening in advance of the time we are to meet. The fact is, ours is the most satisfying conversation either of us has, and we can't bear to give it up even for one week.

Why then, one might ask, do we not meet more often than once a week? The problem is, we both have a penchant for the negative. Whatever the circumstance, for each of us the glass is perpetually half empty. Either he is registering loss, failure, defeat, or I am. We cannot help ourselves.

One night at a party I fell into a disagreement with a friend of ours who is famous for his debating skills. At first I responded nervously to his every challenge, but soon I found my sea legs and then I stood my ground more successfully than he did. People crowded round me. That was wonderful, they said, wonderful. I turned eagerly to Leonard. "You were nervous," he said.

Another time I went to Florence with my niece. "How was it?" Leonard asked. "The city was lovely," I said. "My niece is great. You know, it's hard to be with someone twenty-four hours a day for eight days, but we traveled well together, walked miles along the Arno; that river is beautiful." "That *is* sad," Leonard said. "That you found it irritating to be so much with your niece."

A third time, I went to the beach for the weekend. It rained one day, was sunny another. Again Leonard asked how it had been. "Refreshing," I said. "The rain didn't daunt you," he said.

I remind myself of what *my* voice can sound like. My voice, forever edged in judgment, that also never stops registering the flaw, the absence, the incompleteness. My voice that so often causes Leonard's eyes to flicker and his mouth to tighten.

At the end of an evening together one or the other of us will impulsively suggest that we meet again during the week, but only rarely does the impulse live long enough to be acted upon. We mean it, of course, when we are saying goodbye—want nothing more than to renew the contact immediately—but going up in the elevator to my apartment, I start to feel on my skin the sensory effect of an eveningful of irony and negative judgment. Nothing serious, just surface damage—a thousand tiny pinpricks dotting arms, neck, chest—but somewhere within me, in a place I cannot even name, I begin to shrink from the prospect of feeling it again soon.

A day passes. Then another. I must call Leonard, I say to myself, but repeatedly the hand about to reach for the phone fails to move. He, of course, must be feeling the same, as he doesn't call either. The unacted-upon impulse accumulates into a failure of nerve. Failure of nerve hardens into ennui. When the cycle of mixed feeling, failed nerve, and paralyzed will has run its course, the longing to meet again acquires urgency, and the hand reaching for the phone will complete the action. Leonard and I consider ourselves intimates because our cycle takes only a week to complete.

Yesterday I came out of the supermarket at the end of my block and, from the side of my eye, registered the beggar who regularly occupies the space in front of the store: a small white guy with a hand perpetually outstretched and a face full of broken blood vessels. "I need something to eat," he was whining as usual. "That's all I want, something to eat, anything you can spare, just something to eat." As I passed him, I heard a voice directly behind me say, "Here, bro. You want something to eat? Here's something to eat." I turned back and saw a short black man with cold eyes standing in front of the beggar, a slice of pizza in his outstretched hand. "Aw, man," the beggar pleaded, "you know what I . . ." The man's voice went as cold as his eyes. "You say you want something to eat.

Here's something to eat," he repeated. "I bought this for you. *Eat it!*" The beggar recoiled visibly. The man standing in front of him turned away and, in a motion of deep disgust, threw the pizza into a wastebasket.

When I got to my building, I couldn't help stopping to tell José, the doorman—I had to tell *someone*—what had just happened. José's eyes widened. When I finished he said, "Oh, Miss Gornick, I know just what y'mean. My father once gave me such a slap for exactly the same thing." Now it was my eyes that widened. "We was at a ball game, and a bum asked me for something to eat. So I bought a hot dog and gave it to him. My dad, he whacked me across the face. 'If you're gonna do a thing,' he said, 'do it right. You don't buy someone a hot dog without you also buying him a soda!'"

I have always lived in New York, but a good part of my life I longed for the city the way someone in a small town would, yearning to arrive at the capital. Growing up in the Bronx was like growing up in a village. From earliest adolescence I knew there was a center of the world and that I was far from it. At the same time, I also knew it was only a subway ride away, downtown in Manhattan. Manhattan was Araby.

At fourteen I began taking that subway ride, walking the length and breadth of the island late in winter, deep in summer. The only difference between me and someone like me from Kansas was that in Kansas one makes the immigrant's lonely leap once and forever, whereas I made many small trips into the city, going home repeatedly for comfort and reassurance, dullness and delay, before attempting the main chance. Down Broadway, up Lexington, across Fifty-Seventh Street, from river to river, through Greenwich Village, Chelsea, the Lower East Side, plunging down to Wall Street, climbing up to Columbia. I walked these streets for years, excited and expectant, going home each night to the Bronx, where I waited for life to begin.

The way I saw it, the West Side was one long rectangle of apartment houses filled with artists and intellectuals; this richness, mirrored on the East Side by money and social standing, made the city glamorous, and painfully exciting. I could taste in my mouth world, sheer world. All I had to do was get old enough and New York would be mine.

As children, my friends and I would roam the streets of the neighborhood, advancing out as we got older, section by section, until we were little girls trekking across the Bronx as though on a mission to the interior. We used the streets the way children growing up in the country use fields and rivers, mountains and caves: to place ourselves on the map of our world. We walked by the hour. By the time we were twelve we knew instantly when the speech or appearance of anyone coming toward us was the slightest bit off. We knew also that it excited us to know. When something odd happened—and it didn't take much for us to consider something odd, our sense of the norm was strict—we analyzed it for hours afterward.

A high school friend introduced me to the streets of Upper Manhattan. Here, so many languages and such striking peculiarities in appearance—men in beards, women in black and silver. These were people I could see weren't working class, but what class *were* they? And then there was the hawking in the street! In the Bronx a lone fruit-and-vegetable man might call out, *Missus! Fresh tomatoes today!* But here, people on the sidewalk were selling watches, radios, books, jewelry—in loud, insistent voices. Not only that, but the men and women passing by got into it with them: "How long'll that watch work? Till I get to the end of the block?" "I know the guy who wrote that book, it isn't worth a dollar." "Where'd ya get that radio? The cops'll be at my door in the morning, right?" So much stir and animation! People who were strangers talking at one another, making each other laugh, cry out, crinkle up with pleasure, flash with anger. It was the boldness of gesture and expression everywhere that so captivated us: the stylish flirtation, the savvy exchange, people sparking witty, exuberant response in one another, in themselves.

In college, another friend walked me down West End Avenue. He told me that in the great stone buildings that lined the street lived musicians and writers, scientists and émigrés, dancers and philosophers. Very soon no trip downtown was complete without a walk on West End from 107th Street to 72nd. For me, the avenue became emblematic. To live here would mean I had arrived. I was a bit confused about whether I'd be the resident artist-intellectual or be married to him—I couldn't actually see myself signing the lease—but no matter; one way or another, I'd be in the apartment.

In summer we went to the concerts at Lewisohn Stadium, the

great amphitheater on the City College campus. These concerts came to an end in the mid-sixties, but in the late fifties, sitting on those stone bleacher seats July after July, August after August, I knew, I just *knew*, that the men and women all around me lived on West End Avenue. As the orchestra tuned up and the lights dimmed in the soft, starry night, I could feel the whole intelligent audience moving forward as one, yearning toward the music, toward themselves *in* the music: as though the concert were an open-air extension of the context of their lives. And I, just as intelligently, I hoped, leaned forward too, but I knew that I was only mimicking the movement. I'd not yet earned the right to love the music as they did. Within a few years I began to see it was entirely possible that I never would.

I grew up and moved downtown, but nothing turned out as expected. I went to school, but the degree did not get me an office in midtown. I married an intellectual, but then quickly got divorced. I began to write, but nobody read me above Fourteenth Street. For me, the doors to the golden company did not open. The glittering enterprise remained at a distance.

Among my friends, I am known for my indifference to acquisition. People make fun of me because I seem to want nothing; neither do I know the name of anything, nor can I readily differentiate between the fake and the genuine, the classy or the mediocre. It isn't high-minded disinterest, it is rather that things have always sent me into a panic; a peasantlike discomfort with color, texture, abundance—glamour, fun, playfulness—is the cause of my unease. All my life I've made do with less because "stuff" makes me desperate.

Leonard has developed a style of living that seems the direct obverse of my own but, truth to tell, I think is its mirror image. Overflowing with Japanese prints, Indian rugs, eighteenth-century furniture upholstered in velvet, his place feels like a set of museum rooms of which he is the curator. I see that he is filling in the physical surround as desperately as I am not. Yet he's never been at home in his apartment any more than I am in mine; he too needs to feel concrete beneath his feet.

For me, New York, the real New York, always meant Manhattan, but for Leonard, who'd also grown up in the Bronx, it was still the neighborhoods. From the time I first knew him—more than thirty years ago now—he walked the streets as I never had, into Brooklyn, Queens, Staten Island. He knew Sunnyside, Greenpoint, Red Hook, Washington Heights, East Harlem, the South Bronx. He knew the meaning of a shopping street in Queens with half the stores boarded up, a piece of Brooklyn waterfront restored, a garden lot in Harlem full of deranged-looking flowers, a warehouse on the East River converted to a third-world mall. He knew which housing projects worked and which were a devastation. And it wasn't just the streets he knew. He knew the piers, the railroad yards, the subway lines. He had Central Park and Prospect Park by heart. He knew the footbridges on the East River; the ferries, the tunnels, the beltways. He knew Snug Harbor and City Island and Jamaica Bay.

He often reminded me of the street-urchin protagonists in postwar Italian movies: those handsome, ragged children of Rossellini's who imprint on Rome by knowing the city inside out. Leonard always looked like that to me when we took one of our long hikes through the boroughs: hungry, as only a working-class kid can be, for information; the kind of information that makes the ground beneath your feet yours. With him as my guide, the neighborhoods spread out for miles in all directions, often looking to my uninformed eye like wasteland until I began to see them as Leonard did: an incomparable sea of ghettos forever bleeding new life into a rectangle of glamour and prosperity.

On these treks of ours the character of time and space often changed as we walked. The concept of "hours" evaporated. The streets became one long ribbon of open road stretched out before us, with nothing to impede our progress. Time expanded to resemble time in one's childhood, when it seemed never to end, as opposed to time now: always scarce, always pressing, always a marker of one's emotional well-being.

At a New Year's party Jim comes rushing toward me. Sarah nods and turns away. A year ago I was tight with one, two years ago with the other. Tonight I realize I haven't seen him in three months, her in six. A woman who lives three blocks from me appears, her eyes shimmering. "I miss you!" she breathes wistfully, as though we're lovers in wartime separated by forces beyond our control. Yes, I nod, and move on. We'll embrace happily, me and all these people: not a glance of grievance, not a syllable of reproach among us. And, indeed, there is no call for grievance. Like pieces in a kaleidoscope that's been shaken, we've all simply shifted positions in the pattern of intimate exchange. Many of us who not so long ago were seeing each other regularly will meet now more often by accident than by design: in a restaurant, on the bus, at a loft wedding. Ah, but here's someone I haven't seen in years. Suddenly a flare of intensity and we're meeting once a week for the next six months.

I am often reminded of the tenement friendships in my childhood, circumstantial one and all. Round, dark-eyed women, filled with muted understanding for the needs of the moment. What difference did it make if the next-door neighbor was called Ida or Goldie when you needed someone to lend you ten bucks or recommend an abortionist or nod her head during an outburst of marital rage? It mattered only that there was a next-door neighbor. These attachments, as Sartre might have put it, were contingent rather than essential.

As for us: never before in history has so much educated intelligence been expended on the idea of the irreplaceable—the essential—self; and never before has devotion to the slightest amount of psychological discomfort allowed so many to be treated as the contingent other.

Michel de Montaigne describes the great friendship of his youth with Étienne de la Boétie as one in which a perfect communion of the spirit made the "soul grow refined." In the 1790s, Samuel Taylor Coleridge worshipped an idea of friendship that embodied the same ideal. Living at a time when persons of sensibility yearned for communion of the spirit, its frequent failure to materialize in friendship made Coleridge suffer, but the pain did not threaten his faith, not even when he lost the friendship that defined all others.

Coleridge and Wordsworth met in 1795, when they were, respectively, twenty-three and twenty-five years old. Wordsworth—grave, thin-skinned, self-protective—was even then steadied by an inner conviction of his own coming greatness as a poet; Coleridge, on the other hand—brilliant, explosive, self-doubting to the point of instability—was already into opium. Anyone except them could see that they were bound to come a cropper. In 1795, however, a new world, a new poetry, a new way of being was forming itself, and at that moment both Wordsworth and Coleridge, each feeling the newness at work in himself, saw proof of its existence reflected in the person of the other.

The infatuation lasted a little more than a year and a half. At the end of that time, the chaos within Coleridge doubled its dominion; the pride in Wordsworth stiffened into near immobility. The person each had been for nearly two years—the one who had basked in the unbroken delight of the other—was no more. It wasn't exactly that they were returned to the persons they had been before; it was only that never again would either feel his own best self in the presence of the other.

One's own best self. For centuries this was the key concept behind any essential definition of friendship: that one's friend is a virtuous being who speaks to the virtue in oneself. How foreign is such a concept to the children of the therapeutic culture! Today we do not look to see, much less affirm, our best selves in one another. To the contrary, it is the openness with which we admit to our emotional incapacities—the fear, the anger, the humiliation—that excites contemporary bonds of friendship. Nothing draws us closer to one another than the degree to which we face our deepest shame openly in one another's company. Coleridge and Wordsworth dreaded such self-exposure; we adore it. What we want is to feel *known,* warts and all—the more warts, the better. It is the great illusion of our culture that what we confess to is who we are.

Every night when I turn the lights out in my sixteenth-floor living room before I go to bed, I experience a shock of pleasure as I see the banks of lighted windows rising to the sky, crowding round me, and feel myself embraced by the anonymous ingathering of city-dwellers. This swarm of human hives, also hanging anchored in space, is the New York design offering generic connection. The pleasure it gives soothes beyond all explanation.

The phone rings. It's Leonard.

"What are you doing?" he asks.

"Reading Krista K.," I reply.

"Who's she?" he asks.

"Who's she!" I say. "She's one of the most famous writers in Eastern Europe."

"Oh," he says matter-of-factly. "What's the book like?"

"A bit claustrophobic." I sigh. "You don't really know where you are most of the time, or who's speaking. Then every twenty pages or so she says, 'Ran into G this morning. Asked him how long he thought we could go on like this. He shrugged. Yes, I said.'"

"Oh," Leonard says. "One of those. Bor-ring."

"Tell me," I say, "don't you ever mind sounding like a philistine?"

"The Philistines were a much-maligned people," he says. "Have you seen Lorenzo lately?"

"No, why?"

"He's drinking again."

"For God's sake! What's wrong now?"

"What's wrong now? What's *right* now? What's ever right for Lorenzo?"

"Can't you talk to him? You know him so well."

"I *do* talk to him. He nods along with me as I speak. I know, I know, he says, you're right, I've got to pull it together, thanks so much for saying this, I'm so grateful, I don't know why I fuck up, I just don't know."

"Why *does* he fuck up?"

"Why? Because if he's not fucking up, he doesn't know who he is."

Leonard's voice has become charged.

"It's unbelievable," he swears on, "the muddle in his mind. I say to him, What do you want, what is it you *want?*"

"Tell me," I cut in, "what do *you* want?"

"Touché." Leonard laughs drily.

There follow a few long seconds of vital silence.

"In my life," he says, "I have known only what I *don't* want. I've always had a thorn in my side, and I've always thought, When this thorn is removed I'll think about what I want. But then that particular thorn would be removed, and I'd be left feeling emptied out. In a short time another thorn would be inserted into my side. Then, once again, all I had to think about was being free of the thorn in my side. I've never had time to think about what I *want.*"

"Maybe somewhere in there is a clue to why Lorenzo drinks."

"It's disgusting," Leonard says softly, "to be this old and have so little information. Now, *there's* something Krista K. could write about that would interest me. The only problem is she thinks information is what the KGB was after."

In the drugstore I run into ninety-year-old Vera, a Trotskyist from way back who lives in a fourth-floor walk-up in my neighborhood, and whose voice is always pitched at the level of soapbox urgency. She is waiting for a prescription to be filled, and as I haven't seen her in a long while, on impulse I offer to wait with her. We sit down in two of the three chairs lined up near the prescription counter, me in the middle, Vera on my left, and on my right a pleasant-looking man reading a book.

"Still living in the same place?" I ask.

"Where'm I gonna go?" she says, loudly enough for a man on the pick-up line to turn in our direction. "But y'know, dolling? The stairs keep me strong."

"And your husband? How's he taking the stairs?"

"Oh, him," she says. "He died."

"I'm so sorry," I murmur.

Her hand pushes away the air.

"It wasn't a good marriage," she announces. Three people on the line turn around. "But, y'know? In the end it doesn't really matter."

I nod my head. I understand. The apartment is empty.

"One thing I gotta say," she goes on, "he was a no-good husband, but he was a great lover."

I can feel a slight jolt in the body of the man sitting beside me.

"Well, that's certainly important," I say.

"Boy, was it ever! I met him in Detroit during the Second World War. We were organizing. In those days everybody slept with everybody, so I did too. But you wouldn't believe it"—and here she lowered her voice dramatically, as though she had a secret of some importance to relate—"most of the guys I slept with? They were no good in bed. I mean, they were bad, really *bad*."

Now I feel the man on my right stifling a laugh.

"So when you found a good one," Vera shrugs, "you held on to him."

"I know just what you mean," I say.

"Do you, dolling?"

"Of course I do."

"You mean they're still bad?"

"Listen to us," I say. "Two old women talking about lousy lovers."

This time the man beside me laughs out loud. I turn and look at him.

"We're sleeping with the same guys, right?" I say.

Yes, he nods. "And with the same ratio of satisfaction."

For a split second the three of us look at one another, and then, all at once, we begin to howl. When the howling stops, we are all beaming. Together we have performed, and separately we have been received.

No one is more surprised than I that I turned out to be who I am. Take love, for instance. I had always assumed that, in this regard, I was like every other girl of my generation. While motherhood and marriage had never held my interest, and daydreaming myself on some revolutionary barricade was peculiar among my classmates, I always knew that one day Prince Passion would come along, and when he did, life would assume its ultimate shape—*ultimate* being the operative word. As it happened, a number of PP look-alikes did appear, but there was no ultimate anything. Before I was thirty-five I had been as much bedded as any of my friends, and I had also been twice married, twice divorced. Each marriage lasted two and a half years, and each was undertaken by a woman I didn't know (me) to a man I also didn't know (the figure on the wedding cake).

It was only after these marriages were over that I matured sexually; that is, I became conscious of myself as a person preoccupied with desiring rather than being desired; and *that* development gave me an education. I learned that I was sensual but not a sensualist; that I blissed out on orgasm but the earth didn't move; that I could be strung out on erotic obsession for six months or so but was always waiting for the nervous excitement to die down. In a word: lovemaking was sublime but it wasn't where I lived. And then I learned something more.

In my late thirties I had an affair with a man I cared for and who cared for me. This man and I were both drawn to the energy of mind and spirit that each of us felt in the other. But for this man too—intelligent, educated, politically passionate as he was—the exercise of his sexual will was central to any connection he made with a woman. There was not a moment when we were together that he wasn't touching me. He never walked into my house that his hand wasn't immediately on my breast; never embraced me that he wasn't reaching for my genitals; never lay beside me that he wasn't trying to make me come. When, after we'd been together some months, I began to object to what had started to feel like an on-automatic practice, he would invariably put his arms around me, nuzzle my neck, and whisper in my ear, "C'mon, you know you like it." As I did genuinely love him and he me—we had memorable times together—I would stare at him at such moments, shake my head in exasperation, but then let it go.

One day he suggested that I let him sodomize me, something we'd not done before. I demurred. Next day he made the same suggestion. Again I demurred. "How do you know you won't like it," he persisted, "if you've never done it?" He wore me down: I agreed to try it once. No, no, he said, I must agree to do it three times and *then* if I said no it would be no. So we did it three times, and truth to tell, I didn't hate the physical sensation as much as I had thought I would—almost against my will my body responded—but I definitely did not like it. "Okay," I said, "I've done it three times, and I don't want to do it anymore." We were lying in bed. He nuzzled my neck and whispered in my ear, "C'mon. Just one more time. You know you like it."

I drew away then and looked directly into his face. "No," I said, and was startled by the finality in my own voice.

"What an unnatural woman you are!" he exploded at me. "You know you want to do it. *I* know you want to do it. Yet you fight it. Or is it me you're fighting?"

Once again I stared at him: only this stare was different from those other stares. A man was pressing me to do something I did not want to do, and pressing me in a manner he would never have applied to another man: by telling me that I didn't know what I wanted. I felt my eyes narrowing and my heart going cold. For the first—but not the last—time, I consciously felt men to be members of a species separate from myself. Separate and foreign. It was as though an invisible membrane had fallen between me and my lover, one fine enough to be penetrated by desire but opaque enough to obscure human fellowship. The person on the other side of the membrane seemed as unreal to me as I felt myself to be to him. At that moment, I didn't care if I never again got into bed with a man.

I did of course get into bed with them—love, quarrel, and bliss out many more times after this man and I parted—but the memory of that fine, invisible separation haunted me; and more often than I like to remember, I saw it glistening as I gazed into the face of a man who loved me but was not persuaded that I needed what he needed to feel like a human being.

In time I came to know other women who would have analyzed the experience differently but immediately understood what I was talking about when I described the invisible curtain. It comes with the territory, most of them shrugged.

Work, I said to myself, work. If I worked, I thought, pressing myself against my newly hardened heart, I'd have what I needed. I'd be a person in the world. What would it matter then that I was giving up "love"?

As it turned out, it mattered more than I had ever dreamed it would. As the years went on, I saw that romantic love was injected like dye into the nervous system of my emotions, laced through the entire fabric of longing, fantasy, and sentiment. It haunted the psyche, was an ache in the bones; so deeply embedded in the makeup of the spirit it hurt the eyes to look directly into its influence. It would be a cause of pain and conflict for the rest of my life. I prize my hardened heart—I have prized it all these years—but the loss of romantic love can still tear at it.

Workmen have erected a wooden barrier on my street around two squares of pavement whose concrete has been newly poured. Beside the barrier is a single wooden plank laid out for pedestrians, and beside that, a flimsy railing. On an icy morning in midwinter I am about to grasp the railing and pull myself along the plank when, at the other end, a man appears, attempting the same negotiation. This man is tall, painfully thin, and fearfully old. Instinctively I lean in far enough to hold out my hand to him. Instinctively he grasps it. Neither of us speaks a word until he is safely across the plank, standing beside me. "Thank you," he says. "Thank you very much." A thrill runs through me. "You're welcome," I say, in a tone that I hope is as plain as his. We each then go our separate ways, but I feel that "thank you" running through my veins all the rest of the day.

It was his voice that had done it. That voice! Strong, vibrant, self-possessed: it did not know it belonged to an old man. There was in it not a hint of that beseeching tone one hears so often in the voice of an old person when small courtesies are shown—"You're so kind, so kind, so very kind," when all you're doing is hailing a cab or helping to unload a shopping cart—as though the person is apologizing for the room he or she is taking up in the world. This man realized that I had not been inordinately helpful, and he need not be inordinately thankful. He was recalling for both of us the ordinary recognition that every person in trouble has a right to expect and every witness an obligation to extend. I had held out my hand, he had taken it. For thirty seconds we had stood together—he not pleading, I not patronizing—the mask of old age slipped from his face, the mask of vigor dropped from mine.

A few weeks ago a woman who lives on my floor invited me to a Sunday brunch. This woman has taught grade school for years, but she looks upon teaching as a day job. In *real* life, she says, she is an actor. None of the people at the brunch—all in their forties and fifties—knew each other well, and some didn't know the others at all, but it soon became clear that everyone at the table also thought of the work they did as day jobs; every one of them saw him- or herself as having a vocation in the arts, albeit one without material achievement. The chatter on that Sunday morning was animated by one account after another of this or that failed audition or publication or gallery showing, each one ending with "I didn't prepare hard enough," or "I knew I should have rewritten the beginning," or "I don't send out enough slides." What was striking was the sympathy that each self-reproach called to life in the others. "Oh, you're too hard on yourself!" was heard more than once. Then, abruptly, looking directly at the last person to say, "You're too hard on yourself," a woman who'd been silent started to speak.

"When I got divorced," she said, "I had to sell the house in Westchester. A couple in the business of importing Chinese furniture and art objects bought the house and began moving things in a week before I was to leave. One night I went down into the basement and began looking through some of their crates. I found a pair of beautiful porcelain vases. On impulse, I took one. I thought, They've got everything, I've got nothing, why shouldn't I? When I moved, I took the vase with me. A week later the husband called and said this funny thing had happened, one of this pair of vases had disappeared, did I know anything about it. No, I said, sounding as bemused as he, I didn't know anything about it, I'd never even seen the vases. I felt awful then. But I didn't know what to do. I put the vase in a closet and never looked at it again. Ten years passed. Then I began thinking about the vase. Soon the thought of the vase began to obsess me. Finally this past year I couldn't stand it anymore. I packed up the vase as carefully as I could and sent it back to them. And I wrote a separate letter, saying I didn't know what had possessed me, why I had taken this thing that belonged to them, and I wasn't asking for forgiveness, but here it was back. A few weeks later the wife called me. She said she'd gotten this strange letter from me, she didn't know what I was talking about, and then this package came, and inside the package was about a thousand shards of something or other. What on earth was it that I had taken and was now sending back?"

At ten in the morning, two old women are walking ahead of me on West Twenty-Third Street, one wearing a pink nylon sweater, the other a blue. "Did you hear?" the woman in pink says. "The pope appealed to capitalism to be kind to the poor of the world." The woman in blue responds, "What did capitalism say?" As we're crossing Seventh Avenue, the woman in pink shrugs. "So far it's quiet."

At noon a man at a grocery counter stands peering at the change in his hand. "You gave me $8.06," he says to the young woman behind the cash register. "I don't think that's right." She looks at the coins and says, "You're right. It shoulda been $8.60," and gives the man the correct change. He continues to stare at his open palm. "You put the six and the zero in the wrong place," he says. "It shoulda been the other way around." Now it's the woman who stares. When at last the man turns away, I shake my head sympathetically. "What I put up with all day long," she sighs, as I pile my purchases on the counter. "Would you believe this? A guy comes up to the counter with an item. It's marked wrong. I can see right away it's the wrong amount. I tell him, Listen, that's the wrong price. Believe me, I know the prices, I been working in the store two years. He says to me, 'That's nothing to be proud of,' and he marches out."

At three in the afternoon, a distinguished-looking couple is standing under the awning of the Regency Hotel on Park Avenue. The man has iron-gray hair and regular features and is wearing an expensive overcoat. The woman is alcoholic thin, has blond, marcelled hair, and is wearing mink. She looks up at him as I pass them, and her face lights up. "It's been a *wonderful* afternoon," she says. The man embraces her warmly and nods directly into her face. The scene excites my own gratitude: how delicious to see people of the upper classes acting with simple humanity! Later I run into Sarah, a tired socialist of my acquaintance, and I tell her about the couple on Park Avenue. She listens with her customary Marxist moroseness and says, "You think she knows what a wonderful afternoon is?"

A friend reads what I've been writing and says to me over coffee, "You're romanticizing the street. Don't you know that New York has lost seventy-five percent of its manufacturing base?" In my mind's eye I stare into the faces of all the women and men with whom I interact daily. *Hey, you people,* I address them silently, *did you hear what my friend just said? The city is doomed, the middle class has deserted New York, the corporations are in Texas, Jersey, Taiwan. You're gone, you're outta here, it's all over. How come you're still on the street?*

New York isn't jobs, they reply, it's temperament. Most people are in New York because they need evidence—in large quantities—of human expressiveness; and they need it not now and then, but every day. That is what they *need.* Those who go off to the manageable cities can do without; those who come to New York cannot.

Or perhaps I should say that it is I who cannot.

It's the voices I can't do without. In most cities of the world, the populace is planted in centuries of cobblestoned alleys, ruined churches, architectural relics, none of which are ever dug up, only piled one on top of another. If you've grown up in New York your life is an archaeology not of structures but of voices, also piled one on top of another, also not really replacing one another.

On Sixth Avenue, two small, dark-skinned men lean against a parked cab. One says to the other, "Look, it's very simple. A is the variable costs, B is the gross income, C is the overhead. Got that?" The other man shakes his head. "Dummy!" the first man cries. "You gotta *get* it!"

On Park Avenue a well-dressed matron says to her friend, "When I was young, men were the main course, now they're a condiment."

On Fifty-Seventh Street a delicate-looking man says to a woman too young to know what he's talking about, "These days my life feels like a chicken bone stuck in my craw. I can't swallow it and I can't cough it up. Right now I'm trying to just not choke on it."

As the cabbie on Sixth Avenue said, someone's gotta get it; and late in the day someone does.

I am walking along Eighth Avenue during the five o'clock crush, daydreaming, and somewhere in the forties, I don't notice the light turning red. Halfway into the path of an oncoming truck, I am lifted off my feet by a pair of hands on my upper arms and pulled back onto the curb. The hands do not release me immediately. I am pressed to the chest of the person to whom the hands belong. I can still feel the beating heart against my back. When I turn to thank my rescuer, I am looking into the middle-aged face of an overweight man with bright blue eyes, straw-colored hair, and a beet-red face. We stare wordlessly at one another. I'll never know what the man is thinking at this moment, but the expression on his face is unforgettable. Me, I am merely shaken, but he looks as though transfigured by what has just happened. His eyes are fixed on mine, but I see that they are really looking inward. I realize that this is *his* experience, not mine. It is he who has felt the urgency of life—he is still holding it in his hands.

Two hours later I am home, having dinner at my table, overlooking the city. My mind flashes on all who crossed my path today. I hear their voices, I see their gestures, I start filling in lives for them. Soon they are company, great company. I think to myself, I'd rather be here with you tonight than with anyone else I know. Well, almost anyone else I know. I look up at the great clock on my wall, the one that gives the date as well as the hour. It's time to call Leonard.

LAWRENCE JACKSON

Slickheads

FROM *n+1*

For Donald and AK

AROUND MY WAY we really tripped over two things: the beef with them Woodlawn whores in '85; then four years later, when stick-up boys shot Sonny.

In high school, me, Charm Sawyer, and Piccolo Breaks got up a social club called the Oxfords. More or less just the little guys with round glasses from our block, plus an off-brand or two from the Avenue—North or Wabash—or from the Heights—Liberty or Park.

I pimped in the fine honey from church to the jam. Tanya, Carla, Kim, Lisa, Stacy, all of them dying to get out of the house. I was about fifteen when I booked out, and it took every bit of two years to get snug. But it had started in middle school with me and Rodney Glide freaking the white girl in the basement and him working her skirt up.

I wasn't really built like that. Check it out. Back in the day I loaded dirt and wood chips at a garden supply store on Wabash. One time a church girl gave me a ride home after work and I told her wait while I caught a quick shower. Since the old-school play was to answer the Jehovah Witness knock at the door in a towel, any girl at your house was supposed to get open-fly treatment. Church girl called her mother telling her why she was hold up. Her old mother, an ex-opera contralto, started fussing. "Kim, use common sense. Even little Lair's trying to get some!" I took it as a compliment. Her mother didn't think I was gay the way her unafraid daughter did when I stepped from the shower, still in a towel. That's when I started liking older women, because they always act like, given the chance, you might knock them down. And I got it backwards, since all what she said really did was start me on eating out.

The Oxford clique came together for an obvious reason. When we still footed it to parties and up Rhythm Skate, we needed a whole crew or a connect to get by in the world of yo boys and slickheads. As time went on, the Oxfords put it together for real. Even though all us from out the row house—a snatch of grass in front and the #51 bus chugging by, floods and bugs in the basement, alleyways of blackness out back—all us little men had turned out the next Timex Social Club.

Woodlawn niggers called us the Pajama Crew for spite, because we draped our fathers' old trench coats, that winter of '85. Them County slickheads wore tight their Adidas nylon sweatsuits, silk BVDs, and herringbone gold chains, flexing power. But the real Oxford contribution to the B-More scene was the DC Go-Go haircut—the flattop—or sometimes just faded, Jerseyed, Phillied. Bear in mind that your average yo boy from off the corner cut his naps down to the scalp. That's why we called them unremarkable niggers slickheads.

To me, slickheads lacked imagination, and their haircut was only the beginning of that emptiness. When I was first learning about it, slickhead behavior seemed inhibited, closed down, and reactionary. Like when I was prancing at the Harbor with my merry-go-round honey Sade, me ragging in a cycling cap, moccasins, bleached jeans, and an Ocean Pacific T of a man surfing on a beach I had never seen, and some slickhead called to her, "A yo, drop that prep and get with this slick." They had no class, and if I hadn't thought he would have shot me I might have banged him in his mouth. Then again, he wasn't talking to me, and I was into women's lib, eating out and everything.

The Oxfords went for exhibition and fullness, the whole way, and took it straight to those break-dancing older slickhead clowns from Woodlawn. Yeah, they was popping and breaking, helicopter and all that, but that shit is for tourists. Our thing was the leg dances, speeded-up jigs. I copped our step from this old head who rocked coach's shorts and a touring cap, and who gave up the flow downtown every summer. At the Inner Harbor, near the water-taxi line, seven or eight of us would break into the Oxford Bop, a crisscross reel, while we shouted the lyrics to Status IV's "You Ain't Really Down."

"Said you were my lady . . . And your love was true . . . !"

More attention than pulling your thing out.

The Oxfords liked a Roman holiday. Pretty Ricky brother crashed through the top of the telephone booth at the Harbor. Charm jumped from the second-floor balcony onto the reception desk in the Comfort Inn lobby. James Brown leapt through a car windshield, hind parts first. But mainly we threw cranking jams and released our boredom into the laps of the Oxford Pearls. All them was getting down, especially the girls from Catholic school. Even though we modeled ourselves on the old-time Negro fraternities, chanting "O-X!" through dim basement corridors pulsating with Chip E. Inc. stutter-singing "Like This," the Oxfords could also function like that—like a gang. Coming up in 21215—Bodymore, Murderland—attending public schools, we only did what we had to do. Anyway, a homeboy of a homeboy kicked some slickhead in the chest over a girl at a high school party at a fraternity house on Liberty Heights, and the war against Woodlawn jumped off.

The jam was a cranker, Darrin Ebron spinning "Al-Naafiysh," "Set It Off," and "Din Da Da" over and over; naturally it was honey heaven. I was wedging my knees between so many willing thighs that I never saw Pretty Ricky cousin Jerome and Ron J guff. First thing I knew the music cut off and Pretty Ricky and Mighty Joe Young were shuttling back and forth from the Kappa House to the phone booth in the 7-Eleven parking lot and Charm Sawyer was popping cash shit. I looked out into the mild May night, and it was enough shell-toes and silk BVDs to stop four lanes of traffic. Me and my homeboys were wearing moccasins and corduroy shorts. I had a pound of Dax in my hair, dripping like Shabba Doo's but faded like a prep's.

I loaded all of my men into the car and left the scrum thinking I was just helping out, like Jesus would do. I had a Monte Carlo, an orange EXP, an IROC-Z, and a Cressida on my ass—a slickhead caravan in hot pursuit. Then I thought I got lucky.

Northwest Baltimore's finest had been called about the scrap and I braked when the blue lights spun behind me. I pulled over and I told the police everything I knew, which was that some grown men were following me and I was scared. But you know how Five-O handled his bit.

"I want you out my ju-risdiction! Get your ass out of my sight!"

You know how Five-O cuss you when he through with you. Then he drove off.

It was six of us in the AMC Sportabout, a car about as good for driving as open-toed shoes for running ball. Besides the fact that the starter on my people's car was iffy, the windows didn't operate, and the door handle on the driver's side was broke. That night I put that old yellow wagon to the test. I headed down Liberty Heights back to Garrison Boulevard, and I learned what Pretty Ricky had been doing on the telephone. He had reached out to his wild cousins, some hoppers who ain't mind popping tool. I took Garrison and that baby right turn by the firehouse to Chelsea Terrace, to fetch some gun-slinging boy from out his house. After Five-O shammed on me, I was needing Ricky's cousin to appear with that .357 Magnum that Hawk carried on *Spenser: For Hire.* Instead a jive compact cat hopped into the old station wagon with barely a .25 in his dip.

Now, I had seen some young boys around my way with tool. I think one of them even got into *Time* for showing up strapped at Garrison or Pimlico, the local junior high schools. In fact it had been the cats from my year at middle school, the twins from Whitelock Street now going up Walbrook with Charm, who had brought tool to #66, setting the trend right at the beginning of the 1980s. They had got put out for a couple of days for that stunt. The next year, at Harlem Park Middle, them boys had burned up a cat for his Sixers jacket. I had seen a couple niggers pulled off of a public bus and beaten before. I held my ground standing next to a boy from Cherry Hill who had got his head opened up with a Gatorade bottle at a track meet, and I had gone with Charm to square off at some boys' houses who had been running their mouths too much. And of course I had fought with everybody in my crew except Ricky, who was getting too much ass to fight, because if he won he could double destroy your ego. The best one to fight was Sawyer's brother Chester, who was always threatening you with a nut session or worse. I hoped that the beef would get squashed, but I thought that it would take a big-time older head to do it, and I thought he would have needed a .12-gauge or something with some heat. Because on that night, Woodlawn was coming thick.

We were just idling in the middle of the street, nigger shit, everybody talking at once, planning to fail, when the IROC-Z came up from behind and the Monte Carlo and the EXP drove up from the other direction. The motherfuckers had some kind of CB or headphone communications. A crabapple-head big boy marched out of the Monte Carlo shouting, got up to my face, and started yanking on the door handle. I know it: I had that pleading, begging look on my face. He swung on me anyway and then tried to rip me out from the AMC Sportabout, but the broken door handle saved me. My people, my people. Mighty Joe Young was riding shotgun, and he shouted at me, "Drive!" I hit the gas and thread a needle through the IROC-Z–Cressida–EXP posse, racing my way down Chelsea Terrace. It was ride-or-die down the hill to Gwynns Falls Trail, Walbrook Junction, the briar patch for Charm, Pretty Ricky, and Knuckles.

Knowing the Junction better than our foes, we got back to our block unscathed. I let out Ricky and his cousins, and then we cooled out in an alley. First the slickheads got Ricky's address from some girl and tried to raid his people's house, but they were in the middle of the block and Woodlawn couldn't get to a window or through the front door. I thought I had made a safe passage until the next morning my father woke me up and asked did anything happen. I told him no, and he walked me outside to the ride. Late that night, them damn County yos had chucked a wedge of concrete through the windshield of the wagon.

A couple of days later a homeboy who worked at the McDonald's on Liberty Heights, just over the line in the County, got banked. Charm and Knuckles stopped going up the 'Brook because Simon, the concrete thrower, had promised them a bullet. A week after that Pretty Ricky fought the cruelest of the host, Carlos Gallilee and Dante Rogers, in the middle of Reisterstown Road. For a cat known throughout the city as a gigolo, a guy with slanted eyes and a Puerto Rican look, Rick had a whole lot of heart. He knocked the knees out of his jeans beating those dogs off and he stayed with his cousins in Philadelphia for a couple of weeks after that.

The war went on at high schools, parties, football games, festivals, and public events. About two weeks after the chase, in the parking lot of the all-girls public senior high school where Muhammad, Dern, and I chilled out every day after track practice, this boy Meechee was sitting in the back of a green Thunderbird steady loading a .38 while his homeboys, a lanky bastard about six-foot-nine and some other culprit, leaned on us. They cornered Muhammad on the hood of his Sentra.

"Where Ricky at? Where your boy at?"

I was wanting to run away with my whole body, but my feet got so heavy in the quicksand of his pistol that I could only look longingly in the direction of the administration building. My heart was pumping Cherry Coke the whole way, but I was proud of Muhammad for how he kept the fear out of his voice. The next day Muhammad and Dern got their family arms and we went all tooled up to high school. They took it as far as slinging iron in their sport coats. The day after that, we cut school altogether for marksmanship class in Leakin Park, an abandoned grassland just west of the Junction that had become a desolate zone. The Pearls were jive giddy. I just blasted into the creek, but I had to stop Sawyer, who never had a whole lot of sense, from shooting the pistol right behind my ear. To my mind, nothing is as loud as the roar of that .38.

The war changed the landmarks of our scene. Up to that time I had been keen to play in the County, and I could have cared less about my grimy, down-on-its-heels hometown. Now that we had to go everywhere in groups for safety, Reisterstown Road Plaza Mall and Security Mall in the County, the places where we used to flock to scoop out the honey, were less inviting. Our neighborhood mall, Mondawmin, became safe—if we toned our flamboyance down a little—and we started falling through Mondawmin, the Harbor, even Old Town Mall on the East Side. We kept linking up with city cats we'd gone to school with or had been in summer programs with, guys I had known from church at Lafayette Square, or the Druid Hill Avenue YMCA, where my father had been the director. Plus the girls I knew from those parts of town were slinging enough iron to take care of a boy. We went to our cousins and neighbors from around our way to get our back, to hustlers I had worked with at minimum-wage jobs all over the city, who came from tiny-ass streets crammed with thousands of brick row houses. The kind of music a cat listened to, or how he cut his fade, became unimportant compared to if he was from the city, how good he was with his hands, and, especially, if he had heart. That was how Sonny got down with the clique, because even though he was a young boy, he had all of the above.

Heads from around my way cut their teeth on the Woodlawn beef. The hoppers, the young boys we never had room for in the car, they headed straight up to Bell and Garrison to build themselves up. The hustle on Garrison, or, even more big-time, Park Heights and Woodland, was strictly Fila and Russell. Man, them cats bumped. From then to now it must be something like three thousand cats shot on Garrison between the Junction and Pimlico—that's one boulevard in one section of one chocolate American city. Plus ain't nobody ever see a bustling swaggering yipping corner like Park Heights and Woodland in its prime. Serving 'em well, boy and girl, serving 'em well. Knuckles and Mighty Joe Young knew how to get by around there. I never caught on and only went up to The Lot, the neighborhood McDonald's on Reisterstown Road, a couple of times. I wouldn't throw quarters away on Pac-Man or Space Invaders. I was spending my money on rugged-sole Timberlands and twelve-inch records so I could become a club dancer. Same as slick, the corner was insular and monotonous, unless you had a taste for street fighting and raw booty. Anyway, the hoppers wound up getting tight with cats who the corner was all they had. Like Ringfrail's brother Clyde, who wore brass jewelry, or Taiwan, an adolescent beggar who graduated to being a teenage beggar. Or Little Toby, who had started smoking too early and would always be short and skinny. I think (and was glad) Wookie was already gone by then. I know, and was sad, that Monty was. Every time I go home and walk to the Korean store to get some Utz or Tastykake, I run into them all.

The young boys of course had to take it serious. I only had a year left of high school, but they were going to be in this thing for a long time. Pretty Ricky's younger brother Maceo started going to war on his own, against anybody at all. At the corner store on Wabash and Sequoia he stabbed Richard Franklin, who then followed Maceo back to his house and sent him three-quarters of the way to their family's funeral home with the same knife. Some vet's old bayonet. Kind of intimate, being punctured with the same steel that still has your victim's blood on it. When Five-O locked up Chucky Blue that same night, Chucky, on something like love boat, almost turned the paddy wagon over. That was pure dee

Chuck Blue, living out the Myth. I'd never seen a motor vehicle rock from side to side on two wheels like that before.

It was curious. I found out a lot more about my neighborhood, and was surprised to know that I had a place in it. Slickheads from around the way, cats known for hanging on the corner, mad ill dynamite-style cats like Darius, who rode his Honda Elite scooter in Fila slippers—they respected preps from the city, as long as us cats carried that thing original, which was to say never perpetrated no fraud. It meant taking pride in where you're from. And we did. The Oxfords off Wabash were gaudy preps: pink shirts, green pants, bright-colored track shoes, and Gumby haircuts. Plus there was no bourgeoisie contingent at the schools we mainly attended. Loyola, Walbrook, City College, Carver, Cardinal Gibbons, and Forest Park. To go to school there, you couldn't stand out more than to be an African American prep from the city. I might have eaten humble pie on a bus ride or two, but plenty of times I strutted the city like the word *Hero* was stitched on my chest. And the best-known cat in the clique for that air of confidence was Sonny.

But then our style became a casualty in the war that went off and on for years. On account of the Woodlawn beef, everybody began to ease on down the road to slick, Russell sweats and Filas, bald head and sullen, gold in your mouth, pass the reefer. All of a sudden it seemed like slick had something serene you needed to get through life, a good way to not mind being an outlaw. I didn't like it on a number of levels. And I was always the historian—the identity *yo* was too much connected to the *yo-ski* thing from the 1970s, when the kids ran "What's up yo-ski?" into the fucking ground. And as I got more black and proud, the *ski* part of it sounded too close to the Polack-Johnny level, the citywide hot dog stand. Corny for us to follow the hick klan from Dundalk and Highlandtown.

I never even knew all of exactly how we survived. I had a play cousin from Edmondson Village, slick as a wax floor and known throughout the city as The Ninja. He had jumped with the airborne in Grenada. One story went that he jogged up at a park on Woodlawn with an Uzi and told them to lay off. Another tale had it that the big-time boys from up the top of our street, who owned Yummy's at North and Gold, took an arsenal up to the courts at Bedford, where everybody from the County ran ball, and said they was holding so-and-so personally responsible for whatever went down. I admit, a couple of years later, one night we did have Carlos Gallilee all by himself up at Club 4604 on Liberty Heights. Darius, who had the distinction of having popped tool at the LL Cool J concert, wild Chuck Blue, and the ill James brothers were there, really wanting to hurt somebody. I just talked to Carlos, not feeling it was sporting to bring all of that wrath down on him on a night he was acting humble. But then again, he was an actor and today he's set himself up in Hollywood.

Funny how the slickheads didn't fare well in the end. Rocky, the mastermind—who had said up the Kappa House, not to me, just in my general direction, "You and your homeboys is just fucked!"—shot in the head. Muscleman Dante, whose girl I stole, ended up strung out after sitting down for ten at Jessup. Simon, the lunatic concrete-block man, gunned down at a police roadblock. I think pistol-loading Meechee fell into the dirt too—and if he did, then that's too much like right.

Then again, now that I think of it, these were mainly city guys, who had hung strong with Woodlawn, eighteen and nineteen and, like me, trying anything to get out to the suburbs. Slickheads and their expensive tennis did win the style war; but really, it was just that the city guys lost.

That summer, about ten weeks after the beef got under way, I learned that the police was the slave patrol and the Confederate Army extended. I had been surprised when they refused to protect me from the Woodlawn slickheads, but I hadn't known that my category was on their assassination list.

My father replaced the yellow wagon with a Japanese compact car, used, but with a tape deck and a sunroof, a real surprise. Somehow I had the car in the early afternoon, and me, Charm, and Mighty Joe Young were skylarking around the neighborhood, telling lies about the fine honey, bumping "The Dominatrix Sleeps Tonight." I noticed two white guys and a brother in a Chevrolet Cavalier near the library on Garrison, but I wasn't on the corner so it only seemed odd, not a personal threat. We stared them down and, three deep, drove off to the Plaza, doubling back and through, around Garrison Boulevard and Wabash Avenue.

At Reisterstown Road and Fords Lane I reached the traffic light. All of the sudden it seemed like a car was smashing into the side of me. A Highlandtown cracker pushed a heavy revolver through the sunroof and up to my head, his other hand reaching for the steering wheel. I could count the bullets in the chambers and see the tiny indentations in the cones of the soft lead. I wet my lap. For real. I was preparing to die. The angry man was shouting, "Move over!" and "Git out the car! Git the fuck out the car!" Then, with some time, I thought to myself that he must be a damn bold car thief. It was broad daylight. And even though we had just bought the sporty little Toyota, I couldn't see why he'd be so amped up for a $7,890 car. In a minor key, I thought that a cool hustler would probably find some way to drive off.

I tried to throw the car in park and slide away from the gun at the same time, but I couldn't get past Charm Sawyer's legs in the passenger seat. Charm had been yoked halfway out of the window by the black gloved hand of . . . Five-O? I heard commotion in the back, and next thing I knew Mighty Joe Young had his teeth on the asphalt. Then I noticed a silvery patch swinging from the chest of the man from Highlandtown with the dirty beard, and he demanded my license and registration.

After about fifteen minutes the dirty white man came back to the car.

"You ran a red light back there but my buddy doesn't have enough time to write you a ticket. Beat it."

I looked around fumbling with my mouth open and managed to get the Toyota away from the intersection. We got to the next block and pulled over, me and Charm shaking and crying from relief and shame and Mighty Joe Young mouthing Who-Struck-John. Never will get that dirty white man and that giant .38 from my mind.

When I told my father about it, I could see in his face and his demeanor that there was no authority to appeal to. When I was just a kid, I had been robbed by some bullies and had reluctantly confessed that humiliation to my dad. In his house shoes he stalked out into the middle of the avenue, attempting to find the boys who had wronged his child. But this new violation was just a new burden to shoulder. I knew enough to sense him crying on the inside. We were father and son inside of our house, but outside we were black males in America, with the same honor and respect as No. 1 crabs in season.

I guess prep or slick wasn't all that.

The Pell grants and the Maryland scholarships got cut off

around this time, and all of a sudden nobody was going to college out of state. The money went out as fast as the dope came in. That ride to Edwin Waters or Cheney or Widener, that had been wish fulfillment in the past. By the second half of the '80s, if you went to school, it was either down the street to the community college or up to Morgan, the old state college for Negroes where my parents and Charm's parents had been sent, at the end of the #33 bus line. Most of my homeboys, their parents would let them try it out for a semester. Our people believed in control. In our neighborhood fathers would brag to each other, "I'm never letting that nigger drive my car," meaning their own sons. Young boys like Dan Redd and Darryl and Mark were smart, but they couldn't get to school out of state and get that big jump on life from out the neighborhood. I got into college three hundred miles away—and those last weeks when the beef was running fast and furious, I tried not to be so simple-minded as to jeopardize a chance.

About two weeks before I was supposed to go off to Connecticut, a year now after the chase, the fellas wanted me to drive the brigade down to the Inner Harbor to square off against Woodlawn one last time. Remembering how my father's car had got kissed by the concrete block, I chilled. I heard that when it went down, it wasn't like a Murphy Homes versus Lexington Terrace scrap. Woodlawn had sent mainly the little boys. The police got into the fight before anybody got stomped or thrown into the water. Still, everybody began their adult criminal record that night in '86, and later it helped me that I wasn't there. But I saved the car one night and burned it up the next. When I got back after my freshman year in college, still dropping off into sleep after six weeks on line for Kappa, I passed out at the wheel and hit a neighbor head-on. I never drove again until I was on my own.

They were dog years between the end of high school and the end of college. Time folded every summer: scrapping in '86, macking in '87, bent in '88, and banging a gun in '89. I wouldn't want to live through '89 again, bringing all of that time together. We weren't Oxfords so much anymore—just homeboys now—and only rocking the prep style as a kind of occasional comment on the absurdity of our condition. The world had turned Slick with a capital *S*. To me the hi-top fade had its funeral rites when the cornball Toms at Duke started wearing it. I even stopped collecting house music and let the Blastmaster speak for me with that record "Ghetto Music."

We knew what time it was, but used the powerful narcotics to keep ourselves from the numbers. Heroin was flowing like water that summer, and Saddlehead and Jidda, Paris and Los, all of them good ole North and Poplar Grove boys could get it. Poplar Grove. Longwood. Bloomingdale. The Junction. Then we started falling further down. In the wee hours we used to slumber outside some spot at Lombard and Arlington, not far from ole H. L. Mencken's, blunted, waiting for Troy and Stanley to finish sniffing that dope. The world of joogy. Around my way they call it *boy* or *joogy. Girl* is *Shirl* caine—after Shirley Avenue where you go get nice. If you live in a town with a lot of joogy, everything else, like girl, seems real regular, jive legal. Joogy got me down from the psychedelics that they pumped up at college. Put it like this: in a world of disarray, joogy helps you to carry that thing.

That summer, back from college, every time I left out the house I saw somebody with tool, and one time I'm making eye contact with this lean slickhead, shooting a .45 into the air to keep street fighters tearing up a park festival from scratching his Benz. When I caught his eye I thought he was going to finish me. No question, joogy helps keep that begging, crying look off of your face. It got to the point where the police would be detaining me for walking down the street, and I'm getting ill to handle the stress, which everybody say is imaginary. That summer of '89 people was cross and fussing and we used to wear our Africa medallions at these pro-black rallies organized by Public Enemy. The next summer all the music was about killing each other over colored rags.

The summer Sonny got shot my right hand Charm Sawyer had to hit a boy who was holding a pistol on him, and even though I was making speed toward a degree, I doubted it was fast enough. Hanging out with Sawyer was scrapping every night, which wasn't really my style, especially after he busted my head on Muhammad's basement floor. Plus it's tough on your gear, my main way to get notice from the ladies. "A yo, Lair, hold my glasses," he'd say as he sized up someone for a scrap. "Imma piece that nigger." I would take them. Then he'd smirk and start throwing the dogs. He started out with skinny light-skin boys, but he was working his way up to short, wiry, dark-skin men. When we went out, he would always say that he would either get some pussy, beat a nigger, or get blind ill by the time the sun came up. I didn't understand his rage at the ceiling of possibility until a little later.

Charm got took over by the Myth, which had a couple of ingredients. The Myth meant crazy outrageous athleticism in every activity. It helped the style of it if the head of your thing went past your navel, but it all came together in an attitude of defiant obdurateness that we called Hard. I would try to cool him out, because I was being taught something different at school, but every time I wasn't around, he would trip the fuck out. At a party he shucked off all his gear and swung around ill until he got what he was looking for. One night Charm fouled a catatonic girl's mouth to stop niggers from running a train on her, but she still had to leave the city. He was getting known and some people were afraid of him. He had mastered the art of drilling any girl, no matter her look, no matter her size, at any time. Like, Pretty Ricky had written a book on the art of seduction. He had this snakelike way of peering into the eyes of the slinkiest, the trickiest, the flyest—the LaShawns, Letitias, Sheilas, and Keishas—the girls who had had so much exposure to slick that I didn't even know what to say to them. I only tried to win by light touch. But Charm didn't work in a whole lot of small talk or eye contact or hand-holding. He went on the Mandingo principle. He knocked down big China up against the freezer in my basement and she clawed grooves into his back. It took years for me to know what he did to make her cry out and lose control like that. She was so wide open every time we went with armloads of Guess apparel to the department store counter where she worked, it was like cashing a check.

I got a strong dose of the Myth too, the dreamworld life of super-nigger. One night of the dream me and Charm drank a couple of quarts of Mad Dog and picked up some wild ill broads from the Brook down at the Harbor. I only had one condom, used it on the girl I knew was out there, and ran raw in Sheba, thinking the odds were better because it was her time of the month. I thought another threshold of existence was at hand. Even the girls laughed about it, lil Lair happy cause he trimmed twice. The ill vibe kept clicking, though. At a party in the Junction Charm hit this boy in the face and broke his nose, and the jam was at the house of the broke-nose boy cousin. We had to fight Charm to get him out of there. Then, sitting five deep in a two-door Sentra trying to cool out, two hoppers came up on us. One skinny boy was on the street side, and a bald-headed light-skin boy with a shimmer in his mouth stood in the back. Skinny boy tapped the window with something metal. I heard a crack and the glass breaking, and we were all shouting to Pretty Ricky, "Drive!" "I'm hit!" I was pushing Charm and Knuckles so hard to peel away from that hot one searching for my ass. Decades of nightmares about that gunman.

About a week later, Sawyer and Sonny were throwing a cranker on Maryland Avenue, the little club district anchored by old-school Odell's (*You'll Know If You Belong,* the T-shirt used to say), house music Cignel's, and citywide Godfrey's Famous Ballroom. All the young hustlers and fly girls hung out in that zone. I was a little late getting to the jam.

I'd get the feeling of supreme confidence and contentment, just walking up the street and wading into a real players' crowd. Hundreds deep with hustlers and fly girls—herb bumping—passing quarts of Mad Dog and Red Bull malt liquor. Knowing my hair was faded right and I was getting dap from the players and intimate touches from Sheila, Kim, Lisa, and Tanya. "The Sound" by Reese & Santonio filling the air with our versions of the djembe, dundun, kenkeni, and sangban. Taking everybody way back. It's better than caine. Demerara. Ouagadougou.

Mighty Joe Young and me was nice, dipping up Murlin Avenue, near the bridge, gandering over to the zone from the Armory subway stop. All of a sudden, Ed from Bloomingdale drove by us and shouted, "Sonny got shot!" Old school, we ran the mile or two down the street. Ten minutes later we're outside the operating room at University Shock Trauma, screaming on the state trooper and the young Asian lady doctor who said, "Your friend didn't make it." She spat out that shit to me like I put the gun on Sonny.

I felt like the hospital was run by people with the slickhead mentality, that mentality that claims a nigger ain't shit. Me, I always wanted to redeem a nigger. The state trooper, a brother who understood, saved that bitch's Chinese ass. I wanted to do something. Sonny's parents came in a few minutes later. Crushed. Crying scene. Me and Mighty Joe Young walked down to the central police station where they were taking Sawyer's statement. We were amped up, spreading the word at hangouts like Crazy John's and El Dorado's, where we ran into some of our people.

Sawyer had been standing next to Sonny when they got stuck up. Sawyer's antsy brother Chester had a few dollars on him and gated up the alley, so Sawyer and Sonny, on the other side of the car, booked for it too. Rodney, Birdman, Dern, and Rock could only stand with their hands in the air while the runners gave it up. Sonny and a guy sitting on some steps got shot by a .22 rifle.

A lot of people blamed Sawyer for Sonny's murder, but I told him I was happy he had made it. He was my boy. We had been lightweight wilding up until then. No QP, no Z, no eight-ball, no stick-up, no home invasion, no pop tool, no cold-blooded train. Sawyer, James Brown, and Rock had taken a white boy for bad once. And Sawyer had been seen running down the street with a television, which had kind of got the police looking. Omar had taken a girl's telephone and her father's horse pistol. Sawyer and I had run a couple of gees on some wild young girls, and one time a grown woman did start fussing, but it was his cousin. I remember, because I left my high school graduation watch at her house. I thought if you were going to do the do, you had to take off everything. One night a little boy who had connections had tried to kill James Brown with a bat down at Cignel's, and we beefed over our heads, but James Brown let the thing go. I don't know how many times I got in a car with folk I ain't really know, on their way from or to do I don't know what. It was all right there. Rock, Darius, Worly, Chucky, Taft, Fats, Paris, Wood, Flip, Yippy, Champ, Ringfrail, Hondo, Reds. A whole lot of people got caught up in the mix.

What really hurt everybody was that Sonny had a whole lot of heart. He was a stand-up cat who had the will to make a difference. Shirt-off-his-back type of cat. Break a bottle over a big nigger's head for you cat. If the police looked for the killers, three men and a woman, they never found anybody. I had been in the Five-O palace on Baltimore Street and seen them lounging like they were on the whites-only floors. I had seen an office with a Confederate flag in it and some other of that old-timey, Frederick County shit. They always acted like Sonny's murder was "drug-related," like half of three hundred other murders that year. It hurts to think about his unsolved killing, twenty years later.

After Sonny's funeral, we started linking with cats who had hurt people, hoping to luck up onto that stick-up boy with the letter *G* on his hat who had gunned him down. The night after they shot Sonny we ganged into a dark room lit by the dutchy going around. A powerfully muscled old head addressed the mourning circle. "I gits a nut every time I pull the trigger." None of us ever forgot his sincerity. He said it to us like he was confessing something deep and personal, something that came out of the soul. I believed him.

Since Sonny had finished a year at Morehouse, the less stand-up guys figured that life wasn't worth struggling for. They started to get ill after the funeral like it was a paying job. I knew I didn't have as much heart as Sonny, so I did my share in the dim rooms. The morning after the funeral me and Clifton tried to run a gee on a young girl with a glass eye, not knowing she was five seconds from tricking on the corner—and Clifton months away hisself from the cemetery. Sometimes you would even pity a cat and bip half that bag of dope so that they wouldn't get hooked. One reason I stopped getting high was that Rock, my man from the bus stop days, pulled me up strong about looking weak, chasing. Sometimes you need to see yourself through the eyes of someone who has looked up to you. Then he got caught with a package and sat down at the Department of Corrections at Jessup, so I really tried to pull my pants up. After about eighteen months, overdoses began and cats started heading out of state to get away. Then there were the guys among us who thought that joogy wouldn't get to them, since they weren't shooting it up. But next thing they started flashing pistols to the countergirl at Roy Rogers. That gets you a seven-year bit at Hagerstown, or you could get lucky and go to Jessup where people at least can visit you.

A couple of the cats really tried to make a fortune. If Sawyer was my right hand, then Muhammad was my heart. When I decided to make a break for school in 1990, after my father went back to Guinea, Muhammad told me soberly, "Lair. Imma make a million dollars this year." The hustler thing was in the air. All of the rap music was trying to help you know the I Ching of Rayful and Alpo and our hometown man Peanut King. We all knew by heart the DC anthem "Stone Cold Hustler" and G Rap's "Road to the Riches." But I was so deep into reading about the COINTELPRO thing and what they did to Dr. Martin Luther King Jr. that none of the stories about stacking chips could reach me. Besides the fact that all the New York cats at school would be flipping out over the Bodymore stories I was telling, or the time my homeboys fell through for a visit, joogy-deep. Anyway, Muhammad acted hurt when I looked away from him.

For about two years we didn't have that much rap for each

other, a homeboy blood problem. Meanwhile Muhammad tried to get water from the rock with Rodney Glide. They stretched out until they tripped. Eventually the state of Pennsylvania took the wind out of Glide's sails for eight years, twenty-nine miles west of Philly at Graterford. I remember reading the newspapers about the old crew when I was in graduate school in California, a million miles away.

Sawyer turned the Myth in a new direction. He laid up with a Jamaican sister, got back in school, and earned a degree. He won an internship with a congressman from the streets who knew where he was coming from. He started working with the hoppers at George B. Murphy Homes high-rises, before it got blown up to make way for condos and the university hospital, where they work on getting the bug out. Just going down to Murphy Homes was a trip to us back in the day, where life and death, crime and punishment was wide open, like at my cousin's house on Myrtle Avenue, where Carmello's from. "Fat Boy's out! Fat Boy's out! Girl on green. Girl on green," is how the touts would run it down.

Sonny dying like he did definitely motivated me to finish graduate school and teach at the university level. But going to college for eleven years was no doubt the most sterile experience I had known. It was feeling all balled up like an English walnut. An experience that seemed designed to make me question who I was, if I was a man or not, if I was doing something worthwhile or not. On top of it all, it trained you to appreciate everything about old master and them, right down to studying their trifling distinctions, which is why I guess not that many brothers, when they know this thing about the war, bother with school.

After some years in the trenches, Sawyer got hooked up by George Soros. Now he has a company trying to help "at risk" young people. I guess he helped himself. Sawyer stood for one thing, and I got down with him on it. "Just put it out there. No matter who it hurts, whether it's a lie or not, right or wrong, good or bad. Never stop putting it out there."

LESLIE JAMISON

The Devil's Bait

FROM *Harper's Magazine*

FOR PAUL, IT STARTED with a fishing trip. For Lenny, it was an addict whose knuckles were covered in sores. Dawn found pimples clustered around her swimming goggles. Kendra noticed ingrown hairs. Patricia was attacked by sandflies on a Gulf Coast beach. Sometimes the sickness starts as blisters, or lesions, or itching, or simply a terrible fog settling over the mind, over the world.

For me, Morgellons disease started as a novelty: people said they had a strange ailment, and no one—or hardly anyone—believed them. But there were a lot of them, reportedly 12,000, and their numbers were growing. Their illness manifested in many ways, including fatigue, pain, and formication (a sensation of insects crawling over the skin). But the defining symptom was always the same: fibers emerging from their bodies. Not just fibers but fuzz, specks, and crystals. They didn't know what this stuff was, or where it came from, or why it was there, but they knew—and this was what mattered, the important word—that it was *real.*

The diagnosis originated with a woman named Mary Leitao. In 2001 she took her toddler son to the doctor because he had sores on his lip that wouldn't go away. He was complaining of bugs under his skin. The first doctor didn't know what to tell her, nor did the second, nor the third. Eventually they started telling her something she didn't want to hear: that she might be suffering from Münchausen syndrome by proxy, which causes a parent or caregiver to fabricate (and sometimes induce) illness in a dependent. Leitao came up with her own diagnosis, and Morgellons was born.

She pulled the name from a treatise written by the seventeenth-century English physician and polymath Sir Thomas Browne, who described

> that Endemial Distemper of little Children in Languedock, called the Morgellons, wherein they critically break out with harsh hairs on their Backs, which takes off the unquiet Symptoms of the Disease, and delivers them from Coughs and Convulsions.

Browne's "harsh hairs" were the early ancestors of today's fibers. Photos online show them in red, white, and blue—like the flag—and also black and translucent. These fibers are the kind of thing you describe in relation to other kinds of things: jellyfish or wires, animal fur or taffy candy or a fuzzball off your grandma's sweater. Some are called goldenheads, because they have a golden-colored bulb. Others simply look sinister, technological, tangled.

Patients started bringing these threads and flecks and fuzz to their doctors, storing them in Tupperware or matchboxes, and dermatologists actually developed a term for this phenomenon. They called it "the matchbox sign," an indication that patients had become so determined to prove their disease that they might be willing to produce fake evidence.

By the mid-2000s, Morgellons had become a controversy in earnest. Self-identified patients started calling themselves Morgies and rallying against doctors who diagnosed them with something called delusions of parasitosis (DOP). Major newspapers ran features posing some version of a question raised by the *New York Times* in 2006: "Is It Disease or Delusion?" The Centers for Disease Control and Prevention (CDC) launched a full-scale investigation soon afterward.

In the meantime, an advocacy organization called the Charles E. Holman Foundation started putting together an annual Morgellons conference in Austin, Texas, for patients, researchers, and health-care providers—basically, anyone who gave a damn. The foundation was named for a man who devoted the last years of his life to investigating the causes of his wife's disease. His widow runs the conference. She's still sick. The conference offers Morgies refuge from a world that generally refuses to accept their account of why they suffer. As one presenter wrote to me:

> It is bad enough that people are suffering so terribly. But to be the topic of seemingly the biggest joke in the world is way too much for sick people to bear. It is amazing to me that more people with this dreadful illness do not commit suicide . . .

The CDC finally released its study, "Clinical, Epidemiologic, Histopathologic and Molecular Features of an Unexplained Dermopathy," in January 2012. Its authors, in association with the so-called Unexplained Dermopathy Task Force, had investigated 115 patients, using skin samples, blood tests, and neurocognitive exams. Their report offered little comfort to Morgellons patients looking for affirmation:

> We were not able to conclude based on this study whether this unexplained dermopathy represents a new condition . . . or wider recognition of an existing condition such as delusional infestation.

The authors suggested, with some delicacy, that patients might be treated for a number of "co-existing conditions," such as drug abuse and psychosomatic disorders.

The bottom line? Probably nothing there.

The Westoak Woods Baptist Church, on Slaughter Lane, is a few miles south of the Austin I'd imagined, an Austin full of Airstream trailers selling gourmet doughnuts, vintage shops crammed with taxidermied animal heads and lace, melancholy guitar riffs floating from ironic cowboy bars. Slaughter Lane is something else. It's Walgreens and Denny's and eventually a parking lot sliced by the spindly shadow of a twenty-foot-tall cross.

The church itself is a low blue building. A banner for the 2012 conference reads, SEARCHING FOR THE UNCOMMON THREAD. By the entrance a cluster of friendly women greet new arrivals. On each of their matching shirts, the letters *DOP* are slashed out in red. Most of the participants at the conference, I will come to realize, give the wholesome, welcoming impression of no-nonsense midwestern housewives. I will also learn that 70 percent of Morgellons patients are female—and that women are especially vulnerable to the isolating disfigurement and condescension that accompany the disease.

The greeters direct me past an elaborate buffet of packaged pastries and into the sanctuary, which is serving as the main conference room. Speakers stand at the pulpit with their PowerPoint slides projected onto a screen behind them. Each cloth-covered pew holds a single box of Kleenex. The room has one stained-glass window—a dark-blue circle holding the milky cataract of a dove—but its panes admit no light.

This gathering is something like a meeting of alcoholics or Quakers. Between speakers, people occasionally just walk up to the pulpit and start sharing. Or else they do it in their chairs, hunched over to get a better look at one another's limbs. They swap cell-phone photos. I hear people talk about drinking Borax and running sound waves through their feet, about getting the disease from their fathers and giving it to their sons. I hear someone talk about what her skin is "expressing." I hear someone say, "It's a lonely world."

I discover that the people who can't help whispering during lectures are the ones I most want to talk to; that the coffee station is useful because it's a good place to meet people, and also because drinking coffee means I'll have to keep going to the bathroom, which is an even better place to meet people. The people I meet don't at first glance look disfigured. But up close, they reveal all kinds of scars and bumps and scabs.

I meet Dawn, a nurse from Pittsburgh, whose legs show the white patches I've come to recognize as formerly scabbed or lesion-ridden skin. Antibiotics have left a pattern of dark patches on her calves that once got her mistaken for an AIDS patient. Since her Morgellons diagnosis, Dawn has continued working.

"I was so angry at the misdiagnoses for so many years," she says, "being told that it was anxiety, in my head, female stuff. So I tried to spin that anger into something positive. I got my graduate degree. I published an article in a nursing journal."

I ask her about this phrase, "female stuff." It's like heart disease, she explains. For a long time, women's heart attacks were misdiagnosed or even ignored because doctors assumed that these patients were simply anxious or overly emotional. I realize Dawn's disease has been consistently, quietly embedded in a tradition that goes all the way back to nineteenth-century hysteria. She says her coworkers—the nurses, not the doctors—have been remarkably empathetic. Now they come to her whenever they find something strange or unexpected in a wound. She's become an expert in the inexplicable.

I ask Dawn what the hardest part of her disease has been. At first she replies in hesitant, general terms—"Uncertain future?"—but soon she settles on a more specific fear. "With the scars and stuff that I have from this," she says, "what guy's gonna like me?"

When Dawn talks about her body as something that's done her wrong, I fall into the easy groove of identification. Her condition seems like a crystallization of what I've always felt about myself—a wrongness in my being that I could never name and so pinned on my body, my thighs, my face. This resonance is part of what compels me about Morgellons.

But my willingness to turn Morgellons into metaphor—a physical manifestation of some abstract human tendency—is dangerous. It obscures the particular and unbidden nature of the suffering in front of me. I feel how conveniently these lives could be sculpted to fit the metaphoric strictures of the essay itself.

I once had a specimen of my own. It was a worm in my ankle—a botfly larva from Bolivia—that was too far under the skin to see. I remember my voice in the Yale–New Haven ER saying, "There's a worm," and I remember how everyone looked at me: kindly and without belief. Their doubt was like humidity in the air. They asked if I'd recently taken any mind-altering drugs. The disconnect felt even worse than the worm itself—to live in a world where this thing *was,* while other people lived in a world where it wasn't.

It was almost a relief to finally see the worm, bobbing out of my ankle like a tiny white snorkel. I finally knew it was real. It's the Desdemona Problem facing Othello: fearing the worst is worse than knowing the worst. You eventually start *wanting* the worst to happen.

I still remember the shrill intensity of my gratitude when a doctor verified the worm's existence. Desdemona really had fucked Cassio. It was a relief. The doctor pulled out the worm and gave it to me in a jar. The simultaneity was glorious: the worm was gone and I'd been right about it. I had about thirty minutes of peace before I started suspecting there might be another one.

I spent the next few weeks obsessed with the open wound on my ankle, looking for signs of a remaining worm. None emerged, but I didn't give up looking. Maybe the worm was tricky. It had seen what had happened to its comrade. I inspected the incision relentlessly for signs of eggs or movement. Anything I found was proof: a stray bit of Band-Aid, a glossy patch of bruised skin or scab.

It's easy to forget how Sir Thomas Browne insisted on the value of those "harsh hairs" covering the backs of his Languedoc urchins. He suggested that these strange growths quelled the "unquiet Symptoms of the Disease." Which is to say: physical symptoms can offer their own form of relief—they make suffering visible.

I don't know what causes the pain of Morgellons, the rustling on the skin, the threads and lesions. I only know what I learned from my botfly and its ghost: it was worse when I didn't have the worm than when I did.

A woman named Kendra, from Memphis, called a Morgellons hotline thinking she might be crazy. Now she's here at the conference. She sits on the church steps and smokes a cigarette. She says she probably shouldn't be smoking—gesturing at the church, and then at her scarred face.

Her cheeks show sores covered with pancake makeup. But she's pretty and young, with long, dark hair and a purple boatneck shirt that makes her look like she's headed somewhere else—the swimming pool, maybe—not back into a dim Baptist church to talk about what's living under her skin.

She says the scientific presentations have all gone over her head but that she's looking forward to tomorrow's program, an interactive session with a high-powered microscope. That's why she came all this way. She's seen things—what she initially mistook for hairs and now thinks are fibers—but the microscope will see more. She'll get proof. She can't get it anywhere else. She doesn't have medical insurance, and doctors don't believe her anyway. "I've messed with a part of my chin," she confesses. "It's almost like trying to pull out a piece of glass." Something raw and reddish has been chalked with beige powder.

She makes a point of telling me she never had acne as a teenager. She wasn't one of the facially marred until suddenly she was. Now, at the conference, she's among others like her, and this helps.

Folie à deux is the clinical name for shared delusion. Morgellons patients all know the phrase—it's the name of the crime they're charged with. But if folie à deux is happening at the conference, it's happening en masse: an entire churchful of folks having the same nightmare.

I ask Kendra if she ever doubts herself. Maybe she's afraid of something that's not actually happening?

"It's a possibility," she says, nodding. "But at the same time, you know, I think I've got a pretty good head on my shoulders. I don't think I've totally lost all my marbles."

She admits that coming here has made her a little bit afraid. In two years, will she be showing up in the emergency room with all the skin peeled off her chin? Spitting up bugs in the shower? In twenty years, will she still find her days consumed by this disease?

"Everyone who is born holds dual citizenship," Susan Sontag writes, "in the kingdom of the well and in the kingdom of the sick." Most people live in the former until they are forced—for certain spells of time—to take up residence in the latter. Right now Kendra is living in both. She tells me she's meeting a friend downtown for sushi tonight. She can still understand herself outside the context of this disease: someone who does ordinary things, looks forward to the events of an ordinary life.

But Kendra feels a growing affinity with this community, the refuge and consolation that it offers. "We can't all be delusional," she says.

Before the afternoon session begins, we get a musical interlude. A young man wearing jeans and flannel—somebody's Texan nephew-in-law—performs a rockabilly song about Morgellons. "We'll guarantee you tears and applause," he sings. "Just take on our cause." It seems like he's only doing this as a favor to his wife's step-aunt. Yet he launches bravely into each new song, most of them some combination of battle cry, rain dance, punch line, lament. "Doctor, doctor, won't you tell me what's the matter with me?" he sings. "I got things going wild in my body, can't you see?"

The star of the session is a physician from Laurieton, New South Wales, known casually around the conference as "the Australian." In his talk he responds directly to the recent CDC report, which he calls a "load of hogwash" and a "rocking-horse-dung pile." He contrasts the good guys (doctors who listen) with the bad guys (doctors who don't). The Australian listens. He is one of the good guys.

He aims to get the crowd fired up, and he succeeds. He offers himself to the room as a fighter. He coins a new piece of jargon: DOD, for delusions of doctors. This gets applause and a couple of hoots from the back.

The Australian might be an egomaniac or a savior, probably both. But what matters is the collective nerve he hits, the specter he summons—of countless fruitless visits to countless callous doctors. One senses a hundred identical wounds across this room. Not just from glass and fibers but also from smirks and muttered remarks, hastily scribbled notes, cutting gazes. I'm moved less by the mudslinging than by the sense of liberation underneath the crowd's applause.

This isn't an essay about whether Morgellons disease is real. That's probably obvious by now. It's an essay about what kinds of reality are considered prerequisites for compassion. It's about this strange sympathetic limbo: Is it wrong to speak of empathy when you trust the fact of suffering but not the source?

Calling Morgellons "real" generally means acknowledging that there is actual, inexplicable stuff coming up through human skin. "Real" means a fungus, parasite, bacterium, or virus—anything that might persuade the skeptical medical establishment that these patients aren't simply making the whole thing up.

The notion of "making it up" is also complicated, and could mean anything from intentional fabrication to hypochondria to an itch-scratch cycle that's gotten out of hand. Itching is powerful: the impulse that tells someone to scratch lights up the same neural pathways as chemical addiction. An itch that starts in the brain feels just like an itch on the skin, and it can begin with something as simple as a thought. It can begin from reading a paragraph like this one. Itching is a feedback loop, and it testifies to the possibility of symptoms that dwell in a charged and uneasy space between body and mind.

That's why "self-excoriation" is such a taboo phrase here, and why patients are so deeply offended by any accusation that they've planted fibers in their own skin. These explanations pin the blame back on *them*, suggesting not only that the harm inflicted is less real, but also that it's less deserving of compassion or aid. In contrast, parasites and bacteria are agents of otherness, granting the legitimacy of external struggle.

This insistence on an external source of damage implies that the self is a single coherent entity, a unified collection of physical, mental, and spiritual components. When really, the self—at least as I've experienced mine—is much more discordant and self-sabotaging, neither fully integrated nor consistently serving its own good.

During one discussion of possible bacterial causes of Morgellons, a woman raises her hand to make what initially seems like an incongruous point. "Maybe there *are* no autoimmune diseases," she says. "They just don't make sense." Why, after all, would a body fight itself? Perhaps, she suggests, what seems like an autoimmune disorder is simply the body anticipating a foreign invader that hasn't yet arrived. This logic too is predicated on a vision of the self as a whole, united, its parts working in concert—yet it betrays a lurking sense of the body's treachery, a sense of sickness as mutiny.

What does it look like when the self fights itself? When a human being is broken into warring factions? Perhaps it looks like the experimental cures I see here: scraping or freezing the skin, hitting it with lasers or defibrillators, dousing it with acid or lighter fluid, taking cocktails of antiparasitic medicines meant for animals three times our size.

But I wonder why this fracturing of the self shouldn't warrant our compassion just as much as a diseased body. Or maybe even more.

I duck out of the second afternoon session and fall into conversation with two men involved in a tense exchange near the cookie tray. Paul is a blond Texan wearing a silver-studded belt and stiff jeans. Lenny is from Oklahoma, a well-coiffed man with a curled mustache and a dark tan. Both wear flannel shirts tucked into their pants.

Paul is a patient, and Lenny is not. Lenny's here because he thinks he may have found the cure. A woman came to him with the disease all over her knuckles and he treated it with a laser. "I turned it on that," he says, "and it killed it."

I ask if he's a dermatologist.

"Oh no!" he says. "I'm an electrician."

This woman had two years of pain, Lenny says, and nothing helped her until he did. About twenty minutes into the conversation, he also mentions that she was a meth addict. He assures us that his laser cleaned her out until there was "no sign left" of any fibers. Paul has a strange look on his face as Lenny describes the cure. "You didn't heal her," he says finally. "It's a virus."

Lenny nods, but he's clearly taken aback. He wasn't expecting resistance.

"I've been dealing with this for eight years," Paul continues. "And I would've chopped off my hand if that would have stopped it from spreading to the rest of my body."

Paul looks worse than anyone else I've seen. He has his own name for his illness—the Devil's Fishing Bait—because, he says, he got it on a fishing trip. Sometimes he refers to it as a virus, other times as a parasitic infestation, but the sense of sinister agency remains the same.

Paul's disease is different in that you can see it. His right ear is the most obvious sign of his affliction. It's a little twisted, almost mashed, and it has the smooth, shiny texture of scar tissue all along the juncture between ear and jaw. His face is dotted with red pockmarks; the skin is stained with milky patterns, and he's got teardrop scars around his eyes.

Paul says he came home from the fishing trip with his legs covered in chigger bites. "You could feel the heat coming out of my pants," he says. His whole body was inflamed. I ask about his symptoms now. He simply shakes his head: "You can never tell what's coming next."

I ask whether he gets support from anyone in his life. He does, he says. That's when he tells me about his sister.

At first she wasn't sympathetic. She assumed Paul was on drugs when he told her about his symptoms. But she was the one who eventually discovered Morgellons, just about a year ago, and told him about it.

"So she's become a source of support?" I ask.

"Well," he says, "now she has it too."

They experiment with different treatments and compare notes: freezing, insecticides, dewormers for cattle, horses, dogs. A liquid-nitrogen compound he injected into his ear. Lately, he says, he's had success with root beer. He pours it over his head, his face, his limbs. He tells me about arriving at the ER one night with blood gushing from his ear, screaming because he could feel them—*them* again, uttered with such force—tearing him up inside. One of the ER doctors did a physical examination and noted that his mouth was dry. Paul told the doctor it was from shouting at them for help.

Paul doesn't seem overly impressed with the conference. Mainly because it hasn't offered up a cure, he says, though there's a trace of satisfaction in his disappointment, as if certain suspicions have been confirmed.

I sit behind him during the day's final presentation. I can see he isn't paying attention to the speaker. He's looking at photographs on his computer. They're all images of his face, mostly in profile, focused on his ear. He shows them to the middle-aged woman sitting beside him, and points to a photo of a small metal implement that looks like a pair of tongs: a Taser. A few moments later I hear him whisper, "These were all eggs."

When I leave the church, I find sunlight waiting outside our windowless rooms. The world has been patient. Springtime in Austin is grackles in the trees, a nearly invisible fluttering of bats under the Congress Avenue Bridge, and a waft of guano in blue-washed twilight. Austin is beautiful women everywhere, in scarves and boots, and windblown oak leaves skittering across patios where I eat oysters on ice. People with narrative tattoos smoke in the heat. I find a grotto dedicated to the Virgin Mary with an empty beer bottle and a bag of Cheez-Its buried in the gravel.

I walk among the young and healthy and I am more or less one of them. I am trying not to itch. I am trying not to take my skin for granted. But I can't quiet the voices of those who no longer feel they belong anywhere. I spend a day in their kingdom and then leave when I please. It feels like a betrayal to come up for air.

Doubting the existence of Morgellons hasn't stopped me from being afraid I'll get it. Before the conference, I told my friends, "If I come back from Austin thinking I have Morgellons, you have to tell me I don't." Now that I'm here, I wash my hands a lot. I'm conscious of other people's bodies.

Then it starts happening, as I knew it would. After a shower, I notice small blue strands like tiny worms across my clavicle. I find what appear to be minuscule spines, little quills, tucked into the crevice of a fortune line on my palm.

If you look closely enough, of course, skin is always foreign—full of bumps, botched hairs, hefty freckles, rough patches. The blue fibers are probably just stray threads from a towel, or from my sleeve, the quills not quills at all but smeared ink on the surface of the skin. But it's in these moments of fear that I come closest to experiencing Morgellons the way patients do. Inhabiting their perspective only makes me want to protect myself from what they have. I wonder if these are the only options available to my crippled organs of compassion: I'm either full of disbelief or I'm washing my hands in the bathroom.

I'm not the only person at the conference thinking about contagion. One woman stands up to say she needs to know the facts about how Morgellons is really transmitted. She tells the crowd that her family and friends refuse to come to her apartment. She needs proof that they can't catch the disease from her couch. It's hard not to speculate. Maybe her family and friends are afraid of catching her disease—or maybe they're keeping their distance from what they understand as her obsession.

Kendra tells me she's afraid of getting her friends sick whenever she goes out to dinner with them. I picture her at the sushi place—handling her chopsticks so carefully, keeping her wasabi under strict quarantine, so that this *thing* in her won't get into anyone else.

The specter of contagion serves a curious double function. On the one hand, as with Kendra, there is a sense of shame at oneself as a potential carrier of infection. But on the other hand, the possibility of spreading this disease also suggests that it's real—that it could be proven to exist by its manifestation in others.

This double-edged sword of fear and confirmation is on full display at the Pets with Morgellons website, one of the oddest corners of the Morgellons online labyrinth. In a typical entry, a cat named Ika introduces herself and her illness:

> I have been named [for] the Japanese snack of dried cuttlefish . . . Typically I am full of chaotic energy, however lately I have been feeling quite lethargic and VERY itchy. My best friend/mommy thinks that she gave me her skin condition, and she is so very SAD. I think she is even more sad that she passed it on to me than the fact that she has it covering her entire face.

The litany of sick animals continues. A sleek white dog named Jazzy sports itchy paws; two bloodhounds are biting invisible fleas; a Lhasa apso joins his owner for stretches in an infrared sauna. Another entry is an elegy for an Akita named Sinbad:

> It appears that I got the disease at the same time that my beautiful lady owner got it. And after many trips to the vet they had to put me down. I know it was for my own good, but I do miss them a lot. I can still see my master's face, right up close to mine, when the doc put me to sleep . . . I could sniff his breath and feel the pain in his eyes as tears rolled down his face. But, it's ok. I'm alright now. The maddening itching is finally over. I'm finally at peace.

Who knows what happened to Sinbad? Maybe he really did need to get put down; maybe he was old, or sick with something else. Maybe he wasn't sick at all. But he has become part of an illness narrative—like lesions, or divorces, or the fibers themselves. He is irrefutable proof that suffering has happened, that things have been lost.

The second day of the conference kicks off with a Japanese television documentary about Morgellons—known over there as cotton-erupting disease. We see a woman standing at her kitchen counter, mixing a livestock antiparasitic called ivermectin into a glass of water. The Japanese voiceover sounds concerned, and a conference participant reads an English translation: the woman knows this drug isn't for human consumption, but she's using it anyway. She's desperate. We see a map of America with patches of known cases breaking out like lesions over the land, a twisted manifest destiny.

Just as fibers attach to an open wound—its wet surface a kind of glue—so does the notion of disease function as an adhesive, gathering anything we can't understand, anything that hurts, anything that will stick. "Transmission by Internet," some skeptics claim about Morgellons: message boards as Pied Pipers, calling all comers. It's true that the Internet made it possible for knowledge of Morgellons to spread and transformed its sufferers into a self-contained online community.

A woman named Sandra pulls out her cell phone to show me a photo of something she coughed up. It looks like a little albino shrimp. She thinks it's a larva. She photographed it through a jeweler's loupe. She wants a microscope but doesn't have one yet. She put the larva on a book to provide a sense of scale. I try to get a good look at the print; I'm curious about what she was reading.

Sandra has a theory about the fibers—that the organisms inside her are gathering materials to make their cocoons. This explains why so many of the fibers turn out to be ordinary kinds of thread, dog hair, or cotton. Creatures are making a nest of her body, using the ordinary materials of her life to build a home inside her.

Once I've squinted long enough at the shrimpish thing, Sandra brings up a video of herself in the bathtub. "These are way beyond fibers," she promises. Only her feet are visible, protruding through the surface of the water. The quality is grainy, but it appears the bath is full of wriggling larvae. Their forms are hard to feel sure about—everything is dim and a little sludgy—but that's what it looks like. She says that a couple of years ago, there were hundreds coming out of her skin. It's gotten a little better. These days when she takes a bath, only two or three come out.

I'm at a loss. I don't know whether what I'm seeing are worms, or where they come from, or what they might be if they're *not* worms, or whether I want them to be worms or not, or what I have to believe about this woman if they aren't worms—or about the world, or human bodies, or this disease, if they *are.* I do know that I see a bunch of little wriggling shadows, and for now I'm glad I'm not a doctor or a scientist, because leaning into this uncertainty lets me believe her without needing to confirm my belief. I can dwell with her—for just a moment, at least—in the possibility of those worms, in that horror.

I catch sight of Kendra watching Sandra's phone. She's wondering if this is what her future holds. I want to comfort her, to insist that everyone's disease turns out a little different. She tells me about sushi last night: it was good. Turns out she bought a painting. She shouldn't have, she says. She can't afford it. But she saw it hanging at the restaurant and couldn't resist. She shows me a picture on her phone: lush, braided swirls of oil paint curl from the corners of a parchment-colored square.

I think but don't say, Fibers.

"You know," she says, voice lowered, "it reminds me a little of those things."

I get a sinking feeling. It's that moment in a movie when the illness spreads beyond its quarantine. Even when Kendra leaves this kingdom of the sick, she finds sickness waiting patiently for her on the other side. She pays $300 she can't afford just so she can take its portrait home with her.

*

The organizers are holding a lottery to give away some inexpensive microscopes: a handful of miniature ones like small black plums, and their larger cousin the EyeClops, a children's toy. I win a mini, but I'm sheepish as I head up to the stage to claim it. What do I need a scope for? I'm here to write about how other people need scopes. Everyone knows this. I'm given a small, square box. I imagine how the scene will play out later tonight: examining my skin in the stale privacy of my hotel room, facing that razor's edge between skepticism and fear by way of the little widget in my palm.

I give my miniscope to Sandra. I give it to her because she is sick of using her jeweler's loupe, because she is sad she didn't get one, and because I feel self-conscious about winning one when I wasn't even looking for fibers in the first place.

"That's so generous," she says.

But maybe it wasn't generous. Maybe it was the opposite. Maybe I'd just taken hours of her life away and replaced them with hours spent at the peephole of that microscope, staring at what she wouldn't be able to cure.

"I can be myself only when I'm here" is something I heard more than once at Westoak. But every time I left the church, I found myself wishing these patients could also be themselves elsewhere, could be themselves anywhere. I think of Kendra, terrified by the same assurances that offered her validation. She had proof of fibers in her skin but no hope of getting them out, only a vision of what it might look like to be consumed by this disease entirely—a thousand bloody photographs on a laptop, or a soup of larvae on her phone.

A confession: I left the conference early. I actually, embarrassingly, went to sit by the shitty hotel pool. I baked bare-skinned in the Texas sun, and I watched a woman from the conference come outside and carefully lay her own body, fully clothed, across a reclining chair in the shade.

I've left the kingdom of the ill. Dawn and Kendra and Paul and Sandra remain. But I still feel the ache of an uncanny proximity. "Some of these things I'm trying to get out," Kendra told me, "it's like they move away from me." Sometimes we're all trying to purge something, and what we're trying to purge resists our efforts. These demons belong to all of us: an obsession with our boundaries and visible shapes, a fear of invasion or contamination, an understanding of ourselves as perpetually misunderstood.

But doesn't this search for meaning obfuscate the illness itself? It's another kind of bait, another tied-and-painted fly: the notion that if we understand something well enough, we can make it go away.

Everyone I met at the conference was kind. They offered their warmth to me and to one another. I was a visitor to what they knew, but I have been a citizen at times, and I know I'll be one again. Now my skepticism feels like a violation of some collective trust. The same researcher who told me about "the biggest joke in the world" also told me this: "When I heard of your interest, I felt genuine hope that the real story would be told accurately and sensitively." I can't forget this hope. I don't want to betray it.

"Sit down before fact as a little child," wrote the nineteenth-century biologist Thomas Huxley, in a passage quoted by one of the speakers at Westoak, "and be prepared to give up every preconceived notion, follow humbly wherever and to whatever abyss Nature leads, or you shall learn nothing."

I want to follow humbly; I want to believe everyone. But belief isn't the same thing as compassion, or sorrow, or pity. It wasn't until the seventeenth century that the words *pity* and *piety* were completely distinguished. And what I feel toward this disorder is a kind of piety—an obligation to pay homage, or at least accord some reverence to these patients' collective understanding of what makes them hurt. Maybe it's a kind of sympathetic infection: this need to go-along-with, to nod-along-with, to agree.

Paul said, "I wouldn't tell anyone my crazy-ass symptoms." But he told them to me. He's always been met with disbelief. He called it "typical." Now I'm haunted by that word. For Paul, life has become a pattern and the moral of that pattern is, *You're destined for this.* The disbelief of others is inevitable and so is loneliness; both are just as much a part of this disease as any fiber, any speck or crystal or parasite.

I went to Austin because I wanted to be a different kind of listener than these patients had generally known: doctors winking at their residents, friends biting their lips, skeptics smiling in smug bewilderment. But wanting to be different doesn't make you so. Paul told me his crazy-ass symptoms and I didn't believe him. Or at least I didn't believe him the way he wanted to be believed. I didn't believe there were parasites laying thousands of eggs under his skin, but I did believe he suffered as if there were. Which was typical. I was typical. In writing this essay, how am I doing something he wouldn't understand as betrayal? I want to say, *I heard you.* To say, *I pass no judgments.* But I can't say these things to him. So instead I say this: I think he can heal. I hope he does.

ARIEL LEVY

Thanksgiving in Mongolia

FROM *The New Yorker*

MY FAVORITE GAME when I was a child was Mummy and Explorer. My father and I would trade off roles: one of us had to lie very still with eyes closed and arms crossed over the chest, and the other had to complain, "I've been searching these pyramids for so many years. When will I ever find the tomb of Tutankhamun?" (This was in the late seventies, when Tut was at the Met, and we came in from the suburbs to visit him frequently.) At the climax of the game, the explorer stumbles on the embalmed pharaoh and—brace yourself—the mummy opens his eyes and comes to life. The explorer has to express shock, and then says, "So, what's new?" To which the mummy replies, "*You.*"

I was not big on playing house. I preferred make-believe that revolved around adventure, featuring pirates and knights. I was also domineering, impatient, relentlessly verbal, and, as an only child, often baffled by the mores of other kids. I was not a popular little girl. I played Robinson Crusoe in a small wooden fort that my parents built for me in the back yard. In the fort I was neither ostracized nor ill at ease—I was self-reliant, brave, ingeniously surviving, if lost.

The other natural habitat for a child who loves words and adventure is the page, and I was content when my parents read me *Moby-Dick, Pippi Longstocking,* or *The Hobbit.* I decided early that I would be a writer when I grew up. That, I thought, was the profession that went with the kind of woman I wanted to become: one who is free to do whatever she chooses. I started keeping a diary in third grade and, in solidarity with Anne Frank, gave it a name and made it my confidante. To this day I feel comforted and relieved of loneliness, no matter how foreign my surroundings, if I have a pad and a pen with which to record my experiences.

I've spent the past twenty years putting myself in foreign surroundings as frequently as possible. There is nothing I love more than traveling to a place where I know nobody, and where everything will be a surprise, and then writing about it. The first time I went to Africa for a story, I was so excited that I barely slept during the entire two-week trip. Everything was new: the taste of springbok meat, the pink haze over Cape Town, the noise and chaos of the corrugated-tin alleyways in Khayelitsha township. I could still feel spikes of adrenaline when I was back at my desk in New York, typing, while my spouse cooked a chicken in the kitchen.

But as my friends, one after another, made the journey from young woman to mother, it glared at me that I had not. I would often listen to a Lou Reed song called "Beginning of a Great Adventure," about the possibilities of imminent parenthood. "A little me or he or she to fill up with my dreams," Lou sings, with ragged hopefulness, "a way of saying life is not a loss." It became the soundtrack to my mulling on motherhood. I knew that a child would make life as a professional explorer largely impossible. But having a kid seemed in many ways like the wildest trip of all.

I always get terrified right before I travel. I become convinced that this time will be different: I won't be able to figure out the map, or communicate with non-English-speakers, or find the people I need in order to write the story I've been sent in search of. I will be lost and incompetent and vulnerable. I know that my panic will turn to excitement once I'm there—it always does—but that doesn't make the fear before takeoff any less vivid. So it was with childbearing: I was afraid for ten years. I didn't like childhood, and I was afraid that I'd have a child who didn't either. I was afraid I would be an awful mother. And I was afraid of being grounded, sessile—stuck in one spot for eighteen years of oboe lessons and math homework that I couldn't finish the first time around.

I was on book tour in Athens when I decided that I would do it. My partner—who had always indicated that I would need to cast the deciding vote on parenthood—had come with me, and we were having one of those magical moments in a marriage when you find each other completely delightful. My Greek publisher and his wife took us out dancing and drinking, and cooked for us one night in their little apartment, which was overrun with children, friends, moussaka, and cigarette smoke. "Americans are not relaxed," one of the other guests told me, holding his three-year-old and drinking an ouzo. Greece was falling apart. The streets of Athens were crawling with cats and dogs that people had abandoned because they could no longer afford pet food. But our hosts were jubilant. Their family didn't seem like a burden; it seemed like a party. The idea bloomed in my head that being governed by something other than my own wishes and wanderlust might be a pleasure, a release.

I got pregnant quickly, to my surprise and delight, shortly before my thirty-eighth birthday. It felt like making it onto a plane the moment before the gate closes—you can't help but thrill. After only two months, I could hear the heartbeat of the creature inside me at the doctor's office. It seemed like magic: a little eye of newt in my cauldron and suddenly I was a witch with the power to brew life into being. Even if you are not Robinson Crusoe in a solitary fort, as a human being you walk this world by yourself. But when you are pregnant you are never alone.

My doctor told me that it was fine to fly up until the third trimester, so when I was five months pregnant I decided to take one last big trip. It would be at least a year, maybe two, before I'd be able to leave home for weeks on end and feel the elation of a new place revealing itself. (It's like having a new lover—even the parts you aren't crazy about have the crackling fascination of the unfamiliar.) Just before Thanksgiving, I went to Mongolia.

People were alarmed when I told them where I was going, but I was pleased with myself. I liked the idea of being the kind of woman who'd go to the Gobi Desert pregnant, just as, at twenty-two, I'd liked the idea of being the kind of girl who'd go to India by herself. And I liked the idea of telling my kid, "When you were inside me, we went to see the edge of the earth." I wasn't truly scared of anything but the Mongolian winter. The tourist season winds down in October, and by late November, when I got on the plane, the nights drop to twenty degrees below zero. But I was prepared: I'd bought snow pants big enough to fit around my convex gut and long underwear two sizes larger than I usually wear.

To be pregnant is to be in some kind of discomfort pretty much all the time. For the first few months, it was like waking up with a bad hangover every single morning but never getting to drink—I was nauseated but hungry, afflicted with a perpetual headache, and really qualified only to watch television and moan. That passed, but a week before I left for Mongolia I started feeling an ache in my abdomen that was new. "Round-ligament pain" is what I heard from everyone I knew who'd been pregnant, and what I read on every prenatal website: the uterus expanding to accommodate the baby, as he finally grew big enough to make me look actually pregnant instead of just chunky. That thought comforted me on the fourteen-hour flight to Beijing, while I shifted endlessly, trying to find a position that didn't hurt my round ligaments.

When my connecting flight landed in Mongolia, it was morning, but the gray haze made it look like dusk. Ulaanbaatar is among the most polluted capital cities in the world, as well as the coldest. The drive into town wound through frozen fields and clusters of felt tents—*gers,* they're called there—into a crowded city of stocky, Soviet-era municipal buildings, crisscrossing telephone and trolley lines, and old Tibetan Buddhist temples with pagoda roofs. The people on the streets moved quickly and clumsily, burdened with layers against the bitter weather.

I was there to report a story on the country's impending transformation, as money flooded in through the mining industry. Mongolia has vast supplies of coal, gold, and copper ore; its wealth was expected to double in five years. But a third of the population still lives nomadically, herding animals and sleeping in *gers,* burning coal or garbage for heat. Until the boom, Mongolia's best-known export was cashmere. As Jackson Cox, a young consultant from Tennessee who'd lived in Ulaanbaatar for twelve years, told me, "You're talking about an economy based on yak meat and goat hair."

I got together with Cox on my first night in town. He sent a chauffeured car to pick me up—every Westerner I met in U.B. had a car and a driver—at the Blue Sky Hotel, a new and sharply pointed glass tower that split the cold sky like a shark fin. When I arrived at his apartment, he and a friend, a mining-industry lawyer from New Jersey, were listening to Beyoncé and pouring champagne. The place was clean and modern, but modest: for expats in U.B., it's far easier to accumulate wealth than it is to spend it. We went to dinner at a French restaurant, where we all ordered beef, because seafood is generally terrible in Mongolia, which is separated from the sea by its hulking neighbors (and former occupiers) China and Russia. Then they took me to an underground gay bar called 100 Per Cent—which could have been in Brooklyn, except that everyone in Mongolia still smoked indoors. I liked sitting in a booth in a dark room full of smoking, gay Mongolians, but my body was feeling strange. I ended the night early.

When I woke up the next morning, the pain in my abdomen was insistent; I wondered if the baby was starting to kick, which everyone said would be happening soon. I called home to complain, and my spouse told me to find a Western clinic. I e-mailed Cox to get his doctor's phone number, thinking that I'd call if the pain got any worse, and then I went out to interview people: the minister of the environment, the president of a mining concern, and, finally, a herdsman and conservationist named Tsetsegee Munkhbayar, who became a folk hero after he fired shots at mining operations that were diverting water from nomadic communities. I met him in the sleek lobby of the Blue Sky with Yondon Badral—a smart, sardonic man I'd hired to translate for me in U.B. and to accompany me a few days later to the Gobi, where we would drive a Land Rover across the cold sands to meet with miners and nomads. Badral wore jeans and a sweater; Munkhbayar was dressed in a long, traditional *deel* robe and a fur hat with a small metal falcon perched on top. It felt like having a latte with Genghis Khan.

In the middle of the interview, Badral stopped talking and looked at my face; I must have been showing my discomfort. He said that it was the same for his wife, who was pregnant, just a few weeks further along than I was, and he explained the situation to Munkhbayar. The nomad's skin was chapped pink from the wind; his nostrils, eyes, and ears all looked as if they had receded into his face to escape the cold. I felt a little surge of pride when he said that I was brave to travel so far in my condition. But I was also starting to worry.

I nearly canceled my second dinner with the Americans that evening, but I figured that I needed to eat, and they offered to meet me at the Japanese restaurant in my hotel. Cox was leaving the next day to visit his family for Thanksgiving, and he was feeling guilty that he'd spent a fortune on a business-class ticket. I thought about my uncomfortable flight over and said that it was probably worth it. "You're being a princess," Cox's friend told him tartly, but I couldn't laugh. Something was happening inside me. I had to leave before the food came.

I ran back to my room, pulled off my pants, and squatted on the floor of the bathroom, just as I had in Cambodia when I had dysentery, a decade earlier. But the pain in that position was unbearable. I got on my knees and put my shoulders on the floor and pressed my cheek against the cool tile. I remember thinking, *This is going to be the craziest shit in history.*

I felt an unholy storm move through my body, and after that there is a brief lapse in my recollection; either I blacked out from the pain or I have blotted out the memory. And then there was another person on the floor in front of me, moving his arms and legs, alive. I heard myself say out loud, "This can't be good." But it *looked* good. My baby was as pretty as a seashell.

He was translucent and pink and very, very small, but he was flawless. His lovely lips were opening and closing, opening and closing, swallowing the new world. For a length of time I cannot delineate, I sat there, awestruck, transfixed. Every finger, every toenail, the golden shadow of his eyebrows coming in, the elegance of his shoulders—all of it was miraculous, astonishing. I held him up to my face, his head and shoulders filling my hand, his legs dangling almost to my elbow. I tried to think of something maternal I could do to convey to him that I was, in fact, his mother, and that I had the situation completely under control. I kissed his forehead and his skin felt like a silky frog's on my mouth.

I was vaguely aware that there was an enormous volume of blood rushing out of me, and eventually that seemed interesting too. I looked back and forth between my offspring and the lake of blood consuming the bathroom floor and I wondered what to do about the umbilical cord connecting those two things. It was surprisingly thick and ghostly white, a twisted human rope. I felt sure that it needed to be severed—that's always the first thing that happens in the movies. I was afraid that if I didn't cut that cord my baby would somehow suffocate. I didn't have scissors. I yanked it out of myself with one swift, violent tug.

In my hand, his skin started to turn a soft shade of purple. I bled my way across the room to my phone and dialed the number for Cox's doctor. I told the voice that answered that I had given birth in the Blue Sky Hotel and that I had been pregnant for nineteen weeks. The voice said that the baby would not live. "He's alive now," I said, looking at the person in my left hand. The voice said that he understood, but that it wouldn't last, and that he would send an ambulance for us right away. I told him that if there was no chance the baby would make it, I might as well take a cab. He said that that was not a good idea.

Before I put down my phone, I took a picture of my son. I worried that if I didn't, I would never believe he had existed.

When the pair of Mongolian EMTs came through the door, I stopped feeling competent and numb. One offered me a tampon, which I knew not to accept, but the realization that of the two of us I had more information stirred a sickening panic in me, and I said I needed to throw up. She asked if I was drunk, and I said, offended, *No, I'm* upset. "Cry," she said. "You just cry, cry, cry." Her partner bent to insert a thick needle in my forearm and I wondered if it would give me Mongolian AIDS, but I felt unable to do anything but cry, cry, cry. She tried to take the baby from me, and I had the urge to bite her hand. As I lay on a gurney in the back of the ambulance with his body wrapped in a towel on top of my chest, I watched the frozen city flash by the windows. It occurred to me that perhaps I was going to go mad.

In the clinic there were very bright lights and more needles and IVs and I let go of the baby and that was the last I ever saw him. He was on one table and I was on another, far away, lying still under the screaming lights, and then, confusingly, the handsomest man in the world came through the door and said he was my doctor. His voice sounded nice, familiar. I asked if he was South African. He was surprised that I could tell, and I explained that I had spent time reporting in his country, and then we talked a bit about the future of the ANC and about how beautiful it is in Cape Town. I realized that I was covered in blood, sobbing, and flirting.

Soon he said that he was going home and that I could not return to the Blue Sky Hotel, where I might bleed to death in my room without anyone knowing. I stayed in the clinic overnight, wearing a T-shirt and an adult diaper that a kind, fat, giggling young nurse gave me. After she dressed me, she asked, "You want toast and tea?" It was milky and sweet and reminded me of the chai I drank in Nepal, where I went backpacking in the Himalayas with a friend long before I was old enough to worry about the expiration of my fertility. It had been a trip spent pushing my young body up the mountains, past green-and-yellow terraced fields and villages full of goats, across rope bridges that hung tenuously over black ravines with death at the bottom. We consumed a steady diet of hashish and Snickers bars and ended up in a blizzard that killed several hikers but somehow left us only chilly.

I had been so lucky. Very little had ever truly gone wrong for me before that night on the bathroom floor. And I knew, as surely as I now knew that I wanted a child, that this change in fortune was my fault. I had boarded a plane out of vanity and selfishness, and the dark Mongolian sky had punished me. I was still a witch, but my powers were all gone.

That is not what the doctor said when he came back to the clinic in the morning. He told me that I'd had a placental abruption, a very rare problem that, I later read, usually befalls women who are heavy cocaine users or who have high blood pressure. But sometimes it happens just because you're old. It could have happened anywhere, the doctor told me, and he repeated what he'd said the night before: there is no correlation between air travel and miscarriage. I said that I suspected he was being a gentleman, and that I needed to get out of the clinic in time for my eleven o'clock meeting with the secretary of the interior, whose office I arrived at promptly, after I went back to the Blue Sky and showered in my room, which looked like the site of a murder.

I spent the next five days in that room. Slowly it set in that it was probably best if I went home instead of to the Gobi, but at first I could not leave. Thanksgiving came and went. There were rolling brownouts when everything went dark and still. I lay in my bed and ate Snickers and drank little bottles of whiskey from the minibar while I watched television programs that seemed as strange and bleak as my new life. Someone had put a white bathmat on top of the biggest bloodstain, the one next to my bed, where I had crouched when I called for help, and little by little the white went red and then brown as the blood seeped through it and oxidized. I stared at it. I looked at the snow outside my window falling on the Soviet architecture. But mostly I looked at the picture of the baby.

When I got back from Mongolia, I was so sad I could barely breathe. On five or six occasions I ran into mothers who had heard what had happened, and they took one look at me and burst into tears. (Once this happened with a man.) Within a week the apartment we were supposed to move into with the baby fell through. Within three, my marriage had shattered. I started lactating. I continued bleeding. I cried ferociously and without warning—in bed, in the middle of meetings, sitting on the subway. It seemed to me that grief was leaking out of me from every orifice.

I could not keep the story of what had happened in Mongolia inside my mouth. I went to buy clothes that would fit my big body but that didn't have bands of stretchy maternity elastic to accommodate a baby who wasn't there. I heard myself tell a horrified saleswoman, "I don't know what size I am, because I just had a baby. He died, but the good news is, now I'm fat." Well-meaning women would tell me, "I had a miscarriage too," and I would reply, with unnerving intensity, "He was *alive*." I had given birth, however briefly, to another human being, and it seemed crucial that people understand this. Often, after I told them, I tried to get them to look at the picture of the baby on my phone.

After several weeks I was looking at it only once a day. It was months before I got it down to once a week. I don't look at it much anymore, but people I haven't seen in a while will say, "I'm so sorry about what happened to you." And their compassion pleases me.

But the truth is, the ten or twenty minutes I was somebody's mother were black magic. There is no adventure I would trade them for; there is no place I would rather have seen. Sometimes, when I think about it, I still feel a dark hurt from some primal part of myself, and if I'm alone in my apartment when this happens I will hear myself making sounds that I never made before I went to Mongolia. I realize that I have turned back into a wounded witch, wailing in the forest, undone.

Most of the time it seems sort of okay, though, natural. *Nature.* Mother Nature. She is free to do whatever she chooses.

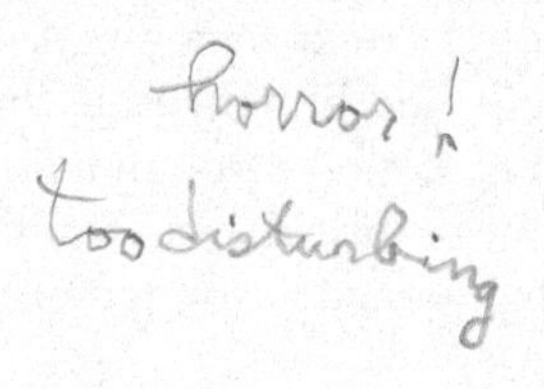

YIYUN LI

Dear Friend, From My Life I Write to You in Your Life

FROM *A Public Space*

1.

My first encounter with *before and after* was in one of the fashion magazines my friends told me to subscribe to when I came to America. I duly followed their advice—I had an anthropologist's fascination with America then. I had never seen a glossy magazine, and the quality of the paper and the printing, not to mention the trove of perfumes waiting to be unfolded, made me wonder how the economy worked for the magazine to make a profit, considering I paid no more than a dollar for an issue.

My favorite column was on the last page of the magazine, and it featured celebrity makeovers—hairstyle and hair color, for instance—with two bubbles signifying before and after. I didn't often have an opinion about the transformation, but I liked the definitiveness of that phrase, *before and after,* with nothing muddling the in-between.

After years of living in America, I still feel a momentary elation whenever I see an advertisement for weight-loss programs, teeth-whitening strips, hair-loss treatments, or even plastic surgery, with the contrasting effects shown under before and after. The certainty in that pronouncement—for each unfortunate or inconvenient situation, there is a solution to make it no longer be—both attracts and perplexes me. Life can be reset, it seems to say; time can be separated. But that logic appears to me as doubtful as traveling to another place to become a different person: altered sceneries are at best distractions, or else new settings for old habits. What one carries from one point to another, geographically or temporally, is one's self: even the most inconsistent person is consistently himself.

2.

A few years ago I was about to go teach a class when an acquaintance, who lived across the country in New Hampshire, called my office. She had traveled to a nearby city. I talked to her for no more than two minutes before telling my husband to go find her. He spent twelve hours with her, canceled her business appointments, and saw to it that she flew back home. Two weeks later her husband called and said she had jumped out of her office on a Sunday evening. He asked me to attend her memorial service; I thought for a long while and decided not to.

Our memories tell more about now than then. Doubtless the past is real; there is no shortage of evidence: photos, journals, letters, old suitcases. But we choose and discard from an abundance of evidence what suits us at the moment. There are many ways to carry the past with us: to romanticize it, to invalidate it, to furnish it with revised or entirely fictionalized memories; the present does not surrender so easily to manipulation.

I don't want the present to judge the past, so I don't want to ponder my absence at her memorial service. We had come to this country around the same time. When I told her that I was going to quit science to become a writer, she seemed curious, but her husband said that it was a grave mistake. "Why do you want to make your life difficult?" he asked.

3.

I have had a troublesome relationship with time. The past I cannot trust because it could be tainted by my memory. The future is hypothetical and is to be treated with caution. The present, what is the present but a constant test: in this muddled in-between one struggles to understand what about oneself has to be changed, what to be accepted, what to be preserved; unless the right actions are taken, one seems never to pass the test to reach the after.

4.

Last winter, during a difficult period, I went to a program for those whose lives had fallen apart. Often someone would say—weeping, shaking, or dry-eyed—that he or she wished to go back in time and make everything right again.

I wished too that life could be reset, but reset from when? From each point I could go to an earlier point—warning signs neglected, mistakes aggregated—but it was useless to do so, as I often ended up with the violent wish that I had never been born.

I was quiet most of the time, until I was told that I was evasive and not making progress. But my pains were my private matter, I thought; if I could understand and articulate my problems, I wouldn't have been there in the first place.

Do you want to share anything, I was prompted when I had little to offer. By then I felt my hope had run out: I saw the revolving door admitting new people and letting old people out into the world; similar stories were told with the same remorse and despair; the lectures were on the third repeat. What if I were stuck forever in that basement room? I broke down and could feel a collective sigh: my tears seemed to prove that finally I intended to cooperate.

I had only wanted to stay invisible, but there as elsewhere invisibility is a luxury.

5.

I've been asked throughout my life, What are you hiding? The question baffles me because I don't know what I'm hiding, and the more I try to deny it, the less trustworthy people find me. My mother used to comment on my stealthiness to our guests. A woman in charge of admission at the public bathhouse often confronted me, asking what I was hiding from her; nothing, I said, and she would say she could tell from my eyes that I was lying.

One hides an affair if one is unfaithful in a marriage; one hides a misdeed—people hide to make things not difficult for themselves. But reticence is a natural state; it is not hiding. People don't show themselves easily and equally to all.

There is a distance that comes with being reserved, but it does not make one feel lonely the way hiding does. Still, that distance must be hard for other people: it can invalidate the importance of others; hiding, however minor, can be blamed on the one who hides.

6.

There are five time zones in China, but the nation uses a unified time—Beijing time. When the hour turns, all radio stations sound six beeps, followed by a solemn announcement: "At the last beep, it is Beijing time seven o'clock sharp." This memory is reliable because it does not belong to me but to generations of Chinese, millions of us: at seven o'clock, the beeping and announcement were amplified through loudspeakers in every people's commune, school, army camp, and apartment complex.

But underneath this steadfastness, time is both intrusive and elusive. It does not leave us alone even in our most private moments: in every thought and feeling about life time claims a space. When we speak of indecision, it's an internal deadline that we're afraid of both meeting and not meeting. When we speak of moving on—what a triumphant phrase—it's what we pack up so we can carry on. And if one seeks kindness from time, it slips away tauntingly or, worse, indifferently. How many among us have said that to others or to ourselves: if only I had a bit more time . . .

7.

One hides something for two reasons: that one feels protective of it, or one feels ashamed by it; and then it's not always the case that one can separate the two possibilities. If my relationship with time is difficult, if time is intrusive and elusive, could it be that I am only hiding myself from time?

I used to write from midnight to four o'clock. I had young children then, various jobs (from working with mice to working with cadaver tissue to teaching writing), and an ambition to keep writing separate from my *real* life. When most people were being ferried across the night by sleep, unaware of time, unaware of weather, I felt the luxury of living on the cusp of reality.

Night for those sound sleepers was a cocoon against time; for me, I wanted to believe, it was even better: time, at night, was my possession, not the other way around.

8.

A few years ago I visited Beijing for the first time in ten years. A friend came to see me, and we talked about her real estate investments and our old schoolmates, and then half an hour after she left my parents' apartment, she called: she hadn't wanted to mention it in person, but a boy who had been close to me when we were teenagers had committed suicide, along with a lover.

My first reaction was wonderment, that my friend would wait until we were out of each other's sight to tell me. My next reaction was still wonderment, as though I had always been waiting for this news.

Our dead friend had had an affair, and both he and the woman had gone through difficult divorces but had been ostracized as adulterers.

"It'd have been better had he gone to America," my friend said.

Why, I asked. In college he had already been doing well as a self-trained designer—often he would mail, along with his letters, cut-out ads from newspapers and magazines: brand-name garments, imported mints, cashmeres. He was someone who would have made a good life in the country's developing economy.

My friend sighed. "You're the only one more impractical than he was. You should know this is not a country for dreamers."

My friendship with the boy existed largely in correspondence. It was a different era, thoughts and feelings traveling by mail, urgency conveyed by telegrams. My family did not have a telephone until I was in college; e-mail came much later, when I was in America. I still remember the days when the engine of a motorcycle disturbed the quietest night—only a telegram announcing a death or a looming one would lead to such an intrusion. Letters, especially those bearing too many stamps, carried the weight of friendship.

I can recall only a few things in those letters: a crush on the girl sitting next to him in class; a Chekhovian political satire he wrote, featuring Gorbachev and an East German general and a pistol going off in Act 3—this was in 1988, and communism still retained its hold in part of Europe; it was in that year too that we last saw each other.

But I do remember that before he had found an outlet for his artistic obsession and sent those profitable ads, there had been endless car models he dreamed up, designed, and named carefully; there had also been odd assortments of pistols, rifles, spacecraft, and household appliances, as well as abstract graphics: all the drawings were meticulously done, sometimes in their fifth or sixth drafts, and their details used to fill me with awe and impatience.

Perhaps when I say I was expecting his suicide, it's only memory going back to revise itself. There is no reason an artistic and sensitive boy could not grow into a happy man. Where and how things went amiss with him I do not know, though even as a teenager, I recognized his despondency when the production of his play earned him jeers, and a special exhibition of his car designs estranged him from his classmates. He was the kind of person who needed others to feel his existence.

9.

A dreamer: it's the last thing I want to be called, in China or in America. No doubt when my friend in Beijing used the term, she was thinking of traits like persistence, single-mindedness, willfulness, and—particularly—impracticality, which she must have seen plenty of in me. Still, that one possesses a dreamer's personality and that one has dreams does not guarantee that one knows how to dream.

The woman in New Hampshire and I, and many like us, came to this country with the same goal—to make a new life here. I wouldn't call it a dream, not even an ambition. She had followed the scientist's path and had a secure job at a biomedical company. I had drifted away, choosing a profession that makes hiding less feasible, if indeed I am a habitual hider.

I don't wonder what my life would've been had I stayed in China: not leaving had never felt like an option since elementary school. For a decade there had been a concrete *after* ingrained in everything I did: the day I arrived in America I would become a new person.

But there is the possibility that I might never have taken up writing. Had I stayed a scientist, would I have turned out differently: calmer, less troubled, more sensible? Would I have stopped hiding, or become better at it?

10.

A few months before my friend's suicide, he had found me on the Internet. In his e-mail he told me about his divorce, and I told him about giving up science for writing. He wrote back, "I congratulate you: you've always been a dreamer, but America has made your dream come true."

Recently someone pointed me out onstage as an example of the American dream. Certainly I have done that too, putting myself on a poster of before and after. The transformation, however, is as superficial and deceitful as an ad placed on the back of a bus.

Time will tell, people say, as though time always has the last word. Perhaps I'm only resisting that notion as I've resisted those who want the power to have the last word about others.

11.

I would have liked to be called a dreamer had I known how to dream. The sense of being an imposter, I understand, is a natural feeling that occurs for many people, and those who do not occasionally feel so I find untrustworthy. I wouldn't mind being taken as many things I am not—a shy person, a cheerful person, a cold person—but I don't want to be called a dreamer when I am far from being a real one.

12.

What I admire and respect in a dreamer: her confidence in her capacities, her insusceptibility to the frivolous, and her faith that the good and the real shall triumph and last. There is nothing selfish, dazzling, or preposterous about dreamers; in everyday life they blend in rather than stand out, though it's not hiding. A real dreamer must have a mutual trust with time.

Apart from feeling unqualified to be called a dreamer, I may also be worrying about being mistaken as one of those who call themselves dreamers but are merely ambitious. One meets them often in life, and at the center of their ambitions—smaller than dreams, more commonplace, in need of broadcasting, and dependent on the recognition of this particular time—are their trivial selves. If they cause pain to others, they have no trouble writing off those damages as the cost of their dreams. Timeliness may be one thing that separates ambitions from real dreams.

13.

The woman in New Hampshire was neither a dreamer nor an ambitious person. She had hoped for a solid and uneventful life in an American suburb, but loneliness must have made her life a desert.

My dead friend in Beijing was ambitious because he understood his talents; he had dreams too. I must have been part of his dream once—why else would he have written if not seeking kinship with another dreamer.

14.

I came to this country as an aspiring immunologist. I had chosen the field—if one does not count the practical motives of wanting a reason to leave China, and having a skill to make a living—because I had liked the working concept of the immune system: its job is to detect and attack nonself; it has memories, some as long-lasting as life; its memories can go awry, selectively or worse, indiscriminatingly, leading the system to mistake self as foreign, as something to eliminate. The word *immune* (from the Latin *immunis, in-* + *munia,* services, obligations) is among my favorites in the English language, the possession of immunity—to illnesses, to follies, to love and loneliness and troubling thoughts and unalleviated pains—a trait that I have desired for my characters and myself, knowing all the same the futility of such a wish: only the lifeless can be immune to life.

15.

One's intuition looks for immunity to two kinds of people: those who confirm one's beliefs about life, and those who turn one's beliefs into nothing. The latter are the natural predators of our hearts, the former made into enemies because we are, unlike other species, capable of not only enlarging but also diminishing our precarious selves.

16.

I had this notion, when I first started it, that this essay would be a way to test—to assay—thoughts about time. There was even a vision of an *after,* when my confusions would be sorted out.

Assays in science are part of an endless exploration: one question leads to another; what follows confirms or disconfirms what comes before. To assay one's ideas about time while time remains unsettled and elusive feels futile: just as one is about to understand one facet of time, it presents another to undermine one's reasoning.

To write about a struggle amidst the struggling: one must hope that this muddling will end someday.

17.

"But what more do you want? You have a family, a profession, a house, a car, friends, and a place in the world. Why can't you be happy? Why can't you be strong?" These questions are asked, among others, by my mother.

There was a majestic mental health worker in the hospital where I stayed, who came with perfect lipstick, shining curly hair, and bright blouses and flats of matching colors. "Young lady," she said every time she saw me, "don't lose that smile of yours."

I had liked her, and liked her still after she questioned my spiritual life. I could see that the godless state of my mind concerned her, and that my compliance made me a good pet project. "Don't mind her," my roommate, a black Buddhist, said. "She's from an evangelical background."

I don't, I reassured her. Being preached to did not bother me.

Then I had a difficult day. At dinnertime the majestic woman asked, "Young lady, why did you cry today?"

"I'm sad."

"We know you're sad. What I want to know is, what makes you sad."

"Can't I just be left alone in my sadness?" I said. The women around the table smiled into their plates: the good girl was having a tantrum.

18.

What makes you sad? What makes you angry? What makes you forget the good things in your life and your responsibilities toward others? One hides from people who ask these unanswerable questions only to ask oneself again and again.

"I know you don't like me to ask what's brought you here," in the hospital my roommate said. "But can you describe how you feel? I don't have words for how I feel."

I had several roommates—another revolving door—but I liked the last one. Raised in a middle-class African American family in upstate New York, she was the only adopted child among six siblings. She married for love, but on her wedding day she realized she had made the mistake of her life. "For the whole first dance he didn't look at me once," she said. "He looked into every guest's face to make sure they knew it was his show."

By the time she told me the story, her husband was overweight, paralyzed by strokes, and blind from diabetes. She took care of him along with a hired nurse; she watched TCM with him because he remembered the exchanges in the old movies. Still, she said she was angry, because the marriage, his illness, everything in their life was about him.

Had she ever thought of leaving him, I asked.

She said she had throughout the marriage, but she would not. "I don't want my children to grow up and think a man can be abandoned in that state."

Yet she had tried to kill herself in the farthest corner of Target's parking lot—an abandonment of both her husband and her children. But this I did not say, because it was exactly what many people would say to a situation like that. One has to have a solid self to be selfish.

19.

There is this emptiness in me. All the things in the world are not enough to drown out the voice of this emptiness, which says, *You are nothing.*

Perhaps I am only hiding my nothingness from people. I worry that they have been deceived by me: the moment they see my nothingness they will leave me.

This emptiness doesn't claim the past, because it is always here; it doesn't have to claim the future, as it blocks out the future. It's either a dictator or the closest friend I've ever had. Some days I battle it until we both fall down like injured animals. That is when I wonder, what if I become less than nothing when I get rid of this emptiness? What if this emptiness is what keeps me carrying on?

20.

On another day my roommate said she noticed that I became quiet if she talked about Buddhism with me. "I don't mean it as a religion. For instance, you can try to meditate."

I didn't explain that I had read Buddhist scriptures from the age of twelve to twenty-three. The teaching of nothingness in those texts—for the longest time they were the most comforting words, because they diluted the intensity of that emptiness.

My father taught me meditation when I was eleven. Imagine a bucket between your open arms, he told me, and asked me to listen to the dripping of the water into the bucket and, when it was full, water dripping out from the bottom. "From empty to full, and from full to empty"; he underlined the words in a book for me. "Life before birth is a dream, life after death is another dream. What comes between is only a mirage of the dreams."

21.

My father is the most fatalistic person I've ever known. In a conversation last year he admitted that he had not felt a day of peace in his marriage and expressed his regret that he had never thought of protecting my sister and me from our mother, who is a family despot, unpredictable in both her callousness and her vulnerability.

But the truth is, he tried to instill this fatalism in us because it was our only protection. For years I've been hiding behind that: fatalism, being addicted to, can make one look calm, capable, even happy.

22.

I read Katherine Mansfield's notebooks when I was having difficulties last year. "Dear friend, from my life I write to you in your life," Mansfield wrote in one entry. I cried when I read the line. It reminds me of the boy from years ago, who could not stop sending the design of his dreams in his letters. It reminds me too why I do not want to stop writing: the books one writes—past and present and future—are they not trying to say the same thing: *dear friend, from my life I write to you in your life.* What a long way it is from one life to another: yet why write if not for that distance; if things can be let go, every before replaced by an after.

23.

It's not fatalism that makes one lose hope, I now understand. It's one's rebellion against fatalism; it's wanting to have one's time back from fatalism.

A fatalistic person cannot be a dreamer, which I still want to become one day.

24.

"The train stopped. When a train stops in the open country between two stations it is impossible not to put one's head out of the window and see what's up," Mansfield wrote at the end of her life. This is the inevitability of life: the train, for reasons unknown to us, always stops between a past and a future, both making this *now* look as though it is nowhere. But it is this nowhere-ness that one has to make use of. One looks outside the window: the rice paddies and alfalfa fields have long been the past, replaced by vineyards and almond groves. One has made it this far; perhaps this is enough of a reason to journey on.

BARRY LOPEZ

Sliver of Sky

FROM *Harper's Magazine*

ONE DAY IN THE FALL of 1938, a man named Harry Shier entered the operating room of a Toronto hospital and began an appendectomy procedure on a prepubescent boy. He was not a trained surgeon; he nearly botched the operation, and the boy's parents reacted angrily. Suspicions about Shier's medical credentials had already surfaced among operating-room nurses, and the hospital, aware of other complaints related to Shier's groin-area operations on young boys, opened a formal investigation. By the time the hospital board determined that both his medical degree, from a European university, and his European letters of reference were fraudulent, Harry Shier had departed for the United States.

A few years later, a police officer in Denver caught Shier raping a boy in the front seat of his automobile. Shier spent a year in prison and then slipped out of Colorado. In the late 1940s, he surfaced in North Hollywood, California, as the director of a sanitarium where he supervised the treatment of people with addictions, primarily alcoholics. In the summer of 1952, at the age of seven, I was introduced to him when I visited the sanitarium with my mother.

At the time I lived with her and my younger brother in nearby Reseda, a town in the San Fernando Valley. My parents had recently divorced, and my father had moved across the country to Florida. To support the three of us, my mother had taken a day job teaching home economics at a junior high school in the city of San Fernando and also a job teaching dressmaking two evenings a week at Pierce Junior College in Woodland Hills, on the far western edge of the Valley.

Early that summer my mother had somewhat reluctantly agreed to take in a houseguest, her first cousin Evelyn Carrothers. Evelyn, who was my mother's age, lived an hour away in Long Beach and was struggling with a drinking problem. Her marriage was also in trouble. Mother couldn't accommodate Evelyn for long in our one-bedroom house, so she began inquiring among her friends about other arrangements. People advised her to call Alcoholics Anonymous. Someone in the organization's Los Angeles office suggested that she contact the North Hollywood Lodge and Sanitarium.

One morning Mother drove us all to the facility at 12003 Riverside Drive, known then around the Valley, I would later learn, as "Shier's dryer." In those years Shier was renowned as someone who could "cure" alcoholism. He was also able to relate sympathetically to the families of alcoholics. When we arrived at the clinic, Mother introduced my four-year-old brother and me to "Dr." Shier. We shook hands with him, and he escorted the two of us to the sanitarium's kitchen, where we each selected a fresh doughnut from an array laid out on trays for the patients—frosted, sugared, glazed, covered with sprinkles. A nice man. I remember the building's corridors reeked that morning of something other than disinfectant. Paraldehyde, I was later informed, which Shier used liberally to sedate his patients.

Shortly after Evelyn had, in Shier's estimation, recovered enough to return to Long Beach—she would begin drinking again and, a year later, would return to his facility—he started dropping by our home in Reseda. He had gotten to know something of Mother's marital and financial situation from Evelyn, and during one of his early visits he told Mother that he was concerned: her income was not, in his view, commensurate with her capabilities. He said he might be able to do something about that. (Mother's divorce settlement required my father to send her ten dollars a month in child support—an obligation he rarely met, according to correspondence I would later find.) Shier said that one of his former patients was in a position to speak with the school board about Mother's value to the school system. This appeal was apparently made, and a short while later she received a small increase in salary.

She was grateful. Harry was pleased to help. Shier conducted himself around Mother like someone considering serious courtship. She was a handsome woman of thirty-nine, he a short, abrasively self-confident, balding man of fifty-six. He complimented her on the way she was single-handedly raising her two polite, neatly dressed sons. He complimented her on her figure. Occasionally he'd take her hand or caress her lightly on the shoulder. After a while, Shier began dropping by the house in the evening, just as my brother and I were getting into our pajamas. He'd bring a tub of ice cream along, and the four of us would have dessert together. One evening he arrived without the ice cream. He'd forgotten. He suggested I accompany him to the grocery store, where I could pick out a different dessert for each of us.

A few minutes after we left the house, he pulled his car up alongside a tall hedge on an unlit residential street off Lindley Avenue. He turned me to the side, put me facedown on the seat, pulled down my pajama bottoms, and pushed his erect penis into my anus. As he built toward his climax he told me, calmly but emphatically, that he was a doctor, that I needed treatment, and that we were not going to be adding to Mother's worries by telling her about my problem.

Shier followed this pattern of sexual assault with me for almost four years. He came by the house several times a month and continued to successfully direct Mother's attention away from what he was doing. It is hard to imagine, now, that no one suspected what was going on. It is equally difficult, even for therapists, to explain how this type of sexual violence can be perpetuated between two human beings for years without the victim successfully objecting. Why, people wonder, does the evidence for a child's resistance in these circumstances usually seem so meager? I believe it's because the child is too innocent to plan effectively, and because, from the very start, the child faces a labyrinth of confused allegiances. I asked myself questions I couldn't answer: Do I actually need protection in this situation? From what, precisely? I was bewildered by what was happening. How could I explain to my mother what I was doing? Physical resistance, of course, is virtually impossible for most children. The child's alternatives, as I understand them, never get much beyond endurance and avoidance—and speculation about how to encourage intervention.

An additional source of confusion for me was the belief that I had been chosen as a special patient by Harry Shier, an esteemed doctor and the director of a prestigious institution. A weird sense of privilege was attached to Shier's interest in me, and to the existence of an unspecified medical condition too serious or exotic to share with Mother. Also, being the elder son in a lower-middle-class and fatherless family, I came to feel—or he encouraged me to feel—that I was shouldering an important responsibility for my family.

I understood that I was helping my family, and he complimented me on my maturity.

When Shier came to our house he would inform Mother that we were just going out to get some ice cream together, or, on a Saturday afternoon, that he was going to take me to an early movie, and then maybe out to dinner at the Sportsmen's Lodge on Ventura Boulevard in Studio City. We would say goodbye and he would walk me to his car and we would drive off. If it was dark, he'd pull over soon in a secluded spot and rape me in the front seat; or we'd go to the movie and he'd force my head into his lap for a while, pushing at me through his trousers; or it would be dinner at the restaurant, where we'd hook our trout in a small pool for the chef to cook, and then he'd drive on to the sanitarium, where he'd park behind the single-story building. He'd direct me up an outside staircase to a series of rotting duckboards that led across the clinic's flat roof to a locked door, the outside entrance to a rooftop apartment, where I was to wait. He'd enter the front of the building, check on his patients, say goodnight to the nurses, and ascend an inside staircase to reach the interior door of his studio-size quarters. I'd see the lights go on inside. A moment later he'd open the door to the roof and pull me in.

One night in these chambers, after he was through with me, he took a medical text from a bookshelf. He sat me down beside him on the edge of the bed and showed me black-and-white photographs of men's genitals ravaged by syphilis. This, he said, was what came from physical intimacy with women.

In bed with him, I would try to maneuver myself so I could focus on the horizontal sliver of sky visible between the lower edge of the drawn blinds and the white sill of the partially open window. Passing clouds, a bird, the stars.

From time to time, often on the drive back to my home, Shier would remind me that if I were ever to tell anyone, if the treatments were to stop, he would have no choice but to have me committed to an institution. And then, if I were no longer around for my family . . . I'd seen how he occasionally slipped Mother a few folded bills in my presence. It would be best, I thought, if I just continued to be the brave boy he said I was.

I know the questions I initially asked myself afterward about these events were not very sophisticated. For example: Why hadn't Shier also molested my younger brother? My brother, I conjectured, had been too young in 1952, only four years old; later, with one brother firmly in hand, Shier had probably considered pursuing the other too much of a risk. (When we were older, my brother told me that Shier had molested him, several times, in the mid-1950s. I went numb with grief. After the four years of sexual violence with Shier were over, what sense of self-worth I still retained rested mainly with a conviction that, however I might have debased myself with Shier, I had at least protected my brother—and also probably saved my family from significant financial hardship. Further shame would come after I discovered that our family had never been in serious financial danger, that Mother's earnings had covered our every necessity, and more.)

My mother remarried in 1956. We moved to New York City, where my stepfather lived, and I never again saw the malachite-green-and-cream-colored Pontiac Chieftain pulling up in front of our house on Calvert Street. After we moved into my stepfather's apartment, I felt a great sense of freedom. I was so very far away now from Harry Shier. A new school, a new neighborhood, new friends. I had surfaced in another ocean. This discovery of fresh opportunity, however, which sometimes gave way to palpable euphoria, I nevertheless experienced as unreliable. I couldn't keep a hold on it. And then, two years after we moved east, when I was thirteen, Harry Shier flew into New York and my sense of safety collapsed. He arrived with my stepfather at our vacation home on the Jersey Shore one summer evening in 1958. He was my parents' guest for the weekend. A surprise for the boys.

Weren't we pleased?

The next morning, a Saturday, while my parents were preparing breakfast in the kitchen, Shier eased open the door of my attic bedroom and closed it quietly behind him. He walked wordlessly to the edge of my bed, his lips twitching in a characteristic pucker, his eyes fixed on mine. When he reached under the sheet I kicked at him and sprang from the bed, grabbing a baseball bat that was leaning against the headboard. Naked, cursing, swinging at him with the bat, I drove him from the room and slammed the door.

While I dressed, he began a conversation downstairs with my parents.

Eavesdropping on them from the hallway next to the kitchen door, I heard Shier explain that I needed to be committed. He described—in grave tones, which gave his voice a kind of Delphic weight—how I was prone to delusions, a dangerous, potentially violent boy. Trouble ahead. Through the hinge gap in the doorway, I studied my mother and stepfather seated with him at the breakfast table. Their hands were folded squarely on the oilcloth. They took in Shier's measured, professional characterization with consternation and grief. In that moment, I couldn't bring myself to describe for them what he had done. The thought of the change it would bring to our lives was overwhelming; and, regardless, my own situation felt far too precarious. Having abruptly gained the security of a family with a devoted father, I could now abruptly lose it.

I left the house without delay, to play pickup baseball with my friends. In the afternoon I rode off alone on my bicycle to the next town inland. When I returned that evening, I learned that Shier had asked my stepfather to drive him straight back to New York that morning so that he could catch a plane west from Idlewild. I had insulted the doctor, my mother told me, and embarrassed the family. She presented his analysis of my behavior. When I tried to object, her response was, "But he's a *doctor!*"

Shier, she said, would confer with her and my stepfather in a few days by telephone, about accommodations for me in Los Angeles.

I was not, finally, sent to California, though the reason for this was never discussed with me. If my parents harbored any misgivings about Shier, I didn't hear them. I studied hard, came home on time, did my chores: I continued to behave as a dutiful son, a boy neither parent would willingly give up.

The trauma stayed with me, however, and in the spring of 1962, when I was seventeen, I gave in to a state of depression. I had become confused about my sexual identity and was haunted by a sense of contamination, a feeling that I had been rendered worthless as a man because of what I had done.

When I was immobilized in the elaborate web of Shier's appetites and undone by his ploys to ensure his own safety, I had assumed that I was the only boy he was involved with. It was the sudden realization that there might have been—probably were—others, and that he might still be raping boys in California, that compelled me to break my silence and risk, I believed, disastrous humiliation. I phoned my stepfather at his office. He agreed to meet me in the lobby of the New York Athletic Club on Central Park South, where I thought he would feel comfortable.

He strode impatiently into his club that afternoon and took a seat opposite me in one of the lobby's large leather chairs. He was a busy man, but he was prepared to listen. I gave him a brief account of Shier's behavior and of my history with him, and I made two requests of him. First, that he never tell anyone what had happened; if he ever came to believe that Mother had to know, he was to let *me* tell her. Second, that he help me stop Shier. He listened with rising interest and increasing ire. He was especially angry, I later realized, at the idea that he had been duped by Shier that summer in New Jersey.

Early the next morning he took a plane to Los Angeles, and late that same afternoon he met with two LAPD detectives. When he returned to New York three days later, my stepfather told me that the detectives he'd spoken with were going to scrutinize everything—the North Hollywood Lodge and Sanitarium, Shier's criminal record, his network of acquaintances. They were going to gather all the evidence. I only needed to be patient. The detectives would contact us.

That week gave way to another. My stepfather waved off my anxious inquiries. He was in touch with the detectives, he said. They were working on it. When I finally confronted him, he admitted that, in consultation with the detectives, he had decided it would be too great an undertaking for me to go up against such a clever deviant, to endure cross-examination in a trial. So he was choosing not to press charges. Besides, he said, Shier had bolted as soon as he had suspected an investigation was under way.

A week or so later, my stepfather told me that he had just heard from the LAPD detectives that Harry Shier had been killed—an automobile accident in Arizona. This was, I now believe, my stepfather's preemptive effort to force closure.

In 2003, forty-one years after these conversations with my stepfather and some years into my own effort to comprehend the psychological effects of what had happened to me, I phoned the LAPD. An officer there, an intermediary, was able to locate one of the two long-retired detectives who had begun the investigation of Shier in 1962. The detective did not want to speak with me directly, but he authorized the intermediary to pass on his recollections. (Because this information is at best third-hand, I cannot be certain about either the dates or the circumstances surrounding Shier's early criminal history. The police department's official records of the case, including the detectives' notes from their conversations with my stepfather, were destroyed, along with other inactive records from that time.) The officer informed me about the botched operations at the hospital in Toronto and the sodomy charge in Colorado, gave me the approximate dates, and confirmed that the investigation had ended soon after it began because Shier had fled the state. The detective also recalled that Shier might have been killed shortly after he left California, possibly in South America, but he could not remember precisely.

In 1989, years before this conversation with the LAPD officer took place, I interviewed Evelyn Carrothers at her home in Studio City about her experiences with Shier. She said that "behind a façade of solicitous concern," Shier was a "mean man." A bully. She had never liked him, she said, but he had been very successful treating alcoholics in the Los Angeles area in the 1950s, and she herself had referred many people to him over the years. At the time I spoke with her, Evelyn had not only been sober a long while but had become a prominent member of Alcoholics Anonymous in Southern California. She was upset, I thought, by my revelation that Shier was a pedophile, but she wouldn't give me the names of anyone who might have known him. She said she never knew what became of him, but she was sure he was dead. She even argued a case for Shier: whatever wrong he might have done in his private life, he had been of great value to the larger community.

I've never been able to comprehend Evelyn's sense of the larger good, though her point of view is a position people commonly take when confronted with evidence of sexual crimes committed by people they respect. (A reputation for valued service and magnanimous gestures often forms part of the protective cover pedophiles create.)

A more obvious question I asked myself as I grew older was, How could my mother not have known? Perhaps she did, although she died, a few years after she was told, unwilling to discuss her feelings about what had gone on in California. I've made some measure of peace with her stance. When certain individuals feel severely threatened—emotionally, financially, physically—the lights on the horizon they use to orient themselves in the world might easily wink out. Life can then become a series of fear-driven decisions and compulsive acts of self-protection. People start to separate what is deeply troubling in their lives from what they see as good. To use the usual metaphor, they isolate the events from one another by storing them in different rooms in a large hotel. While these rooms share a corridor, they do not communicate directly with one another.

I'm not able, today, to put the image I have of my mother as her children's attentive guardian together with the idea of her as an innocent, a person blinded by the blandishments of a persistent pedophile. But for whatever reason, she was not able, back then, to consider what might be happening in the hours after she saw Shier drive away, her son's head, from her point of view on the porch, not quite clearing the sill of the car window as the two of them departed.

In June 1970 my stepfather related to my mother, without my knowledge, a distorted and incomplete version of what her friend Harry Shier had done, breaking the promise he had made to me that day eight years before when I'd spoken to him. They were having lunch together in midtown Manhattan; she became hysterical and was taken from the restaurant by ambulance to a hospital. When she called me that evening, all she could bring herself to say, in a voice resigned and defeated, was, "I know what happened. I know what happened to you."

And then she never spoke of it again.

Six years later, in July 1976, as my mother was dying of lung cancer, I asked her whether she wanted to speak to me about California. She lay on her bed in a private room at Manhattan's Lenox Hill Hospital, rocking her head slowly back and forth like a metronome. Her face averted, she wept silently while I sat mute in a chair by the bed. She would not take my hand.

Some of the pathways of a debilitating sexual history are simply destined never to be mapped.

The reasons monstrously abusive relationships persist between people are as complex, I think, as the mathematics of turbulence. The explanation I gave myself for decades, partly to avoid having to address any question of my own complicity, was that I had done this in order to keep our family safe and intact. After my father abandoned us, my mother told me that I would now be the man of the house. I took her remark literally. I began to double-check the locks on the doors at night. I mowed and weeded the lawn and took the trash out to the incinerator in the back yard to burn. I got the day's mail from the box on the street. Whenever Shier showed up at the door, I would bear down on myself: Just see the business with Shier through, I said to myself. Maybe another man, one of the more likable men Mother dated, would come and stay with us. And this one wouldn't walk out. Standing in the shower in Shier's filthy apartment, washing the blood and semen off my legs, I hammered this thought into my mind: You cannot quit.

I bottled the anger. I hid the blood. I adamantly focused anywhere else.

What my stepfather actually did when he went to California in 1962, and how he presented Shier's crimes to the detectives, I will never know. And though I know he saw Evelyn at that time, I don't know what he discussed with her. Over the years, right up to his death, whenever I asked him about what he'd done, he became evasive. In an effort to seem sincere, he would occasionally recall a forgotten detail from one of his conversations with the detectives. This additional fact would sometimes shift my basic understanding of the longer story he had already told, raising new questions. Or, alternatively, trying to demonstrate compassion, he might suddenly recall a fact meant to soothe me but that made no sense. He told me once, for example, that during his 1962 visit Evelyn had taken him to see Shier's grave at the Forest Lawn Memorial-Park in Glendale—several weeks before Shier was supposedly killed in an out-of-state automobile accident.

My stepfather, a recovering alcoholic, became, like Evelyn, a regionally prominent figure in Alcoholics Anonymous in the late 1960s. Whenever I inquired, in those early weeks of the investigation, about what sort of progress the detectives were making, he would find a way to mention how many alcoholics Shier had helped. Alcoholism, he said, was a "terrible disease," a more pervasive and serious issue, he wanted me to understand, than pedophilia. He suggested that I would benefit from a slightly different perspective on all this. Shier, he conceded, was an awful man—but he had done a lot of good. I should consider, instead, how well I was doing. At seventeen I was student body president at my Jesuit prep school. I had the highest academic average in my class senior year; I was lettering in two sports; I was escorting debutantes to balls at the Plaza, the Sherry-Netherland, the Pierre. Whatever might have occurred in California, he said, things had actually worked out all right. I should let it go.

For thirty years this was exactly the path I chose. Silence. I believed that in spite of Shier's brutalizations I could develop a stable, productive life, that I could simply walk away from everything that had happened.

The conclusion I eventually reached about my stepfather's refusal to pursue charges against Shier was that he did not want the family to be embarrassed by a trial. He was unable to understand that the decision to face cross-examination in a courtroom was not his to make. He could not appreciate that the opportunity to stand up in a public forum and describe, with Shier present, what he had done, and what he had forced me to do, was as important to me as any form of legal justice. Not to be allowed to speak or, worse, to have someone else relate my story and write its ending was to extend the original, infuriating experience of helplessness, to underscore the humiliation of being powerless. My stepfather's ultimate dismissal of my request for help was an instance, chilling for me, of an observation that victims of child molestation often make: If you tell them, they won't believe you. Believing you entails too much disruption.

From what I have read over the years in newspapers and magazines about scandals involving serial pedophiles, I have gathered that people seem to think that what victims most desire in the way of retribution is money and justice, apparently in that order. My own guess would be that what they most want is something quite different: they want to be believed, to have a foundation on which they can rebuild a sense of dignity. Reclaiming self-respect is more important than winning money, more important than exacting vengeance.

Victims do not want someone else's public wrath, the umbrage of an attorney or an editorial writer or a politician, to stand in for the articulation of their own anger. When a pedophile is exposed by a grand-jury indictment today, the tenor of public indignation often seems ephemeral to me, a response generated by "civic" emotion. Considering the number of children who continue to be abused in America—something like one in seven boys and one in three girls—these expressions of condemnation seem naive. Without a deeper commitment to vigilance, society's outrage begins to take on the look of another broken promise.

Up until the time I interviewed Evelyn in the late 1980s, I had grown to more or less accept my stepfather's views about what had happened in California—which was, of course, my own form of denial. Whatever had been done to me, I held to the belief that things had actually turned out fairly well. By the time I was forty I had experienced some national success as a writer. I was friends with a large, if geographically scattered, group of people. And I was living happily in a rural, forested area in western Oregon with my wife of twenty years. Significantly, since I had moved to this mountainous place in 1970, the emotional attachment I felt to my home had become essential to any ongoing sense of well-being I had. My almost daily contact there with wild animals, the physical separation of the house from the homes of my neighbors, the flow of a large white-water river past the property, the undomesticated land unfolding for miles around, the rawness of the weather at the back door—all of it fed a feeling of security.

During the years of "traumatic sexual abuse," the term psychologists use for serial sexual abuse, the deepest and sometimes only relief I had was when I was confronted with the local, elementary forces of nature: hot Santa Ana winds blowing west into the San Fernando Valley from the Mojave Desert; Pacific storm surf crashing at Zuma and the other beaches west of Malibu; winter floods inundating our neighborhood when Caballero Creek breached its banks on its way to the Los Angeles River. I took from each of these encounters a sense of what it might feel like to become fully alive. When I gazed up beneath a flock of homing birds or listened as big winds swirled the dry leaves of eucalyptus trees or sat alone somewhere in a rarely traversed part of the Santa Monica Mountains, waiting for a glimpse of a coyote or a brush rabbit, I would feel exhilaration. Encouragement.

But deep inside, I knew things remained awry. (It is relatively easy today—it wasn't then—to find pertinent and explicit information about childhood sexual trauma. How one interprets that information or chooses to act on it remains a perilous second step.) I could not, for example, shake the old thought that by not having acted sooner I was somehow responsible for what happened to other boys after I left California. According to my stepfather, one of the investigating detectives said I had been lucky to walk away in 1956. Continuing their investigation after Shier disappeared, my stepfather told me, the detectives had located three other boys, "none of whom had fared well." The detectives' advice to my stepfather had been that neither he nor I should inquire further into what Harry Shier had been doing with young boys during his years in North Hollywood.

When I began a deliberate inquiry into my past, starting in 1989, I thought of myself as a man walking around with shrapnel sealed in his flesh, and I wanted to get the fragments out. The doubts and images I had put aside for years were now starting to fester. I felt more or less continually seasick, confronting every day a harrowing absence within myself. I imagined it as a mine shaft of bleak, empty space, which neither the love of a spouse nor the companionship of friends nor professional success could efface. The thought began to work on me that a single, bold step, however, some sort of confrontation with the past, might sufficiently jar this frame of mind and change it. I could, I thought, dramatically cure myself in this way.

I phoned Forest Lawn Memorial-Park. No, there was no Harry Shier buried in any of their cemeteries. I couldn't find an obituary for him in any of the Southern California papers either. I called Evelyn and asked whether I could come to California and interview her. I would begin my healing, my ablution, by speaking with someone who had known him well. And on that same trip, I decided, I'd drive the rental car to 12003 Riverside Drive in North

Hollywood. If the sanitarium was still there, I'd walk through the front door.

Shier's rooftop apartment, nearly hidden behind the branches of several Norfolk Island pines, remained just visible from the sidewalk. I parked in the shade of a pepper tree on Ben Street and walked through the main entrance of the white stucco building, which now housed a private secondary school, a yeshiva. No one took any notice of me standing in the foyer. If someone had come up to inquire about my business, I was prepared to say that I had been a patient in this place thirty years earlier, when it had been a hospital. But I seemed to be invisible.

I walked down the main corridor. In rooms to my right, where I'd once seen the bedridden lying in dim shadow, lights now blazed. Attentive students sat at desks, avidly scribbling while someone lectured. I arrived at an intersection and suddenly found myself staring at the foot of an interior staircase. The door to the stairs, slightly ajar, revealed steps winding upward to the left. My throat clenched like a fist in my neck.

I left the building as soon as I was able to turn around. I ran across Riverside Drive into an outdoor nursery with a fence around it. I went down a pea-gravel path, past potted camellias and oleanders, past blooming primroses and azaleas. After a few minutes, breathing easily once more, the rigidity gone out of my back muscles, I crossed back to where I'd parked the car and drove away.

Later that afternoon, at the Central Library on West Fifth Street in downtown Los Angeles, I gathered several San Fernando Valley phone books from the 1950s, trying to remember the names of my mother's friends, guessing at the spellings—Emery, Falotico, Ling, Murray—hoping to dislodge a memory, to find a thread to follow. When my right index finger came to Shier's name, it halted there below the stark typeface. My bowels burst into my trousers.

In the men's room, I threw my undershorts into a waste bin and washed my pants in the sink, trying to keep the wet spot small. I was in my stocking feet, putting my pants back on, when a guard entered abruptly and stood alert and suspicious in the doorway. He informed me that the library was closing. *I'll be only another moment,* I assured him.

A few minutes later, shielding the wet seat of my pants with my briefcase, I met a friend for dinner nearby. When the maître d' asked whether we preferred eating outdoors or in, I suggested we sit outside. I didn't tell my friend where I'd been that day.

Over the years, I'd spoken to very few people about Shier—my brother, serious girlfriends, my wife, a few close friends. I didn't feel any need to be heard, and the chance of being misunderstood, of being taken for no more than the innocent victim, long ago, of a criminal's heinous acts seemed great. Pity, I thought, would take things in the wrong direction for me. What I wanted to know now was, *What happened to me?*

In the months following my visit to the building on Riverside, I placed an occasional call to state and county agencies in California, trying to track down some of the details that might have framed my story. Doing this, I came to suspect that I was missing the memory of certain events. I could recall many scenes from my childhood in the Valley, even remember some vividly; but I also became aware of gaps in that period of time from which nothing surfaced.

In the fall of 1996, I visited a therapist for the first time. I'd briefly seen a psychiatrist when I was in college, but we were not able to get anywhere. Years later, I understood it was because I hadn't been capable at the time of doing the required work. My expectation was that she would somehow simply fix me, get me over the anxiety, over the humiliation.

I chose therapy because my own efforts to clarify my past seemed dramatically unproductive, and because I was now, once again, of a mind that something was wrong with me. I had begun to recognize patterns in my behavior. If I sensed, for example, that I was being manipulated by someone, or disrespected, I quickly became furious out of all proportion. And I'd freeze sometimes when faced with a serious threat instead of calmly moving toward some sort of resolution. I suspected that these habits—no great insight—were rooted in my childhood experience.

Also, a persistent, anxiety-induced muscular tension across my shoulders had by now become so severe that I'd ruptured a cervical disc. When a regimen of steroids brought only limited relief, my doctor recommended surgery. After a second doctor said I had no option but surgery, I reluctantly agreed—until the surgical procedure was drawn up for me on a piece of paper: I'd be placed facedown and unconscious on an operating table, and a one-inch vertical slit would be opened in the nape of my neck. I said no, absolutely not. I'd live with the pain.

From the beginning the therapist encouraged me to move at my own pace through the memories I was able to retrieve, and to resist the urge to fit any of these events into a pattern. I remember him saying in one of our first sessions, with regard to my apparent inability to protect myself in complex emotional situations such as my stepfather's betrayal, that I did "not even understand the concept of self-protection." I resented the statement. It made me feel stupid—but it also seemed like a start.

We worked together for four years. I described for him the particulars of the abuse: the sandpaper burn of Shier's evening stubble on my skin; his antic Chihuahua, which defecated on the floor of the apartment and raced around on the bed when we were in it; Shier's tongue jammed into my mouth. I described the time he forced me to perform fellatio in my home while my mother and brother were away. Shier lay back on Mother's sleeping couch, self-absorbed, palming my head like a melon, supremely at ease. I told the therapist about my inability to break off the relationship with Shier, and about my mother's apparent intention to look the other way.

At the start of therapy, I speculated that the real horror of those years would prove to be the actual acts of abuse—my choking on his semen, the towel forced over my face to silence me, the rectal bleeding. After a while I began to see that the horror was more elusive, that it included more than just betrayals and denials and being yanked around in Shier's bed like a rag doll. The enduring horror was that I had learned to accommodate brutalization. This part of the experience remained with me long after I walked out of Shier's apartment for the last time.

Caught up in someone else's psychosis, overmatched at every turn, I had concentrated on only one thing: survival. To survive I needed to placate. My response to emotional confrontation in the years following that time, I came to see, was almost always to acquiesce, or to overreact angrily, with no option in between. Therapy led me to comprehend that I had not, as I wanted to believe, been able to tough out the trauma. I had succumbed, and others besides me had experienced the consequences of my attempt to endure. I had ahead of me now a chance to do better, to be a person less given to anger.

I visited the therapist twice a week to start with, occasionally for double sessions; then it was once a week or less frequently until we decided we'd come to a resting place. In our final sessions, I fitted the pieces of my story together differently, creating "another narrative," as therapists are wont to say, of the early years in California, a broader context for the physical and emotional damage. After that, long-term sexual abuse no longer organized the meaning of my life as it had during the years I believed that I'd simply walked away from it.

One night in 1998, driving from the town where I had been seeing the therapist forty miles upriver to my home, I suddenly felt flooded with relief. The sensation was so strong I pulled over and got out of the truck. I walked to the edge of what I knew to be an unfenced, cultivated field. At first I thought I was experiencing physical relief, the breakdown of the last bit of tension in my upper back, which, after many weeks of physical therapy, no longer required surgery. But it was something else. A stony, overbearing presence I'd been fearful of nearly all my life wasn't there anymore. I stood in the dark by the side of the road for a long while, savoring the reprieve, the sudden disappearance of this tyranny. I recalled a dream I'd had midway through my therapy. I burst through a heavy cellar door and surprised an ogre devouring the entrails of a gutted infant, alive but impassive in the grip of his hand. The ogre was enraged at being discovered. What seemed significant was that I had broken down the door. It didn't matter whether it was the door into something or the door out.

Therapy's success for me was not so much my coming to understand that I had learned as a child to tolerate acts of abuse. It was discovering a greater capacity within myself to empathize with another person's nightmare. Most of the unresolved fear and anger I once held on to has now metamorphosed into compassion, an understanding of the predicaments nearly everyone encounters, at some level, at some time, in their lives.

A commonplace about trauma, one buried deep in the psyches of American men, is that it is noble to heal alone. What I've learned in recent years, however, is that this choice sometimes becomes a path to further isolation and trouble, especially for the family and friends of the one who has been wounded. I took exactly this path, intending to bother no one with my determined effort to recalibrate my life. It took a long while for me to understand that a crucial component of recovery from trauma is learning to comprehend and accept the embrace of someone who has no specific knowledge of what happened to you, who is disinterested.

We need others to bring us back into the comity of human life. This appears to have been the final lesson for me—to appreciate someone's embrace not as forgiveness or as an amicable judgment but as an acknowledgment that from time to time private life becomes brutally hard for every one of us, and that without one another, without some sort of community, the nightmare is prone to lurk, waiting for an opening.

I'm not interested any longer in tracking down the details of Harry Shier's death, or in wondering how, if it is still there, I might reenter his apartment above the building on Riverside Drive to gaze out at the sky through the corner window. I'm on the alert now, though, for an often innocuous moment, the one in which an adult man begins to show an unusual interest in the welfare of someone's young son—especially if it's my grandson. He still, at the age of nine, reaches out for my hand when we start to cross a dangerous street.

CHRIS OFFUTT

Someone Else

FROM *River Teeth*

BY THE TIME I was fourteen, my family was accustomed to my absences—wandering the woods, sleeping in town, eating at other people's homes. What mattered to my parents were academic grades. I maintained all A's, an easy task in Appalachia during the sixties and seventies. Of equal importance was granting utter obedience to Dad, and never causing my mother public embarrassment. With this veneer of civility thus attended to, I was free.

I don't remember how I met the fatman. I assume he approached me. He lived in town on the second floor of a small building, where he rented a single room with a bathroom in the hall. He was nice. He bought me candy bars and bottles of pop, which my parents never allowed me to have. I told him about my life and girls I liked. At four feet eleven inches, I was the shortest kid in high school, with the longest hair, reputed to be the smartest but lousy at sports. The fatman listened to me. He offered a kind of sympathy and attentiveness that I needed. He accepted that I wanted to be an actor or a comic book artist when I grew up, and he believed such aspirations weren't ridiculous. He didn't talk about himself but implied that he'd experienced life beyond the confines of Rowan County, and that I would like it out there when I finally left.

I was vulnerable, I suppose, although not a dire misfit. I was open and friendly, having gone through eight years of grade school with the same small group of kids, then riding the bus ten miles to high school. One by one my classmates began losing the habit of attending school. It was not expected but certainly accepted, and of little concern. After all, we were from Haldeman, the community farthest from town, site of the main bootlegger, weekly drag strips, occasional shootings and arson. We were at the bottom of a pecking order that didn't start very high. Bused into town, we became aware of our status. Some of us responded by staying at home, changing our style of dress, or becoming withdrawn. I explored town.

The fatman's room was small, with no chair, and we both had to sit on the bed. The whole time I pretended it was happening to someone else. Afterward, the fatman said he liked me. He gave me money. I left the room and walked to the drugstore, where my mother picked me up after shopping for groceries. I bought a lot of comic books at the drugstore. She didn't ask where I got the money.

I don't remember his name or what he looked like. I don't recall the print on the wallpaper or the color of the bedspread. What I do remember is the overhead light fixture, a plain bisected globe in a ceramic setting that emitted a dim yellowish light. Surrounding the globe and painted over many times were plaster rosettes with narrow leaves. I remember the light because I spent all my time staring at it and waiting until I could leave.

When I returned, I climbed the steps very slowly, trying not to make any noise because I didn't want to get the fatman in trouble. A clot of tension rose along my spine, vibrating like an embedded blade. I felt hollow—my heart pounding, sweat trickling down my sides, mouth dry, my stomach congealed to stone. The fatman opened the door and ushered me in. The bed sagged when he sat down. The money lay in sight on the bedside table. Time stopped as I slid away from my body to rove the air, imagining a life beyond the hills. I would be a movie actor. Beautiful women would throw themselves at me as I left French cafés. I was the mayor's son, the governor's nephew. I was secretly adopted. I inherited a Lexington horse farm. I was anyone but a lonely kid feeling the dampness of fat fingers.

Just before I started being someone else, I decided my parents would be proud of my open-mindedness in such a small town. They considered themselves progressive. My mother wore miniskirts and my father had a tidy beard. They traveled often, leaving me in charge of my younger siblings for a few days at a time. They went to exotic locales for science-fiction conventions—Cincinnati, Louisville, St. Louis, Nashville, once even Florida. I thought that what I was doing with the fatman made me similar to my parents. They wrote porn. They had affairs. If they knew about the fatman, they would respect me, maybe even like me.

The fatman took me to the movies. We stood in line but didn't have to buy tickets. The fatman looked at the owner, put his hand on my shoulder, and nodded once. The owner looked at me without changing expression and let us in free. I felt important.

The fatman bought a large buttered popcorn and gave it to me. I was not allowed to have popcorn at the movies because my father said it was too expensive. Occasionally Mom made popcorn at home, but she never put butter on it. I felt special eating buttered popcorn and watching *The Godfather,* which affected me in a very powerful way. I'd never seen a movie that long or that slow. The world was utterly foreign but I understood its insular nature, the power dynamics, the violence and loyalties. After the movie the fatman gave me a dime because I insisted on calling my father and telling him that if anything ever happened to him, I would avenge his death. I was crying into the phone. My father said little.

The fatman wanted me to touch him in his bed, but I refused. I explained that I liked girls, though I'd never been with one. I'd kissed three and touched one's bra strap, but never got any further. The fatman offered me two hundred dollars to help him make a movie. They'd shoot the whole thing in a hotel room nearby, but I'd have to touch a man, maybe another boy about my age. I told him that I really wanted to be with a girl, and suggested we make that kind of movie instead. He said that if I made a movie with a man, he would provide me with a girl to be with afterward. I told him no. He told me to think about it, but I didn't. Instead I looked at the light fixture and went away in my mind. I'd developed the ability to go rapidly, to vanish from the circumstances and enter a trancelike state in which I was a prince with a personal garrison at my command, a lavish kingdom to rule, and a harem of lovely women. I fell in love with a commoner and abandoned all my riches for her. We lived by the sea in Italy. Our eyes never left each other. We were together throughout the ages, each era presenting its version of our love. Abruptly I was back in the dim room. My legs were bare and cold, my body tense. The fatman was breathing hard. I took the money and left.

The last time I went to the room, I encountered another boy

on the steps. He was a year older than me, with long hair, new to school. I'd seen him before, outside the building, but we pretended like we didn't see each other. This time he was crouching on the steps. He motioned me to be quiet. I joined him, moving silently. We were midway up the staircase. The bathroom was at the top of the stairs and the door was not fully closed. Through it we could see the fatman standing in the shower, his vast naked bulk exposed. He was vomiting and defecating simultaneously. It was a sickening sight, so repulsive that it was hard to stop staring. I realized the fatman was crying. Not just weeping but an uncontrollable sobbing that made his shoulders quake, his torso ripple. He leaned on the wall as if in surrender.

The other boy and I slipped down the stairs and laughed about what we'd seen. What else could we do? We laughed at the hideous sight. We never talked about it later, and he soon quit school. It took me many years to wonder if the other boy made a movie at the motel. By then he was dead of an overdose. The fatman had once suggested that I bring my brother to visit, and I got very angry. The only good that I can find in all this now is that I protected my brother. At least I did that.

The fatman left town as suddenly as he'd appeared. I didn't speak to anyone about him. Instead I began to shoplift. Every time I entered a store I walked around as if browsing while secretly examining lines of sight and avenues of getaway. I was a meticulous planner. The best technique was to set what I wanted to steal near the door, then buy something cheap that required a shopping bag. On my way out of the store, I'd surreptitiously slip the preset goods into the bag. I got very scared as I walked to the door, my body encased in the same adrenalized state as when climbing the steps to the fatman's room. I breathed slowly through my mouth, sweating inside my clothes. On the sidewalk outside, I felt the euphoria of relief at having gotten away. Stealing supplied an intensity to life that was absent. It later left me feeling bad about myself, but that didn't matter, because by then feeling bad felt normal.

I skipped school and began spending all my time at the pool hall. I learned to shoot a good stick. I also learned to make marijuana pipes from an empty toilet paper tube, a Coke can, an apple, anything I could punch two holes in. Some cool older boys gave me acid. Next I tried Valium. I began taking amphetamines and breaking into cars. I never got caught. I never stole anything good. I dropped out of high school and joined the army, but they didn't want me. I went to college.

In a psychology class I read an article that defined victims of sexual abuse. This made me feel uneasy, because I knew the whole fatman business was my fault. I didn't like the idea of being a victim. Nobody forced me to enter that building and climb those stairs and push open the dark wooden door. I went there freely. I went there more than once. I felt special. I felt bad. I wondered if I was gay. I dropped the psychology class and got stoned, then drunk, and stayed that way for a good while.

Twenty-five years later I began talking about the fatman. I thought I might feel relieved, or unburdened, but I didn't. I told my wife. I told my parents and siblings in a group letter, which I suppose was cowardly, perhaps even cruel. It was shocking enough that no one knew how to respond. My father, surprisingly, called. He wanted to know if the fatman still lived in the county. In fact, Dad evoked *The Godfather,* saying that he would send Vito and Luigi to kill the man. I didn't have the heart to tell him how that particular movie had figured into things so long ago.

After revealing my old secret, I mainly felt embarrassed. Worse things happened to other people, and much worse things happened to women. I was never forced or hurt. It was a long time ago. I understood the fatman had probably been abused as a child. I also knew that I should find it in myself to forgive him, an act which would ultimately benefit me. But I couldn't do it. I'd spent too many years hoping the fatman went to prison. I hoped every inmate spat on him in the corridors. I wanted them to fill his food with poison, smack him around in the yard, and ambush him in the shower. I wanted him to be scared and alone. I wanted his life to be so miserable that he spent every day wishing he was someone else. I wanted him to memorize the dim flat light fixture in his cell. I wanted him as dead as I felt, as dead as I still feel sometimes, as dead as the other boy I saw on the steps will always be.

ZADIE SMITH

Joy

FROM *The New York Review of Books*

IT MIGHT BE USEFUL to distinguish between pleasure and joy. But maybe everybody does this very easily, all the time, and only I am confused. A lot of people seem to feel that joy is only the most intense version of pleasure, arrived at by the same road—you simply have to go a little further down the track. That has not been my experience. And if you asked me if I wanted more joyful experiences in my life, I wouldn't be at all sure I did, exactly because it proves such a difficult emotion to manage. It's not at all obvious to me how we should make an accommodation between joy and the rest of our everyday lives.

Perhaps the first thing to say is that I experience at least a little pleasure every day. I wonder if this is more than the usual amount? It was the same even in childhood, when most people are miserable. I don't think this is because so many wonderful things happen to me but rather that the small things go a long way. I seem to get more than the ordinary satisfaction out of food, for example—any old food. An egg sandwich from one of these grimy food vans on Washington Square has the genuine power to turn my day around. Whatever is put in front of me, foodwise, will usually get a five-star review.

You'd think that people would like to cook for, or eat with, me—in fact I'm told it's boring. Where there is no discernment there can be no awareness of expertise or gratitude for special effort. "Don't say that was delicious," my husband warns, "you say everything's delicious." "But it was delicious." It drives him crazy. All day long I can look forward to a popsicle. The persistent anxiety that fills the rest of my life is calmed for as long as I have the flavor of something good in my mouth. And though it's true that when the flavor is finished the anxiety returns, we do not have so many reliable sources of pleasure in this life as to turn our nose up at one that is so readily available, especially here in America. A pineapple popsicle. Even the great anxiety of writing can be stilled for the eight minutes it takes to eat a pineapple popsicle.

My other source of daily pleasure is—but I wish I had a better way of putting it—"other people's faces." A redheaded girl, with a marvelous large nose she probably hates, and green eyes and that sun-shy complexion composed more of freckles than skin. Or a heavyset grown man, smoking a cigarette in the rain, with a soggy mustache, above which, a surprise—the keen eyes, snub nose, and cherub mouth of his own eight-year-old self. Upon leaving the library at the end of the day I will walk a little more quickly to the apartment to tell my husband about an angular, cat-eyed teenager, in skinny jeans and stacked-heel boots, a perfectly ordinary gray sweatshirt, last night's makeup, and a silky Pocahontas wig slightly askew over his own Afro. He was sashaying down the street, plaits flying, using the whole of Broadway as his personal catwalk. "Miss Thang, but off duty." I add this for clarity, but my husband nods a little impatiently; there was no need for the addition. My husband is also a professional gawker.

The advice one finds in ladies' magazines is usually to be feared, but there is something in that old chestnut "shared interests." It *does* help. I like to hear about the Chinese girl he saw in the hall, carrying a large medical textbook, so beautiful she looked like an illustration. Or the tall Kenyan in the elevator whose elongated physical elegance reduced every other nearby body to the shrunken, gnarly status of a troll. Usually I will not have seen these people—my husband works on the eighth floor of the library, I work on the fifth—but simply hearing them described can be almost as much a pleasure as encountering them myself. More pleasurable still is when we recreate the walks or gestures or voices of these strangers, or whole conversations—between two people in the queue for the ATM, or two students on a bench near the fountain.

And then there are all the many things that the dog does and says, entirely anthropomorphized and usually offensive, which express the universe of things we ourselves cannot do or say, to each other or to other people. "You're being the dog," our child said recently, surprising us. She is almost three and all our private languages are losing their privacy and becoming known to her. Of course, we knew she would eventually become fully conscious, and that before this happened we would have to give up arguing, smoking, eating meat, using the Internet, talking about other people's faces, and voicing the dog, but now the time has come, she is fully aware, and we find ourselves unable to change. "Stop being the dog," she said, "it's very silly," and for the first time in eight years we looked at the dog and were ashamed.

Occasionally the child too is a pleasure, though mostly she is a joy, which means in fact she gives us not much pleasure at all but rather that strange admixture of terror, pain, and delight that I have come to recognize as joy and now must find some way to live with daily. This is a new problem. Until quite recently I had known joy only five times in my life, perhaps six, and each time tried to forget it soon after it happened, out of the fear that the memory of it would dement and destroy everything else.

Let's call it six. Three of those times I was in love, but only once was the love viable, or likely to bring me any pleasure in the long run. Twice I was on drugs—of quite different kinds. Once I was in water, once on a train, once sitting on a high wall, once on a high hill, once in a nightclub, and once in a hospital bed. It is hard to arrive at generalities in the face of such a small and varied collection of data. The uncertain item is the nightclub, and because it was essentially a communal experience I feel I can open the question out to the floor. I am addressing this to my fellow Britons in particular. Fellow Britons! Those of you, that is, who were fortunate enough to take the first generation of the amphetamine ecstasy and yet experience none of the adverse, occasionally lethal reactions we now know others suffered—yes, for you people I have a question. Was that joy?

I am especially interested to hear from anyone who happened to be in the Fabric club, near the old Spitalfields meat market, on a night sometime in the year 1999 (I'm sorry I can't be more specific) when the DJ mixed "Can I Kick It?" and then "Smells Like Teen Spirit" into the deep house track he had been seeming to play exclusively for the previous four hours. I myself was wandering out of the cavernous unisex (!) toilets wishing I could find my friend Sarah, or if not her, my friend Warren, or if not him, anyone who would take pity on a girl who had taken and was about to come up on ecstasy who had lost everyone and everything, including her handbag. I stumbled back into the fray.

Most of the men were topless, and most of the women, like me, wore strange aprons, fashionable at the time, that covered just the front of one's torso, and only remained decent by means of a few weak-looking strings tied in dainty bows behind. I pushed through this crowd of sweaty bare backs, despairing, wondering where in a super club one might bed down for the night (the stairs? the fire exit?). But everything I tried to look at quickly shattered and arranged itself in a series of patterned fragments, as if I were living in a kaleidoscope. Where was I trying to get to anyway? There was no longer any "bar" or "chill-out zone"—there was only dance floor. All was dance floor. Everybody danced. I stood still, oppressed on all sides by dancing, quite sure I was about to go out of my mind.

Then suddenly I could hear Q-Tip—blessed Q-Tip!—not a synthesizer, not a vocoder, but Q-Tip, with his human voice, rapping over a human beat. And the top of my skull opened to let human Q-Tip in, and a rail-thin man with enormous eyes reached across a sea of bodies for my hand. He kept asking me the same thing over and over: *You feeling it?* I was. My ridiculous heels were killing me, I was terrified I might die, yet I felt simultaneously overwhelmed with delight that "Can I Kick It?" should happen to be playing at this precise moment in the history of the world, and was now morphing into "Smells Like Teen Spirit." I took the man's hand. The top of my head flew away. We danced and danced. We gave ourselves up to joy.

Years later, while listening to a song called "Weak Become Heroes" by the British artist The Streets, I found this experience almost perfectly recreated in rhyme, and realized that just as most American children alive in 1969 saw the moon landings, nearly every Briton between sixteen and thirty in the 1990s met some version of the skinny pill-head I came across that night in Fabric. The name The Streets gives him is European Bob. I suspect he is an archetypal figure of my generation. The character Super Hans in the British TV comedy *Peep Show* is another example of the breed, though it might be more accurate to say Super Hans is European Bob in "old" age (forty). I don't remember the name of my particular pill-head but will call him Smiley. He was one of these strangers you met exclusively on dance floors, or else on a beach in Ibiza. They tended to have inexplicable nicknames, no home or family you could ever identify, a limitless capacity for drug-taking, and a universal feeling of goodwill toward all men and women, no matter their color, creed, or state of inebriation.

Their most endearing quality was their generosity. For the length of one night Smiley would do anything at all for you. Find you a cab, walk miles through the early-morning streets looking for food, hold your hair as you threw up, and listen to you complain at great length about your parents and friends—agreeing with all your grievances—though every soul involved in these disputes was completely unknown to him. Contrary to your initial suspicions, Smiley did not want to sleep with you, rob you, or con you in any way. It was simply intensely important to him that you had a good time, tonight, with him. "How you feeling?" was Smiley's perennial question. "You feeling it yet? I'm feeling it. You feeling it yet?" And that *you* should feel it seemed almost more important to him than that *he* should.

Was that joy? Probably not. But it mimicked joy's conditions pretty well. It included, in minor form, the great struggle that tends to precede joy, and the feeling—once one is "in" joy—that the experiencing subject has somehow "entered" the emotion, and disappeared. I "have" pleasure, it is a feeling I want to experience and own. A beach holiday is a pleasure. A new dress is a pleasure. But on that dance floor I *was* joy, or some small piece of joy, with all these other hundreds of people who were also a part of joy.

The Smileys, in their way, must have recognized the vital difference; it would explain their great concern with other people's experience. For as long as that high lasted, they seemed to pass beyond their own egos. And it might really have been joy if the next morning didn't always arrive. I don't just mean the deathly headache, the blurred vision, and the stomach cramps. What really destroyed the possibility that this had been joy was the replaying in one's mind of the actual events of the previous night, and the brutal recognition that every moment of sublimity—every conversation that had seemed to touch upon the meaning of life, every tune that had appeared a masterwork—had no substance whatsoever now, here, in the harsh light of the morning. The final indignity came when you dragged yourself finally from your bed and went into the living room. There, on your mother's sofa—in the place of that jester spirit-animal savior person you thought you'd met last night—someone had left a crushingly boring skinny pill-head, already smoking a joint, who wanted to borrow twenty quid for a cab.

It wasn't all a waste of time, though. At the neural level, such experiences gave you a clue about what joy not-under-the-influence would feel like. Helped you learn to recognize joy, when it arrived. I suppose a neuroscientist could explain in very clear terms why the moment after giving birth can feel ecstatic, or swimming in a Welsh mountain lake with somebody dear to you. Perhaps the same synapses that ecstasy falsely twanged are twanged authentically by fresh water, certain epidurals, and oxytocin. And if, while sitting on a high hill in the South of France, someone who has access to a phone comes dashing up the slope to inform you that two years of tension, tedious study, and academic anxiety have not been in vain—perhaps again these same synapses or whatever they are do their happy dance.

We certainly don't need to be neuroscientists to know that wild romantic crushes—especially if they are fraught with danger—do something ecstatic to our brains, though like the pills that share the name, horror and disappointment are usually not far behind. When my wild crush came, we wandered around a museum for so long it closed without us noticing; stuck in the grounds, we climbed a high wall and, finding it higher on its other side, considered our options: broken ankles or a long night sleeping on a stone lion. In the end a passerby helped us down, and things turned prosaic and, after a few months, fizzled out. What looked like love had just been teen spirit. But what a wonderful thing, to sit on a high wall, dizzy with joy, and think nothing of breaking your ankles.

Real love came much later. It lay at the end of a long and arduous road, and up to the very last moment I had been convinced it wouldn't happen. I was so surprised by its arrival, so unprepared, that on the day it arrived I had already arranged for us to visit the Holocaust museum at Auschwitz. You were holding my feet on the train to the bus that would take us there. We were heading toward all that makes life intolerable, feeling the only thing that makes it worthwhile. That was joy. But it's no good thinking about or discussing it. It has no place next to the furious argument about who cleaned the house or picked up the child. It is irrelevant when sitting peacefully, watching an old movie, or doing an impression of two old ladies in a shop, or as I eat a popsicle while you scowl at me, or when working on different floors of the library. It doesn't fit with the everyday. The thing no one ever tells you about joy is that it has very little real pleasure in it. And yet if it hadn't happened at all, at least once, how would we live?

A final thought: sometimes joy multiplies itself dangerously. Children are the infamous example. Isn't it bad enough that the beloved, with whom you have experienced genuine joy, will eventually be lost to you? Why add to this nightmare the child, whose loss, if it ever happened, would mean nothing less than your total annihilation? It should be noted that an equally dangerous joy, for many people, is the dog or the cat, relationships with animals being in some sense intensified by guaranteed finitude. You hope to leave this world before your child. You are quite certain your dog will leave before you do. Joy is such a human madness.

The writer Julian Barnes, considering mourning, once said, "It hurts just as much as it is worth." In fact, it was a friend of his who wrote the line in a letter of condolence, and Julian told it to my husband, who told it to me. For months afterward these words stuck with both of us, so clear and so brutal. *It hurts just as much as it is worth.* What an arrangement. Why would anyone accept such a crazy deal? Surely if we were sane and reasonable we would every time choose a pleasure over a joy, as animals themselves sensibly do. The end of a pleasure brings no great harm to anyone, after all, and can always be replaced with another of more or less equal worth.

ELIZABETH TALLENT

Little X

FROM *The Threepenny Review*

MEN THEN WERE MORE ALIKE than they are now. In their alikeness, which the time required, they had a conscientious, replicable beauty—boy cleanliness, haircuts that showed their ears, white shirts, black ties. Fresh handkerchiefs. Shoes whose shine needed vigilance. In winter, imposing overcoats that made them seem like soldiers in the army of seriousness and made it hard to tell them apart, especially from a distance, so that if a child saw her father far down the winter sidewalk, she would have trouble knowing for sure it was her father and she would stand in her oversized rubber boots, using one mitten as a gas mask to diffuse the freezing air, until it was him or it wasn't. This was long ago, during the war known as *Cold.* The early-morning unison of the fathers' departure would have shamed a flight of blackbirds; under the vaults and domes of the Capitol, behind locked doors, at the fathers' gray steel desks, at the ends of their pencils, the war was going well, it was going badly, it was a matter of interpretation, it was work. The daylight absence of the men, the fathers, imbued the suburb with the suspense of desertion. Every blade of grass in every lawn was waiting. Every wife was waiting, every dog with pricked-up ears and metal tags tinking on its collar was waiting, and each blade of grass, each wife, each dog and child, whatever else they did, held still. Whatever else it was for, the suburb was for holding still. Look: black circles have been cut from the lawns and into these circles have been inserted slim upward-striving trees. Against the possibility of their flying away to unite with other trees they are tethered to the earth with wires.

*

The explaining voice pauses; the pause is not a lull, not neutral, but active and soliciting; the voice belongs to the movie you are watching, and watching is what has been asked of you so far, but you learn from the pause that watching no longer suffices and some other engagement is required, but what that might be, you can't say, there isn't time. Over the Hiroshima of the black-and-white classroom movie, the bomb floats from the belly whose riveted steel plates have a homemade Frankenstein crudity: how strange to see how the plane is *made;* that clouds float by; how serenely, with what destined aplomb, the bomb peels away into the long arc of descent. In its scrolling slowness it's left behind in air; it's smaller and smaller and farther and farther behind; it could almost be forgotten about. Below, between parting clouds, a plain, the city-feeling of a grid, a clutteration of tiny roofs, infinite holding still.

Saturday you might see your dad in a T-shirt, your brother might be asked if he'd like *to throw a ball around,* and from a corner of the lawn you might sit and watch, wild with the wrongness of being a girl, *wild* with stoppered grace. Saturdays your dad was his own man, he said. Whose was he when he wasn't his own? Opposing the soft amused handsomeness of his face, his glasses had an architectural authority, the naked lenses dominated by the heavy black plastic bridge and earpieces. His hair memorized its side part. On a high closet shelf lived the hats forsaken when Kennedy took his oath of office bareheaded, trusting in his rashness and eloquence, in how young he was and how that was suddenly what was needed, and how it seemed to mean he could face things without the old inhibition and correctness, with, instead, shameless resourcefulness, undeluded cunning; and how fear relented with the bareheadedness of JFK; how fear was no equal for wind rifling the dark hair of a handsome man.

Deprived of my mother's attention, my father would narrow his eyes lonesomely and try to set something on fire, some dogma or other, till she faced him to argue. His voter registration was discreetly partyless to insure his survival from administration to administration, but he was a Democrat. Wounded by her Republican convictions, offensive not only in themselves but as the emblem of some ultimate elusiveness in his wife, he persisted in the belief that she could be harangued into converting. PhD or not, he came of a long line of forceful soul-savers, river-dunking, hellfire-extolling Baptists. When troubled, he would take nail clippers from his pocket and excruciate tiny parings from his already short nails. He didn't seem to regard this as a private act, and the fact that he wasn't aware this habit repelled other people filled me with wretched solicitude, as if nothing stood between him and disaster. When he took his glasses off it was as if he lifted away his sly intelligence and left a face naive as a sleeper's. When he crossed his legs the striptease shock of the white calf with its intimate corkscrews of black hair alarmed us all (my mother wondered aloud sometimes why no shank showed when JFK crossed *his* legs). He was an avid taker of offense. The word *hillbilly* overheard by chance—in a joke on TV, say—riled him like a just accusation. His gaucheness wasn't completely lost on him, and in the right mood he could mock it with a kidding lightheartedness impossible to reconcile with his prevailing touchiness: my little brother and sister and I longed for these fits of clowning, but they were like weather, immune to coaxing. In the token sartorial task assigned him, his oxfords submitted to the polish-stained shoebrush. The happiness of buffing called for snatches of sinister, lilting Hank Williams. *Oh I know a gal lives over the hill. If she won't do it, her sister will.*

On the coffee table: glorious oversized magazines whose pages exacted from a usually slapdash child the delicate touch and visual insatiability of a curator. Whose arrival was an event—at dinner: "The new *LIFE* came today"—and whose disposal elicited an elegiac tone—"Are we done with that *LIFE*?" There was TV, of course, but TV watching was closely monitored: these magazines were the source of my knowledge of the world beyond the suburb. These pages had held the sullenly unremarkable book depository, the knoll where a father in swiftest reflex had flattened himself against the grass, taking his crewcut sons with him (there was so little touch in our family that I envied those boys, I wanted an instinctive arm to press me down while sirens careened, or maybe just to feel adrenalized protectiveness radiating from a male body—maybe it was Freudian, the wish to be toppled and yanked close while emergency wheeled through the air), Oswald's lean fox face, its expression not much different from the shamed, dissembling insolence of certain boys in my class, boys known for cornering and tormenting, whose meanness was revered. There was Audrey Hepburn in a striped sailor shirt; there was the hammy smile of a chimpanzee in an astronaut suit, harnessed into the padded socket of a space capsule; there was an American soldier, rifle on his knees, watching five slight Vietnamese men, hands bound behind their backs, step barefoot into the narrow boat with him. In those pages Jenny Small and I read that when police entered the apartment of a woman murdered by the Boston Strangler, a record was still spinning on the turntable. From the hulking cabinet stereos in our living rooms we knew the grainy hiss and snap of the needle riding that last groove, the diamond of needle with its gliding listlessness and its failure to notice it had come to the end, and it came home to us on the rattly aluminum-framed faded turquoise-and-white plastic-webbing chaise longue in Jenny's back yard that as girls we were on the way to becoming wanted by rapists. We might *feel* cunning and self-sufficient and male, but look, *none of those things was true.* It was as if we had been two boys till we read that. It was just luck that we read it on Jenny's mother's chaise longue, me on the rickety end where a sunbather's feet belonged, Jenny sitting close to but not leaning against the cranked-up back support, the magazine spread across her lap, a flexing slippery *V* of glossy pages with, on each side, an island of brown knee. I seemed to see the left knee with the keenest focus I had ever brought to bear on any object. The horrifying page that rested against it made that knee exquisite in the composed human beauty of bone under skin. What did what we had read *do* to us? That it was terrible Jenny and I could discern in each other's eyes. We were in this together, but what did being *in it* mean? Later, in the hour after supper when nobody cared where children went, we looked for and found each other (we were not best friends, and didn't possess best-friend telepathy) and went to Jenny's back yard again, behind an overgrown lilac, where, with the Boy Scout knife borrowed from her older brother's drawer and singed for sterilization with matches also found there, Jenny and I nicked *X*'s in the palms of our hands and, sitting cross-legged, held our palms together, interlacing our fingers and gazing nobly into each other's eyes while the *X*'s bled into each other. Only they didn't. One of us noticed and said *Wait, there's not enough and it's not getting into each other.* From the edges of the cuts emerged little rubies, bead after luscious bead, but, true, it wasn't *flowing,* so we rubbed and smeared our palms, and that was the only thing that hurt, the edges of the cuts peeling back, the nervy insideness of one hand in electric contact with another, the streaky fingerpainting mess we were making of our palms, meaning bleeding into each other was not glamorous but messy and determined, amateur and startling. That didn't matter too much compared to the feeling that this was working—that it was doing what we'd wanted it to, hard though it would have been for either of us to explain.

Set apart: time of midmorning departure, time of highways' infinity, time of the gritty-glassy echoey unscrewing of the lid of the red plaid thermos usually reserved for the beach, time of lemonade atilt in the red plastic cup cap. Time of that cup's rim, wiped between turns so no one would die from the other's germs. Time of children's immersion in the atmosphere of their parents' marriage. Time of getting lost and whose fault it was. Time of the hotel swimming pool with its confidence-inspiring stench of chlorine. Time of signs warning that there was no lifeguard, of the cement margins where the chaise longues held sunglassed mothers and fathers whose shy nakedness causes the child's heart to thump in the child's skinny chest from delight at this exposure, which the child feels as a coming closer, a confounding of realities. Every unhappy family is periodically ransacked by joy. It is the way the family haunts itself, through the unknownness that is always, powerfully, in the parents' possession, the unknown whose sudden casual revelation on the chaise longues on the hot cement margins of the hotel swimming pool in a never-before-seen city causes a child's heart to beat hugely in the first intimation of breaking—of the child comprehending why grownups say of something or other that it is *enough to break your heart.*

Where was this? The chainlink fence that warned there was no lifeguard, the mothers who called *No running, I mean it, no running.* The shouted names of other children revealed to us, though our mother, a violent admirer of Jackie Kennedy's widowed composure, would never raise her voice in public. The not-very-distant freeway doing a steady business in semis, cumulus clouds brighter for the level radiance from the west, our shadows' legs marvelously long, our sleek wet heads so alike we were tribal, except within that tribe were the sharper alliances of brother and sister, and in our wet swimsuits we were more brother and sister than we had ever been before, eagerly, competitively, near-nakedly brother and sister, and when he followed me up the fifteen-foot ladder, whose rungs I remember for their wet-metal smell and ascending dangerousness, the flattery of his following so close lit my skin like sunburn and drove my climb to the pinnacle whose galvanized aluminum slide slanted to a glancing, slapping, light-scattering heaven ringed with wavering child-bodies that left an open space for the next slider. My brother was right behind, and right behind him came the oppressive almost-sexiness of other children's wet bodies clambering up the ladder. Maybe he wanted to impress these strange others, maybe too many cartoons whose victims rebounded laughing had led him to believe no real harm would be done (that was to be our parents' theory)—whatever causes converged in his shove, I was off balance, trying to correct the asymmetry of my pose there at the top, and thus went over the metal-pipe railing, the arm thrown in front of my face hitting first, then my knees, and I was slammed flat, silence closing in, circling as if I were a drain it wanted to go down. It was a very quiet thing to be at the heart of an accident. Through wet eyelashes I saw a world peaceful down to the grains of sand or grit on the cement inches from my nose, each grain precisely cherished by its shadow, the grains brightly lit and far apart and astounding as an array of boulders on the moon, and whose meticulousness placed them with this unearthly distinctness—what did that, and did it know about me? Then: voices, grownup voices, grownup feet, confusion, thrilled interrogation, solicitude. Dark fur against gaudy whiteness: those were my father's legs, this was my father crouching to ask questions, but the magnitude of my alertness crushed the desire to answer him. Nobody maintained in those days that you shouldn't move a person who'd fallen, rescue was a more casual prerogative, and I was carried back to our hotel room in my father's arms; this once, his arms. I was left alone on one of the double beds in the air-conditioned gloom while my mother and father conferred outside the door in the gentling heat of early evening, other grownups stopping by, their questions politely deflected, their kids' voices ringing from the pool like clamor from a past life. Standing outside the room in his baggy swim trunks, assailed by well-meaners, my father would feel humiliated and full of blame, these emotions unrelievable by the surgery he habitually inflicted on his nails, but sufficiently disguised by his charm that only I, listening in the dark room, could detect the hazardousness of his mood, which sought, which had to seek, an object. At ten I believed nobody else had real insight into my father, not my brother or sister, who understood hardly anything, not my mother, whose adoration of him outwardly resembled suffering omniscience but who was in fact easily deflected by his contrarieties. Now it was she who intervened. My little brother had not meant to hurt anyone, had he? That tender, harassing spell cast by adults coercing a right answer: it was surprising how instantly we welcomed that (their welcoming it was plain in their voices, and as for my welcoming it, I could feel that). Of all of us, my brother was the only one beloved by the other four, his crying the only heartbreaking crying. Outside the door he was crying now, he was (I closed my eyes and knew this for sure) shuddering, goosefleshed, wet hair sleeked to his skull and pathetic ears jutting out, arms hanging at his sides, shaking his head no, no, no, no, no, no, and in that dark hotel room I was relieved that my mother knew how to manage the questioning by which he could be forgiven, and within relief a doorway opened into sleep.

Enormous suitcases, jade and beige and navy, jammed together in a rattling bulwark smelling of sunstruck plastic, shade a narrow canyon lined with a flannel sleeping bag whose hunters and retrievers alternate with flushed pheasants. The fact that the pheasants are bigger than the hunters and their dogs and if they flew at them instead of away could crush them with a few decisive wingbeats arouses an aesthetic revulsion intense to the point of nausea: I need to correct this, to write a letter to the sleeping-bag people, enclosing a pheasant-setter-hunter drawing so piercingly *right* they would wonder who this girl is and resolve to find her to hire her to design all future sleeping-bag-flannel vignettes. My forehead sweats, the roots of my hair sweat; sweat runs from between my shoulder blades down my spine with a feeling like being crawled on and not minding, and I close my eyes and coax that sensation to the center, where it's the war of slow-sliding creepy arousal versus pain. If you have three children in the back seat, one is always in the middle, nudged and bothered and whisper-taunted from the left and from the right. The answer is always no, but every trip begins with someone begging to ride in the rear of the station wagon, called in our family the Wayfarback, sweet as a vacant house is sweet, as only unclaimed spaces ever are, carpeted in clean scratchiness, offering what can be found nowhere else in our life, the ambiguity of being close yet unseen: a child in the Wayfarback can't be surveilled by glances in the rearview mirror. Can't be seat-belted in, either, making it appealingly dangerous. So why is it mine, this hot rumpled hidey-hole? Attuned to injustice—savage keeners of *No fair!*—my little brother and sister are quiet in the face of this travesty, gratified by their own quietness, which seems grownup and inexplicable. Mother-and-father silence followed my saying plaintively, two or three times before we left the hotel room this morning, *Something's wrong.* With my left arm, with the little finger and the fourth finger and the thumb of my left hand—*Something's wrong it feels really strange.* To which no one said even *It'll be all right in a little while.* Wearing the same clothes as yesterday, I was standing there saying *Look* with my whole incredulous body. My mother who didn't like to touch me helped me work my swollen arm out of the sleeve of my T-shirt, but even then she didn't do the thing I wanted, she didn't look, and because she didn't look it changed into something not quite mine, my arm, and I got a little divorce from it, like getting distance from a lie you're going to disown before long. I couldn't knot the cowboy bandanna I was obsessed with, so she did, though she hated it and was always trying to talk me out of it on the grounds that girls didn't look good with rags around their necks. Then astounding license: *You can ride in the very back.* With the smashing of strictness, the air in the station wagon brightens, my father calls my mother *honey,* which makes everyone feel as if they've been called *honey,* my brother and sister trade the Etch-a-Sketch back and forth, and I lie on my stomach in the Wayfarback, turning the pages of *Smoky the Cowhorse.* It was my rope-callused hand Smoky snatched the apple from, my sunburnt neck the bandanna circled, only now (I suddenly saw) the bandanna could be used to wrap my forearm—a feverish cowboy would do that if he was shot with an arrow. When the wrapping seemed to help, I found the rag used to wipe condensation from the back window and swaddled my hand, figuring out how to encompass the outsize, yammering fingers too, although the thumb remained an orphan with a big, throbbing heartbeat. I wished I had a scrap for it. Eternity could be broken into bearable slabs by the ritual of loosening the bindings and winding them tighter, the baseball game fading and reviving on the radio and my father calling the glorious salute *Attaboy!* and the sun lasering between suitcases to ignite hot stripes on my legs while I slept, and I slept a lot, and when I woke there was a fraction of an instant when my old life was back and all was well, and that was snatched away. How wrong I'd been not to have loved my unbroken arm more. My mother unfolded the map of America with every Howard Johnson's on it. My father said *Shoes on, kids.* The back door swung up, me blinking at the loss of my cave, clambering out to the asphalt where the bare-legged beauty of the other four struck me sharply. Glass doors opened into the mercy of air conditioning in a circus-bright barrage of orange and turquoise, the gauze bow in the small of the waitress's back led us in single file between tables of families, and I held my scarecrow arm close to my body, but more than one waitress raised her eyebrows and would have inquired if she hadn't, in time, registered my parents' unwillingness to engage. There was another hotel-room night; there was bacon and eggs and Tang that astronauts drank. *Look, kids, the Cumberland Gap, your great-great-grandpa rode home through here after he lost his leg at The Wilderness, we'll go there sometime. Rode home one-legged? He could get a prit good hold, his stump was long enough, down to the knee. Bill! Don't go into details!* There was *prit* to evoke the ghost's voice and prove the Civil War had happened; there was fog, the headlights' shafts filled with rolling plumes, the dented guardrail the only thing between us and the abyss; there was my father's tale of the Model A he first learned to drive and the red mud it foundered in, and how it was pulled out with a neighbor's mule who could count and do tricks and would neatly, with its big mule lips peeled back, take an apple from between its owner's wife's teeth; there was my father imitating the mule's grimace, and when my mother didn't laugh, doing it again; there was my mother's Yankee reticence and delicacy and irony, about to become drawbacks in the encounter with my father's family. She was hard to make sense of, in Tennessee.

The fraying, dirty mummification of my arm enchanted my cousins as if I had carried a filthy stray cat into their house and then refused to give it up. This was seen as boldness on my part: the lawlessness they imagined for me was an outline I would have poured myself into if I could. They wanted to touch and poke and unwrap, and since that would earn me more reverent attention of the kind boys pay only to what slightly sickens them, I would have let them. But my aunt said *Boys. Now you leave it alone.* My cousins stuck close, honoring the leprous *it*ness of my arm. Asked by my aunt about the pain, I don't think I was constrained by loyalty to my parents' version, which was that nothing was broken. The doubleness of my vantage point—aware that they were wrong but sure they were perfect—wrecked my awareness of them; where *what they want* belonged, there was a blank, so I was honest with my aunt, and relieved by the distress she let show. Reined in only by my aunt's southern-lady-ness, that distress verged on an indictment of my parents, especially my mother; but my aunt held her tongue and didn't accuse her of anything, not where I could hear, and I think not to anyone, because it wouldn't have served any purpose, not really, or made it any easier to accomplish what she right away determined to do, which was get me to a doctor. My aunt had brown eyes so dark they were often described as black, enviable eyes, as hers was an enviable high-cheekboned black-haired drawling beauty that hadn't gotten her into too much trouble, either because she was naturally sensible or had set out to cultivate happiness. She'd married my father's droll, soft-spoken, easygoing little brother, and their household seemed miraculous to me, so much so that on previous annual visits I had insisted on watching my aunt do every little thing, spellbound by her gentleness and determined to attract as much of it as I could to myself. This greed of mine for my aunt's company didn't go unremarked, and it embarrassed my mother. If she'd liked my aunt less, she might have held it against her, or conjectured to my father late at night when they were finally alone that my aunt was egging me on in my ridiculous infatuation, with the secret aim of making Bill's Yankee wife look bad. My aunt's nature was equable and warm and self-effacing, qualities my restless hypercritical mother did not possess but religiously impersonated. As sometimes happens, two women who seem exactly positioned for mutual loathing ended up forging a spirited conspiracy, whose great staple was discussion of their men, those very different brothers.

At the hospital I was *sugah*ed and *sweetheart*ed, endearments good as opium. The dream of benevolence was pierced by my fear when the doctor bent close. I hadn't bathed since the accident and my skin radiated the stench of fever and chlorine, but the possibility that he would be repelled by me did not concern me—that wasn't it, though what I was afraid of was *like* smelling bad: it was present, like a taint, when the doctor leaned in. It was the possibility of being deeply shamed. With his mannerly Tennessee-slow slightly formal inquisitiveness the doctor might assent to my parents' view that nothing real was wrong, and attention-lover that I was, I would be seen as having impersonated brokenness and spun a fable of pain. Could that be, could I have done that? Across a wall, at adult eye level, ran the sequence of black X-ray sheets, and I gazed up at the frail light of my bones while grownup voices took polite turns, the longest, southernest turn belonging to the doctor. *You know how if you take a little stick and give it a good twist, it will splinter out with the strain but not snap clear through? What's called a greenstick fracture. Fractures here, here, and here too.* The truth of X-rayed bone, the lifted-up feeling of rescue, the sensuousness of the expert winding of plaster-soaked gauze, spindly as layers of papier-mâché, around and around until the hurt arm vanished.

The opposite of hospital order and clarity and decisiveness is the velvet passivity of sinking into the high-backed seats of a darkening theater, but whose whim was this? Down at the thrilling level where children piece together rumors of what adults find *dirty,* this movie was a source of joking and awe and back-yard reenactment: *This bad guy kills women by sneaking in while they're sleeping and painting them gold, all over so their skin can't breathe. They die? If a person's skin can't breathe they die. Wouldn't it wake you up to be painted—you'd feel it? They're just in real deep sleep. The painting happens fast. They used real gold. This one woman, while they were painting they forgot to leave her a patch of bare skin to breathe through and she died. In real life, died, and you get to see her.* For my aunt and uncle as evangelicals, the corruption that could attend moviegoing wasn't taken lightly; how did they ever agree to Bond? I can't explain it, unless the movie was meant as reckless compensation for the ordeal of the hospital, which had left the grownups in a dangerous state of disenchantment with each other. Maybe some unprecedented enchantment was needed, which could embrace them in its scandalous arms—maybe it had to be scandalous or it wouldn't constitute enough of a break, it wouldn't do the trick. Neither can the adults' decision to sit apart from us children be explained, unless their apartness seemed the route to undistracted calm and unity. So: to the gilding and velvet and shushing of southern audience voices, to five cousins in thrall to each other's nearness, alert to every flicker of an eyelid in a cousin's profile. The troubling parts *are going to go right over their heads,* the grownups had decided, a satisfying conclusion all round, for them because it guaranteed them a respite from the strained aura of mutual apology that had overtaken them at the hospital, for us because we fully intended to absorb every bit of sex and violence. In the downfalling twilight I rested my brand-new cast on the armrest and admired its luminous whiteness, the separate aluminum splint that shielded my thumb, the cute pawlike entrapment of my other fingertips showing at the cast's end. Then it was dark. For music there was a moaningly erotic blare of trumpets whose notes were prolonged with a *nyaaaah nyaaaaaah* obnoxiousness well known to children. Bond too was gloriously obvious: he did whatever he wanted. We understood! How beguiled we were to find ourselves surfing the shockwaves of a movie for grownups. We grew bolder, also for some reason indifferent to each other, staring without whispering. Deep in the movie, in the silk sheets where Bond had left her the night before, a woman lay on her side, her hair swerving across a pillow, her back to us, what my dad called *the cheeks of her ass* exposed, just a little string running down between them. Bond came in. Bond sat on the edge of the bed. She was bare bright overpowering gold, the tilt of shoulder declining to the tuck of waist, the hip the high point of a luminous dune tapering to rigid feet. Had she slept through her own death? Or wakened to feel consciousness beat its wings against suffocating skin? How long did it take? What came next? In his white pajamas, his back straight, Bond extended his fingertips to the glazed throat. No thudding, no pulse, only calm metal *thing*ness like a tin can's, a car fender's. We sat there hushed and oppressed and sorry. My cousins hadn't moved a fraction of an inch, but they had gotten farther away. Maybe to my cousins, maybe to something else, I directed an inarticulate wish along the lines of *Come back, come back.* The wish could do nothing. It was a trammeled, locked-in wish beating against other people's unknownness. It wasn't going to work. Aloneness wasn't going anywhere. While my soul hung waiting for the next part of my life, I looked down at my arm, emerging into visibility as the lights came up. Under plaster and gauze was the ghost of the *X* where I had once bled into somebody and she had bled into me, and it worked, that *X,* and if it worked once, it could work again, or something like it could, the *X* of one body held to the *X* of another, and this notion stirred me, though

I didn't know enough about bodies to make the desire any more authoritative or detailed than that, I didn't know this was sex. But I knew it was a way out. *Find Jenny and ask her if she loves you and when she says yes say good because I do too.* And like magic, I did. Love her.

They were *reality.* Like everybody's parents, they were the most real thing there was. It was not possible to blame them, it would not have occurred to me at ten. The truth is I was sickened by myself for being a child they wanted not to know about. I repudiated myself because I could find no way to matter, it was my failure, and I understood that another, more beautiful child could have had a hold on them. Yet it seemed possible that by force of will I could become this other, more beautiful child. Was it a thing a nonbeloved child could figure out—could replicate? How long would it take? This was an emergency. I was wrong, in my wrongness I was alienating them, and either I was doing things wrong or I was imbued with wrongness, irretrievably wrong, a wrong self, and that could not be changed, and it could not be borne. Therefore it must be the case that I was doing things wrong, and if I was doing things wrong, then it was only a matter of beginning to do things right, and I could do that, I would, I had to, it was life or death to me to be loved by them, so I would do things beautifully, beginning now.

If they have both been lost to me by death, gone for years, that hasn't changed things: death, it turns out, can't touch the deep aura of waiting, the lifelong spell that is the need for them to *see.*

WELLS TOWER

The Old Man at Burning Man

FROM *GQ*

THE LAND, THE VERY atmosphere out there, is alien, malignant, the executioner of countless wagon trains. I am afraid to crack the window. Huge dervishes of alkaline dust reel and teeter past. The sun, a brittle parchment white, glowers as though we personally have done something to piss it off. An hour out here and already I could light an Ohio Blue Tip off the inside of my nostril. One would think we were pulling into this planet's nearest simulation of hell, but if this were hell, we would not be driving this very comfortable recreational vehicle. Nor would there be a trio of young and merry nudists capering at our front bumper, demanding that we step out of the vehicle and join them. These people are checkpoint officials, and it is their duty to press their nakedness to us in the traditional gesture of welcome to the Burning Man festival, here in Nevada's Black Rock Desert.

The checkpoint nudists are comely and embraceable, in the way that everyone ten years younger than me has lately begun to seem comely and embraceable—the women's dolphin smoothness still undefeated by time and gravity; the men bearing genial grins and penises with which I suppose I can cope: neither those lamentable acorns one pities at the gym, nor fearsome yardage that would be challenging to negotiate at close quarters. But here is the question: Do I want some naked strangers to get on me? Or, more to the point, do I want them to get on me with my father watching? This quandary is no quandary for my father. He is already out of the vehicle, standing in the coursing dust, smiling broadly, a stranger's bosom trembling at his chin.

My father and I are staid, abstracted East Coast types without much natural affinity for bohemian adventures. But we are here less for the festival itself than in service of an annual father-son ritual. Fourteen years ago my father was diagnosed with an exotic lymphoma and given an outside prognosis of two years. When we both supposed he was dying, we made an adorable pledge—if he survived—to take a trip together every year. Thanks to medical science, we've now followed the tradition for a solid decade, journeying each summer to some arbitrarily selected far-flung destination: Greenland, Ecuador, Cyprus, etc. This year we've retooled the concept and departed instead on a bit of domestic ethnography. We have joined the annual pilgrimage of many thousands who each year flee the square world for the Nevada desert to join what's supposed to be humanity's greatest countercultural folk festival/self-expression derby. Or it used to be, before people like my father and me started showing up.

Now I too am in the daylight, being hugged by a small, bearded Mr. Tumnus of a fellow, and also by a bespectacled lady-librarian type with a scrupulously mown vulva. "Welcome home," they murmur in my ear. "Home" this is decidedly not. Whether it is good to be here, we shall discover in the coming week. Still, I reply, "Uh, it's good to be home."

At the adjacent welcome booth, dreadlockers, having been duly greeted, are trudging back to their hippie wagon. "I hope it doesn't suck this year," one of them says, eyeing our vast and foolish RV. "We're surrounded by all these bougie people."

"I'm so fucking *stoned,*" complains a bikini-clad girl wearing a fedora snugged over dreadlocks stout as table legs. "Man, I gotta focus. Gotta get ready for the Slut Olympics."

We climb back aboard, tracking pounds of dust into the RV. My dad is enlivened. "What a nice greeting that was," he says. "Did you know that woman didn't have any trousers on? I was so focused on her breasts I didn't notice she was naked until after the ceremony."

When I mentioned to friends that I was going to Burning Man with my sixty-nine-year-old father, *Good idea* were the words out of no one's mouth. Perhaps this was a poor idea. Mere moments here and my emotional machinery, specifically the feelings-about-my-family manifold, is beginning to smoke, creak, and blow springs with a jaw-harp *bwaaaang!*

The root causes of my embarrassment, unsurprisingly, naturally, track back to my childhood, a montage of my father perpetually falling short of the dull, decorous Ward Cleaver ideal I imagined everyone else had for a dad. Because my father is constitutionally incapable of being embarrassed, I spent much of my early life being embarrassed on his behalf. In elementary school I was embarrassed by his car, a mulch-colored Datsun coupe which, when the clearcoat gave out, my father repainted, with brushes, a pupil-puckering shade of kelly green. I was, and am, embarrassed by his house. After my parents divorced (I was six), the home became a tribute to unreconstructed bachelorhood, a place where the dominant cuisine was ramen noodles, where the dirty-clothes hamper was a delta of fragrant laundry on the kitchen floor, and where, when the furnace broke, it went unrepaired for the better part of a decade. For much of my adult life, my father's house has existed in a state of entropy so ideal that were a band of vandals or a flood to hit the place, it could only enhance the house's orderliness.

I was embarrassed by my father's fearlessness about his body—how, for example, when we met for a tennis game, he never bothered to change ahead of time or repair to a restroom but instead shucked his trousers off in the parking lot without a care for who observed him in his sagging BVDs. I was embarrassed, and also sort of impressed, one day when I was seven when I saw him drink some of my pee. The setup was this: I'd spent the morning pissing in a Collins glass I'd hidden in the garage, which I intended to take down the street to show a neighbor friend, for reasons unclear to me now. In any case, I set it on the kitchen table while I went to find my shoes. When I returned, my father was hoisting the glass to his lips and uttering these words: "What's this, apple juice?"

I recall yelling, "Noooooooooo," in slo-mo basso. Too late. He took a generous slug. Then he set the glass down, turned to me, and said only this: "Don't ever, ever do that again."

But I think what I'm feeling now is the opposite of the old embarrassed feeling, more a kind of petulant recognition that my father's heedlessness, his lack of inhibition, are in fact virtues that I failed to inherit. Did I mention that my father is no free-ranging hippie papa but a professor of economics who once voted for George W. Bush? Yet when I asked my father to come with me to Burning Man, though he'd never heard of Burning Man, "Absolutely" was his prompt response. Never mind that his immune system is faltering. He now requires monthly transfusions of immunoglobulin. His chronic chest cold seems to be getting worse. His doctor recently noticed sulfurous halos around my father's pupils, inspiring worries that he may someday soon go blind. His mouth has lately broken out in ulcers, part of a painful accumulation of signals that this year's trip could be our last one together.

And yet, while I love my father, these trips with him are not always enjoyable for me. It is not just that he likes to dry his sink-scrubbed underclothes by flying them from the antenna of the rental car. It is also the sleeping arrangements. My father is the sort of thrifty traveler who stays at hotels with hourly rates. Once, in a jungle in New Zealand, we got drunk and passed out on the corpse of a decomposed rat. My father insists on sleeping nude, even when we share a room, sometimes even when we share a bed, and this sort of closeness can be difficult to bear.

And so it's probably wise that this year we have included two auxiliary homeboys in our party: my father's first cousin Cam Crane, and a grad-school buddy of my father's, a Canadian professor of economics in his emeritus years whose actual name is James Dean.

Cam is fifty-seven years old and is among the kindest and most capable people I know. He is the sort of person who, on camping trips, always brings two of everything in case somebody else needs his spare. Both of Cam's parents were dead of alcoholism before Cam was twenty-three, and he has lived his life in an underparented, not-all-who-wander-are-lost sort of way. Cam is widely loved among members of our family, but we are sometimes confused by the life choices he makes. For example, Cam spent this past year staying in the spare room at the house of his ex-girlfriend and her husband to care for their quadriplegic dog as it died of Lou Gehrig's disease. His duties involved manually voiding the dog's bladder and bowels and "walking" the creature by means of a little cart built for this use. The dog, whose name was Sierra, was at last put down the week before Cam set out for Burning Man, to Cam's mixed relief. Cam acknowledges that his life probably needs to tack in a new direction. "I really think Burning Man could change my life," he said to me on the phone a few weeks back. How? "Well, to be around these people all getting together for a common reason—it might help me focus on my own path."

Then there's my father's old friend James Dean, who views the week a bit less ingenuously. Dean, seventy-one, is famous among his friends for a lifetime of resounding successes with women, if not wives. He plays the saxophone and rides a big motorcycle, and if he didn't you would say, "That guy ought to play the saxophone and ride a big motorcycle." He does not expect Burning Man to change his life: "I think it's probably just a sexed-up art party" is his take on the week ahead.

Black Rock City—temporary home this year to nearly 60,000 souls—comes into view. It spans more than two miles, with concentric "streets" laid out around an open expanse of desert or "playa" where stands the eponymous Man (a sort of neon stick figure atop a plywood mansion). The city is breathtaking, especially if your thing is tarps and ropes and improvised shade structures. The dominant aesthetic is hardcore post-apocalyptic sun-retardant functionality: PVC-and-Tyvek Quonset huts, moon-base yurts made of foil-faced foam core, army-surplus wall tents—all lashed to rebar pilings sledgehammered deep into the hardpan. No camp seems to lack a soundly anchored shade structure, an appurtenance that we've heard constitutes the difference between having a good time at Burning Man and roasting miserably in your RV. Winds here crest at sixty miles an hour. Thanks to Cam's foresight, we've at least got masks and goggles against the frequent dust storms, but shadewise, all we've brought is a crappy little steel-and-nylon awning from Walmart. Roving past the pro-grade battenings of the other campers, Cam, our logistics man, says, "I think we might be fucked."

And the genuinely sort of scary thing about Burning Man is that if you've fucked yourself in the food, water, or shade-structure departments, you are quite fucked indeed. According to the principles set down by Larry Harvey, who inaugurated the festival twenty-six years back by torching some art on San Francisco's Baker Beach, nothing may be bought or sold at Burning Man. (After the festival outgrew California and relocated to the desert, an amendment was made for coffee and ice.) "Gifting," as you've probably heard, is the soul of the Burning Man economy, which is helpful if you're in the market for some ecstasy or a chakra balancing, but stuff like rebar, rope, and triple-gusseted tarps is too heavy and precious to hand out for free.

But what really distinguishes Burning Man from Bonnaroo or

any other festivals on the indie-bohemioid trail is that there's no main attraction: no famous bands or beer tents or dreamcatcher salesfolk. At Burning Man the attraction is the mass of fellow campers, each of whom is doing his bit by, say, hosting the Slut Olympics, or giving a lecture on Foucault, or knitting a Buddhist stupa out of pubic hair and setting it on fire. And the art (if that's the word for a flaming neon hoagie on wheels) has gotten a good deal more elaborate since the first beach bonfire. Among the hundreds of visual extravagances in store this year: an actual-size replica of an eighteenth-century shipwreck, a diesel-powered cast-iron dinosaur, a snowstorm in the desert, plus a menagerie of flammable installations (a plywood cathedral, a multistory effigy of Wall Street) to be torched in celebration of life's transience and other arty ideals. The whole thing defies expectations pretty spectacularly, especially if what you expected, as I did, was a Grateful Dead parking lot with no bands and more intense personal filth.

It is, in short, worth the lamentably expensive ticket price ($240 to $420, depending on when you buy). The ticketing system's supposed to accommodate veteran Burners, but somehow things got screwed up this year, and a full third went to people like me and my dad—here, the old-timers fear, to party and gawk and score free shit but not to "contribute" to the festival in any real way.

We pick a campsite in a quiet neighborhood on an outer ring of the city. To one side of us, some rather abject fraternity gentlemen cower in the lee of their Subaru having Heineken brews. Our closest neighbors are several women in their thirties whom James Dean promptly diagnoses as "horny" by means of divination lost on the rest of us.

The professors mix up a batch of gin and tonics while Cam and I lash our miserable little Walmart gazebo to the chassis of the RV. I am tempted to nap in its washcloth-sized patch of shade, but my father has other plans. My father is dressed in adventure sandals, cargo shorts, a muslin tunic he bought in Thailand, and a nouveau legionnaire's chapeau complete with trapezius snood. Through a pair of dime-store spectacles ($4.99 price tag still on the lens) he is reading today's schedule of events. We have a happy range of activities from which to choose. Something called the Adult Diaper Brigade is welcoming participants. There is also "Make a Genital Necklace," "Fisting With Foxy," "3rd Annual Healthy Friction Circle Jerk," and "Naked Barista." Not all the offerings are lascivious. Some are educational ("Geology of the Black Rock Desert"), creative-anachro-geeky ("Excalibur Initiation and Dragon Naming Ceremony"), culinary ("FREE FUCKIN' ICE CREAM!!"), and spiritual ("Past Life Regression Meditation"). None of these options are seriously entertained.

"I think I'll go to the Naked Barista and have a naked cup of coffee," says my father.

"I'm coming with you, Ed," says James. "Are you going to get naked?"

"I think that's the arrangement," he says. "You have to get naked to get your cup of coffee."

"You don't think you're going native a bit prematurely?" I say.

"I don't see what the big deal is," he says. "I'm quite confident no one will look at me."

We set off. We have brought bicycles. Black Rock City contains miles of byways, and to travel on foot would be a sure way to turn yourself into a Slim Jim. Only when we leave the camp does it begin to register how very astounding this whole thing is. The sun is setting, and the dusty avenues teem with weird life. A golf cart made to resemble a bluefin-sized sperm crosses our path (this year's theme is Fertility 2.0), followed by a hay wagon belching fire. Men cycle past wearing destroyed tuxedos, monkey outfits, suits of armor made of gold lamé, or T-shirts beneath whose belly hem bare genitals wag. (This is known as "shirtcocking" in the local argot.) Women wear, uniformly, their underwear. Or the vast majority do. In real life these women are bankers, substitute teachers, receptionists at gravel quarries, but here they have all entered into a common sisterhood of underpants in a collective mission to make the playa a place of beauty and terrible longing. God bless them.

I am now feeling the onset of an unpleasant sort of tourist panic. As one of the people who siphoned off tickets from the regular Burners, I'm gone in this guilty little fugue: *Wow, you know, I thought this was going to be a half-assed and risible demon-sticks-and-reefer-and-Himalayan-salts dipshit convention, but afoot is a pageant of trippy ingenuity and gorgeousness that must have taken a hell of a lot of work and money and gymnasium hours to bring off and that can only be diminished by the gawking presence of guys like us—whom the etiquettician Amy Vanderbilt once described as "decrepit extra males."*

We creak along. The Naked Barista occupies a shanty alongside a jungle gym under which people are applying henna tattoos to one another. Under the shanty a hairy man is foaming a latte. In line is a naked older guy who I know is from Southern California because his buttocks exactly resemble a sun-dried seal's corpse I once saw on a Santa Barbara beach.

This is not my father's scene. "I may have seen enough of this," he says. "Only the men seem to be naked."

It is happy hour in Black Rock City, and I, for one, think that some sort of very stiff, inhibition-destroying cocktail is in order. Nearby, something called Homojito is going on, which Cam rejects.

"No one is giving away blowjobs," laments James Dean. "There ought to be a barter station."

I explain that there is no bartering in Black Rock City, only gifting.

"Yeah, but there's always an implicit barter, or I guess it depends on whether you belong to the Chicago School or not," says James Dean, professor of economics.

Onward through the shifting dust to a camp where a woman in a wedding dress is pumping on a swing. Behind her a shirtless Chippendales guy in a gold harlequin mask appears to be handing out free booze. Uncertain of proper mooching etiquette, we grin and cringe around the premises for a quarter of an hour before the Chippendales guy waves us over for a dose. He's not just giving it away, though. He explains that I have to first spin an arrow on a little cardboard dial listing a menu of chores and humiliations. The card commands me to bare my breasts, which I do. The bartender grimaces. "What's second prize?" he says.

In return for this degradation, I am treated to the vilest cocktail in all of Christendom: a crimson sludge consisting of gummy bears deliquesced in vodka. Okay, so having now logged my first transaction in the Burning Man economy, it seems pretty clear that the festival's utopian, pan-inclusive rhetoric doesn't extend much past the promotional literature. I mean, *What's second prize?* I thought this whole thing was about Larry Harvey's Principle No. 5, radical self-expression, i.e., showing people your tits and stuff. Which I guess applies if you're a sexy underpant woman or a Nautilus-hewn Los Angeles–based life form. But if you're a schlubby white dude with a pale belly and sort of sucky tits, then it's junior high school redux: *What's second prize?*

This private tantrum is halted by the sound of my father's laughter. He is being spanked by a Cleopatra in a stressed bikini. He knocks back his shot and then heads to an après-ski-theme party across the way. Folk in toboggans and little else dance beneath a shower of synthetic snow. Where is my father? He is roving the crowd, dispensing tiny little key-chain flashlights, our meager yet handy contributions to the gift economy. And here he is now, clinking cups with a topless woman in white faux-fur chaps, having a splendid time. He gives her a flashlight. "That was a rather unusual toast," he says. "She said, 'Here's to your hemorrhaging anus.' And then I gave her a light, and I said, 'The better to see it with.'"

My father, repartee king. In five minutes with the anus woman, he has uttered more words than I have in the past two hours.

Cranky. Why am I in despair among these fluffy pals? I suppose because this is supposed to be it, this is supposed to be Xanadu, miles and miles from the uptight squares and cultural toxins of late capitalism, free to make weird remarks to strangers about their anuses, free to shirtcock or to don a pair of underpants with the words *Permission to Come Aboard* blazoned on the ass. But what if you do not care to don such a pair of underpants? What if you do not care to reveal your genitals to strangers? Well, my friend, then you are part of the problem, a cultural toxin, a dreary spy from what is known in Black Rock City as "the default world." You should not have come here. You should be at home, buying consumer durables on the World Wide Web.

And now the sun is going down, tinting the sky and the brown hills with Easter-egg hues. My father takes a great portion of desert air into his lungs and lets it out in a staticky, bronchitic sigh. "I think this is spectacular," he says. "This works. People are pleasant. They like having their picture taken. This is wonderful. It's absolutely wonderful! What is it that motivates it all? The urge to be unique!"

We awake to the sound of the RV's tin hide—*tick-tick-tick*—deforming in the sun. Sleeping arrangements are these: Cam and I split the big rubber mattress in the RV's master bedroom. James Dean sleeps in the little roost over the cockpit. (Dean's body philosophies are not far from my father's. To retract suddenly the curtains to Dean's roost is a good way to get an eyeful of scrotum.) My father, Ed the Uncomplaining, Ed the Jolly Receiver of the Short End of the Stick, sleeps very happily on the RV's hard and sticky floor.

The professors rose early and are just now returning from a trip to the plaza of portable toilets a couple of blocks away. But isn't there a toilet in the RV? Yes, there is, but as the uptight captain of this vessel, I have levied an edict against deucing in the vehicle for fear of cumulative odors. The Burning Man organizers have done a fair job of placing toilet villages at convenient intervals throughout the city, but the toilets are not pleasant. They radiate a smell that registers in the nose not as merely bad but dangerous, like a shipwrecked supertanker of tainted smelling salts. Step inside one of these Porta-Johns and flashbulbs explode behind your eyes.

James Dean returns from the toilet in his underpants, carrying his shorts at arm's length. An unexplained misadventure took place at the commode. Still, it sounds like the fellows enjoyed themselves at the latrine plaza.

"Your father is very good at walking up to bare-breasted women and asking if he can take their photograph," Dean tells me.

"They're extremely gracious," my father confirms. "Even when they desperately have to poop."

"You just walk up and ask them?" I say, quite astonished.

"I just ask them, yeah. My first thought was to do it surreptitiously, but then I discovered that tattooed naked boobs like to be photographed."

Now the team reviews the program of events to plot a course for the day. Other than Saturday, when the Man goes up in flames, there aren't really any marquee events. You basically find your way through offerings of individual camps listed in the program.

"This might be worth going to: Critical Dicks," says Dean. "I think it's a dick contest. It starts at noon, and it lasts for two hours."

"You're going to compete, James?" I ask.

"No, but perhaps your father would."

Dad is pondering other possibilities. "There's the Romp of the Tranny Goddesses. There's the Human Playapede: 'Now join playapede friends ass to mouth to ass.' I'm not sure I want to participate in that one. There's also Anal Probe."

"That wouldn't be my first choice," says Dean. "Here's one we should go to: How to Drive a Vulva. Pussy ninja tricks at Camp Beaverton."

Agreed. We make for Camp Beaverton. But seconds after mounting his bike, my father realizes he has forgotten a seat cushion he bought at the Las Vegas Walmart. Executing a slow turn in the lane, he falls hard into the dirt, his bare legs tangled in his bike frame. He gazes up at me with a dazed expression of embarrassment and mild shock.

"Are you okay?"

"Yeah, yeah, yeah. I tripped."

He rights his bike and moves along.

Cam and I watch him go. "My mom used to do a lot of stuff like that, falling down or whatever," he said. "It was usually alcohol-related, but still, it's sort of a weird wake-up call. You know they're not going to be around that long. But Ed's been doing okay. He's keeping up all right. I hope he's going to be with us a while."

"I hope so too," I say.

Bicycle caravans are a challenge at Burning Man. By the time Cam and I get to Camp Beaverton, my father and Dean are nowhere to be seen. How to Drive a Vulva isn't all it's cracked up to be anyway, just some nervous lesbians saying stuff like "Talk to your partner" to a crowd too vast for the tent they've got. We get bored and move on. The afternoon's a bit of a drag. I am so peevish and abstracted that three times people approach me wanting to be high-fived and three times, assuming they've got their hands up for someone behind me, I leave them hanging and they go, "Awww, man!"

I return to the safety of the RV after several hours roving the playa. My father is MIA. I picture him on a gurney, succumbing to a bronchial attack. Maybe lost in a dust storm, pedaling out into the desert's lethal infinitude. Close to dinnertime, he returns, and in the manner of some nagging spouse, I commence to chew his ass. "Where the hell did you go?"

He shoots me a blank and rather guilty look. "James and I went to the Naked Tiki Bar," he says.

"You got naked?"

"I certainly did," he says. "It was a remarkably friendly place. And I actually found it very liberating to see these enormously fat women being perfectly willing to bare everything. It was fun to see all of that voluptuality. What did you discover?"

"We waited for you at How to Drive a Vulva, and then when you didn't turn up, I came back and waited for you here."

"I'm sorry."

"You ditched me."

"I didn't mean to. I'm really, really sorry."

My little nag sesh is mercifully cut short by a visit from an old friend of mine. He is a fellow known as Mur-Dog, an actor and voice-over man who has been coming to Burning Man for some number of years. He is a believer. My project of writing about it is, in the opinion of Mur-Dog, doomed. "You can't explain this experience in words," says Mur-Dog. "This is about getting outside yourself, giving up your fears, giving yourself over to the impermanence of everything. We've got so much of society in us: trying to impress people, worrying about what our friends think. Then here it's total freedom. Give up the fear. The fear of death, the fear of whatever's limiting you. Why *not* fuck that girl? Why *not* take your pants off and run around screaming? You come into this thinking it's gonna be this hippie rave party, but it goes so much deeper. It goes to the base of some deep human stuff. It's for everybody. I mean, I motorboated some huge-titted woman last night. It was so magical."

"You did what?" my father asks.

"When you put your face between a woman's breasts and go *brbb-brbb-brbb*."

"It really is a remarkably friendly place," says Dad.

"You will be transformed here," says Mur-Dog. "Ed, by Saturday you'll be wearing a dress. No, you'll be walking around buck naked with a sock over your dick."

"Actually, I was naked very recently at the Naked Tiki Bar. I enjoyed myself."

I acknowledge to Mur-Dog that while my father has more or less gone native, I have yet to surrender to the experience.

"All right," says Mur-Dog. "Tonight you're coming out with me. We're going dancing."

I inform Mur-Dog that in my late teens, after serially disgracing myself to the strains of "Groove Is in the Heart," for the good of all mankind I incinerated my dancing shoes.

"Fuck that," says Mur-Dog. "Tonight you're going to dance until your legs hurt, then you're gonna dance some more. We're gonna see the sun rise. You've gotta liberate yourself. Leave the notebook at home."

Very well. I resolve to accept the teachings of Mur-Dog. That evening, when the professors are readying themselves for bed, Cam and I rendezvous with Mur-Dog on the open playa. The playa at night is a vision unlike anything else in the known world, and it is impossible to describe without resorting to psychedelic clichés. It is like being in a malarial brain. It is like a synapse-level view of an acid trip. It is like a voyage through a violently bioluminescent deep-sea-scape designed by Peter Max and Wavy Gravy and ravers and dragons and gay Martians. The playa is a mile expanse of indigo blackness across which traverse such things as pirate ships, a car disguised as windup teeth, an octopus blasting huge jets of flame, a bunch of other unrecognizable things blasting even huger jets of flame. The soundtrack is screams and diesel engines and propane detonations and several hundred really good sound systems going full blast. Thousands of cyclists and pedestrians, beribboned in traceries of incandescent technology, float and course through the distance. Some people, to their own peril, have disdained to wear lights. These people are known in the local idiom as "darktards."

As per Mur-Dog's instructions, I left the notebook at home, so I'm reconstructing here, but this is what basically went down: Mur-Dog led us across the playa to something called Opulent Temple, which was a great arena of seething humanity where confusing music blared and green lasers gridded the sky and the ecstatic sweat of dancing underpant people glowed orange in intermittent blorps of propane flame. Mur-Dog wore a trucker hat and a red blazer and no shirt and a tie, and he danced like a madly romping puppet. I wore, I dunno, some bunny ears or some shit and tried to dance like some teenagers I saw, I think, in a TV ad for breath mints. Cam and I drank of Mur-Dog's champagne. We drank of his bourbon and apple juice. I was offered and accepted three different illicit substances—including a drug called molly that I'd never heard of before—and though I more or less swore off recreational drugs back in high school, in the interests of achieving immediacy (Principle No. 10) and psychological surrender I ingested them all.

The group's experience was mixed. A tribe of the nearly nude hauled Mur-Dog onto some scaffolding to dance with them. Cam wandered around, smiling and shrugging. I danced my breath-mint dance with a tiny Asian woman dressed as a butterfly, by which I mean I stepped on her several times. And how was my dope journey? It never left the driveway. Or if it did, it didn't carry me into transcendent mortal-fear-abandoning head spaces. It carried me into a head space whose inner monologue was this:

"Is there not something deeply embarrassing and sad about a man on the verge of forty doing a breath-mint dance, moving his unexcellent body to tuneless, lyricless, thudding music he finds both baffling and bad? If this music is not about robots fucking, then what in God's name *is* it about? Well, it seems to express a kind of high-tech erotic vehemence, which the crowd reflects via complex dance maneuvers that are sort of lonely in their virtuosic self-orientation. *'Oh, if only someone were as good a dancer as me, then I might have sex with that person, but it shall never be'* would be a fine subtitle for most of the dancers in the observable vicinity. And what does it mean when the beat breaks and, prefatory to an intensification of the pounding, the music goes silent save for this rising tone akin to the noise of a bottle being filled, and the flames spurt high, and everyone pumps their fists as though to say, *'Oh yes, oh yes, the bottle-filling noise has come again, this bottle-filling noise, a most profound and excellent thing with which I am very much of a piece'*? And now here is Mur-Dog, making a hoisty-hoisty pump-up-the-volume gesture at me with his palms, an exhortation to dance like no one's watching. Oh, but Mur-Dog, don't you see? If no one were watching, I would not dance at all."

At last, when the champagne was gone, we left. "Was that a rave?" Cam asked me.

"I think so, more or less," I said.

"I'd always wondered what one was."

Shortly after 4 A.M. we made it back to the RV, whose farting, snoring squalor was a comforting familiarity, a relief.

"So how'd it go last night?" James Dean asks in the morning.

I give him a synopsis. "Sounds as though you had your first middle-aged experience," he says.

"I did," I say. "It was sort of upsetting."

Professor Dean offers these words of condolence: "Get used to it."

By day three our filthiness is profound. There is no part of my body I cannot rub with my thumb to raise a gray cigar of silt. On the recommendation of James Dean, I proceed with my father and Cam to PolyParadise, an encampment of polyamorists whose gift to the community is something called the Human Carcass Wash. It is an open tent with a tarp floor, where perhaps fifty nudists have queued. Until now, if given the choice, I'd have preferred to have a hole of large diameter drilled in my foot rather than be naked among strangers. But I am trying here, friends, so there is nothing to be done but to remove one's clothes. I disrobe brusquely, a little angrily.

My hope is for a simple shower. This thing is not that. Before the wash begins, we are broken into little cadres to receive instruction from the (also naked) administrators of the Carcass Wash. A very genial blond man with an air of ecclesiastical gentility and a somehow angelic blond pubic bush delivers the disappointing news that we are not here merely to be scrubbed by polyamorists and sent on our way. We will first wash others, dozens of them, before we are washed ourselves. The washing of the carcasses will happen not with hose or sponge. We will mist bodies with spritz bottles and squeegee carcasses dry with cupped palms. It is a ritual, we are told, that has its roots in cultures other than our own, where, when a visitor arrives, his hosts will honor his body by stripping him nude and manually laving his sweaty creases. Which cultures? I think he said *Persian*. Really? And here I'd thought Tehran was more the sort of place where trying to loofah a stranger's taint would get you a scimitar in the neck. Is that how they kill people there? Let's puzzle this out. Pay no attention to the devastatingly lovely young woman next to you, whose flawless left gazonga is bulging a little bit against your right triceps. All thoughts on the ayatollah.

After the briefing, we are dispatched to the lavage gauntlet. So, you ask, did I touch the penises of other men for the first time in my life? I did. And did I also touch the vaginas and breasts and buttocks of women, and was that experience erotic? Well, sort of I did, and no, it was not, so scrupulous was I to be a good scrubber and not a lecherous busyfingers impersonating a good-faith body honorer. But did I not also lay hands on drastic cases of keratosis like burnt raisins sprouting from people's hides and weird patches of wiry hair and surgically crafted transgenitalia that haunt my imagination even still? Excuse me, but the Human Carcass Wash is a privileged space where people come to have their bodies honored, not to be judged in print by a sneaky media poisoner, so I will not answer that.

So, you ask, did I wash my father's body? And in light of his doctor's recent concerns, did I feel as though I were washing his living corpse and murmur lines from Ecclesiastes: *As he came forth from his mother's womb, naked shall he return to go as he came.* And did my father take my naked body into his arms? And was he teleported back to 1973, when he held for the first time a child he was not sure he was ready for or necessarily wanted? And, most importantly, did my father rinse my pecker? For some reason I was afraid of that. Not that my father would, as a going concern, want to rinse it. But I'm saying that if he found himself in a squad of strangers, all of whom were rinsing my pecker in a totally body-honoring Californian manner, my father is such a sweet guy that he might start to worry that he was being a bad dad by not getting in on the body honoring. Well, the answer to all of that is no. To sidestep that whole problem, I made sure I got into a different corral of nudists, and I didn't see my father until we got out the other side.

By the time I emerge from the gauntlet, my father is already clothed. He stands tentside in his Thai tunic and his legionnaire's cap with the trapezius snood, tucking into a rusty half-eaten apple he stowed in his backpack. And the gorgeous woman whose breast I drew nigh to, and whom I spent my entire HCW experience trying hard not to look at? My father is regarding her as a sixteenth-century pilgrim to the Vatican must have admired his first stained-glass window. Chomping and watching. Full-fed in body and soul.

"Botticelli-esque," he murmurs. "Remarkable how some of us have let ourselves go and others of us have taken very good care of our bodies."

"How was your carcass-wash experience?" I ask.

"I thought it was quite wonderful," he says in a faraway voice.

We step out into the boulevard, still damp. The wind blows up, and in an instant we are battered like fish sticks in alkaline dust.

On the north side of the playa, at a remote remove from the lasers and fire leapers and bare-flesh frolics and booths where you can receive a cookie after having your ass struck with a paddle, stands a structure known as the Temple. The Temple is a splendid simulacrum of a Siamese palace made of plywood laser-cut to lacework that would shame a doilymaker. Large enough to accommodate many dozens, it is a structure of such intricacy and beauty that I am glad I will not be here to see it incinerated on Sunday night, the evening after the Man burns.

At the Temple's gate, you're checked by a silence that seems to thicken the air and halt the wind. And inside, you see people asquat under the central spire with tears runneling the dust on their cheeks. You see a young woman lying in the lap of her friend, her spine bucking with the force of her sobs. You see a guy trying for some reason to snug a latex glove onto a piece of driftwood and to lay the gloved driftwood onto a shrine, which is one of perhaps thousands of little shrines—feathers, bandannas, booze bottles, Nalgene tankards, cheesy studio portraits, snapshots—lashed and propped and taped and stapled to the Temple's ornate walls.

Letters to dead parents: "Beautiful dreams, mummy and daddy."

"Goodbye, Dad, you are a great father. I love you."

"Fuck you dad, suicide . . . isn't [obscured]."

"Love you, dad." (This in a mini-coffin containing also a dildo and a photo of a man in a leather vest blowing someone and also, it looks like, being penetrated.)

Letters to dead infants.

Lots of letters to dead pets:

"To the world you were just a dog, but to us you were the world."

A general outpouring of emotion that would, in the default world, strike an East Coast media poisoner as cloying, sentimental, and precious. But here it affects you as you are sometimes affected upon entering a church, when an emo wad thickens in your throat, not because you believe, necessarily, in God but because it is forcefully heartbreaking to witness our strange species trying to reckon with its curse, its knowledge of death. You are in no way tempted to laugh at the hippie guy who is standing amid the crouched and huddled crowd, weeping and saying, "I'm here today because my cat died. He liked drinking rainwater, and he liked drinking tuna water. I miss my small, furry, gentle friend. I miss my pookie. What can I give to have him purr in my ear one more time?"

What happens is something weird, a new sensation coalescing this week in some not wholly conscious part of your brain. Perhaps it's an effect of being here with your elderly father, or your late-breaking awareness of your arrival at middle age, but you become abruptly, terrifiedly conscious of the terrible velocity of time, of life, a kindred sensation to the instant you sometimes experience during a commuter jet's descent, when your nervous system suddenly alerts itself to the preposterous number of MPHs at which the ground is hurtling up at you and you begin to twitch and shudder under a fusillade of thoughts like these:

"I do not do volunteer work. I am a poor carpenter. I give very little money to charity. My hair is thinning. I am a miserly Captain Bligh of an RV skipper, having forbidden the men from deucing, or even showering, in the RV out of fear of depleting the battery and water reserves. I am bad about returning e-mails. I love my father. My father is dying and will leave no worthy successor. My life is at least half over. Out of cowardice masquerading as prudence, I have sired no children and nourished no lifelong commitment to a member of the opposite sex. My dog's halitosis is noxious and incurable. The ivory-billed woodpecker is almost certainly extinct. Super-PACs are destroying American democracy. The Milky Way is whorling into a huge black hole. They eat dolphins in Japan. I'm getting muffin tops."

And in the shadow of this splendid monument to cut-rate sentiment, you go somewhat to bits. A mortifying brine gouts from your eyes and pools in your dust-retardant goggles.

It takes a moment to collect yourself, to prepare a face to rejoin your group over by the gate, where James Dean is saying, "I don't know what to make of all that. One minute we're dwelling on anal hygiene and sexual fetishes, and then there's this temple and this air of quiet spirituality. Where does religion come into all this?"

"I thought it was intense," says Cam, whose own eyes are damp (he tells me later) with remembrance of Sierra, his ex's hospice-patient dog.

"I don't know that it's religious," says my father, gazing contemplatively at the Temple's gold-lit steeple. "It's just amazing the lengths people go to, to be thought of as special. I never imagined that a crew of folks could build a temple as elegant as this, only to burn it down."

"I'm just trying to find the common theme, and the only common theme, I think, is that this could only happen in the United States," says Dean the Canadian. "Both in its excesses and its excellence. Some people look at America as a nation of vulgarity and excess, and others think it's the most creative country in the world. I think it's both. Who else would burn a sculpture that took a year to build? But Ed, you and I know you can't run an economy this way."

"I don't think it's about running an economy," says Cam. "It's about freedom. It's about celebrating creativity, the human spirit."

"Yes," says Dean. "But for most of us, we've channeled our creativity into purchasing excessive camping supplies at Walmart."

But Dean's diegesis is halted by a sudden explosion. A fleur-de-lis of fireworks erupts across the playa, where one can see the sperm car chasing a vagina barge.

Saturday night. Tonight the Man burns. A little after dusk, we make our way to the playa. The city, already, is beginning to decay, with spots of bare ground between camps. The festival's commandment to "leave no trace" is losing out to the selfish pragmatism of the default world. Several folks have left unpleasant traces in the form of water jugs topped up with dark amber tinkle.

Down, down across the playa, the hordes are gathering around the Man, who stands above a multistory plywood mansion shaped much like a drill chuck. We take our seats. I very quickly hand out a hundred or so of our camp's tiny flashlights. Even in this, I fall short. My manner is efficient, peremptory. "Would you like a tiny flashlight? Of course you would. They're extremely convenient."

When I return, Cam seems to be maybe making time with a hippie matron in a leopard-print halter and rainbow-glo ligatures about her neck and chest. Good man.

My father, somehow, appears to be in animated grinning rapport with a young woman in minuscule shorts, brassiere, and pierced tongue. "I'm nineteen," I think I hear her say.

Out before the Man, a gang of tribal majorettes brandish flaming batons. My father and his young friend take note, but it does not halt the flow of language between these two. What are they saying? Something naughty? Is my father—horrible! miraculous to imagine!—getting some sort of *angle* going here? I draw near to them. She is telling my father that she is interested in doing something to do with environmentalism. My father is getting the opposite of an angle going. He is saying, "Yeah, but I worry that all that environmental stuff is going to inhibit trade." She is saying that she would like to go to Africa someday. "I once calculated fertilizer subsidies in Malawi" is his reply.

This is why I love my father. Probably ninety-nine out of a hundred men in the vicinity would be trying to persuade this girl out into the dark of the evening with talk of "Baby, let's bump uglies.

Let me fly my freak flag with you." But of course that particular flag, the lecherous-septuagenarian-horndog flag, is not freaky at all. Much freakier, much more radically self-expressive, when you are down in the dust with some winsome young lady, is to ply her instead with talk of fertilizer subsidies and not take it there at all.

The fire dancers retreat. The drill-chuck-mansion pedestal goes up in a great pumping beefheart of flame. My father sits in a rain of cinders big as playing cards, more than sufficient to ignite the infant wisps of his remaining hair. Unconcerned, he gawps at the flames. The danger is unreal to him, or not as important as the splendid inferno before him. In childhood, I knew my father as a man to cringe at loud noises, to wince, cower, shield his precious carcass when you raised your fists to him, as I did at least once in my teenage years. That man is not this man, to whom the risk of minor incineration is worth an extra instant of beauty. The transformation dates, I think, to the cancer treatment. There is likely some best-selling wisdom here, à la *Everything I Need to Know I Learned from My Christ-Bitten Kindergartner.* If not a bankable bathroom title, the inferno begs at least some modest, affirming revelation. *Don't fear the reaper. Regret not the past. Stand in the flames. Hide not your genitalia. Naked boobs like to be photographed.*

But my mind, unfortunately, is dwelling not on life's precious evanescence but on the eight-hour traffic jam we've been told to expect in the postburn exodus. Instead of getting into a soul communion with my father, I am screaming at him, "Move! Move! Move!"

We speed back to the RV and beat the traffic handily.

"Well, I thought that was extraordinary," says my father. We are riding south through the Great Basin Desert in the small hours of the night. "A fine capstone to our adventures. I hope not, but perhaps."

He is returning to the real world, to thoughts of his faltering immune system, his racking cough, the sores in his mouth, the rings around his pupils.

As it turns out, these troubling symptoms are unlikely to kill him. The pupil halos turn out to be benign. His lung infection proves treatable. The doctor doubles his transfusions of immunoglobulin, and when I see him next, he's looking healthy and feeling fine. We ponder a trip next year to Myanmar.

And Cam. I almost forgot about Cam. Cam stayed at Burning

Man, still on the lookout for a new community, a desert sweetheart, a sense of clarity and closure to his curious year. On Sunday evening the Temple burned, and Cam had a good, exhausting cry over the decline and death of Sierra the dog. By the pulsing light of the embers, Cam met a lovely young woman, a "playa goddess," in his description. By gosh, he and the playa goddess hit it off, and by his own account he got to third base with her. One Californian wrinkle was that two other people were also getting to third or some other base with her at the time Cam stepped onto the field. But that was okay, that was cool. The only truly disappointing thing about the evening was that when the playa goddess started trying to get to third base with Cam, that project got derailed because Cam was wearing some high-concept outdoorsman's trousers that had no zipper access. Still, no regrets. He got more out of the week than he'd honestly expected. He's going back next year. He will be wearing different pants.

JERALD WALKER

How to Make a Slave

FROM *Southern Humanities Review*

GATHER SCISSORS, CONSTRUCTION paper, crayons, popsicle sticks, and glue. Take them to the den, where your thirteen-year-old sister sits at the table thumbing through your schoolbook on black history. Smile when she notices you and turns to the pre-marked page with a photo of Frederick Douglass. It's one from his later years, when his Afro was white. Realize you need cotton balls. Leave and return with them a moment later to see that your sister has already cut from the construction paper a circle that will serve as Douglass's head. Start gluing popsicle sticks together to make his body. As you work silently, your sister tells you basic facts about slavery and abolition that you will present to your class. You'll end the presentation by saying with passion that Frederick Douglass is your hero, which will not be true because you are only ten and the things you are learning about black history make it difficult to feel good about his life, and sometimes yours.

But feel good about the beating he gave his master. Your classmates feel good about it too. They cheer when you describe it, as they cheered seconds earlier when you recited Douglass's famous line: *You have seen how a man was made a slave; you shall see how a slave was made a man.* "I wouldn't have taken that stuff either," one of your classmates says after school. Forget his name in a few years but remember his skin was so dark that you and your friends had no choice but to call him Congo. Congo explains how he would have gouged out his master's eyes, and then other boys break their masters' legs and amputate their arms, and when someone curls his fingers into a claw and twists off his master's balls everyone cups his crotch in agony before laughing. Enjoy how wonderful it feels to laugh at that moment, and as you walk home, with Douglass staring somberly out of your back pocket, wish black history had some funny parts.

Find a funny part. One has been captured on an FBI wiretap of Martin Luther King, Jr., in which he's in a hotel having sex and at the right moment yells, "I'm fucking for God!" The funniness is not immediately apparent, though, because you are twenty-five now and King *is* your hero and the woman with whom he is performing God's work is not his wife. Wonder with indignation how he could do such a thing, but while smoking the second of three bongs come to terms with the complexity of humankind and the idea of moral subjectivism. Now it is clear that the important thing here is not the messenger but rather the message. It is also clear that the message bears repeating.

After you repeat it, your girlfriend looks confused. She opens her mouth as if to respond but all she does is stare up at you, not even blinking when a bead of sweat falls from your forehead onto hers. Try to explain that you are only quoting some black history but be overtaken by the giggles and conclude that this is a conversation for a different time, when you have not smoked three bongs and are not doing God's work. And maybe it is a conversation for a different person too, because this one is white and does not like to talk about race. She does not even *see* race, she has said, having taught herself to judge individuals solely by their character and deeds. She is postracial, the first postracial person you have ever known, but because the term has not yet been invented you just think she's stupid. And because you are the first person she has ever known who has taught himself to see race in everything, she thinks you are stupid too. In time, you both seek and find smarter companions.

Yours, like Frederick Douglass, is, to use a phrase from that earlier era, a mulatto. This appeals to you a great deal because you know mulattos give race a lot of thought, and so this girlfriend probably will not mind helping you see it in places you might have missed. And maybe she can understand it in ways you cannot, since her perspective was not shaped by a stereotypical ghetto experience, like yours, but by a stereotypical suburban experience, like the Fonz's.

"It wasn't quite like his," she says.

The schools she attended were excellent; her neighborhood

was safe; the parks and streets were pristine; racial diversity was negligible; the community had its own Fourth of July parade. As you remind her of these facts, sense her getting uptight, and diffuse her discomfort with a wide grin and a bad joke, something along the lines of her only run-in with the police being with an officer named Friendly.

She nearly smiles.

Give her two thumbs up at the hip and say, *"Aeyyyyyyy!"*

She does smile as she calls you a moron. "But seriously," she continues, and do not interrupt when she relates some of the challenges she faced as one of the few black kids in high school. You have been disappointed by how little she talks about race, to say nothing of her inability to see it everywhere, so her self-pity is a rare treat. Nod sympathetically when she broadens her grievances to include her family; the stares and snickers her parents faced in restaurants; how her brother was routinely followed by mall security; how her sister had trouble getting a date for the prom. Say that while these are excellent blemishes on her community, they are relatively benign. Some people, like you, for instance, lived in communities with drugs, gangs, crime, bad schools, police brutality, and the collective view that white people were and would always be racists. Let the conversation end as she concedes that, should you have children, her stereotype is preferable to yours.

Have children, two boys, two years apart, and decide that neither stereotype will do. The ghetto was never an option, but do not be thrilled about raising your sons to be Fonzies. Want a racially diverse, progressive, urban community, but instead move to one that is 96 percent white, conservative, and rural. It is in a college town near Boston where you and your wife land professorships, the primary appeal being that your house is only a block from campus. It is also, the realtor tells you, on the parade route. Buy four lawn chairs. Sit in one next to your wife and sons on the Fourth of July and wave American flags at the procession. Enjoy this. Your boys are happy.

Later that evening, wrestle with this question: How long will your boys be happy in a 96 percent white, conservative, rural town near Boston?

The answer for your older son, now five, is sixty-eight more days.

That is when you come home from teaching one afternoon and

your wife informs you that one of his classmates told him that people with his skin color are stinky. Your son reported this incident while crying, but that night he appears to be fine, based on your observations of him, conducted from his bedroom closet. For the twenty minutes you have been in there, he and his little brother have lain in their adjacent beds chatting about cartoon characters and imaginary friends and a new fire truck they wish to own. When they finally fall asleep you sneak out and report the good news to your wife, though you caution that more observations will be necessary. In the meantime, you say, that classmate of his should be disciplined. Curl your fingers into a claw and tell your wife you are twisting off his tiny, five-year-old balls.

"First of all," your wife responds, "the person who said it is a girl. Second, let's not make a big deal out of this. I've already told him that she was just being silly. I'm sure he's already forgotten the whole incident."

Dispute this. Tell her that kids remember these sorts of things, sometimes for decades. Tell her about Congo. Imagine Congo's father learning of his son's nickname and later that night hiding in his closet, watching to see if he cries.

A few weeks pass and your son has not cried again. Decrease but do not suspend the observations. Remain on edge, as there are many kids out there who at any moment could say something potentially harmful with long-term consequences.

This is exactly what happens. And this time the culprit is your older son's little brother. He recently started preschool and has noticed that his skin color more closely resembles the other kids' than his brother's, and that his brother's skin color more closely resembles yours than your wife's, and that your wife's skin color is closer in resemblance to his than to his grandmother's, and that his grandmother's skin color is exactly the same as that of the kids in preschool, except for the brown spots on her hands. He turns to his six-year-old brother and asks, "Why is skin different colors?"

A beat passes before your older son responds, "I don't know."

Wonder if this is the moment to have your first important discussion with your sons about race. You can do it by revisiting that "stinky" comment, for starters, and then by warning them of other insults they'll likely receive, though be sure to note that insults, relatively speaking, are not much compared to what they'll learn studying a history that is not very funny. Determine that yes, the time for this talk has come, and then watch it evaporate when your sons scream bloody murder as you emerge—perhaps too quickly—from their closet. Fail at your attempts to calm them before your wife hurries into their room and catches the full rush of their bodies. She sits with them on the bed as they wail through tears that you frightened them. Your wife gives you a look that foretells a coming drought of affection, and your boys give you looks that make you seriously wonder if you have the capacity to be a good father. Conclude that you probably do not, but decide to give yourself a fighting chance by ending your subjection to race. Tonight the boys will sleep with their mother, and you will sleep alone in their room, but tomorrow evening, while the boys are in the den playing with their new fire truck, find your wife. She will be sitting at the kitchen table grading papers. Scoop her a dish of mint ice cream. Lower yourself across from her. Stare into her eyes and say this: *You have seen how a man was made a slave; you shall see how a slave was made a man.* She will look confused. Explain.

PAUL WEST

On Being Introduced

FROM *The Yale Review*

ONCE THE PERSON introducing me bit his tongue so badly that blood poured over his necktie onto the index card on which he had inscribed my entire life. Another time one of the more combative younger poets introduced a colleague in terms so stark and acidulous the speaker seemed struck dumb: "If I were you," our host opined, "I'd go do something else, not listen to this genius's gibberish; he screws better than he writes." One day at the University of Tulsa, my introducer actually read aloud my entire curriculum vitae, taking up some thirty minutes, smitten at the outset by parroty echolalia and devastating nerves. Even as he spoke, on and on, I ran a 2B pencil through paragraphs of comparable length in my speech. Indeed, given time enough, we could have exchanged roles completely; the introduction would have supplanted the speech. I cannot think why someone has not attempted this—suddenly the audience twigs it that the introducer is the real draw after all and the ostensible speaker is a figment, a ghost who will slink away when no one is looking.

Stanley Elkin, never the master of the gentlest turn of phrase, used to proffer an introduction of such glistening eloquence, such magisterial authority, such daunting length that the speaker, humbled, only mumbled, aching to get off and away, not having been warned what he or she would have to follow. In the same neck of the woods, St. Louis, on the campus of Washington University, William H. Gass used to do a similar thing, reading an introduction even more resplendent than anything of Elkin's, achieving something between encyclopedia entry and red-hot book review, leaving you more or less to flounder (or shine) in the afterglow, but with one plus: he left behind him a cloud of menthol and eucalyptus from the big toffee on which he had sucked to clear his tubes. So even as you trotted up into that aroma and began, your sinuses behaved, and you excelled. Or choked by newly descended phlegm, you coughed on your finest phrases.

Gass, that formidable introducer, had (no doubt still has) another trick, however. Having studied temptation, he lays on something you cannot resist, a treat for having sung for your supper—in my case a huge iced chocolate cake, perhaps to keep me from speaking ever again, such was its sleek sweet softness.

You see how, as memory spins and serves things up, the worst evokes the best, calling in from the periphery of aversion the silliest goings-on, I have been introduced, in my time, as a former test pilot, a professional cricketer, and an expert on cheese. I have had the introducer who interrupts you halfway through to pose a question, the introducer who fell off his chair, having been driven to sleep by my speech, and the one who set me up as Paul Weiss. You never know what's coming, what's in the water, whether the reading light will work. Once at Binghamton University, mine host led me up several flights of steep stairs so that I arrived too breathless to speak, not that it mattered anyway; we entered a room wholly in darkness, with nonetheless a murmur of people at the front and who knew how many behind them. The power had failed. So had the mike, the lights. He nonetheless maneuvered me into a chair in what I recalled as a Bob Hoskins motion from *The Cotton Club* (in which movie he is always *positioning* people) and began his introduction without a pause, getting the facts right and even paying tribute in the dark to things I'd written. I was then supposed to get on with my reading: no flashlight, no academic flare. For a few moments I fudged in the dark, heard appreciative glottal sounds, and stopped dead. Then the lights came on in dazzling anticlimax.

I once saw the classical scholar Michael Grant introduce himself in Latin, having waited in vain for his host to show up, and what an urbane, concise job he made of it. Had it been me, I'd have spoken it in Greek—given Grant's linguistic mastery, of course. Carlos Fuentes, handed a minibottle of Tang or some such to slake his thirst, tried it before beginning and treated us all to an agonized rictus of the mouth that merged loathing and disgust with hauteur and warned us not to do anything else vulgar or he would stalk off back to the Mexican embassy. One speaker, who must remain nameless, arrived in a wheelchair and, perhaps made nervous by his introduction, wheeled himself gradually backward as he spoke, destined to cannon against the blackboard as the hour ended. Yet another speaker, introduced in a blaze of NASA light, clawed at her crotch the instant the lights went down for her slide show, and kept doing so whenever darkness descended, fired up by the occasion.

There is something artificial about the speaker confronting an audience, and there is something painful about the speaker, badly introduced, who with an aggrieved twitch wants to correct the introducer instead of giving the announced spiel. Once again, I think, it should be done, just to widen the experience of audiences, to develop their compassion for the focus of solitary palaver. When called upon myself to introduce someone I have not yet offended, I try to subordinate myself to the occasion, with often ghastly results, and that is how you get the various looks that say *This is about me, not you* or *Why do you have to be funny?* Some introducers, not I, like to read aloud something you have written, and that feels like dentistry, with all the stresses in the wrong place, the rhythm bumpy, some words mispronounced, some phrases omitted altogether in what seems a last-minute attempt at censorship. The best introducer I ever had was my French translator, who, having introduced, read a portion of my work in his own exquisite French; I then read the same text in English (this was in Paris) with a feeling of *English sounds so oafish in comparison.*

Have your glasses ever fallen off? Have you ever dropped your script? Or brought the wrong one? Or, as I on a couple of occasions have while mine host looked on aghast and unrequited, fallen into one of those dumbstruck spells of critical reverie in which you see a better way of saying what you have put in print? Have you revised, in total silence, on the hoof? Only the other night, under strong lights, with a text enlarged on the Xerox machine and powerful glasses to help, I just could not see what a certain word was and so made various stabs at it; some crystalline fleck in the paper was shining fit to beat the band and the Formica ridge that a bit of black rested on was creating an ambiguity all its own. *Impale* or *impala*? Come on, *you* wrote it, don't you know from memory?

No, I did not. But these hazards are not the introducer's fault, even though they mesmerize the audience with a glimpse of hit or miss. How many felicities owe their charm to a misreading, I wonder.

Who holds the record for the best apparition on the stage, right after the introducer finishes? In my book, Dame Edith Sitwell, who, before launching into *Façade,* tested her loud-hailer or megaphone (like the one the little dog used to listen to on HMV records). Looking like some bleached macaw, bird of semi-demi-paradise, she tooted into the mouthpiece her version of *Testing, testing,* and then let out a screech at the introducer, who had clearly offended in a thousand ways. I thought she was declaring war and was going to rip out his eyes, but she just as suddenly went back to business and made even weirder sounds into the orange cone she held to her mouth. Michael Rennie introducing Gort in *The Day the Earth Stood Still* would have had an easier task than whoever it was launching Dame Edith in front of the peasants of her own Derbyshire, there out of courtesy during a harvest gala.

I am thinking of designing a little card such as hotels often inflict upon you when you leave, asking you to pick certain evaluations. Would you rate your introducer as A., accurate; B., articulate; C., bumptious; D., slanderous; E., certifiable? Something like that. Would you like this person to introduce you again? No, I would like to write my own intro; but the very phrase—*being introduced*—has winning overtones of a foreign body invading the mucous membranes or of spies being parachuted into occupied countries. Amid all this bumbling, fumbling, faking and croaking, preening and posting, there is a heroic art form going to waste. Call it the oral overture, the informative preliminary, or barker's bite, it echoes the boxing announcer's blurry histrionic "Let's get ready to rumble!" and that ancient, little-honored literary form, the prologue, once a vogue, now an epitome of lost things in a revved-up world.

JAMES WOOD

Becoming Them

FROM *The New Yorker*

NIETZSCHE SAYS SOMEWHERE that the industrious, virtuous English ruined Sundays. I knew this at the age of twelve—that is, the Sunday part and the ruination part. When I was growing up, Sunday morning was all industry and virtue, a religious bustle: the dejected selection of formal clothes (tie, jacket, gray trousers); a quick pre-ecclesiastical breakfast; lace-up shoes handed to my father, master of the polishing arts (that oily Kiwi cake, glistening in its tin like food). Then the eternal boredom of church, with its ponderously enthusiastic adults. And, after that, Sunday lunch, as regimented as the Hapsburg Sunday lunches of brisket of beef and cherry dumplings that the Trotta family eats week after week in *The Radetzky March*. A joint of beef, or of lamb, or of pork, with gravy, roast potatoes, and a selection of fatally weakened vegetables (softened cauliflower, tattered Brussels sprouts, pale parsnips, all boiled punitively, as if to get the contagion out of them). It was the 1970s, in a small town in the north of England, but it could almost have been the 1870s. The only unusual element in this establishment was that my father cooked lunch. He cooked everything for our family, and always had; my mother was never interested in the kitchen, and gladly conceded that territory.

After lunch, tired and entitled—but sweetly, not triumphantly—my father sat in the sitting room and listened to classical music on the record player. He fell asleep gradually, not really intending to succumb. He wanted to be awake for one of his favorite composers, a narrow but rich cycle of Beethoven (piano sonatas and string quartets), Haydn (string quartets), and Schubert (lieder, especially "Die Winterreise"). These three masters were almost as unvarying as the rotation of Sunday beef, lamb, and pork. My brother and sister and I were all musical children, so we would be appealed to, as we crept toward the door. "Don't go quite yet—you'll miss the next one, 'Der Lindenbaum,' which Fischer-Dieskau does very well. He has the advantage over Peter Schreier." My father's musical discussion involved grading performances; though an intelligent auditor, he didn't play a musical instrument. So my memory of those Sunday afternoons is as much a memory of names as of music: "No one has really approached the young Barenboim, in those late sonatas, except Kempff. But of course Kempff is a completely different pianist. Solomon, whom I heard playing the last two sonatas in London, when I was still at school, was tremendously fast and powerful." Richter, Kempff, Schnabel, Barenboim, Brendel, Ogdon, Pollini, Gilels, Arrau, Michelangeli, Fischer-Dieskau, Schreier, Schwarzkopf, Sutherland, Lott, Vickers, Pears—all the precious names of childhood.

I thought of those Sundays when Dietrich Fischer-Dieskau died, some months ago. Some of the obituaries rightly suggested that he became a brand name for a kind of smooth, dependable quality. That is how he functioned in our household (which isn't to deny his beauty as a singer, or the validity of my father's admiration of him). I grew a bit suspicious of that rich emollience of tone, that tempered, bourgeois liquidity. Just as intolerantly, I grew restless with the way my father would look up from his armchair and calmly utter the double-barreled guarantee: "Fischer-Dieskau, of course . . . Marvelous." The name had the shape and solidity of some dependable manufacturer or department store, a firm that would never go bust. Aston Martin, Rolls-Royce, Harvey Nichols, Austin Reed, Royal Enfield. My father had great faith in reliable British companies, often against the evidence, it should be said. It was a joke in our family. Once, at dinner, a wall plug and socket exploded, with a mild, odorous flash. Imperturbable, my dad went to the wall and examined the plug, like the scientist he was. "M.K. and Crabtree," he said, intoning the names of the manufacturers. "Totally dependable." We all laughed at this stolid evenness of response, while perhaps gratefully aware that this was the kind of man you would want around in an actual crisis. Fischer-Dieskau, like M.K. and Crabtree, was totally dependable, though inconveniently German.

Boredom, headachey Sunday boredom: I blamed Christianity.

On those English Sundays, the knowledge that all the shops were religiously shut (even the little back-alley record shop where my best friend and I fingered the new LPs) simmered like a sullen summer heat and made me lethargic. There was nowhere to go, nothing to do. My brother was somehow more adept than I at slipping away to sin; he made it to his bedroom, and I would hear Robert Plant whining up there, the euphoric, demonic, eunuch antidote to Fischer-Dieskau's settled baritone. ("I should have quit you, long time ago.") My sister was too young to count as audience. My mother steered clear. So I would sit with my father, and sometimes when he fell asleep I would fall asleep too, in companionable torpor.

For ages I associated those three composers with that Sunday world. Haydn was killed for me. Even now I can't listen to him, despite the adulatory testimony of several musicians and composers I know. For quite a long time I thought of Schubert only as the composer of snowy, trudging lieder. I refused to hear the limpid beauty of the songs, or the dark anguish; I knew nothing about the piano sonatas, now among my favorite pieces. Most terribly, I thought of Beethoven as the calm confectioner of the *Moonlight* Sonata; I heard the beauty, but not much more. It was music to go to sleep to. An idiotic assessment, of course. All the tension and dissonance, the jumpy rhythms, the fantastic experimental fugues and variations, the chromatic storms, the blessed plateaus (the sunlit achievement, once you have got through the storms, as at the end of Opus 109 and Opus 111)—in short, all the fierce complex modernity of Beethoven was lost to me.

And then Beethoven came back, as probably my father knew he would, in my early twenties, at a time of solitude and anxiety—came roaring back with the difficult romanticism that my incuriosity had repressed in childhood. I can't now imagine life without Beethoven, can't imagine not listening to and thinking about Beethoven (being spoken to by him, and speaking with him). And, like my father, I have quite a few recordings of the piano sonatas, especially the last three, and I listen to the young Barenboim playing, and think to myself, as my father did, Not quite as lucid as Kempff, but much better than Gould, who's unreliable on Beethoven, and perhaps more interesting than Brendel, and, yes, I think I just heard him make a little mistake, which Pollini certainly never does . . .

Sometimes I catch myself and think, self-consciously, You are now listening to a Beethoven string quartet, just as your father did. And at that moment I feel a mixture of satisfaction and rebellion. Rebellion, for all the obvious reasons. Satisfaction, because it is natural to resemble one's parents, and there is a resigned pleasure to be had from the realization. I like that my voice is exactly the same pitch as my father's, and can be mistaken for it. But then I hear myself speaking to my children just as he spoke to me, in exactly the same tone and with the same fatherly melody, and I am dismayed by the plagiarism of inheritance. How unoriginal can one be? I sneeze the way he does, with a slightly theatrical whooshing sound. I say "Yes, yes" just as he does, calmly. The other day I saw that I have the same calves, with the shiny, unlit pallor I found ugly when I was a boy, and with those oddly hairless patches at the back (blame for which my father unscientifically placed on trouser cloth rubbing against the skin). Sometimes, when I am sitting doing nothing, I have the eerie sense that my mouth and eyes are set just like his. Like him, I am irritatingly phlegmatic at times of crisis. There must be a few differences: I won't decide to become a priest in my fifties, as he did. I'm not religious, and don't go to church, as he does, so my Sundays are much less dull than those of my childhood (and the shops are all open now, a liberty that brings its own universal boredom). I'm no scientist (he was a zoologist). I am less decent, less ascetic, far more materialistic (*pagan* would be my self-reassuring euphemism). And I'm sure he's never Googled himself.

This summer I happened to reread a beautiful piece of writing by Lydia Davis, called "How Shall I Mourn Them?" It is barely two and a half pages long, and is just a list of questions:

> Shall I keep a tidy house, like L.?
> Shall I develop an unsanitary habit, like K.?
> Shall I sway from side to side a little as I walk, like C.?
> Shall I write letters to the editor, like R.?
> Shall I retire to my room often during the day, like R.?
> Shall I live alone in a large house, like B.?
> Shall I treat my husband coldly, like K.?
> Shall I give piano lessons, like M.?
> Shall I leave the butter out all day to soften, like C.?

When I first read this story (or whatever you want to call it), a few years ago, I understood it to be about mourning departed parents, partly because a certain amount of Davis's recent work has appeared to touch obliquely on the death of her parents. I think that the initials could belong to the author's friends—seen, over the years, falling into the habits of grief. It is a gentle comedy of Davis's that those habits of grief are so ordinary (piano lessons, leaving out the butter) that they amount to the habits of life, and that therefore the answer to the title's question must be "I can't *choose* how to mourn them, as your verb, *shall,* suggests. I can mourn them only haplessly, accidentally, by surviving them. So I shall mourn them just by living." But I spoke recently to a friend about this story, and she thought that I had missed something. "Isn't it also about *becoming* one's parents, about taking on their very habits and tics after they disappear? So it's also about preserving those habits once they've disappeared, whether you want to or not." My friend told me that before her mother died she had had very little interest in gardening (one of her mother's passions); after her mother's death, she began to garden, and it now brings her real happiness.

If you are mourning your parents by becoming them, then presumably you can mourn them before they are dead: certainly I have spent my thirties and forties journeying through a long realization that I am decisively my parents' child, that I am destined to share many of their gestures and habits, and that this slow process of becoming them, or becoming more like them, is, like the Roman *ave atque vale,* both an address and a farewell.

My parents are still alive, in their mid-eighties now. But in the past two years my wife has watched both her parents die—her father quickly, of esophageal cancer, and her mother more slowly, from the effects of dementia. She bore one kind of grief for her father, and she bore a slightly different grief for her mother, for an absence that was the anticipation of loss, followed finally by the completion of that loss—grief in stages, terraced grief. I say to her, "I haven't yet had to go through any of what you've gone through." And she replies, "But you will, you know that, and it won't be so long."

My parents know much better than I do that *it won't be so long;* that their life together is precarious, and balances on the little plinth of their fading health. There is nothing unique in this prospect: it's just their age, and mine. Twice this year my father has been hospitalized. When he disappears like that, my mother struggles to survive, because she has macular degeneration and can't see. The second time I raced over to damp Scotland, to find her almost confined to the dining room, where there is a strong (and pungently ugly) electric fire, and living essentially on cereal; the carpet under the dining table was littered with oats, like the floor of a hamster's cage. When my father returned home, he had a cane for the first time in his robust life, and seemed much weaker. My brother took him around the supermarket in a wheelchair.

I spent a week at my parents' home, helping out, and it took a couple of days for me to register that something was missing. It nagged at me, faintly, and then more strongly, and finally I realized that there was no music in the house. In fact, it occurred to me, there had been no music during several previous visits I'd made. I asked my father why he was no longer listening to music, and was shocked to discover that his CD player had been broken for more than a year, and that he had put off replacing it because a new one seemed expensive. He was much less perturbed than I was by this state of affairs. I could hardly imagine my parents' life without thinking of him sitting in an armchair, while Haydn or Beethoven or Schubert played. But of course this idea of him is an old memory of mine, and thus a picture of a younger man's habits—he is the middle-aged father of my childhood, not the rather different old man whom I don't see often enough because I live three thousand miles away, a man who doesn't care too much whether he listens to music or not. So even as I become him, he becomes someone else.

Most likely he is simply too busy looking after my mother to have time to relax. He is the cook, the driver, the shopper, the banker, the person who uses the computer, who gets wood or coal for the fire, who mends things when they break, who puts the cat out, and who locks up at night. Perhaps he is too busy being anxious about my mother, being slightly afraid for both of them, to sit as he used to, triumphant and calm and secure.

Or perhaps this is just my fear projected onto him. When I was a teenager, I used to think that Philip Larkin's line about how life is first boredom, then fear, was right about boredom (those Sundays) and wrong about fear. What's so fearful about life? Now, at forty-seven, I think it should be the other way around: life is first fear, then boredom (as perhaps the fearful Larkin of "Aubade" knew). Fear for oneself, fear for those one loves. I sleep very poorly these days; I lie awake, full of apprehensions. All kinds of them, starting with the small stuff and rising. How absurd that I should be paid to write book reviews! How long is *that* likely to last? And what's the point of the bloody things? Why on earth would the money *not* run out? Will I be alive in five years? Isn't some kind of mortal disease likely? How will I cope with death and loss—with the death of my parents, or, worse, and unimaginably, of my wife or children? How appalling to lose one's mind, as my mother-in-law did! Or to lose all mobility but not one's mind and become a prisoner, like the late Tony Judt. If I faced such a diagnosis, would I have the courage to kill myself? Does my father have pancreatic cancer? And on and on.

There is nothing very particular about these anxieties. They're banal, even a little comic, as the mother in Per Petterson's novel *I Curse the River of Time* understands when some bad medical news is delivered. She had lain awake, night after night, worried about dying of lung cancer: "And then I get cancer of the stomach. What a waste of time!" It's just the river of time, and a waste of time. But there it is. And sometimes I murmur to myself, repetitively, partly to calm myself down, "How shall I mourn them?" How indeed? For it sounds like the title of a beautiful song, a German lament, something my father might have listened to on a Sunday afternoon, when he still did.

BARON WORMSER

Legend: Willem de Kooning

FROM *Grist*

A YOUNG MAN decides to stow away. He could scrape together the money and buy a ticket. Many people have done that so they could go to America, people much poorer than he. They sold whatever they had—a donkey, a table, a necklace. They borrowed. They stole. He is improvident, however, an instinctive romantic. He detests the very notion of saving. Or he feels that there is nothing to save. There is endless movement; light and air cannot be saved. He understands the word *ontology*. In his quiet way he revels in metaphysics, but he doesn't care about definitions. He cares about paint, though not as a fine artist. He makes signs and paints houses. Paint cares for the world. Paint is practical.

Like everyone, he has notions about America. Largely they stem from the movies. America is the land of fantasy, of Chaplin and Keaton. He likes the humor, the drollery, the commerce between the possible and the impossible, the grimace of longing. Even from afar he understands the loneliness of the place, all those little human molecules bouncing off one another as they pursue the chimera of happiness. Yet the absence of any overarching goal reassures him. Europe is the home of kings and their great, grinding purposes. Chaplin and Keaton have no purposes. The beauty they make is contingent on the mere fact of their being human, their walking down a street, looking in a window, eyeing a woman, tipping a battered hat, waving a cane. They have no apologies to make. Their vulnerability goes without saying; lacking as Americans do an aristocracy, their pretensions have no pretense. Despite the many stories he has read as a child about Indians and buffalo hunters and pioneers, the bravery of Americans does not impress him. They could not help themselves in that regard; the vastness of the continent demanded tenacity. It is their innocence that impresses him, their smiling blindness, their offhand candor. He sees all that on the screen while he sits in the stale dark and chuckles and roars. Chaplin fiddles with his tie; Keaton stretches his mouth until it is a sort of prairie. He, the viewer, can laugh until he cries; he understands what genius is.

Where he wants to go isn't the width and breadth of America, all those strangely named states he barely can remember; it's the former Dutch enclave of New York City. Among the advertisements and crowds, he can be who he wants to be. He can't define what that will be, but he can say what he doesn't want to be. He doesn't want to be another bourgeois. He doesn't want to pretend to be more solid than he is. He doesn't want to surrender his life to history. There is the feeling in Rotterdam of trying to hold on to something that has died already. That is what makes his mother violent and his father distant. They are trying to live, but they have no room to breathe. So they try harder and breathe less. They barely exist, but they keep trying.

If he can see no further than the next New York City block, that is fine. The last thing he wants to do is wander and look. He does that inside of himself enough already. Amateur painters make a fetish of looking so intently at this flower and that tree. They don't understand how greedy the eyes are; how they subdue the hand, how they enforce imitation. See: it is a command more than a question. It insinuates authority: see what I see, see what society sees, see what you are told to see. He prefers the question.

The modest amount of space infested by gargantuan buildings that distinguishes New York City pleases him. For him it is best that the rest of the nation remain in novels and histories. Like too much turp in the paint being elsewhere would thin out the feeling. When he sits in a movie theater in Rotterdam and sees the cowboys galloping across the plains, he senses that that may be one of America's dilemmas—the distances are bound to mock any feeling. The hero is always looking into the distance beyond the woman who stands there pleading. When he tells his friends about his plans, they laugh and ask, "Ter Texas?" "Neen Texas," he replies.

Like everyone in his nation, he has lived his life not far from the sea. Though he loves the sea, when he thinks of the painting he loves it is an interior or a portrait. When a painter renders the sea by itself, there is the difficulty of what is faceless and the difficulty of where to begin. To frame the sea is a joke. The horizon appalls. The depths are unthinkable, the surface ungraspable. Faced with this chthonic indifference, the painter offers his puny industry.

There were ways, of course, to win the game. When Vermeer painted his *View of Delft,* the sea—still as a blanket on a bed—capitulated, yet what was gained? Vermeer's homage was an act of exquisite revenge—enormity economized. There was no conceit in that painting (Vermeer was far beyond that), but the scale of the human—those figures that must be in the foreground pointing at this or expostulating about that—was so modest as to be laughable. Perhaps that was Vermeer's wisdom. The Netherlands was a nation of bustling havens. A viewer might think those painted people could walk on that water behind them.

The ships on the sea are toys. The sailors on the ships are less than toys. A stowaway is less than a sailor, yet a stowaway must emulate the sea's silence. When he tramps around Rotterdam in pursuit of nothing special, he practices that silence. It isn't hard. Though he is gregarious enough, he has cultivated silence. It is the margin of his dignity. And paint is inarticulate. No one expects a painter to say much.

He wants to imagine himself into the world. but it is hard. He doesn't have much to go by—poverty, lovelessness, anger, the callous maxims of realism. Those days and nights can turn a boy who is becoming a man into one more human projectile. To land as any projectile must land is to be impaled by more of the same, to live in another tiny room and smell the cabbage being fried and the raised voices. He has heard more arguments than there are stars in the heavens. He has been in his share of them. He has shut his eyes and raised his own voice. He has shaken his fists. Yet even as he did it, he felt there must be more to being human than this.

Imagination is an imperative and a siren too. The ships in the harbor are not much to look at—floating beasts of burden—but they offer escape. First a person has to escape before anything can happen. He has prospects enough in his homeland. He can make furniture. He can draw. He can design. He can paint anything.

None of that adds up to imagination, however. It adds up to one week paying another. It adds up to the beggared love of begetting a child on some young woman desperate with desire. Or she may not even be desperate. She may be calculating. He has heard plenty of those stories. He wants women all the time, but he is wary. Women have their own imaginations. They can turn men into pawns. Imagination must not be naive.

How many days has he stood by the sea and stared, as if waiting for an answer? How many days has he gone to Amsterdam to the Rijksmuseum and stared, as if the paintings could speak to him? They do, of course. That is what great paintings do. They tell him of the impossibility of perfection, the semblance of it and the goad of it, the wanting. They tell him of darkness—so many of the paintings are obscured by shadows and night and a background that dissolves into black vapor. He sketches, the way countless acolytes sketch. He does not feel compromised by those who came before him. The past doesn't frighten or belittle him. If he is experiencing the past as he stands there, then it isn't the past. When one day he tells this to his mother, she says he is conceited. He knows better, though. If the paintings stank of the past, they wouldn't be on the museum walls. They would be in oblivion, where most of the past resided, the detritus of moments and hours and days. Painting and drawing offer a release from that. They are a practical heaven.

On the ship to America there is no time for drawing. At first he hides behind some cargo boxes and then when the ship is at sea he emerges. The sailors laugh, spit at the floor, and tell him they will put him to work. It isn't a luxury cruise; an extra hand is always welcome in the boiler room. None of the higher-ups has to be informed. "Nothing worse than a snitch," an old sailor observes to the nods of the other men. Whether he has paid for his berth or hasn't makes no difference to their pay. If he helps them, he makes their work easier. If he looks down out of awkwardness and shyness when they make jokes about him, that makes their jokes all the better. If he thanks them for whatever leftovers they bring him from the dining table, that is something out of the ordinary—someone thanking someone for something.

Late at night he is able to get above deck. He feels excited yet sad. What has his life been thus far? If he threw himself overboard, who would mourn him? And the thought of how the sea would devour him frightens him. Still, he lingers for those minutes when he knows the watchman is elsewhere. He tries to stand back from himself and see himself the way someone else might see him, there at the ship's rail. Not much comes of it: the only thought that visits him is his wishing he were taller. It is laughable, but that is what he thinks. When he hears steps, he retreats. No one hails him. If he doesn't officially exist, he is not there.

If a romantic knows that he is a romantic, is he still a romantic?

He has brought nothing with him. Though long planned, his departure has been sudden. Now a friend of his tells him and that is that. On the ship one sailor gives him an old shirt; another gives him a change of underwear. He becomes a mascot to the men in the boiler room. They know this is only a passage. They will never see him again. He understands that too. This is how life works, he thinks. I have nothing and that is good. He wants to make things, but he wants to hold on to nothing. Or he doesn't want the making to ever finish.

The boat docks; the stowaway slips off, averting his face from any faces that might chance to look at him. A few sailors hoot and try to call attention to him. He walks faster down the gangplank. He sets foot in the New World. He exhales. There is nothing to constrain him. That is ignorance but also truth. His shirt and underwear are in a paper bag.

He is right about New York. It is his proper home. It is careless in ways Rotterdam never could be careless. Everyone seems to know where they are headed. Everyone is in a rush but everyone is heedless too, busy thinking the next thought, living the next moment, ahead of themselves, in pursuit. He can feel that. He doesn't have to think it; he can feel it on a street corner while he waits for a traffic light to change. If he stands still for too long, people assume something is wrong with him. No one says anything, but they eye him. He must be a foreigner. The eyeing lasts only for a moment. Then they are off to wherever they are going.

New Yorkers need signs to tell them what to do and see and buy. He is good at making those signs, at making displays too for store windows. He is an artisan, though that is not an American word. His bosses appreciate the quality of his work, though some want him to work faster. "Cut corners" is one of the first phrases he learns. "We need to cut some corners, Bill." He feels not just the hopelessness of trying to adapt to a different rhythm of work but also the hopelessness of idioms. Still, he tries. Will do. Roger. Got you. The phrases spin through his head. People like it when he uses them. They smile. He smiles back. It is a little demeaning, but only a little. He knows that enthusiasm is important. He can be enthusiastic. He can reassure. Got you.

His melancholy would sing to him, but it is hard to hear that voice in the hubbub of the city. That is, as they say, okay. He must be resolute. Yet what he feels inside himself is not so resolute. It is not doubt but longing, not only for a woman—women are attracted to him—but for a life's work. He believes his hands will lead him there. Sometimes when he is washing his hands, after work or when he rises, he pauses and examines them. They are not beautiful but they are perfectly strong. He trusts them. Who else to trust? They are part of the body's persevering sanity, millennia of adaptation. One reason he loves to paint is because he loves to grip the brush. That sensation gets overlooked, but never by him. Before the painting there is this blessed gripping.

Because of the new language he is a child again. His accent is amusing—his *th* tends to be a *t, think* is *tink*—but he is definitely not a child. He could allow himself the resentment of humiliation but refuses. To quarrel with good humor is foolish, and the Americans he meets at work are good-humored. Working people are working people the world over. They know what the hour hand is, what a cup of coffee is, and what a boss is. And he delights in their vocabulary. One day someone says, "Hot diggity dog." The phrase throws him into a paroxysm of confused delight. He doesn't understand it, but he intuits the excitement. It is a ridiculous yet sensible superlative. A few days later he says the phrase. His workmates laugh. They get him.

When he buys a new suit to wear on Sunday outings, he feels as though he is being reborn. He goes to have dinner with a friend he has made at work and the man's family—a wife and two children. They all sit around a table and eat meat and potatoes and talk about nothing special—other people, movie stars, athletic events. Again he realizes this is part of his passage, but he is on dry land now. He is moving forward. He is one among many. At home he felt too close to zero. However overwhelming the American numbers are, the fact of one remains staunch. When he returns to his tiny room, he pauses and admires himself in the cracked mirror on the back of a door. He runs his hands over the jacket. He looks trim. He looks sharp. He can allow himself to smile.

He doesn't worry. He has money. He meets a woman who is good for him. Whether he is good for her never enters his head. He isn't like that. He explains to her that life is like a teeter-totter: the two people are together on it, but one is up and one is down. Both can't be up at the same time. She smiles at him and shakes her head. He is charming; it is a rare woman who does not want to be charmed. He knows that but is not conceited. He is too intent on whatever is in front of him to be conceited.

What is the new nation telling him? What art is possible here? Everything must be useful here—that is the work of the nation—and he agrees but only up to a point. After he has taken the time to commend the cars and record players and elevators, he understands that that is not all there is for him. He must go past that point. Such going can make a person doubt himself. He doesn't come from the privileged classes. No one has handed him fine art on a plate and welcomed him to partake. He has studied at an academy back home, but that was more like the nineteenth century, the assured century, the century before the frame was shattered. In America to speak about art to any casual acquaintance is to invite a large pause in the conversation.

Gradually he does meet people who want to talk about art and who practice it. They often are displaced people too. "Washed up here," one of them puts it, as if he and others were flotsam and jetsam, what the sailors threw overboard on the ship from Rotterdam. He wants to laugh at that but recognizes the truth. To imagine that other people, the people milling around him on any midtown Manhattan street corner, would be interested in what displaced people do is hard to believe. That, however, is no reason not to start painting and talking with others who paint. He needs to do that. He must do that. The desire is like a fire in his gut. It is stronger even than sex.

These painters believe in modern times but not as something that can be made, advertised, and sold. They believe in modern times as a metaphysical enterprise, a challenge. New times demand new ways of seeing and acting. The challenges are daunting, though. How does one invent a tradition? Tradition is something that is handed down and agreed upon. It isn't individual. And where does one find the authority to move ahead? To be obsessed is fine in its way. He can bear being poor. He can bear going hungry. That is how he grew up. He has fled Europe, but he never would flee from himself. There must be, though, more than obsession. Obsession can limit as much as it can enrich.

The talk among the displaced painters is vivid and affirming. They face the same difficulties; revere the same contemporaries, even if sometimes it feels that everything is contained in the protean name Picasso. Over and over again they come to his door and stand amazed. They also go to the museum on Fifth Avenue and look at the tradition. Other people wander by the paintings talking of where they will eat lunch or shop, but the painters stand for long minutes and observe an Ingres or Chardin. They are not interested in likenesses. They are extracting essences, critiquing forms and geometries and lines and proportions and edges and centers and compositions and brushstrokes and paint and shadows and volumes and foregrounds and backgrounds and space. And that is only a fraction of it. What goes into the making is bottomless. In its way, that is reassuring. They are like swimmers launched upon a vast lake. Reaching the other shore may be a delusion, but that is all right. They belong there with the paintings in the museums. However obscurely, they feel that someday their own paintings may hang there. It is absurd—just look at their clothes and listen to their speech—but it is not absurd. America is an unsettled place where anything can happen. Like Picasso, it must continually reinvent itself. When the painters walk outside of the museum and stand in the late-afternoon light on the great steps leading down to the street, they breathe deeply. The exhaust being spewed from cars, buses, and buildings is good. There is more life here than they ever can get down on canvas. That too is reassuring.

His own painting is wan. It is easy to say that the grays and rusts are part of the shabby, hopeless era, the lines of identical-seeming men looking for work or waiting patiently for a bowl of soup, but it is his soul that is gray and rusty. He labors at each painting but destroys most of what he does. He has guiding notions in his head—the masters are alive for him—but the gap between his head and the canvas seems unbridgeable. It would be easy for him not to trust himself. That happens sometimes. He bulls ahead, hoping that the hard work which he adores and to which he is inured will save him. It doesn't. What is left are painterly ashes.

Other painters who see his work don't feel that way. They realize something exquisite is present. They realize that there is more sensitivity than anyone might know what to do with. The painters talk with him, but however invigorating the talk is, it remains talk. The essential thing is to figure out how to be modern in ways that are convincing and individual and profound. The painters and he don't say that exactly, but they feel it and they know it is in part silly. No one anymore could be Michelangelo. There is no pedestal of spirit to stand on. At best they can be grandly assertive in the way Picasso is grandly assertive. That is not all Picasso is, but that is part of it—the willingness to engage everything through the medium of painting. When they see his *Guernica* they weep inside. The power and the broken glory of it are irrefutable. That is what they tell one another art should be—irrefutable. Yet the world they live in practices its refutations daily. All he has to do is open the window of his studio and listen to the automobile horns. He doesn't despise the horns, but their tidings are empty ones.

He whistles while he works. He is full of good cheer despite what the paintings look like. He is like a harlequin, always wearing two or more colors. His inner weather is the mist and cold that come off the North Sea. His inner weather is joy in the physical facts of existence. He would not change anything and has, accordingly, little interest in the leftism of his friends. Progress seems foolish to him. The issue is to appreciate what has happened already and what is here now. Looking ahead is a bromide, what the purposeful will tells the anarchic soul. His whistling is habit, but it is feeling too. He likes Stravinsky and jazz and folk tunes. He owns an impressive record player good for the parties he and his wife give occasionally. Everyone dances at these parties. Full of fun, he dances too.

It is not just painting he faces. It is the task of the painting, how it seeks to maintain its history, how it must be fresh yet not at all, as they say in America, born yesterday. History's shadow is a welcome one to him, though that makes him, to use the strange word of Americans, un-American. As an immigrant he is nervous about that. Other artists make pronouncements, but he is inclined to speak in riddles, axioms, and parables. Part of that is uncertainty; part of that is humility; part of that is covert ambition, and part of that is how he sees the world. Each day he is busy with his brushes defining the indefinable. No wonder he paints over endlessly, changes what is before him endlessly, and then discards most of what he creates. He wants the painting to come alive and be still at the same time. He wants to make his own miracles. Is that too much to ask?

He sits in restaurants and eats good meals and indifferent ones. He goes to cafeterias late at night and over a cup of strong coffee talks more. Sometimes he goes into a bar where other painters go and has a drink or two. People brag, people gossip, people complain. What he prefers above all is to walk the narrow downtown streets alone. If someone he knows recognizes him, they exchange greetings, but he doesn't linger to talk. He is possessed by a quiet torment. It can't be any other way. He is the one who fell out of the cradle long ago. There is no crawling back in, no telling himself that he is someone else. He is doomed to return to the painting at hand.

He loathes his own melodrama. Walking the streets in the quiet, after midnight hours, he whistles in the dark.

He succeeds. Like a slot machine, the three matching images come up at the same time: critical acclaim, museums and patrons who want to buy his paintings, and the work itself. He becomes someone whose name is known to people who are strangers to him. He has worked hard all his life to hold on to himself. At times this has made him seem selfish and cold. Now he has lost his hold. Strangers come up to him and start talking. Women lie down for him. Acquaintances act as though they are ancient friends. Friends look warily at him. He has been identified, yet the whole gist of his painting is not to be identified with any one particular, to keep moving, searching, pursuing and resisting identity. Identity means that you are more *was* than *is*. To combat that, you must prove yourself continually. It is wearying. You are supposed to be perpetually excited about who you are. But you aren't that person.

That person is someone like the artist he calls Andy Asshole. Andy is unexcited about himself, which translates into ironic excitement, the excitement of anti-excitement. Andy adores identity. Andy's work mocks any notions of inwardness. Everyone is a product. Externals are externals. There is nothing below or beneath or within. By accepting and glorifying the beast of commerce, Andy has tamed it. He has given the world a canny, heaping portion of nothingness. The efforts of a painter trying to get some strokes and forms to come to magical life might as well be going on millennia ago. The modernist Willem de Kooning might as well be a cave painter.

One thing replaces another in America, even if the thing is a person.

He drinks for days on end. He wanders the streets of lower Manhattan and hangs out with derelicts. He looks like a derelict himself. He starts fights. He collapses on sidewalks. He knows he is playing out a grisly notion of the romantic artist. He knows the truth of his squalor, however, in ways few people know. How could they? They believe that achievements make a person secure and important. They don't understand that there are no achievements. There is only the restlessness of the work, of trying to get the impossible right. They aren't haunted. The purpose of the country he has made his homeland is to allow people to live lives that are not haunted. The oblivion of alcohol recommends itself all the more.

What saves him is the sea. It is, after all, the same vast sea that took him to America, the sea that awed, frightened, and consoled him. Now he can gaze at it to his heart's content. It wants nothing from him. The consolations of nature are part of what lie at the center of painting—the dynamic between resisting and accepting those consolations. Painting is so human, so fraught with indecision, so laden with time. The sea offers its eternal terms. The sea teaches humility. If he must be someone who answers to recognition, he must be able to bow his head before all that dwarfs recognition.

He bicycles. He goes for walks. He makes paintings. He has rid himself of the excitement machine. If people want to see him as serene or wise or masterful, that is their business. He would like to say that he likes the world less, but he is an honest man who would never say that. He still feels a definite enchantment in the morning's light, in the colors on his palette and outside his window. He still feels the power in moving his brush. He still marvels at his hands and the tactile wonder of paint. There did not have to be paint, he likes to say to his assistants. Considering that he is a famous person, he seems to those assistants almost childlike.

"He's the painter," he overhears someone say one day in the local post office.

"Imagine that," another person says.

Contributors' Notes

Notable Essays of 2013

Contributors' Notes

TIMOTHY AUBRY is an English professor at Baruch College, CUNY. He is the author of *Reading as Therapy: What Contemporary Fiction Does for Middle-Class Americans* (2011). His essays have appeared in *n+1*, the *Point, Paper Monument,* and the *Millions.*

WENDY BRENNER is the author of two short story collections, *Phone Calls from the Dead* and *Large Animals in Everyday Life,* which won the Flannery O'Connor Award for Short Fiction. She is currently completing a book of essays, *Misfits.* Her work has appeared in *Travel + Leisure, Allure, Seventeen, Mississippi Review, New England Review,* and *Ploughshares,* among other magazines, and has been anthologized in *Best American Magazine Writing* and *New Stories from the South.* She is the recipient of a National Endowment for the Arts fellowship and is a contributing editor for *Oxford American.* She teaches creative writing in the MFA program at University of North Carolina Wilmington.

JOHN H. CULVER continues to ride a three-legged horse while moving from academic to creative nonfiction and fiction writing. He taught political science at Missouri State University, Fort Lewis College, and then for twenty-eight years at Cal Poly, in San Luis Obispo, California. His publications include four coauthored texts on California politics, American politics, and state judicial politics along with many chapters and articles in scholarly books and journals. After California voters elected Arnold Schwarzenegger as governor in 2002, Culver retired to Durango, Colorado, on the assumption that the state would be better off without one of them. He enjoys outdoor pursuits and spending time doing volunteer work in activities that have a progressive focus. He subscribes to the philosophy that life as a retiree is positive if you don't take everything seriously, can get up after a fall without help, read, and keep trying to figure out what it all means.

KRISTIN DOMBEK is a writer living in Brooklyn. Her essays can be found in *n+1*, the *Paris Review*, and *Painted Bride Quarterly*. The recipient of a 2013 Rona Jaffe Foundation Writer's Award, she writes an advice column called "The Help Desk" for the *n+1* website, and her book on narcissism is forthcoming. She is at work on a book inspired by her essay "How to Quit."

DAVE EGGERS is the author of seven books, most recently *A Hologram for the King*. He is the founder and editor of McSweeney's, an independent publisher based in San Francisco, and cofounder of 826 Valencia, a nonprofit writing and tutoring center for youth.

EMILY FOX GORDON is the author of two memoirs, *Mockingbird Years: A Life In and Out of Therapy* and *Are You Happy? A Childhood Remembered*. She has also published a novel, *It Will Come to Me*, and, most recently, a collection of personal essays, *Book of Days*. She is the recipient of two Pushcart Prizes and is a 2014–2015 Guggenheim Fellow.

MARY GORDON's works of fiction and nonfiction include *Final Payments, The Shadow Man, The Other Side, The Company of Women, Pearl, Seeing Through Places, Circling My Mother, Reading Jesus, The Stories of Mary Gordon,* and *The Love of My Youth*. She is McIntosh Professor of English at Barnard College.

VIVIAN GORNICK's most recent books are a biography of Emma Goldman and a collection of essays, *The Men in My Life*. Her newest memoir, *The Odd Woman and the City*, will be published next spring.

LAWRENCE JACKSON has published essays and criticism in *n+1*, the *Washington Post*, the *Los Angeles Review of Books, Baltimore Magazine, New England Quarterly, Baltimore Sunpapers, Antioch Review,* and *Harper's Magazine*. He has written biographies of Chester Himes and Ralph Ellison and an award-winning history of black postwar writers, *The Indignant Generation*. He teaches in the African American studies and English departments at Emory University.

LESLIE JAMISON is the author of the novel *The Gin Closet*, a finalist for the Los Angeles Times First Fiction Award, and an essay collection, *The Empathy Exams*. Her work has appeared in *Harper's Magazine, Oxford American, A Public Space, Virginia Quarterly Review,* the *Believer*, and the *New York Times*, where she is a regular columnist for the *Sunday Book Review*.

Ariel Levy is a staff writer at *The New Yorker.* She is writing a book based on the essay "Thanksgiving in Mongolia," which won a National Magazine Award. Prior to joining *The New Yorker* she was a contributing editor at *New York* magazine for twelve years.

Yiyun Li grew up in China and came to the United States in 1996. Her debut collection, *A Thousand Years of Good Prayers,* won the PEN/Hemingway Award, the Guardian First Book Award, and the Frank O'Connor International Short Story Award. Her novel *The Vagrants* was shortlisted for the Dublin IMPAC Award. Her second collection, *Gold Boy, Emerald Girl,* was shortlisted for the Frank O'Connor International Short Story Award and was a Story Prize finalist. *Kinder Than Solitude,* her latest novel, was published to critical acclaim. Her books have been translated into more than twenty languages. Yiyun Li has received numerous other awards, including the Whiting Award, a Lannan Foundation residency fellowship, a 2010 MacArthur Foundation fellowship, and the 2014 Benjamin H. Danks Award from the American Academy of Arts and Letters. She was selected by *Granta* as one of the twenty-one best American novelists under thirty-five and was named by *The New Yorker* as one of the top twenty writers under forty.

Barry Lopez, an essayist and short story writer, is the author of fourteen books of fiction and nonfiction. He is the recipient of numerous literary and cultural honors and awards, including the National Book Award for *Arctic Dreams.*

Chris Offutt grew up in Haldeman, Kentucky, a former mining town of two hundred people in the Daniel Boone National Forest. He is the author of two books of nonfiction, *The Same River Twice* and *No Heroes;* two collections of short stories, *Kentucky Straight* and *Out of the Woods;* and one novel, *The Good Brother.* Offutt has published more than seventy stories and essays, including appearances in the *New York Times, Esquire, GQ,* and *Playboy* and on National Public Radio. He has received awards from the Guggenheim Foundation, the Whiting Foundation, the Lannan Foundation, the National Endowment for the Arts, and the American Academy of Arts and Letters. *Granta* included him in their list of the top twenty young American writers. He wrote screenplays for HBO's *True Blood* and *Treme* and Showtime's *Weeds* and TV pilots for Fox, Lionsgate, and CBS. His TV work was nominated for an Emmy. He lives in rural Lafayette County and is a professor of English at the University of Mississippi.

Zadie Smith is the author of four novels: *White Teeth* (2000), *The Autograph Man* (2002), *On Beauty* (2005), which won the Orange Prize for

Fiction, and *NW* (2012). She is also the author of *Changing My Mind: Occasional Essays* (2009) and the editor of a story collection, *The Book of Other People* (2007). She has taught creative writing at New York University since 2010.

ELIZABETH TALLENT's stories have appeared in *The Pushcart Prize: Best of the Small Presses, The Best American Short Stories,* and *The PEN/O. Henry Prize Stories.* Her novel *Museum Pieces* and her collections *In Constant Flight, Time with Children,* and *Honey* will be reissued as e-books this year. She teaches in Stanford University's creative writing program.

WELLS TOWER is a correspondent for *GQ* magazine and the author of *Everything Ravaged, Everything Burned,* a collection of short fiction. He lives, on average, in North Carolina.

JERALD WALKER is the author of *Street Shadows: A Memoir of Race, Rebellion, and Redemption,* recipient of the PEN New England/L. L. Winship Award for Nonfiction. His essays have appeared in numerous periodicals and anthologies, including three previous times in this series, and his memoir about growing up in a doomsday cult will be published in 2015. Walker is an associate professor of creative writing at Emerson College.

PAUL WEST is the author of fifty books, including *My Father's War: A Memoir,* the novels *The Tent of Orange Mist* and *The Immensity of the Here and Now,* and a collection of poems, *Tea with Osiris.* Among other awards, he has been honored by the French government with a Chevalier of the Order of Arts and Letters.

JAMES WOOD is a staff writer at *The New Yorker* and professor of the practice of literary criticism at Harvard University. He has written three books of essays, *The Broken Estate, The Irresponsible Self,* and *The Fun Stuff;* a critical study, *How Fiction Works;* and a novel, *The Book Against God.*

BARON WORMSER is the author or coauthor of thirteen full-length books and a poetry chapbook. He has received fellowships from the National Endowment for the Arts, Bread Loaf, and the John Simon Guggenheim Memorial Foundation. From 2000 to 2006 he served as poet laureate of the state of Maine. He teaches in the Fairfield University MFA program and is director of educational outreach for the Frost Place in Franconia, New Hampshire.

Notable Essays of 2013

SELECTED BY ROBERT ATWAN

RAYMOND ABBOTT
A Warm Spring Rain, *Open 24 Hours*.

SUE ALLISON
Additional Tenses You Should Know, *Apt*, no. 3.

MARY MARGARET ALVARADO
Dear Joshua, *Wag's Revue*, Fall.

AARON APPS
Barbecue Catharsis, *Carolina Quarterly*, Fall.

CHRIS ARTHUR
How's the Enemy? *Literary Review*, vol. 56, no. 1.

RILLA ASKEW
Rhumba, *Tin House*, Fall (no. 57).

LINDA ATWELL
Three Seconds, *Perceptions: A Magazine of the Arts*, May.

KAREN BABINE
An Island Triptych, *New Hibernia Review*, Spring.

NICHOLSON BAKER
Wrong Answer, *Harper's Magazine*, September.

POE BALLANTINE
The Tyranny of Paradise, *The Sun*, June.

LINDA BAMBER
The Miracle of My Freedom, *Kenyon Review*, Spring.

JUDITH BARRINGTON
An Aristocratic Murder, *1966: A Journal of Creative Nonfiction*, vol. 1, no. 1.

TIM BASCOM
Picturing the Personal Essay: A Visual Guide, *Creative Nonfiction*, no. 49.

EMILY BASS
Zulu Love Story, *Slice*, no. 12.

RICK BASS
The Thinness of the Soil, *Ecotone*, Spring.

CONGER BEASLEY, JR.
Wind Dancers, *New Letters*, vol. 79, nos. 3 and 4.

ELIZABETH BENEDICT
My Inheritance, *Salmagundi*, Winter.

CHARLES BERNSTEIN
Disfiguring Abstraction, *Critical Inquiry*, Spring.

JEREMY BERNSTEIN
A Song for Molly, *American Scholar*, Winter.

Leo Bersani
"I Can Dream, Can't I?" *Critical Inquiry,* Autumn.

Warner Berthoff
Memories of Okinawa, *Sewanee Review,* Winter.

Ellis J. Biderson
A Complete Thought, *Tampa Review,* no. 45/46.

Chelsea Biondolillo
Phrenology: An Attempt, *Hayden's Ferry Review,* Fall/Winter.

Kate Jarvik Birch
One More Artificial Organ, *Indiana Review,* Winter.

Sven Birkerts
One Long Sentence, *Threepenny Review,* Summer.

Eula Biss
Sentimental Medicine, *Harper's Magazine,* January.

Buzz Bissinger
My Gucci Addiction, *GQ,* April.

Lucienne S. Bloch
The Machine and I, *Southwest Review,* vol. 98, no. 2.

Amy Boesky
The Ghost Writes Back, *KROnline,* January 16.

Marc Bookman
The Confessions of Innocent Men, *The Atlantic,* August.

Marianne Boruch
Boredom, *Yale Review,* January.

James Braziel
The Ballad of JD, *Southern Humanities Review,* Fall.

Kevin Brockmeier
Dead Last Is a Kind of Second Place, *Georgia Review,* Winter.

Catharine Savage Brosman
Islands of Our Years, *Sewanee Review,* Fall.

Garrett J. Brown
Galileo in the Uecker Seats: Reflections on Failed Observations, *Black Warrior Review,* Spring/Summer.

Laura Lynn Brown
Fifty Things About My Mother, *Iowa Review,* Winter.

William Broyles
My Son and the Bear, *Outside,* June.

Erick Brucker
How to Get Home in Arequipa, *Jelly Bucket,* no. 4.

Robert S. Brunk
A Samuel Beckett Song, *Michigan Quarterly Review,* Fall.

Frank Bures
The Secret Lives of Stories, *Poets & Writers,* January/February.

Katie Burgess
Rahab's Thread, *Pembroke Magazine,* no. 45.

Gabrielle C. Burton
East of East, *Southern Indiana Review,* Fall.

Katy Butler
A Full Life to the End, *Wall Street Journal,* September 7–8.

Bonnie Jo Campbell
Crimes Against a Wrecker Driver, *Southern Review,* Spring.

Mary Cappello
My Secret, Private Errand (An Essay/Memoir on Love and Theft), *Salmagundi,* Fall.

Ron Capps
Writing My Way Home, *Delmarva Review,* October.

Charles Caramello
Henry James Goes to War, *Denver Quarterly,* vol. 47, no. 4.

Emily Arnason Casey
Laughing Water, *Upstreet,* no. 9.

Mauricio Castillo
Do Not Brainstorm!, *American Journal of Neuroradiology,* July.

Alicia Catt
On Saliva, *1966: A Journal of Creative Nonfiction,* vol. 1, no. 2.

Mary Ann Caws
Thinking North, *Raritan,* Winter.

CHRIS CHAN
It's Time We Demanded More, *Gilbert Magazine,* September–October.

KATHLEEN CHAPLIN
The Death Knock, *New England Review,* vol. 34, no. 1.

JAMES M. CHESBRO
From the Rust and Sawdust, *Superstition Review,* Fall.

JOSEPH CHINNOCK
Legally Ted, *Gettysburg Review,* Spring.

JILL CHRISTMAN
Borrowed Babies, *Iron Horse,* vol. 15, no. 3.

KELLY CLANCY
Who Are Not, but Could Be, *Massachusetts Review,* Summer.

BRUCE COHEN
(Closed) American Barber Shop, *Upstreet,* no. 9.

CHARLES COMEY
The Love We Use, *The Point,* Fall.

ELI CONNAUGHTON
Sisters, *Carolina Quarterly,* Spring.

KATIE CORTESE
Winning Like a Girl, *Sport Literate,* vol. 8, no. 2.

TRACI COX
Missed, *Masters Review,* no. 2.

PAUL CRENSHAW
Work, *Alaska Quarterly Review,* Fall/Winter.

MARIAN CROTTY
It's New Year's Eve, and This Is Dubai, *New England Review,* vol. 34, no. 2.

PATTI CROUCH
Sea Change, *Bellingham Review,* Spring.

JOHN CROWLEY
Squeak and Gibber, *Lapham's Quarterly,* Fall.

BRENT CUNNINGHAM
Last Meals, *Lapham's Quarterly,* Fall.

RENEE E. D'AOUST
You Move Away. You Move Closer, *Trestle Creek Review,* no. 27.

ADAM DAVIES
The Loneliest Lemur on Earth, *Sarasota,* September.

SARAH DE LEEUW
Soft Shouldered, *Prism,* Fall.

JEREMY DENK
Every Good Boy Does Fine, *The New Yorker,* April 8.

MARCIA DESANCTIS
The Slow Language of Sculpture, The Fast Language of Words, *The Millions,* April 17.

BONNIE DEVET
Prince Christian Sound: Iceberg Canyon of the North, *hackwriters .com,* May.

JAQUIRA DIAZ
Girl Hood: On (Not) Finding Yourself in Books, *Her Kind,* January.

MORRIS DICKSTEIN
My Life in Fiction, *Threepenny Review,* Fall.

BRIAN DILLON
Attention! Photography and Sidelong Discovery, *Aperture,* Summer.

KRISTIN DOMBEK
How to Quit, *n+1,* no. 15.

BRIAN DOYLE
Dawn and Mary, *The Sun,* August.

REGINA DREXLER
Stealing Mannequins, *West Branch,* no. 72.

BRIAN DUCHANEY
The Man I Killed, *War, Literature, & the Arts,* no. 25.

PETE DUVAL
Adhesion, *Massachusetts Review,* Spring.

CAROL EDGARIAN
Savages, *Narrative Magazine,* Stories of the Week 2012–2013.

John M. Edwards
A Trace of Thrace: A Balkan Adventure, *Europe Revisited,* October.

Mickey Edwards
What Is the Common Good? The Case for Transcending Partisanship, *Daedalus,* Spring.

Pia Z. Ehrhardt
The Owls of Solomon Place, *Oxford American,* no. 82.

Jonathan Fink
The Holy Land Experience, *Southwest Review,* vol. 98, no. 3.

Carole Firstman
Objects of Affection, *South Dakota Review,* no. 50.

Bruce Fleming
Small Hard Things, *Yale Review,* April.

Robert Long Foreman
Guts, *The Cossack,* Winter.

Patricia Foster
Contingencies: Iowa City, IA, *Antioch Review,* Fall.
In Transit, *The Sun,* January.

Thomas Frank
Academy Fight Song, *The Baffler,* no. 23.

Ian Frazier
The One that Got Away, *Outside,* September.

Camillia Freeman
Cartesian Anxiety in a Bleeding I, *Indiana Review,* Winter.

Patrick French
After the War, *Granta,* Autumn (no. 125).

Bonnie Friedman
The Discipline of the Notebook, *Image,* no. 76.

Molly Gallentine
Jell-O, *CutBank,* no. 78.

J. Malcolm Garcia
My Middle Age, *Tampa Review,* no. 45/46.

Philip Gerard
Freedom Fighter, *Our State,* March.

Merrill Joan Gerber
The Found Desk, *Salmagundi,* Winter.

David Gessner
Meet the Keatles, *Oxford American,* no. 81.

Nancy Geyer
Black Plank, *Georgia Review,* Spring.

Dagoberto Gilb
Pride and Prejudice, *Texas Monthly,* February.

Gary Gildner
Tearing Down the Barn, *Georgia Review,* Fall.

D. Gilson
On Faggot: An Etymology, *Indiana Review,* Summer.

Corey Ginsberg
Miami Redux, *Third Coast,* Fall.

Peter Godfrey-Smith
On Being an Octopus, *Boston Review,* May/June.

Anne Goldman
Souvenirs of Stone, *Southwest Review,* vol. 98, no. 3.

Lucy Bryan Green
Melt, *So to Speak,* Spring.

Alvin Greenberg
Visiting the Maharaja, *Ascent,* August 7.

Karl Taro Greenfeld
My Daughter's Homework, *The Atlantic,* October.

Gordon Grice
A Stiller Ground, *This Land,* November 15.

Gail Griffin
The Messenger, *Chattahoochee Review,* Fall/Winter.

Robert Hahn
Becoming Unknown, *Southern Humanities Review,* Spring.

BRIAN HALL
Study Bible: The Great Commission, *Memoir,* no. 12.

JEFFREY HAMMOND
Night Watch, *Gettysburg Review,* Winter.

SILAS HANSEN
Blank Slate, *Colorado Review,* Spring.

JIM HARRISON
Courage and Survival, *Brick,* Winter.

KATHRYN HARRISON
Incest: The Epilogue, *More,* October.

STEVEN HARVEY
The Vanishing Point, *Southern Review,* Winter.

LINDA M. HASSELSTROM
Rabid, *New Letters,* vol. 79, nos. 3 and 4.

ROBIN HEMLEY
The Writer Across the Table, *Southern Humanities Review,* Fall.

BEN HEWITT
Lessons from the Hayfield, *Yankee,* July/August.

PATRICK HICKS
Treblinka, *Beecher's,* no. 3.

KARRIE HIGGINS
Partial Match, *Diagram,* September 1.

J. A. HIJIYA
Numbers, *Raritan,* Spring.

GRAHAM HILLARD
The Complainers: Online with *The Chronicle of Higher Education, Los Angeles Review of Books,* September 4.

AMANDA HILLES
Breathless, *Midwestern Gothic,* Fall.

JEN HIRT
Hour Thirteen, *Colorado Review,* Fall/Winter.

EDWARD HOAGLAND
On Friendship, *American Scholar,* Winter.

ALYSHA HOFFA
Colorless Life: An Essay in Grayscale, *Southern Indiana Review,* Spring.

LINDA HOGAN
Ways of the Cranes, *Image,* Fall (no. 79).

B. J. HOLLARS
Death by Refrigerator, *Normal School,* Fall.

SARAH HOLLENBECK
A Goldmine, *Dogwood,* no. 12.

CLAUDIA HONEYWELL
Street Life, *War, Literature, & the Arts,* no. 25.

MARY HOOD
Breaking It, *Georgia Review,* Spring.

MARYA HORNBACHER
Strip, *Fourth Genre,* Spring.

CAROLINE HORWITZ
Bare, *Summerset Review,* September 15.

GAIL HOSKING
The ABCs of Parting, *Post Road,* no. 24.

EDWARD HOWER
What Can You Do, *Alaska Quarterly Review,* Spring/Summer.

EWA HRYNIEWICZ-YARBROUGH
Europa, Europa, *Agni,* no. 77.

SONYA HUBER
Love and Industry, A Midwestern Workbook, *Terrain.org,* Winter.

BARBARA HURD
Fracking: A Fable, *Brevity,* March.

SAMUEL HYNES
Keeley Rules or How to Play Tennis on Social Security, *Sewanee Review,* Spring.

JUYANNE JAMES
Table Scraps, *Bayou,* no. 60.

KRISTOPHER JANSMA
Why Do We Write? *Slice,* no. 12.

CARREN JAO
Head Games, *The Magazine,* August 1.

ALEX R. JONES
Matinee, *Santa Monica Review,* Fall.
SHANA CAMPBELL JONES
Family Portraits, with Dogs, *Barely South Review,* Spring.

ANNE KAIER
Maple Lane, *Alaska Quarterly Review,* Spring/Summer.
BETTYE KEARSE
Destination Jim Crow, *River Teeth,* Fall.
GARRET KEIZER
Walt, *Virginia Quarterly Review,* Summer.
THOMAS E. KENNEDY
My White House Days, *New Letters,* vol. 79, nos. 3 and 4.
TIM KEPPEL
My Father's Hands, *Hayden's Ferry Review,* Fall/Winter.
SEAN KILPATRICK
The Buff Ruins, *Hobart,* no. 14.
BARBARA KINGSOLVER
Where It Begins, *Orion,* November/December.
JUDITH KITCHEN
Coda, *Water-Stone Review,* no. 16.
RACHEL KOLB
Seeing the Speed of Sound, *Stanford,* March/April.
JACQUELINE KOLOSOV
Dust, Light, Life, *Bellevue Literary Review,* Spring.
The Inner Life of Pearl: Vermeer's Alchemy, *Fifth Wednesday,* Fall.
MARY KORAL
Lock Up, *Alaska Quarterly Review,* Spring/Summer.
ROBERT KOSTUCK
The Birds of South America, *Zone 3,* Fall.
HARI KUNZRU
Stalkers, *Granta,* Autumn (no. 125).
KIM DANA KUPPERMAN
Strangers on a Plane, *Normal School,* Fall.

MATT LABASH
The Last 24 Notes, *Weekly Standard,* September 16.
ROBERT LACEY
On the Dangers of Hero Worship, *North Dakota Quarterly,* Spring/Summer.
DON LAGO
Three Rings, *Gettysburg Review,* Summer.
ELLEN LAMBERT
"Death Will Abide": A Meditation on an Adolescent Suicide, *Raritan,* Summer.
ALEXANDER LANDFAIR
Facebook of the Dead, *Missouri Review,* Fall.
WILLIAM LANGEWIESCHE
What Lies Beneath, *Vanity Fair,* October.
LANCE LARSEN
The Room in Which I Write, *Southwest Review,* vol. 98, no. 2.
PETER LASALLE
Au Train de Vie, *Missouri Review,* Summer.
KIESE LAYMON
You Are the Second Person, *Guernica,* June 17.
DAVID LAZAR
Playing Ourselves: Pseudo-Documentary and Person, *Antioch Review,* Spring.
JACKSON LEARS
Get Happy!!, *The Nation,* November 25.
MICHELLE LEGRO
A Trip to Japan in Sixteen Minutes, *The Believer,* May.
DANIEL W. LEHMAN
"Proper Names Are Poetry in the Raw": Character Formation in Traumatic Nonfiction, *River Teeth,* Fall.

Sarah K. Lenz
Lightning Flowers, *Colorado Review,* Fall/Winter.

Naton Leslie
My Criminal Past, *Under the Sun,* Summer.

Jonathan Lethem
Here's Looking at You, *Vogue,* November.

Steven Levingston
My Drama, *Washington Post Magazine,* April 7.

Ariel Lewiton
Holiday, *Ninth Letter,* Fall/Winter.

Alan Lightman
Symmetrical Universe, *Orion,* March/April.

Mel Livatino
Dogged by the Dark, *Notre Dame Magazine,* Winter.

Sonja Livingston
Mad Love: The Ballad of Fred & Allie, *Creative Nonfiction,* no. 48.

Beth Loffreda
Dinosaur Monument, *High Desert Journal,* Spring.

Linda Logan
Selfless, *New York Times Magazine,* April 28.

Phillip Lopate
How I Look at Movies, *Normal School,* Fall.

Frankie Lopes
Room for My Knees, *Post Road,* no. 26.

Nancy Ludmerer
Kritios Boy, *Literal Latte,* Winter.

Sarah Macaraeg
Namesake, *TruthOut,* May 31.

Doug Mack
Go Your Own Way, *The Morning News,* May 1.

Karen Maner
Hugo, *Colorado Review,* Summer.

James Marcus
Arrive Without Traveling: India, *Antioch Review,* Fall.

Ann Markle
You Never Expect the Call, *Under the Sun,* Summer.

Miriam Markowitz
Here Comes Everybody, *The Nation,* December 9.

Lee Martin
Spook, *1966: A Journal of Creative Nonfiction,* vol. 1, no. 1.

David Masello
The Boys Who Sailed Away, *Fine Art Connoisseur,* June.

Elizabeth Rosen Mayer
The Portrait, *South Loop Review,* no. 15.

Noreen McAuliffe
Under the Locust Tree, *Baltimore Review,* Winter.

Rebecca McClanahan
Adopt a Bench, *The Sun,* March.

Kevin McGrath
Walking to Windward, *Harvard Review,* no. 44.

Kate McIntyre
Revenge of the Spider King, *Redivider,* vol. 10, no. 2.

Charles McLeod
Steps for Home Tooth Extraction, Berkeley 2006, *Hobart,* no. 14.

Kat Meads
Margaret Mitchell's Dump, *Gargoyle,* no. 60.

Sarah Menkedick
Homing Instincts, *Vela Magazine,* July 1.

Brenda Miller
Dress Code, *Passages North,* Winter.

Ander Monson
Dear Defacer, *A Public Space,* Winter.

Sarah Fawn Montgomery
Lesson in Cartography, *Crab Orchard Review,* Summer/Fall.

Rick Moody
Election Diary 2012, *Black Clock,* Winter/Spring.

DINTY W. MOORE
Of Striped Food and Polar Bears, *TriQuarterly,* January 15.

RUTH MOOSE
A Key as Big as Your Hand, *Southeast Review,* no. 1.

JENNIFER MORGAN
Inshallah, *Event,* vol. 42, no. 3.

FREDERIC MORTON
Othello's Sons, *Harper's Magazine,* September.

NICK NEELY
Nasty, *CutBank,* no. 79.

TAM LIN NEVILLE
The Skirts and Blouses Are Hatched, *New Ohio Review,* Fall.

JACOB NEWBERRY
A Thousand Nations, *Kenyon Review,* Winter.

CAITRIN NICOL
Do Elephants Have Souls? *New Atlantis,* Winter.

DELANEY NOLAN
Soyleyelim, *Chattahoochee Review,* Spring.

JAMES NOLAN
Sixty-Eight, *Boulevard,* Spring (no. 84).

GEOFFREY NORMAN
A Great Battlefield, *Weekly Standard,* July 8–15.

THOR R. NYSTROM
Specter of Silence, *Iowa Review,* Fall.

LAURIE OLIN
From Sundogs to the Midnight Sun: An Alaskan Reverie, *Hudson Review,* Spring.

MARK OPPENHEIMER
Forty Thoughts on a Fourth Daughter, *Medium,* October 23.

ADRIANA PARAMO
Praying Alone in Qatar, *The Sun,* December.

WILLIAM SIDNEY PARKER
I'm No Expert but; or An Idea Among the Laity, *Labletter,* no. 15.

JERICHO PARMS
A Chapter on Red, *Hotel Amerika,* Spring.

DUSTIN PARSONS
Pumpjack, *Crab Orchard Review,* Summer/Fall.

ANITTAH PATRICK
The Math, *Bellingham Review,* Spring.

ANNIE PENFIELD
The Half-Life, *Fourth Genre,* Spring.

SAM PICKERING
Poetry at the Breakfast Table, *Sewanee Review,* Spring.

LESLIE PIETRZYK
Joy to the World, *PMS,* no. 12.

STEVEN PINKER
Science Is Not Your Enemy, *New Republic,* August 19.

NORMAN PODHORETZ
"My Negro Problem—and Ours" at 50, *Commentary,* May.

ROLF POTTS
Why I Follow Football, *Barrelhouse,* no. 12.

CHRISTINE POUNTNEY
Coming Apart, *Brick,* Winter.

RICHARD PRINS
Crying for the Razor in Dar es Salaam, *Transition,* no. 110.

LIA PURPURA
Dot, *Normal School,* Fall.

JILL SISSON QUINN
The Myth of Home, *Ecotone,* Spring.

ANNE RAEFF
Lorca in the Afternoon, *ZYZZYVA,* Fall.

SANDRA RAMIREZ
Stray, *Free State Review,* Summer.

JONATHAN RAUCH
The Case for Hate Speech, *The Atlantic,* November.

WENDY RAWLINGS
Weight Watching, *Cincinnati Review,* Winter.

ANNA REDSAND
Naturalization, *Clockhouse,* Summer.

ADENA REITBERGER
Here Is Always Somewhere Else, *Black Warrior Review,* Fall/Winter.

CHELSIA A. RICE
Tough Enough to Float, *Los Angeles Review,* Spring.

EMILY RICH
On the Road to Human Rights Day, *Little Patuxent Review,* Winter.

COLIN ROBINSON
Paddleball, *Granta,* Winter (no. 122).

WALTER ROBINSON
Nurse Clappy Gets His, *Literary Review,* vol. 56, no. 4.

JOHN G. RODWAN, JR.
Carlessness, *Midwestern Gothic,* Fall.

JAMES SILAS ROGERS
The Sadly Sweet Season, *Notre Dame Magazine,* Autumn.

PEGGY ROSENTHAL
An Apprenticeship in Affliction: Waiting with Simone Weil, *Image,* Spring (no. 77).

EARL ROVIT
The Waning of the Wayne, *Sewanee Review,* Winter.

ANASTASIA RUBIS
Girl Falling, *North American Review,* Summer.

MARY RUEFLE
My Private Property, *KROnline,* October 9.

PAUL RUFFIN
Laying that Awful Burden Down, *Boulevard,* no. 85/86.

KENT RUSSELL
Mithradates of Fond du Lac, *The Believer,* June.

OLIVER SACKS
Speak, Memory, *New York Review of Books,* February 21.

NICK SALVATO
Cringe Criticism: On Embarrassment and Tori Amos, *Critical Inquiry,* Summer.

SCOTT RUSSELL SANDERS
A Writer's Calling, *Chautauqua,* no. 10.

EVA SAULITIS
Nonexistent Black and White Photograph, *Catamaran Literary Reader,* Spring.

GERDA SAUNDERS
Telling Who I Am Before I Forget: My Dementia, *Georgia Review,* Winter.

LYNNE SHARON SCHWARTZ
You Gotta Have Heart, *Agni,* no. 77.

MIMI SCHWARTZ
If You Are Absolutely Certain, I Get Suspicious, *TriQuarterly,* June 3.

KAETHE SCHWEHN
Tailings, *Witness,* Spring.

MARTIN SCORSESE
The Persisting Vision: Reading the Language of Cinema, *New York Review of Books,* August 15.

ROGER SCRUTON
Scientism in the Arts and Humanities, *New Atlantis,* Fall.

DAVID SEARCY
Mad Science, *Paris Review,* Spring.

MICHELLE SEATON
The Jet Set, *Lake Effect,* Spring.

DAVID SEDARIS
Company Man, *The New Yorker,* June 3.

Peter Selgin
My New York: A Romance in Eight Parts, *Missouri Review*, Summer.

Susan Elizabeth Shephard
Wildcatting, *Buzzfeed*, July 25.

Bill Sherwonit
Of Waxwings and Goshawks and Standing Up to Power, *Anchorage Press*, January 17–23.

David Shields
I Can't Stop Thinking Through What Other People Are Thinking, *New Letters*, vol. 79, nos. 3 and 4.

Gary Shteyngart
O.K., Glass, *The New Yorker*, August 5.

Robert Anthony Siegel
Unreliable Tour Guide, *Ploughshares*, Winter.

Floyd Skloot
Elliptical Journey, *Post Road*, no. 24.

John Skoyles
A Stay at Yaddo, *Five Points*, vol. 15, no. 3.

Maura Smith
Omphalos, *Bellevue Literary Review*, Spring.

Patricia Smith
83 Problems, A–Z, *Jabberwock Review*, Winter.

Suzanne Farrell Smith
The Pearl, *Post Road*, no. 25.

Katharine Smyth
Prey, *The Point*, Fall.

Rebecca Solnit
Mysteries of Thoreau, Unsolved, *Orion*, May/June.

Patty Somlo
If We Took a Deep Breath, *Gold Man Review*, no. 2.

Brian Jay Stanley
Odyssey of Desire, *Pleiades*, Winter (vol. 33, no. 1).

Kathryn Starbuck
Nazis, *Sewanee Review*, Winter.

David Stevenson
A Cultural History of the Ice Axe, in Eight Fascicles, *Rock & Ice*, ascent issue.

Deborah Stone
Picking Pebbles, *Boston Review*, May/June.

Susan Straight
What My Brother Left Behind, *The Believer*, March/April.

Ginger Strand
Company Town, *Tin House*, Fall (no. 57).

Hal Stucker
Strapped, *Boston Review*, February.

Ira Sukrungruang
Atlas, Don't Let Me Down, *Southeast Review*, no. 2.

Caroline Sutton
Fin, *Ascent*, April 30.

Barrett Swanson
Perilous Aesthetics, *The Point*, Fall.

Neil Swidey
Restart, *Boston Globe Magazine*, May 12.

Jill Talbot
Autobiographies, *Full Grown People*, December 18.

Deborah Thompson
Scavenger Love, *Chattahoochee Review*, Fall/Winter.

Moritz Thomsen
The Bombardier's Handbook, *ZYZZYVA*, Winter.

Melanie Rae Thon
Galaxies Beyond Violet, *Five Points*, vol. 15, nos. 1 and 2.

Caitlin Thornbrugh
Ahuacatl Agovago. Avocado: The Corrupt Alligator Pear, *Parcel*, Spring.

Sallie Tisdale
An Uncommon Pain, *Harper's Magazine*, May.

LAD TOBIN
My Fifty-Minute Hour, *The Sun,* August.

ALISON TOWNSEND
At the Bottom of the Ocean: Psych Ward, 1986, *Feminist Studies,* vol. 39, no. 2.

WILLIAM TROWBRIDGE
Ode to the Motel, *River Styx,* no. 90.

ZHANNA VAYNBERG
Because a Wall Fell Down, *Michigan Quarterly Review,* Winter.

INARA VERZEMNIEKS
The Last Days of the Baldock, *Tin House,* Fall (no. 57).

NATALIE VESTIN
Forms of Wanting, *Water-Stone Review,* no. 16.

PATRICIA VIGDERMAN
The Real Life of the Parthenon, *Kenyon Review,* Winter.

WILLIAM T. VOLLMANN
Life as a Terrorist, *Harper's Magazine,* September.

JULIE MARIE WADE
Holy Orders, *Zone 3,* Spring.

JESSE WALKER
America the Paranoid, *Reason,* October.

NICOLE WALKER
Antibodies, *Fifth Wednesday,* Fall.

MARK WARREN
The Father You Choose, *Esquire,* August.

JOHN WATERS
The Dress That Changed My Life, *Harper's Bazaar,* September.

MICHELLE WEBSTER-HEIN
Counting Apples, *Ruminate,* Winter (no. 30).

SARAH WELLS
Field Guide to Resisting Temptation, *Brevity,* May.

CAROLYN WHITE
Narrative Supplemental, *Prism,* Spring.

PATTI WHITE
The Sound, *Gulf Coast,* Summer/Fall.

COLSON WHITEHEAD
Loving Las Vegas, *Harper's Magazine,* December.

A. WHITFIELD
The Garden, *Prism,* Fall.

LEON WIESELTIER
Crimes Against Humanities, *New Republic,* September 16.

JESSICA WILLBANKS
On the Far Side of the Fire, *Ninth Letter,* Fall/Winter.

EMILY WITT
What Do You Desire?, *n+1,* no. 16.

MELORA WOLFF
Masters in This Hall, *Normal School,* Spring.

JAMES WOOD
Why?, *The New Yorker,* December 9.

LIA WOODALL
Torn in Two, *South Loop Review,* no. 15.

RUSSELL WORKING
Us, *Narrative Magazine,* Stories of the Week 2013–2014.

AMANDA WRAY
Black Dolls, *American Athenaeum,* Summer.

KAREN WUNSCH
My Mother, Eating; or Dystalgia, a Memoir, *Hotel Amerika,* Spring.

KEVIN YOUNG
Blood Nation, *Virginia Quarterly Review,* Spring.

PAULINE YU
The Number One Funeral Home, *American Scholar,* Autumn.

NAOMI ZACK
More than Skin Deep, *Oregon Humanities,* Summer.

BEATRIZ ZALCE
You Are Here, *Cimarron Review,* Spring.

Notable Special Issues of 2013

American Athenaeum, Things They Carry, ed. Jan Nerenberg, Summer.
Antioch Review, Cartography with a Twist, ed. Robert S. Fogarty, Fall.
Black Warrior Review, Offal Issue, ed. Emma Sovich and staff, Spring/Summer.
Briar Cliff Review, 25th Anniversary, ed. Tricia Currans-Sheehan, no. 25.
Chattahoochee Review, The Animal, ed. Anna Schachner, Fall/Winter.
Chautauqua, Journeys & Pilgrimages, ed. Jill and Philip Gerard, no. 10.
Creative Nonfiction, Issue 50, ed. Lee Gutkind.
Daedalus, American Music, ed. Gerald Early, Fall.
December, Revival Issue, ed. Gianna Jacobson, Winter.
Gulf Coast, The "Issues" Issue, ed. Zachary Martin and Karyna McGlynn, Summer/Fall.
Hudson Review, Literature and the Environment, ed. Paula Deitz, Spring.
Lapham's Quarterly, Animals, ed. Lewis H. Lapham, Spring.
Mānoa, Cascadia: The Life and Breath of the World, ed. Frank Stewart and Trevor Carolan, vol. 25, no. 1.
Massachusetts Review, W.E.B. Du Bois in His Time and Ours, ed. Jim Hicks, Michael Thurston, and Ellen Dore Watson, Fall.
Michigan Quarterly Review, Back to School, ed. Jonathan Freedman, Summer.
Midwestern Gothic, Creative Nonfiction Issue, ed. Jeff Pfaller and Robert James Russell, Fall.
Minerva Rising, Rebellion, ed. Kimberly Brown, no. 3.
North Dakota Quarterly, Going Global, ed. Robert W. Lewis, Spring/Summer.
Oregon Humanities, Skin, ed. Kathleen Holt, Summer.
Oxford American, Southern Music Issue, ed. Roger D. Hodge and Rick Clark, Winter (no. 83).
The Point, What Is Marriage For?, ed. Jon Baskin, Jonny Thakkar, and Etay Zwick, Fall.
Portland, Heroes, ed. Brian Doyle, Spring.
Post Road, Writing the Body: Creative Nonfiction, ed. Amy Boesky, no. 24.
Prairie Schooner, A War Portfolio, ed. Brian Turner, Winter.
The Progressive, Living Our Values, ed. Matthew Rothschild, January.
Ruminate, The Body, ed. Brianna Van Dyke, Winter (no. 30).
Slice, The Unknown, ed. Elizabeth Blachman, Celia Blue Johnson, and Maria Gagliano, no. 13.
Smithsonian, 101 Objects That Made America, ed. Michael Caruso, November.
South Dakota Review, 50th Anniversary Issue, ed. Lee Ann Roripaugh, no. 50.
Southern Humanities Review, Cultural Memoir, ed. Patricia Foster, Fall.
Southern Review, The National Book Award 1963, Revisited, ed. Chris

Bachelder and Emily Nemens, Autumn.

Sport Literate, Body and Mind, ed. William Meiners, vol. 8, no. 2.

Threepenny Review, A Symposium on Revenge, ed. Wendy Lesser, Fall.

Transition, Django Issue, ed. Tommie Shelby, Glenda R. Carpio, and Vincent Brown, no. 113.

Water-Stone Review, Forms of Wanting, ed. Mary Francois Rockcastle, no. 16.

Wired, Inventing a Better World, ed. Bill Gates, December.

Witness, Redemption, ed. Maile Chapman, Spring.

...

Correction: The following essay was inadvertently omitted from *Notable Essays of 2012:* Deja Early, Virgin, *Ruminate,* Winter (no. 22).